**"I want to do this right. I don't
want to screw this up..."**

Ava stared at Griffin. "This is real? I'm not dreaming?" Covering his hand with hers, she pressed it to her face.

"It's real. And...honey, could you maybe not look at me that way?"

She smiled.

"Yeah, don't do that either." He bowed his head and swore under his breath. "This is going to be tougher than I thought."

"So if I can't look at you or smile at you, what can I do?"

"I know it's a lot to ask, but wait for me."

That was easy.

She'd been waiting for him for more than a decade.

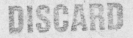

ACCLAIM FOR THE CHRISTMAS, COLORADO SERIES

HAPPY EVER AFTER IN CHRISTMAS

"This charming story of two people struggling to trust their love and build a life together is certain to earn the author new fans."

—Bookpage.com

KISS ME AT CHRISTMAS

"This story has so much humor that at times I found myself laughing out loud, holding my sides and shaking my head...a complete joy to read."

—HarlequinJunkie.com

SNOWBOUND AT CHRISTMAS

"Heartfelt...a laugh-out-loud treat."

—*Publishers Weekly*

"4 1/2 Stars! Mason's brisk pacing and inventive plot define this first-rate entry in her Christmas Colorado series."

—*RT Book Reviews*

ALSO BY DEBBIE MASON

The Harmony Harbor series

Mistletoe Cottage
Christmas with an Angel (short story)

The Christmas, Colorado series

The Trouble with Christmas
Christmas in July
It Happened at Christmas
Wedding Bells in Christmas
Snowbound at Christmas
Kiss Me at Christmas
Happy Ever After in Christmas
Marry Me at Christmas (short story)

Starlight Bridge

DEBBIE MASON

A Harmony Harbor Novel

FOREVER

NEW YORK   BOSTON

Copyright © 2017 by Debbie Mazzuca
Excerpt from *Wedding Bells in Christmas* © 2015 by Debbie Mazzuca

Cover design by Elizabeth Turner
Cover illustration by Tom Hallman
Cover copyright © 2017 by Hachette Book Group, Inc.

Forever
Hachette Book Group
1290 Avenue of the Americas, New York, NY 10104
forever-romance.com
twitter.com/foreverromance

First Edition: February 2017

Forever is an imprint of Grand Central Publishing. The Forever name and logo are trademarks of Hachette Book Group, Inc.

The publisher is not responsible for websites (or their content) that are not owned by the publisher.

The Hachette Speakers Bureau provides a wide range of authors for speaking events. To find out more, go to www.hachettespeakersbureau.com or call (866) 376-6591.

ISBNs: 978-1-4555-3722-8 (mass market), 978-1-4555-3721-1 (ebook)

Printed in the United States of America

OPM

10 9 8 7 6 5 4 3 2 1

Acknowledgments

Thanks once again to my incredibly talented and dedicated editor Alex Logan, who not only makes every book so much better but also gives me the time I need to write the story of my heart. Many thanks to the hardworking sales, marketing, production, and art departments at Grand Central Forever for all their support and efforts on behalf of my books. I'm also grateful to my daughter Jess for reading Ava and Griffin's story through its many stages and to my agent Pamela Harty for always being there when I need her.

Special thanks to the lovely Roberta Capizzi for not only being a fabulous cheerleader for both the Christmas, Colorado series and Harmony Harbor series but also for kindly offering to be my "little Italian helper" and making sure I get the Italian words and phrasing right.

My heartfelt thanks to the wonderful readers, bloggers,

and reviewers who have been so supportive of me and my series. Your lovely e-mails, tweets, Facebook posts, and reviews mean the world to me.

And to my wonderful husband, amazing children, and adorable granddaughters, thank you for all your love and encouragement, and supporting me in doing what I love to do. Love you all so very much.

Starlight
Bridge

Chapter One

♥

Ava DiRossi didn't believe in fairy tales and happily-ever-afters, but right about now, she'd sell her soul for a fairy godmother.

As the elevator shuddered and creaked on its way up to the north tower, Ava removed her black work shoe. The sole had come loose, flapping when she walked. She hammered it against the steel frame of the service cart in hopes it would hold out until the end of her shift. After several good whacks, she stopped to examine the seam. Satisfied the shoe wouldn't fall apart before she got home, she slipped it back onto her foot.

Obviously she didn't need a fairy godmother to take care of her footwear or to provide her with fancy gowns. And Prince Charming? She'd had one of her own. A long time ago. Only he'd turned out to be more princely and charming than she deserved, and she'd ended their fairy-tale marriage. But there was something a fairy godmother could help her with. If Ava had one, she'd ask her to turn back the clock to three months earlier. Her life had been so simple then.

She loved Greystone Manor. It had been her refuge, her sanctuary. She'd been left alone, free to do as she pleased as long as the guest rooms were well and properly cleaned. And they were, because Ava wouldn't have it any other way. She made sure each room sparkled and shone.

But everything had changed the day Colleen Gallagher died and Ava's cousin Sophie had become manager of the manor. It seemed like every time Ava turned around, her cousin was there with a new scheme to improve Greystone's bottom line. One that invariably required Ava's help and was designed to push her out of her comfort zone.

The elevator jerked to a stop. Without thinking, Ava pushed the service cart toward the now-open doors. A jarring pain shot up her arm, and she sucked in a breath through her teeth. That's what she got for letting thoughts of fairy godmothers fill her head. She used her good arm and her hip to push the heavy cart into the deserted hall. As though in judgment of what she was about to do, long-dead Gallaghers looked down at her from the portraits in gilded frames that lined the stone walls.

"I'm not any happier about it than you are," Ava told the portrait of William Gallagher, the family's patriarch. He looked like the pirate he'd been reputed to be. "But Colleen would understand. She'd want me to find her memoirs."

Until the private viewing at the manor three days after Colleen had passed, no one had believed that she'd actually written her memoirs. But during the wake, in a recorded message for the Widows Club—of which Ava was a member, the token divorcée—Colleen had held up the book, proving that it did indeed exist. And not only had Colleen written about her life and her secrets, but she'd also recorded each and every one of theirs. Just before Colleen announced where she'd hidden the book, static filled the screen and the videotape was damaged beyond repair.

There were secrets in the book that Ava couldn't afford to come to light. Secrets she'd confessed to Colleen in a weak moment. Secrets the Gallagher matriarch had promised to take to her grave.

Oh, now, you have a head full of fanciful thoughts today, don't you, Ava my girl?

"Yes, thanks to you and Sophie, my head seems to be full of them these days. And I can tell you I was much happier without them," Ava said as she parked the cart under William's portrait, then sighed when she realized she was talking aloud. Talking to her ex-husband's great-grandmother, who'd died more than two months ago.

It wasn't the first time Ava had caught herself doing so. She wasn't worried she was going crazy though. Her newly acquired habit was a result of stress and exhaustion. There wasn't much she could do about being so tired she could hardly think straight, but she could alleviate part of her stress by finding the book that would reveal the truth about her and that night and the man she'd allowed to ruin her life.

In case someone happened upon her in Colleen's room, Ava tossed two sponges in a bucket and made her way to the walnut-studded door, sliding her passkey into the lock. Colleen had lost her battle with her son Ronan, a historian, over the entry upgrade. She never did like change. If Colleen had gotten her way, Greystone Manor, which had been built in the early nineteenth century and modeled after a medieval castle, would have stayed exactly the same.

Meow.

Ava jumped, pressing a hand to her chest as a black cat wound his way between her legs. Simon, who'd arrived at the manor a week before Colleen died, raised his blue eyes and meowed again. Placing the bucket on the hardwood floor, Ava crouched to scratch behind his ears.

"You miss her, too, don't you?" she said to the cat, realizing that was most likely the reason she'd been talking to a dead woman. She missed Colleen. Ava had worked for her ex-husband's family for more than a decade.

Simon purred, rubbing his head against her leg. She gave him a final pat. "You can come with me, but you have to stay quiet."

Ava picked up the bucket and straightened to open the door. As she did, a sweet, floral scent wafted past her nose. She frowned at the fresh bouquet of pink, yellow, and white roses in a crystal vase on the nightstand beside the canopied bed. Odd. Who would…Jasper, she decided. The older man had been with the Gallaghers for as long as she could remember. He'd been Colleen's right-hand man and confidant. Skinny as a rail with stiff, upper-crust manners, he was a pain in Ava's *culo*.

Her gaze lifted from the roses to the Gothic-style leaded windows that overlooked the gardens. Sleet pelted the windowpanes, and the barren trees swayed in the cold mid-January winds. She wrapped her gray sweater around her while casting a longing glance at the fireplace with a three-tiered wrought-iron candelabra standing in front of it. The fireplace was more for show than heat. So no matter that she could practically see her breath in the room; now wasn't the time to put it to the test and risk an actual fire.

She eyed the hundreds of books lining the walls of the sitting area. More were stacked haphazardly on the antique tables on either side of a well-worn, gold damask love seat with additional piles creating small towers on the hardwood floor. A cluttered white desk with feminine lines sat in the center of the room with a view of the dark, turbulent sea through the French doors that led onto a stone balcony.

The room looked exactly the same as the night she'd searched it with her cousin, her Auntie Rosa, and the rest of the Widows Club. As far as Ava knew, no one had found the book. Though not for lacking of trying. It had to be here, somewhere in this room.

She set the bucket beside the fireplace and walked the perimeter, lifting the heavy, antique-gold drapes and peeking under the oil paintings in search of a safe or secret compartment. Simon meowed from where he stretched out on the back of the love seat, once again drawing Ava's attention to the shelves of books behind him.

They'd been looking for a brown, leather-bound book the night they'd first searched the room—aptly named *The Secret Keeper of Harmony Harbor*. Ava wondered if Colleen had hidden it within another book. She wouldn't be surprised if she had. Colleen had been a cagey old lady.

As Ava catalogued the sheer volume of books, she realized she'd be here longer than she had anticipated. Unconsciously, her hand went to her bruised arm; she couldn't be late again. She reached in her pocket for her earbuds and turned on her iPod. Fitting the buds in her ears, she got to it, leafing through one book at a time. Alone with her music—aside from Simon—Ava felt some of the day's tensions leave her. She liked repetitive, mindless work. She found it calming. Well, it was usually calming. With the book on the loose, it was somewhat less so today.

Someone tapped her shoulder, and she jumped, dropping the book she'd just taken off the shelf. She whirled around, pressing a hand to her chest. "You practically gave me a heart attack."

"Sorry." Sophie grimaced. Ava's cousin wore her uniform of a white blouse and black pencil skirt. "I called out, but you mustn't have heard me. What are you listening to?" She pulled the bud from Ava's ear and held it to hers. "It's loud"—Sophie made a face—"and depressing."

"'Mad World' by Gary Jules. It's not depressing. It's beautiful." Ava reached into the pocket of her black uniform dress and turned off the iPod, then bent to pick up the book she'd dropped. "I, um, was looking for something to read."

Sophie removed the black-framed glasses that held back her long, chestnut-brown hair and put them on, leaning forward to look at the book. She raised an eyebrow. "*Finnegans Wake* by James Joyce. Interesting choice."

"I thought so. It was one of Colleen's favorites."

"You miss her, don't you?" Sophie said with a sympathetic smile.

It wasn't that long ago that her cousin had been as anxious to find Colleen's memoirs as Ava. A fire in Sophie's LA apartment left her and her daughter, Mia, homeless, forcing them to move back to Harmony Harbor. For years, Sophie had kept the true identity of Mia's father a secret. But just a month after arriving home, the truth came out. It had been a difficult time for Sophie and Liam, but in the end, their love for each other prevailed.

So Sophie would understand Ava's need to find the book only too well and would no doubt offer her help. But there'd be a price to pay. Sophie would want to know her secret, and it was a secret Ava would take to her grave. "*Sí*, I do."

Sophie rested her hip against the back of the love seat, absently petting Simon. "Do you think I'm horrible for renting out Colleen's suite?"

Her cousin had announced her plans last night. It was the reason Ava was searching the room. While there was a part of her that didn't want Colleen's private space invaded, she understood why Sophie felt she had to do so.

Within a day of her cousin announcing plans for a bridal show at Greystone, their major competitor, the Bridgeport Marquis, announced plans for their own bridal show. Yesterday, the Marquis's bridal suite had been featured in the *Harmony Harbor Gazette*.

"You know, if Colleen were here, she'd have suggested it herself, Sophie. The bridal suite at the Marquis can't compete with this." Ava lifted her hand to the French doors. "Look at the views."

Sophie nibbled on her thumbnail and nodded. "I know, but maybe I overreacted. The old bridal suite has an ocean view too. It's just not as big as Colleen's. I'll have Dana stage them both. If she thinks the old bridal suite shows just as well, we'll feature it in the *Gazette*. That way we won't have to pack Colleen's things away."

Dana Templeton was a long-term guest at the manor. She'd also become a close friend to both Ava and Sophie. The woman had exquisite taste…and a secret. She was probably as anxious to find Colleen's memoirs as Ava.

"Next on the list is updating the restaurant menu," Sophie added with a look in her golden-brown eyes that was all too familiar.

"It's getting late. I should probably get going," Ava said in hopes of avoiding another conversation about the restaurant. She turned to pick up the books she'd piled on the floor. She adored Sophie, admired the woman she'd become, but her cousin had an almost obsessive need to fix things, including the people she loved. Over the past two months, it had become apparent that Ava was her new pet project.

"You're not walking home. I'll give you a ride. It'll give us a chance to talk about the restaurant," Sophie said brightly.

Ava bowed her head and sighed. Her cousin was like a dog with a bone. "Sophie, no matter how often you ask, my answer will be the same. I can't. My father—"

"Please, just think about it? You're an incredibly talented chef. No, don't wave me off. You are. You know how important the bridal show is for us. I can't have Helga handling the food. I need you, Ava. Greystone needs you."

"No, what you need is a well-trained and experienced chef, and that's not me. I want to save Greystone as much as you do, Sophie, but I can't take over the restaurant. I'll do anything else but that."

"What if I talk to Uncle Gino? I'm sure he'd—"

Fingers of fear crawled up Ava's spine at the thought of Sophie talking to her father. She drew the sleeve of her sweater over her hand, fisting it around the gray wool. "No. *Capisci?*" The words came out more forcefully than she intended, and in Italian. When she was nervous or upset, she slipped back into the language she'd grown up hearing at home.

"No, I don't understand," Sophie said with equal force and a stubborn jut of her chin. "You helped out before, so I don't know why you won't help out again."

There were times when her cousin reminded Ava of her Auntie Rosa, Sophie's mule-headed grandmother. This was one of them. "Because you were desperate." Ava held up a hand when Sophie opened her mouth. "Find someone else. I'm not interested. I'm a maid, Sophie. Not a chef."

"What happened to you, Ava? What happened to the girl I remember?"

Ava had once loved to cook—it had been her passion. But she was no longer the girl her cousin remembered. She didn't want to be. "She grew up. Now, do you think I can get back to my job?"

Sophie made a face. "Fine. Griffin will be arriving within the hour unless his plane was delayed by the weather. It should be enough time for the room to warm up. There's extra firewood in the lobby. I'll go—"

"Griffin…Griffin's staying here? In this room?" Her ex-husband rarely came back to Harmony Harbor. In the past ten years, Ava had only seen him a handful of times. Though that may have been because he'd gone out of his way to avoid her. Granted, she had done the same. But she hadn't been able to avoid him when he'd come home for Colleen's funeral or for Liam and Sophie's wedding.

"I thought I told you he was coming home." Sophie lifted a shoulder as though it had slipped her mind, but Ava saw the hint of a smile playing on her lips. "We needed some extra muscle to help get the ballroom ready for the bridal show. You have to admit Griffin fits the bill."

She wouldn't let her mind go to just how well her ex fit the we-need-muscle bill or allow herself to think about the potential consequences of her tenacious cousin playing matchmaker. Ava would worry about that later. Right now, she was more terrified at the thought of Griffin staying in a room that quite possibly held a book that contained her deepest, darkest secret.

"What's wrong?" Sophie touched Ava's bruised forearm, her brow furrowed with concern. "It's not like when he came home for Colleen's funeral. His ex won't be with him if that's what you're worried about."

At the light pressure of Sophie's hand on her bruised arm, Ava clenched her teeth to stifle a groan and reached for the bucket. "Nothing's wrong. I just have a lot to do before he arrives. I'll get to it now." She prayed her cousin took the hint and left, because for the first time in more than a decade, Ava had no intention of doing her job. She was going to find Colleen's book instead. Or at the very least, ensure that Griffin didn't.

Sophie looked over the room. "I promised Mia and Liam I'd be home for supper, but if you need me to stay—"

"Thank you, but no. I'll get done faster without you."

"Um, are you forgetting I used to work as a maid? I was actually pretty good at—"

Would she never leave? Ava took matters into her own hands and carefully steered her cousin toward the door. "Yes, I'm sure you were the Maid of LA, but I am the Maid of Harmony Harbor, so you can go now. Give Mia a kiss for me."

Sophie laughed. "Okay, okay, I'm leaving. But call me when you're finished, and I'll give you a ride home."

"*Ciao,*" Ava said, and closed the door. Heart racing, she pressed her back against it. Simon sat in front of…the fireplace. The one place none of them had thought to look. Ava raced across the room. She knelt on the floor to move the heavy wrought-iron candelabra, careful not to knock off the candles as she pushed it to the side. Ignoring the pain in her arm, she scrutinized the brick facing for a sign it had been tampered with. When she didn't find any, she ran her fingers along the dark oak frame and mantel.

Simon meowed and padded into the fireplace. He sat on the logs and looked up. Ava stuck her head inside and did the same. It was too dark to see much of anything. She was typically prepared for whatever might come up on the job, but she didn't carry a flashlight, and she didn't have her cell phone. Her father had broken it two weeks before in another fit of temper.

She skimmed her right hand up and down the wall where Simon was staring. Two of the bricks were loose. She pushed her finger between them, touching what felt like soft leather. She held her breath as she tried to lift it and the edges of paper brushed against her finger. It was a book. Her pulse kicked up with excitement, her shoulders sagging with relief.

Her relief was short-lived. No matter how hard she

tugged on the upper brick with her uninjured arm, it refused to budge. Gritting her teeth, she tried using both hands. Her bruised arm protested the movement, but she refused to give up and breathed through the pain.

Fifteen minutes later, she stopped to regroup. There had to be another way. Her hands were blackened with soot, the tips of her fingers raw, and the bricks had barely moved. She looked around the room for something to wedge between them and spied the poker.

"We're in business, Simon. This should do—"

"Tell Grams I'll see her in a bit."

Her gaze shot to the door. She'd recognize that voice anywhere. Griffin was here. Now. Outside the door. She shot to her feet, shoving the candelabra in front of the fireplace.

Meow.

She'd trapped Simon. She grabbed the cat, put him on the floor, and scooped up the bucket and sponges while frantically searching for somewhere to hide. The balcony. She didn't care if she froze to death; she couldn't let him find her here.

As she turned to run, Ava heard the beep of the passkey. She wouldn't make it. She spun around and ran the short distance to the bathroom. Her breath coming in panicked puffs, she stepped inside the bathtub and carefully inched the crimson and gold shower curtain across the rod. She sagged against the tile wall, praying his *in a bit* meant he'd drop his bags off and leave.

If it had been anyone other than Griffin, she'd pretend to be cleaning the room. But she remembered all too clearly the humiliation of being discovered by Griffin and his ex-wife the last time they'd stayed at the manor. He'd looked at Ava like he hadn't known who she was, and his wife had asked for fresh towels, acting as though Ava hadn't done her job.

And then there was the book. She couldn't leave without it.

"How did you get in here?"

Her gaze jerked to the curtain, her heart beating double time. She let out the breath she'd been holding when the bed creaked. Simon. Griffin was talking to the cat. "Better question would be, what have you been up to? Your paws are black. Off the bed, buddy."

Her toes curled in her shoes, a warm, fluttery sensation settling low in her stomach in response to the slow drawl of Griffin's deep voice. He always spoke in that low, unhurried tone. Even when he was angry or when he was whispering how much he loved her or when he was talking her out of her temper. Only then there'd been a hint of laughter too. Her temper used to amuse him. He had a long fuse; she had a short one. She used to, at least.

Her lips curved at the memories; then her wistful smile faded when the consequences of what he'd just said penetrated her lovesick brain. Simon's paws were dirty. All she'd need was for Griffin to start looking for the source. She had to...

There was the rasp of a zipper, then the light thud of something hitting the floor. At the sound of heavy footfalls approaching the bathroom, Ava's eyes went wide, and she pressed her back against the tiled wall. A bare, muscled arm reached past the curtain, a large hand turning on the water. The cold spray from the showerhead hit her in the face, and a small, shocked squeak escaped before she could contain it.

Griffin whipped back the shower curtain. His thick, toffee-colored hair glistened under the fluorescent light, his dazzling, deep blue eyes wide in surprise. She opened her mouth to say something, but the words got stuck in her throat as her eyes drifted down his body. He was completely and gloriously naked. And even more beautiful than she remembered.

Chapter Two

♥

Griffin Gallagher gaped at his ex-wife standing fully clothed under the shower's icy spray. Beneath a dripping wet gray sweater several sizes too big, her uniform clung to her birdlike frame, an ugly pair of shoes on her feet. Her long, jet-black hair plastered to her head, Ava stared at him through the water streaming down her pale, gaunt face.

Despite the changes to the woman he'd once loved more than life itself, he felt a familiar stirring, a familiar heat low in his belly. He was reacting to her as though nothing had changed. With her gaze riveted on the evidence of his body's betrayal, embarrassment and anger coursed through him.

"What the hell are you doing in here, Ava?" He shut off the water with such force that he nearly ripped the lever off the wall.

Her impossibly green eyes jerked to his face, remind- ing him where they'd lingered only seconds before.

Swearing under his breath, he covered himself with the shower curtain and then leaned to his right to grab two towels off the rack. He threw her one. She blinked and caught it before it hit her in the face.

Reeling from the realization that he still wanted her, still felt something for her after all this time, he said through clenched teeth, "Get out. Now," and wrapped the towel around his waist.

"I...I'm sorry. I didn't expect you so soon. I was...I was just cleaning the tiles."

Everything about her was foreign to him—the meek, stammering voice; the way she stood with her shoulders bowed; the raw, chapped hands that trembled as she brought the towel to her face. She looked exhausted, and she was lying.

He opened his mouth to ask her what was going on. Then quickly closed it before he uttered the questions that had been eating at him since he saw her at his great-grandmother's funeral. *Are you okay? What happened to you? What can I do to take the shadows from your eyes?* It was no longer his job, no longer his right.

He'd been there before, a long time ago. And all it had gotten him was a broken heart. It'd taken him years to re-cover. There'd been a time when he didn't think he ever would. With Ava, he'd never again allow his heart to over-rule his head. He needed to get her out of here, and so he hauled her from the tub.

She cried out, and her face crumpled.

He released her immediately and dropped his hands to his sides, taking a step back. "Jesus, I'm sorry. I didn't think I grabbed you that hard, Ava. I didn't mean to hurt you." His gut bottomed out at the thought that he had.

From his time as a Navy SEAL, his body had been trained to be a weapon—powerful, lethal. It was something he never allowed himself to forget. Even when he was angry, he was careful. He'd been careful with her too. He was sure of it.

"You didn't. I hurt my arm yesterday. I'm sorry for…" Her gaze dropped, and his unruly body part perked up at the attention. She slowly raised her eyes back to his face, a hint of pink coloring her prominent cheekbones. She cleared her throat. "…startling you."

He knew she was lying again. Just as he had all those years before. But no matter how much he wanted her gone, he had to make sure he wasn't responsible for the pain that had been clearly etched on her face. "What happened to your arm?"

She turned to grab the bucket. "I hit it on the service cart. It's nothing, really."

"It's not nothing. Let me see." He reached for her, at the same time wondering what he was doing. Why couldn't he just leave it alone?

"No. I…" Her gaze jerked to his hand as he gently wrapped his fingers around her fine-boned wrist. She pulled away from him, wrenching her arm as she did. He noted her desperate attempt to contain the pained gasp, the flash of panic in her eyes.

They were the same, her eyes. They no longer lit up with laughter and passion, but they were just as incredibly beautiful as they used to be. Her eyes were the only thing about her that was remotely familiar. Maybe they were the reason he couldn't let it go. The reason he took her hand, despite her murmured protest, and carefully pushed up the sleeve of her sweater.

His breath hissed through his teeth. Her forearm was almost completely black-and-blue. He raised his gaze to hers. "You didn't get this from banging your arm on the service cart."

She wouldn't meet his eyes as she tried to push her sleeve back down. "I hit it again last night. Please, Griffin, it's just a bruise."

"You sure about that? It looks pretty bad to me. Maybe you have a hairline fracture. Did you let Doc Bishop take a look?"

She pulled away again, and this time he let her go. They hadn't been alone together in a long time. He hadn't stood this close to her or held her hand, and he didn't like the uncomfortable pressure building in his chest. He tried to convince himself that it was nothing—just a reaction to seeing the extensive bruising. His protective instincts were strong. That's all it was. He'd react the same to anyone with a similar injury. But with Ava, he didn't want to feel anything. Not one damn thing.

"I'm not bothering Dr. Bishop about a bruise. I'm perfectly capable of taking care of it myself. But I appreciate your concern. It looks worse than it is. I haven't had a chance to ice it today, that's all."

She probably was qualified to make that call. Two months before she would have graduated as a nurse-practitioner, she'd left school. A month before that, she'd asked him for a divorce, ending their marriage with five words: *I can't do this anymore.* And that's all he got. No matter how much he begged and pleaded for a reason, those five words were all she gave him.

But the anger flaring to life inside him had nothing to do with the past. It was because she *appreciated his concern*, and dammit, he didn't want to be concerned. And he sure as hell didn't want her to think that he was.

"You shouldn't be working. Take a couple days off." His irritation was evident in each word he bit out. It used to take a lot to set off his temper. That had changed after he'd lost Ava and his mother and sister. It had improved some after he met Lexi.

And there it was, the real reason for that uncomfortable pressure in his chest. It didn't have anything to do with Ava, yet it had everything to do with her. His second wife believed he'd never stopped loving Ava. It made it impossible for them to work out their other issues. Impossible for Lexi to stay with him.

Ava blinked as though surprised not only by his suggestion, but also by the harshness with which he'd delivered it. "I can't afford to take time off," she said with quiet dignity.

Once again he felt the unwanted pull of sympathy. Six months after Ava had asked him for a divorce, her father had been badly injured on the job. He'd been left paralyzed from the waist down. Ava's mother had died of cancer when Ava was nine, so the responsibility for her father's care fell solely on her shoulders. But the apology Griffin was about to make got no farther than the tip of his tongue.

Ava saw to that with the next words out of her mouth. "I'll finish your room while you take your shower. I won't be long."

The last thing he wanted to be thinking about was her in his room while he was naked in the shower, but more than that, he kept seeing that bruise. "No. Leave it alone and go home."

She looked like she might argue, then lifted a shoulder and walked to the door. Her shoes squished and sloshed, leaving a trail of water behind her. He was about to suggest she borrow some clothes and shoes from her cousin before heading home but kept his mouth shut. He didn't want Ava to think he was worried about her.

The tension in his shoulders released as the door closed behind her. Maybe now he could get her out of his head. He dropped the towel and reached for the lever to turn on the shower, his attention drawn to the oily, black footprints left behind by her butt-ugly shoes. So much for his plan.

He grabbed a washcloth off the towel rack and got to work on the stains. Getting rid of any trace of her helped work off some of the anger and frustration still rolling around inside him. Only when he finished did he realize his hands were covered in what appeared to be black shoe polish. He looked around for a bar of soap. There wasn't one. Turning the lever to hot, he left the bathroom to retrieve a bar of soap from his kit. He stopped short at the sight of Ava walking across the room carrying an armful of wood.

"What the hell do you think you're doing?"

Her mouth fell open, and she dropped the logs…onto her foot. "Crap. Ow. Crap," she yelped, grabbing her foot and hopping around.

"Ava, let go of your foot. You'll hurt your arm."

She ignored him, swearing in Italian while still holding on to her foot with both hands.

He released an exasperated sigh. "Stubborn as ever," he muttered as he walked toward her and scooped her into his arms. She might be as stubborn as she used to be, but she was at least thirty pounds lighter. When they were together, she'd been all soft, lush curves. She released a surprised gasp and her arms automatically went around his neck. Beneath the smell of damp wool, he caught a whiff of the same perfume she used to wear—D&G Light Blue. It brought back memories of all the times he'd held her in his arms. Seven years of memories, most of them amazing.

He set her on the edge of the bed and cleared his throat. "Do you think your foot's broken?"

She didn't answer; she looked like she might be in shock. He crouched in front of her to remove her wet shoes. The old Ava wouldn't have been caught dead wearing shoes like these. She loved heels, the higher the better. Sexy, strappy shoes that were colorful and blinged out. He never could figure out how she walked in them for hours on end without complaining. But damn, he'd loved watching her do it. He should probably be grateful her taste in footwear had changed too.

This pair though…"For Chrissakes, Ava, there's a hole in the bottom of this shoe, and look at this." He lifted the other shoe, flicking its flapping sole.

She made a small choking sound, her eyes huge in her flushed face.

He frowned. "What's wrong with—"

"You…you're naked."

He scowled and rose to his feet. "It's not like you haven't seen it before," he grumbled, stalking to the bathroom to retrieve a towel. She was gone by the time he came back.

Colleen Gallagher walked straight through the closed door of Jasper's room at the manor, surprised not to feel that disconcerting rush she normally did when passing through doors and such. Then again, her dander was up, so that may well be the reason why she didn't. Or perhaps she was just getting used to this ghost gig. She'd been undead…Well, she wasn't exactly sure what she was, but she'd missed the welcome mat to heaven more than two months before.

At a hundred and four, she'd been anxious to join her loved ones in the great beyond. In the end, though, it was probably for the best she'd missed her ride to heaven. She had to protect the Gallagher legacy.

There was also the small matter of ensuring that, when she eventually met St. Peter at the Pearly Gates, he'd welcome her into heaven instead of sending her straight to hell. She had to make amends for her past mistakes.

All she had to do to save the manor and wipe the sins from her eternal soul was to ensure her plans for her great-grandchildren's love lives came to fruition. Which was easier than it sounded; she'd been quite the matchmaker in her day. Even in her ghostly state, she'd already successfully married off one of her great-grandsons. Liam and Sophie were a shining example of her success. She didn't fool herself that marrying off the next couple on her list would be as easy though.

Especially now that she'd discovered a traitor in their midst.

Ah, there he was, happy as a clam sitting in a brown leather wingback chair wearing a paisley smoking jacket and black satin sleep pants, his burgundy slippered feet crossed and resting on the ottoman. She caught his smirk as he brought the china teacup to his lips.

"You think you're so smart sending me off on a wild-goose chase, don't you, laddie?" She moved to stand between him and his favorite series playing on the television—*Downton Abbey*. Not that it would do her much good. He couldn't hear or see her, but he bloody well sensed her presence. He'd used that to his advantage today.

"Back from your hunt so soon, Madame?"

So soon? She'd spent most of the evening down in the tunnels searching for her memoirs. Which Jasper well knew since he'd been the one who suggested her book might be there. She'd been looking over Ava's shoulder while she leafed through the books in the tower room when Colleen heard a sound outside the door. She'd walked through it…and Jasper, who'd obviously been on the lookout for Griffin, and Colleen.

"I've got your number now. You thought to keep me busy so I wouldn't be about to meddle in Ava's and Griffin's affairs now that he's come home. You're as bad as that Mr. Carson you admire so much on *Downton Abbey*. But you're wrong about Ava. She doesn't deserve your censure. She's suffered more than you'll ever know. And I'll be damned if you'll stand in the way of her and Griffin's happiness."

Oh yes, she had her dander up all right. Admittedly, it wasn't entirely Jasper's fault. He was just trying to protect her great-grandson. Jasper blamed Ava for breaking Griffin's heart. If Colleen had shared Ava's secrets, Jasper would know the truth. She should have shared them before now. At the very least, she should have broken her vow to Ava and told Griffin.

Back then, Colleen had a good reason not to. Ava had shared her heartbreaking secret with Colleen a week before Griffin married Lexi. Colleen liked her great-grandson's then wife-to-be and couldn't bring herself to hurt the girl, even for Ava's sake. Lexi had saved Griffin from himself.

Setting the teacup on the nesting table beside him, Jasper rested his linked fingers on his chest and grinned like a Cheshire cat. "It appears you'll have to set your matchmaking sights on one of your other great-grandchildren, Madame. I have it on good authority that Master Griffin will be leaving in two days' time. Not the fortnight Miss Kitty had planned on and you no doubt had hoped for."

At least she and her daughter-in-law Kitty were on the same page. But the news Griffin planned to leave in two days' time was worrisome at best. "I don't know what you're so happy about. You want to save Greystone from that grasping developer's hands as much as the rest of us do, and we need Griffin's vote. Without Ava to convince him otherwise, the lad's dead set on selling the estate."

Colleen had spent the months leading up to her death fending off local real estate agent Paige Townsend's attempts to steal Greystone and the family's five-thousand-acre estate out from under them. The thirtysomething woman represented the developer who wanted to tear down the manor and build high-end condos.

Colleen's great-grandchildren stood to make millions if they went through with the sale. It's why she'd set up her will the way she did. The estate couldn't be sold unless all her great-grandchildren agreed. To date, only two of them were on the Save Greystone Team.

A scratching sound and then an insistent meow came from the other side of the door.

"Ah, it appears your partner in crime has arrived. Perhaps you should let him in," Jasper said with a smirk in his voice.

She glared at him. He knew darn well she couldn't open the door. These days her hands rarely obeyed her brain. There were some things she'd become quite adept at though. She walked to the television and put her hand through Mr. Carson's face, smiling when static filled the screen. "You'll think twice before pulling another fast one on me, laddie. Enjoy your evening. I have work to do."

"Where have you been, Tomcat?" she asked Simon when she arrived on the other side of the door. The black cat was the only one who could both see and hear her. Sophie and Liam's daughter Mia could see her. Lately, though, Colleen sensed that she was no longer as visible to the child as she used to be.

Simon gave Colleen a testy meow, looking at the spiral staircase that led to the tower and then back at her. Nudging his head before he ran off, he obviously expected her to follow.

"Oh, but you're a bossy one. I'd already planned on paying my great-grandson a visit." She walked to the staircase. There had to be a way to convince Griffin to stay until she found her memoirs.

"Stop your caterwauling. You'll wake the other guests," Colleen said to the meowing Simon as she reached the landing in no time at all. It never ceased to amaze her how quickly and easily she got around these days. The aches and pains of old age were no longer a problem in her ghostly state. A shame she couldn't say the same for her memory.

Simon cast her a smug look when Griffin opened the

door. Colleen rolled her eyes, scooting past her great-grandson, who wore black sweatpants and a T-shirt. He was on the phone.

"It was just Simon, the cat." Griffin grimaced as he shut the door. "Ah, no, I'm staying at the manor. It was my dad's idea, Lex." He sat on the edge of the bed and rubbed the heel of his palm on his forehead. "I don't know why you're getting so bent out of shape."

Simon parked himself in front of the fireplace and me-owed at Colleen. "What's gotten into you? Hush now. I need to hear this. It sounds like Jasper isn't the only one going to give us trouble." She sat on the bed beside Grif-fin, trying to hear what his ex-wife was saying on the other end.

Griffin looked across the room at Simon. "Knock it off. No, not you. I was talking to the damn cat. Hang on."

"Oh, you've gone and done it now. You should have listened to me and stopped while you were ahead. He'll be throwing you out on your ear," Colleen told Simon as she followed her great-grandson to the fireplace. Simon had managed to get himself trapped inside. He stood on top of the logs, meowing at Colleen.

"What is it that's got you in such a dither?" She went down on all fours and pushed her head and the upper half of her body through the wrought-iron candelabra to peer inside.

Griffin scooped up Simon. "If you don't cut it out, you can find somewhere else to spend the night," he told the cat as he put him down. "Sorry, I…What? No, I'm here because my family asked me to come, not because I'm interested in Ava. You can't be serious." He paused and shook his head. "Yeah, yeah, I know what you thought you saw when we were here for GG's funeral, but you're wrong. I'm not in love with Ava, and she's not in love with me."

Colleen glanced over her shoulder, catching the look of frustration on Griffin's handsome face. "Oh yes she is, my boy. That girl never stopped loving you. If I could just find my memoirs, you'd understand why she—"

Simon meowed twice, nudging his head at the fireplace.

"Bejaysus, are you trying to tell me my memoirs are in here?" The cat responded with what could only be described as a get-on-with-it meow. If Colleen still had a heartbeat, it would have quickened.

She pushed all the way inside the fireplace at the same time Griffin said, "Okay, this is the last time I'm going to say this, Lex. There's nothing between Ava and me, and there never will be."

"Never say never, my boy. If I've taught you anything, it should be that," Colleen said, narrowing her eyes on the wall of soot-covered bricks while keeping an ear open to Griffin's side of the conversation with his ex-wife.

"So are you going to tell me why you really called?" Several beats passed before he said, "Sure, but why don't you just tell me now? Okay, fine. I'll give you a call when I'm headed home, and we can get together then." His eyebrows drew inward at whatever Lexi was saying to him. "You sure you're okay? All right, I'll see you in a few days."

Scrubbing a hand over his face, he tossed his phone on the pillow. "Simon, take my advice, stay single and play the field." Griffin came to his feet and walked to the fireplace, rubbing his muscular arms. "Let's get some heat in here."

There was a scratch on the brick, then the smell of sulfur. A small flicker of flame lit the inside of the fireplace. Griffin touched a match to the logs, sparking Colleen's memory. Her memoirs were here. She could see herself fitting them behind the loose bricks for safekeeping one hot summer night.

"No!" she cried. Then realizing Griffin couldn't hear her, she leaned over and blew with all her might. The small flame blinked out. Her great-grandson cursed but was undeterred.

"You always were stubborn," she groused at him after his fifth try. She wasn't sure how much air she had left. As he lit another match, she frantically waved her arms. The small flame sputtered and went out.

Griffin snapped the long matchstick in half, tossing it on the logs. "If I get lucky, the pipes will freeze, and they'll have to get their heads out of their asses. The sooner we sell out, the better."

Chapter Three

♥

The sun had yet to rise when Ava walked from her bedroom through the sparsely furnished living room and into the kitchen. She started the coffeemaker and then bent to retrieve a pot from the bottom cupboard. She turned on the tap, glancing out the window while filling the pot with cold water. The sky looked like an artist's palette with splotches of lavender breaking through the midnight black, streaks of tangerine on the horizon.

When she was younger, she would have taken a moment to appreciate the beauty of the view and watch the white-crested waves breaking against the dock's pylons across the road. Today her eyes automatically went to the thermostat attached to the white window frame, its paint peeling. Her walk to and from the manor would be more pleasant than yesterday's.

She turned off the water and placed the pot on the back burner, flicking it on. The coffeemaker spat and gurgled as she salted the water. She reached for the bag of steel-cut oats, placing it on the yellowed laminate countertop beside the stove. Then she went to the fridge and took out the top round beef and vegetables, placing them on the counter beside the cutting board. She retrieved two sweet onions from the windowsill and removed the skins. Ignoring the ache in her arm, she mechanically chopped the vegetables before moving on to the meat.

Once she was finished, she scraped everything into the Crock-Pot, adding two cups of red wine, several cups of the beef stock she'd made earlier in the week, the leftover tomato sauce from last night's dinner, and a couple pinches of basil, thyme, and marjoram. Setting the Crock-Pot to medium heat, she turned to the water boiling on the stove and added the oats before covering it with the glass lid.

It was a routine she could do in her sleep. Which was probably a good thing since she'd barely gotten two hours last night. Her father had had another bad night. Every night for the past three weeks had been the same. Though Ava doubted she would have slept even if he'd had a good one.

Every time she closed her eyes, she saw Griffin. Her body responded with the same desperate yearning, the same want and need, as it had when he'd opened the shower curtain, when he so easily swept her off her feet, and when his strong, calloused hands had gently wrapped around her ankles to remove her shoes.

The strength of her desire had shocked her. It shouldn't, she supposed. This was Griffin, after all. A man who, with one look, could cause butterflies to take flight in her stomach and her toes to curl. A man whose body she had once known as well as her own.

There had been a time, though—twelve years before—when those rippling muscles and chiseled eight-pack had filled her with something other than desire. Her emotions had been darker and haunted back then. The thought of making love, even with the husband she adored, had filled her with dread, shame, and guilt. Unable to see a way to get past the crippling emotions, she'd asked him for a divorce.

If he discovered the book behind the bricks, he'd know why. For now, she thought she was safe. She would have heard from him if he'd found it. She prayed he'd used all the firewood, inadvertently burning the book in the process.

Reaching for a mug, she recalled the flash of anger in his indigo eyes when he whipped open the shower curtain, the way his upper lip curled in loathing beneath his heavy scruff. After all this time, he still hated her, and she loved him with every fiber of her being. The mug slipped from her fingers and hit the edge of the stove, shattering into a thousand pieces at her feet.

"Can't a man get some sleep in his own home? Keep it down out there!" her father yelled in Italian from the back bedroom, his voice gravelly from lack of sleep and his two-pack-a-day habit.

She crouched to pick up the broken mug, fighting back tears of exhaustion and resentment. Her emotions were bubbling too close to the surface these days. For years, she'd been like a zombie, sleepwalking through her life. Then Colleen died and Sophie became manager of the manor, figuratively holding up a mirror to Ava, forcing her to see the woman she'd become. Ava hadn't liked what she saw, but she couldn't change the past, and she didn't see a way to change her future. The road that lay ahead seemed as bleak as the one she'd been on for the past twelve years.

As she stood up to walk to the garbage, a splinter of glass stabbed the ball of her big toe. She swore and raised her foot, pulling out a thick shard of ceramic. Droplets of blood splashed onto the tile.

"What's wrong?" her father called out.

She grabbed the paper towel roll from the counter, ripping off several pieces to stop the bleeding. "Nothing, Papa."

Wrapping the paper towel around her foot, she straightened to give the pot of oatmeal a quick stir and then removed it from the burner. Once she cleaned the blood droplets off the black-and-white tile floor, she washed her hands before preparing her father's breakfast tray. She scooped several tablespoons of the fruit salad she'd made the night before into a small bowl, sprinkled wheat germ and cinnamon on the oatmeal, and added a glass of freshly squeezed orange juice and a mug of coffee to the tray. She hobbled to the bathroom, cleaned and bandaged her foot, then made her way down the bright blue carpeted hallway to her father's bedroom.

Squaring her shoulders, she forced a smile and entered. "Good morning, Papa."

"What's good about it?" he grumbled, glaring at the breakfast tray. "What is that crap? Where's my bacon and eggs?"

She set the legs of the tray carefully over his hips. "Your cholesterol levels were high at your last appointment. Dr. Bishop recommended—"

"I don't give a good goddamn what Doc Bishop has to say. I want my bacon and eggs. Take it away." He shoved the tray.

Ava gasped, grabbing the juice glass and mug before they toppled over, hot coffee sloshing over her hand and onto her father's beige comforter. What looked to be regret flickered briefly in his green eyes. "I don't have much to look forward to. I should be able to eat whatever I want," he said in a sullen voice, pushing at the tray again, not as hard this time.

Ava nudged aside the framed photographs on the nightstand to set down the glass and mug. Her parents' wedding photo, a photo of the three of them the Christmas before her mother died, and one of Ava and her father taken a few years before his accident.

He was still as ruggedly handsome as the man in the photographs, though his curly hair was more gray than ebony now and his green eyes no longer sparkled with good humor. Unless he was angry, which more often than not he was these days, his eyes were dull and lifeless. The lines that fanned from the corners were deeper and more pronounced, like the ones carved into either side of his down-turned mouth.

His injury had turned her once kind and loving father into a man who could be cruel and vindictive. He wasn't the father she remembered, but as she had done for so many years now, she reminded herself of the man he'd once been and stuffed down the hurt, anger, and resentment. "Eat some of your porridge, and I'll make you bacon and eggs. Only one egg, though, and two slices of bacon. You can have the fruit cup for lunch."

Making a second breakfast for her father messed up

Ava's carefully scheduled routine. By the time she'd showered, gotten ready for work, stripped and remade her father's bed, helped him bathe, shave, and get dressed, it was almost eight o'clock.

At the side door, she pulled on a black knit hat and wrapped a scarf around her neck. "I'm leaving now, Papa. I'll see you at six."

Her father, sitting in his wheelchair watching television, glanced at her. "Don't be late. I'm almost out of smokes and whiskey. Get me a forty-ouncer of Crown Royal this time. No more of the cheap stuff. They're watering it down."

Ava opened her mouth and then closed it. She couldn't tell him she was the one watering it down. She hadn't thought he'd caught on. "Next paycheck. There's red wine in the bottom cupboard. It's better for you anyway." If he'd drink only one glass it would be. "Dr. Bishop wants you to cut—"

"I don't give a good goddamn what Doc Bishop wants. He can kiss my hairy ass. I'll not give up the only things that give me pleasure."

Ava thought about arguing, pointing out he was heading for an early grave. But she was too tired to fight. "All right, Papa. I'll get your Crown Royal."

He picked up his package of cigarettes, looked inside, and frowned. "I thought I had more left. You better get me a couple packs."

Ava had picked up her father's dirty habit. She found it relaxing. Though she limited herself to eight cigarettes a day. She'd taken them from her father's package this morning. Now she'd have to find time to make the long trek to the liquor store and corner store on her lunch hour.

"Papa, why don't you go out today? The fresh air will do you good. The sidewalks have been salted, and I put sand on the ramp last night."

He turned up the volume on the television. Ava sighed and opened the door, the tension in her body releasing as soon as she pulled it closed behind her. She glanced at the ramp. On the off chance he'd actually go out, she scooped another cupful of sand from the bag beside the door and tossed it onto the weather-beaten boards.

The front door of the blue bungalow beside theirs opened, and Dorothy popped her head out. "Do you have a minute to spare, lovey?"

Ava's stomach dropped, afraid this was the day their neighbor said she'd had enough of Gino's verbal abuse. The older woman was a retired nurse and had been Ava's mother's childhood best friend. She'd moved back to Harmony Harbor last month when her husband died. She popped in to check on Gino a couple times a day.

"Of course. Is something wrong?" Ava asked tentatively as she walked along the sidewalk.

"That's what I wanted to talk to you about. Come in, it's freezing." She held the door open. No matter what time of day, the older woman was always well put together. Today was no exception. Dorothy's chin-length blond hair was styled, her lightly lined face made up. She wore black slacks and a fuchsia sweater. "I didn't want to call in case your father picked up the other line."

Ava tried not to let her panic show. "Did something happen when you were over yesterday?"

"It's not just yesterday. He's getting worse, lovey. Surely you out of anyone can see that." She gave Ava's arm a pointed look.

Dorothy knew how Ava had gotten the bruise. Gino had been in a rage when she'd arrived home late from work the other night, and Dorothy had been outside shoveling. She'd heard Gino throwing things around the kitchen and cursing at Ava. The older woman had opened the side door at the same time Ava deflected a cast-iron frying pan with her arm. Dorothy had threatened to call the police. At the thought of everyone in town knowing their business, Ava had begged her not to. She didn't believe her father meant to hurt her. He'd never hurt her purposefully before. Sometimes, he just forgot his own strength.

"It's the weather and being stuck inside. You know how active he was. He lived to be at sea."

"Lovey, stop making excuses for him. He's been in a chair going on twelve years."

"You're right, I know you are. But it doesn't make it any less difficult for him, Dorothy. He was used to being the breadwinner and self-sufficient. Now he's dependent on me. I think it scared him when I was late coming home the other night."

"I'm sure it did, and I have a feeling my stopping by to check on him isn't helping matters. He's gotten it into his head you're getting ready to move on with your life, and I'm your replacement. I suppose I haven't helped by suggesting that's exactly what you should do. Still, there's no excuse for that kind of behavior. He's drinking too much."

Ava fiddled with the zipper on her coat. "I know. I'll talk to him about it tonight." She dreaded the thought of confronting him about his drinking, but Dorothy was right. His mood swings had become more dramatic, his behavior more erratic.

"I don't want you to do it on your own. Call me when you get home, and I'll come over."

Ava wasn't sure having Dorothy there when she talked to her father was a good idea. It would probably make matters worse. Gino was as private as Ava was. But Dorothy was a determined woman, and just like with her father, Ava was too tired to fight. "Okay. There's chicken sandwiches and white bean soup in the fridge for lunch. I made extra for you, and there's stew in the Crock-Pot. I left a container on the counter for you to fill."

Dorothy patted Ava's cheek. "I wish you'd take care of yourself as well as you do your father and me."

"It's the least I can do. I don't know what I'd do without you." She glanced at the clock on the living room wall. "I better get going or I'll be late for work."

"Why don't you let me drive you? Rosa tells me your ex-husband is staying at the manor and helping renovate the ballroom. I'd like to get a look at the man…and the ballroom, of course."

Ava didn't want to think about why her Auntie Rosa was talking to Dorothy about Griffin or why the older woman wanted a look at him. Dorothy had recently joined the Widows Club, of which Rosa was also a member. A month earlier, the group's sole focus had been getting Sophie and Liam together. Which was probably responsible for the nervous hitch in Ava's voice and the reason she avoided any mention of Griffin. "*Grazie*, but the walk will do me good."

Dorothy held the door open. "I can think of several other things that would be good for you, too, and more fun. Your father might be stuck in a chair, but you're as stuck as he is, lovey. Life's short. Don't let it pass you by."

Dorothy's proclamation joined Ava on the walk to work—it made for an uncomfortable traveling companion. She breathed deeply of the frosty morning air as she walked past the pastel-colored Colonials along Main Street, trying not to think about what Dorothy had said. If she did, Ava might start wondering what her life would have been like if she'd made different choices. She wasn't going to let the *what if*s get a toehold in her mind. As far as she was concerned, it was better to stay firmly rooted in the reality of her life than waste precious energy on an impossible dream. If she didn't, she'd become frustrated and bitter.

This was her life, and she'd make the best of it. Things would get back to normal once she ensured Colleen's memoirs had burned and Griffin left town. Other people might not agree that her life was *normal*, but it was the one she'd known for twelve years. Then she remembered the issue of her father self-medicating with alcohol and tonight's upcoming confrontation.

It looked like she could use a fairy godmother after all. One who had a talent for dealing with belligerent fathers. No sooner had the thought crossed her mind than someone knocked on a window. Julia Landon, owner of Books and Beans, was dressed like a fairy and waving her inside.

Ava looked up at the cloudless blue sky. "I don't think you're funny, Colleen. Meddle in someone else's affairs."

"So, does she answer you back or is it a one-sided conversation?" a smooth male voice asked.

Byron Harte, reporter and part owner of the *Harmony Harbor Gazette*, looked at her with a grin on his sunbronzed face. Ava didn't trust his slick, pretty-boy looks. He reminded her of Griffin's childhood best friend

Damien Gray, a man Ava had made the mistake of trusting a long time ago.

Despite wishing the sidewalk would open up and swallow her whole, Ava shrugged. "Depends if she's in the mood to talk or not."

"Fascinating. I've never met anyone who can converse with the dead. I'd love to interview—"

She rolled her eyes. "It was a joke, Mr. Harte."

"Really? That's a shame. I was hoping you'd ask where her memoirs are. Unless...No one's found the book yet, have they?" He held the door open for her.

Ava's stomach dropped at Byron's interest in Colleen's memoirs. "Don't tell me you actually fell for that? Colleen was a hundred and four. She was *pazza*, crazy." She forced a laugh while silently asking for her old friend's forgiveness.

Julia smiled as they entered Books and Beans. She stood behind the small coffee bar at the front of the shop. A few feet beyond the counter and through an arched opening was the bookstore. The walls of the children's section at the back were covered in brightly painted murals. A big, red velvet chair that Julia sat in during children's hour was the focal point of the space. "I thought I missed you, Ava. Your chocolate cinnamon latte is almost ready."

Stopping at Books and Beans for a latte was the highlight of Ava's morning. She supposed she'd be better off saving the money for new shoes and a cell phone, but she justified the expense as her small contribution toward making the bookstore a success. Julia had become a good friend, and their daily conversation and Julia's coffee made Ava happy. And it's not as if she had a lot that made her happy these days. She'd take it where she could get it.

Ava dug in her knapsack for her thermos. "Thank you. I'm running a little late."

"Just a minute more." Julia smiled, then glanced at Byron. "You're looking a little glum this morning. Did you wake up on the wrong side of the bed?"

"Ms. DiRossi just dashed my hopes of a big story. It seems there's no truth to the rumors that *The Secret Keeper of Harmony Harbor* exists."

Julia held Ava's gaze for a moment before giving Byron a bright smile. "Of course there isn't. Colleen was a hundred and four. No one believed she'd actually written the book."

"According to my grandmother, the Widows Club did. And I can tell you so did quite a few other people in town. Most of whom I imagine will be pleased to learn the book doesn't exist."

"There you go. Run the story as a public service announcement."

A slow smile creased Byron's handsome face, and he leaned across the counter. Taking Julia by the shoulders, he kissed her. "You're brilliant."

"I am?" the other woman's voice cracked.

"You are. I know of at least five people who were terrified the book would come to light. Now I just have to find out why." He frowned. "Are you all right, love? You look a little peaked."

"I'm fine." Julia gave him a bright smile. Ava noticed it faltered when she turned to the coffee machine. "You want your usual today, Byron?" Julia asked as she filled Ava's thermos.

"Please." He leaned over the counter again. "Watch your fairy wings, love. You nearly took out the cups. What's on for story hour today?"

With her smile back in place, Julia handed Ava her thermos. "*Cinderella.*"

"Ah, you should have Ms. DiRossi play the lead role. She fits the part perfectly. She's a maid and hides her beauty behind oversized, ugly clothes. One wave of your sparkly wand and, voila, Cinderella. Albeit with black hair."

Ava fumbled the thermos she'd been returning to her bag.

Byron caught the thermos and handed it to her. "You are beautiful, Ms. DiRossi. Stunningly so." He angled his head. "It makes me wonder why or who you're hiding from."

His words felt like a threat, but she didn't see it in his eyes. They were warm and kind. Then again, she hadn't thought Damien was a threat either. She forced a derisive snort. "You're *pazza.*" And handed a fistful of change to Julia. "Have a good day, Julia. You, too, Mr. Harte."

"I'm planning on heading to the manor to check on the ballroom's progress, Ms. DiRossi. If you wait a moment, I'll give you a ride."

"*Grazie*, but no. I prefer to walk."

"I had a feeling you might say that," he said with a half-smile.

"Just a minute, Ava. I nearly forgot." Julia bent down, reappearing with a fistful of flyers. "Can you pass these around at the manor? I'm starting a book club in February. Meetings will be once a month on Wednesday nights. I hope you'll join."

Ava was tempted to say yes. She liked to read when she had the time, and she wanted to support Julia. But her father…"Maybe. We'll see. *Ciao*."

"Where do I sign up?" Byron asked.

The door closed on Julia saying something about it being a women-only club, and Byron arguing against sexism.

Ava hurried down the sidewalk, half walking, half running. She wanted to have at least ten minutes to enjoy her coffee and cigarette at the manor before starting work.

"Hi, Ava." A woman waved a broom outside of Truly Scrumptious, the hood of her parka covering her long, caramel-colored hair.

"Morning, Mackenzie." Ava pointed at the snow piling up on top of the bakery's purple-and-white striped awning. "Be careful. It looks like ice has built up on the right-hand side."

"Thanks, pal. Have a good day."

"You too. Morning, Arianna," Ava called to the stylish blonde standing back from the storefront window a few doors down from Truly Scrumptious.

"Hey, Ava. How does the display look from over there?" Arianna was a designer and owned Tie the Knot. With small purple and pink hearts, she'd created the outline of a large heart that framed a mannequin wearing a stunning bridal gown.

"Gorgeous as always."

"Thanks." Arianna smiled. "I'll see you later. I wanna check out the ballroom."

"Me too. I'll come with you. Morning, Ava." Lily, the owner of In Bloom, called out as she unloaded a box from a delivery truck a few shops down from Tie the Knot.

Ava waved. "I'll see you both later." She said hello to several more shopkeepers who were out salting the sidewalks. If she went down the next street, she could take the shortcut to the manor. It's how she usually walked to work. But there was one problem—DiRossi's Fine Foods was on that particular street. Given that her aunt had filled Dorothy in on Griffin, the last thing Ava wanted was to run into Rosa.

Ava took the long way instead, her heavy black coat and boots weighing her down as she ran up the hill, past the town hall and the copper-domed clock tower. Byron's words kept time with her boots hitting the pavement. Ugly clothes. *Thud*. Beautiful. *Thud*. Hiding. *Thud*. She tried to empty them from her head, but her mind kept flashing images of the voluptuous girl she used to be. Until that long-ago night, she'd loved her body, loved each and every one of her curves. She'd felt feminine and strong. She'd felt beautiful.

Damien had changed how she saw herself, how she felt about herself. Byron was right. She'd tried to disappear, to hide in plain sight. She hadn't wanted to attract attention. She understood why she hadn't then. But more than a decade had passed, and still she wore ugly clothes that were two sizes too big. She didn't care what she looked like. She didn't want anyone to see her—to really see her.

Tears prickled behind her eyelids. She hated Byron. Hated him for asking his stupid question and making her think. She'd destroyed the man she loved and ruined her life. There was no going back. The past had to stay in the past. She had her father to take care of.

She cut through a small opening in the stone fence and

ran across Greystone's half-empty parking lot. Finally, she'd reached her refuge. At the manor, she could simply go about her job and no one would bother her. She sighed. How quickly she forgot about the book, Griffin, and her cousin Sophie.

"*Basta*, enough," she grumbled when thoughts of Gino and Dorothy entered her already overcrowded head.

She ducked behind a tall cedar tree in the frozen garden at the front of the manor and crouched, pulling the thermos from her knapsack and then a cigarette and lighter from her coat pocket. She lit the cigarette, her mind emptying as she deeply inhaled. After two more calming drags, she unscrewed the lid on the thermos, breathing in the chocolate and cinnamon scent with a contented smile. She straightened and leaned against the sand-colored granite wall. These few moments alone with her coffee and cigarette made the rest of the day seem survivable and put the morning from hell in her rearview mirror.

She relaxed and sipped her coffee, savoring its taste and warmth, welcoming the tiny buzz from the caffeine. She took a couple more drags of the cigarette, blowing out lazy smoke rings. At the low rumble of an engine, she leaned to the side. A black truck with an open bed backed toward the walkway. She recognized the honey-brown hair and wide shoulders of the man at the wheel and slid an inch to her left.

She had half a cigarette and coffee to go; the risk was worth it. Griffin had obviously picked up supplies for the ballroom. He'd be too busy lugging them in to notice her.

The truck door slammed, and she took a sip of coffee and then another drag on her cigarette. She waited for the sound of the truck's gate opening. Instead she heard, "What are you doing hiding behind a tree?"

Crapola. She shuffled a little farther to the left. "Enjoying a few minutes of peace and quiet before my shift."

She heard the crunch of Griffin's boots on the snow-crusted ground, and then he was standing in front of her with a bag in his hands. Avoiding his eyes, she drank her coffee while easing her left hand behind her. She knew his opinion of smoking and had no doubt she would have to listen to a lecture.

"Give me that before you set your coat on fire." He reached for her hand.

She lifted the cigarette to her mouth. "Now you don't have to worry about my coat." She put it between her lips.

Griffin plucked it from her mouth. "Now you don't have to worry about your lungs." He tossed the cigarette on the ground, grinding it to dust under his boot.

"You had no right to do that, Griffin Gallagher. If I want to smoke, I will." Furious, she dug in her pocket for the second cigarette and her lighter. She now had a better understanding of how her father felt about people telling him what he shouldn't do and sympathized with him.

"Since when?"

"Since when what?" she asked, placing the second cigarette between her lips. She clamped it between her teeth when he moved his hand toward her. She raised a finger. "Do not even think about taking this cigarette from me."

"Yeah, what are you going to do about it if I do?" he asked, a hint of amusement in his voice.

"I will—" Before she got another word out of her mouth, he'd taken her cigarette and broken it in half.

"You can thank me later."

She looked from him to her cigarette. "Th-thank you… Thank you! You…you," she sputtered, her temper rendering her momentarily speechless.

Griffin grinned and put a finger behind his ear. "You… you what?"

She gasped at his teasing, and all the emotions she'd kept bottled up inside her exploded in a torrent of rapid-fire Italian. She forgot she had her thermos in her hands and threw up her arms, her precious latte ending up on the wall behind her. *"Testa di cazzo!"* she yelled, and picked up her knapsack. Which went to prove just how furious she was. She only ever called him a dickhead when she'd totally lost it.

"And there she is," Ava thought she heard him say as she stormed off, but he no longer sounded amused.

"Ava," he called after her.

"What?" she shouted back.

He held up a finger, a white plastic bag dangling from it. "For you."

She frowned. "No, it's not mine."

His broad shoulders rose on a sigh. "Yeah, it is. They're for you."

"For me?" she asked as she slowly approached him.

"You still wear a size seven?"

"Yes, but what does that have to—"

"Your shoes are falling apart. You needed new ones."

She stared up at him as she took the bag, a familiar warmth spreading in her chest. When they were married, he'd often surprise her with new shoes. "I don't understand. You bought me shoes?" she asked, unable to stop her lips from curving in a tentative smile.

He looked away. "Yeah, it's not a big deal, so don't make it one."

The muttered words replaced her initial pleasure with embarrassment. She handed back the bag. "*Grazie,* but I can buy my own shoes."

"Just take the damn shoes, Ava. You work for us. They're part of your uniform."

"*Grazie,*" she said, adding under her breath, "you're still a high-handed *testa di cazzo.*"

Chapter Four

♥

"Cremation or burial?" Sophie sat behind the formidable mahogany desk in the study, holding up Ava's work shoes with a wry expression on her face. "If you ask me, it's long past time they were laid to rest. What are they, twenty years old?"

"Twelve, and they've served me well. I think I'll bury them," Ava said, placing the empty shoebox and tissue paper back in the plastic bag.

"I was joking. They're ugly, and they're going in the trash." Sophie leaned over and tossed them in the wastebasket.

"So was I, but they were good shoes."

"If you say so, but those are adorable." Sophie nodded at Ava's new shoes. "They look comfortable too. Where did you get them?"

Comfortable didn't begin to describe how wonderful the black leather lace-up booties felt on Ava's feet. They were feather light, the cushioned insoles making it feel like she was walking on air. They were also the prettiest shoes she'd worn in a long time. "Head Over Heels," she responded to Sophie's question while leaving out the most important part.

No way was she telling Sophie that Griffin had bought her the shoes. The last thing she needed was for her cousin to misinterpret the gesture. Something Ava herself was trying not to do. Thinking of Griffin's grumpy manner when he'd given her the shoes made that easier.

Ava stood up. Sophie had waylaid her as soon as she'd walked into the manor, and they'd gotten sidetracked by the shoes, but Ava had to get to Griffin's room and check on the book. "You said you needed to talk to me about something?"

"I did, didn't I?" Sophie clicked away on the keyboard, studiously avoiding Ava's gaze. "Um, we need your help in the ballroom today. I've asked Trudy to take over your rooms."

Ava crossed her arms and waited her cousin out.

Sophie looked up from the computer screen. "It wasn't my idea. It was Kitty's."

At that bit of unwelcome news, Ava slowly lowered herself onto the chair across from Sophie's desk. "Please tell me Kitty is acting alone and Auntie Rosa and the Widows Club aren't involved."

Sophie grimaced. "I wish I could. And they aren't the only ones. Liam and his dad are the reason Griffin's here. They want him to vote to keep Greystone in the family and move back to Harmony Harbor. They've decided that you're the one who can make that happen."

Ava stared at her cousin. "That makes no sense. For years they blamed me for breaking Griffin's heart."

Sophie lifted a shoulder. "Maybe they think you're the only one who can put it back together again."

"Please, Griffin got over me a long time ago. The man has no interest in me whatsoever." She didn't bother adding that she had no interest in Griffin either, because Ava hadn't done a good job hiding her unrequited love from her cousin. "They should be talking to his ex-wife." Thinking back to her conversation with Sophie the day before, Ava narrowed her eyes at her cousin. "You put Liam and his father up to this, didn't you?"

"Me? Of course not, I've been too busy coming up with ways to get you to take over the…"

Ava held her gaze.

"Okay, so I might have encouraged them after the fact," Sophie admitted.

"*Pazze*, everyone has gone crazy." Even her, Ava decided, because for a brief moment when she'd discovered Griffin had bought her a gift, something small and hopeful had stirred to life inside her.

"Well, I doubt you have to worry about them now. In Griffin's opinion, we're wasting time and money fighting a losing battle, and we should cut our losses and accept the developer's offer before he withdraws it."

Of course, that's something Griffin would say. The man was a battle-hardened warrior who attacked every problem as though he were on a mission. He didn't romanticize things. It wouldn't matter to him that Greystone had been in his family for generations. He knew how to shut off his emotions. He'd done the same with her. After trying to get her to talk and change her mind about the divorce, he'd given up and cut his losses.

But she had no intention of allowing him to give up on the manor—even if it did put her in the crosshairs of the Widows Club. Someone had to make the man see reason. Too many people depended on Greystone, including herself. "So, what's the plan?"

Sophie blinked. "But I thought...You're really okay with everyone playing matchmaker?"

"No, of course not. They'd be disappointed anyway. Not to mention embarrassing and annoying. What I meant is how are you planning to get Griffin on the Save Greystone Team?"

"Oh, I...I'm not really sure. You know him better than anyone. Can you think of something?"

"It's been twelve years, Sophie. I don't really know him anymore."

"People don't change that..." She glanced at Ava as though she were proof the old adage didn't always hold true, then cleared her throat. "Okay, for argument's sake, let's say he hasn't."

"His family is his Achilles' heel. He'll do anything for them." Sophie opened her mouth, and Ava raised a hand. "I know what you're going to say. But right now he thinks he's protecting them. Kitty, Liam, and Colin need to show him how important the manor is to them. So do you, and don't be afraid to use your secret weapon."

Sophie wrinkled her nose. "I don't know how Liam would feel if I start flirting with his brother."

Ava snorted. "You're a beautiful woman, but I was thinking about Mia. Griffin loves children, and he adored Riley. Mary used to complain about how much he spoiled her." Riley had been a late-in-life baby. Mary'd had her when she was nearly fifty, and her four sons were in their late teens and twenties, which pretty much guaranteed Riley was doted on.

Sophie frowned. "I didn't think you had anything to do with Griffin's family after the divorce. Other than Colleen and Kitty, I mean."

More than seven years had passed since the night Ava had learned about the horrific accident that had claimed Mary's and Riley's lives. To this day, she couldn't think of them without getting emotional. Her reaction was no different now, and she glanced out the window to hide the tears welling in her eyes. "Mary never gave up hope that Griffin and I would get back together. After my father's accident, she'd stop by every few weeks to check on us. When Riley was born, she'd bring her too," Ava said, surreptitiously running a finger under her bottom lashes.

"Does Griffin know?"

"No, no one does. Mary didn't want it to look like she was taking sides. And like I told you, I was persona non grata as far as Griffin's father and brothers were concerned. Colleen probably suspected, but she never said anything to me." Ava stood up. "I'll try to think of a way for you to bring Griffin around while I'm cleaning the rooms." She had to check on the status of the book before she could think of anything else. "You might want to remind Auntie Rosa and the Widows Club that their priority should be saving the manor, not me."

"Easier said than done," Sophie said, leaning back in her chair to grab two bakery boxes off the wooden filing cabinet. "Speaking of Nonna, she dropped these off earlier and asked that you give them to Griffin." Sophie handed the boxes across the desk to Ava.

If she hadn't already sniffed out her aunt's matchmaking scheme, the scent of icing sugar and vanilla coming from the bakery boxes would have given Rosa's intentions away. Worried that Griffin might get the wrong idea if Ava showed up with his favorite cookies, she considered handing the boxes back to Sophie.

As though her cousin read her mind, she waggled her eyebrows and grinned. "It's for a good cause. Take one for the team."

Ava wasn't sure she liked the gleam in her cousin's eyes, but she'd do whatever it took to get Griffin on board—within reason. Plus, she owed him a more genuine thank-you than the one she'd muttered at him earlier.

The study door opened. "Good morning, my dears," Griffin's grandmother greeted them with a soft lilt in her voice. Kitty was still beautiful for a woman in her seventies. She looked elegant no matter what she wore, and today was no exception. She had on jeans and a blue sweater that matched her eyes. "Rosa said she dropped off…" Kitty's gaze landed on the boxes in Ava's hands. "Wonderful. Just the pick-me-up Griffin needs. He's been working since the crack of dawn. Perhaps you should bring him some coffee with his cookies, Ava."

Ava caught the matchmaking twinkle in Kitty's eyes and had to remind herself how important it was to get Griffin on their side. But right now protecting her secret outweighed protecting her job. "I really need to get the rooms—"

Kitty interrupted her. "I'm sure you remember how he likes his coffee."

Of course she did. Ava remembered everything about him, every moment of every day they'd been together. She'd clung to those memories like a lifeline during the worst of times. Ava nodded, forcing an agreeable smile on her face. And really, it was difficult to be anything but agreeable to Kitty. She'd only ever been kind to Ava.

"Leave your bag and coat here. I'll drop them in the staff's break room later," Sophie offered.

"*Grazie*." Ava had just turned to rest the boxes on the chair while she snuck a cigarette and lighter from her coat pocket when Kitty said, "Ava, your new shoes are darling. I'm so glad Teddy didn't mind opening early for Griffin this morning."

"Wow, Griffin bought you the shoes, Ava? Funny you forgot to mention that. He has great taste, doesn't he? And to think he remembered your size after all this time. Guess some things never change, do they?"

Ava gritted her teeth to hold back a curse at the smug tone in her cousin's voice. Slipping the lighter and cigarette into the breast pocket of her uniform, Ava picked up the boxes and straightened. Without meeting Sophie's gaze, she said, "He does." And that's all she would admit to. "I'll see you both later."

She closed the door of the study as the two women resumed their discussion of Griffin and his taste in footwear. As she walked down the hall and through the lobby, Ava couldn't bring herself to resent her new shoes or Griffin for putting her in the crosshairs of Kitty…and most likely Sophie too.

No longer weighed down by her clunky footwear, Ava didn't trudge across the lobby's gray slate floor like she normally did. Her steps seemed to match her sexy, youthful shoes. She couldn't remember the last time she'd walked with a slight sway to her hips. Odd what something as simple as…

The whirring of drills and banging of hammers interrupted the thought. She'd almost forgotten she had a job to do. Somehow she had to deliver the cookies without Griffin attaching the meaning to them that Rosa no doubt intended him to.

He wouldn't be able to if Ava offered them to the other workers first. She headed for the dining room instead of the ballroom. "Hi, Erin," she greeted the attractive young waitress clearing a table in the empty dining room.

Erin straightened, glancing toward the kitchen, then back at Ava. "Word of advice—you don't want to go in the kitchen. Helga's on a tear."

Ava weighed facing an on-the-tear Helga to handing Griffin two boxes of the same type of cookies she'd made him on their third date. He used to tell anyone who'd listen that he fell in love with her that day. "I'll risk it. I just need a platter for the cookies."

Erin tucked a strand of shoulder-length blond hair behind her ear. "Where are the cookies from?"

"My Aunt Rosa made them for...the men working on the ballroom. Why?"

"Okay, no way are you going in there."

At Ava's raised eyebrow, Erin explained. "Sophie asked her brother to make pizzas for the men's lunch. So if Helga sees you bringing cookies from Rosa...Yeah, I'll get the platter for you. As much for my sake as yours. I'll have to put up with her for the rest of the day."

Ava set the boxes on the waitstaff station and filled two carafes with coffee while she waited for Erin.

Helga's voice followed the waitress out the kitchen door. Erin rolled her eyes. "She threatened to castrate Marco if he steps foot in her kitchen."

The older woman wasn't a fan of the DiRossis, especially Ava, but it sounded like her cousin was at the top of Helga's hit list now. "I'll be sure to warn him. Thanks," she said, accepting the platter from Erin. "Do you mind if I use the dessert cart? I'll bring them coffee too." When Erin bit her lip and shot another worried glance at the kitchen door, Ava added, "I promise, Helga won't even know it's gone. I'll be back in ten minutes." She hoped.

Erin nodded and then smiled. "Lucky you. There's some serious eye candy in the ballroom today. I think I'll hang out there during my break."

Ava imagined Erin wouldn't be the only member of the staff to do so. A large contingent of local firefighters had volunteered their time thanks to Griffin's father, who was Harmony Harbor's fire chief. Liam was a firefighter as well.

Once the cart was ready to go, Ava handed Erin a cookie. "Thanks for your help. I'll see you in a few minutes."

"Anytime." Erin's brow furrowed as she looked more closely at Ava. "There's something different about you today. You seem…taller somehow." Her eyes dropped to Ava's feet. "Oh. My. God, they're adorbs. I seriously need a pair. Please don't tell me they came from Head Over Heels."

Ava made a face and lifted an apologetic shoulder.

Erin groaned. "I should have known. I'll have to save for six months before I can afford a pair." She eyed Ava again and gave her an arch look. "So, does the arrival of one of the most delectable pieces of eye candy to hit Harmony Harbor have anything to do with your new look?"

If the shoes weren't so comfortable, Ava would have

been tempted to throw them in the trash. "I don't have a new look, and even if I did, it would have nothing to do with Griffin."

"I never said it was Griffin," Erin said with a cheeky grin, adding, "But you're right, the man is off-the-charts hot. You know, if you were interested in getting him back, I could totally help with that. I'm really good with makeup and…" She held up her hands when Ava shot her a look. "Okay, okay, I'll zip it. Just, you know, FYI, you might not want to be shooting around that look too often. It's kinda scary."

"I'll take that under advisement," Ava said as she pushed the cart up the ramp with a small smile. She liked Erin. She reminded Ava a little of herself at twenty-one.

Ava's footsteps slowed as she crossed the lobby. She picked out Griffin's voice among all the others. His deep laughter wrapped around her like a bittersweet caress. It had been a long time since she'd heard him laugh.

The wheels of the cart rattled over the gray slate floors as she made her way to the open French doors. Jasper, wearing his standard black suit, stood with his hands clasped behind his back surveying the progress. The work on the ornate ceiling and hardwood floors had been completed last week. Today they'd begun the massive undertaking of replacing each and every individual twelve-by-twelve wooden tile on the walls.

Without Dana, none of the work would have been possible. Greystone operated on a lean budget, and the restoration of the ballroom had been far beyond their means. So Dana had started a GoFundMe campaign. After all, as she argued, the town would be benefiting as much as Greystone. In less than a week, they had enough money to go ahead with the renovations. Ava had a feeling the campaign was a ruse. She was almost positive Greystone's benefactor was none other than Dana herself.

At that moment, the attractive redhead was at the far end of the ballroom speaking to Chase Halloran, who'd been overseeing the work. His family owned a historic preservation and restoration company. Much to his grandmother's delight, Chase had recently moved back home to take over the business. The single women of Harmony Harbor were as delighted as Mrs. Halloran. Ava imagined the members of the Widows Club were, too, since their mandate was to bring the children of Harmony Harbor back home. If that included a little matchmaking while they were at it, so much the better. She wondered if Griffin had any idea what he was up against.

Jasper turned at Ava's noisy approach and raised an eyebrow. "Am I to presume you have completed your rooms for the day, Miss DiRossi?" he asked in a familiar, condescending tone of voice.

He'd never liked her. If he'd had his way, Colleen wouldn't have hired her.

"Kitty asked me to serve the men cookies and coffee," she responded quietly, like a meek little mouse. She startled at the thought, at the seething resentment bubbling up inside her. She'd never let Jasper get under her skin before. She'd just gone about her job, doing her best to stay out of his way. But now...

He waved a dismissive hand. "Get back to work. I'll see to the refreshments."

"You can stop your meowing, Simon. I'm coming," Kitty said to the cat who appeared to be herding her toward the ballroom. She smiled at Jasper and Ava when she reached them. "I don't know what's gotten into him. He wouldn't leave me alone until I followed him here. Ava, dear, I thought you would have given Griffin his cookies by now."

Ava's face heated. She didn't know if it was because Kitty was being so obvious or because Griffin had stopped midconversation with his brother to glance their way. The two men stood a few yards across the room on scaffolding. Griffin wore faded jeans that molded to his muscular thighs, his black T-shirt accentuating his impressive biceps. As his eyes moved over her, the warmth spread from her cheeks to her stomach. So obviously Griffin was responsible for the heat and not Kitty.

"Miss DiRossi has rooms to see to, Miss Kitty. I'll take care of—"

"I need a word with you, Jasper. Off you go, my dear. Ava?"

She blinked, pulling her gaze from Griffin's. "Sorry, yes, I'll get back to work." She turned to walk away.

Kitty stopped her with a hand on her bruised arm. "No, dear, I meant serve the cookies. Griffin looks ravenous, don't you think?"

With the way his brow furrowed and his eyes narrowed, Ava thought he looked more angry than hungry. But whatever emotion he was feeling appeared to be directed at her. More specifically, her arm. She must have winced when Kitty touched her. Leave it to Griffin to catch it. Those all-seeing eyes of his never missed much.

She wondered if that was the reason for the butterflies in her stomach. She was nervous he was going to make a big deal of her injured arm in front of everyone. Other than Griffin and Dorothy, no else knew she'd been hurt.

She wanted to keep it that way. But as she offered the cookies to the three men working a few feet from Griffin, the butterflies no longer felt like they were freaked out, they felt like they were turned on. It didn't seem to matter that hers and Griffin's interactions in the past twenty-four hours hadn't gone particularly well; she was anxious to be near him, to gaze at his handsome face, look into his beautiful eyes, and remember how it felt to be loved by Griffin Gallagher.

Foolish woman, she berated herself, forcing a smile for the three firefighters helping themselves to the cookies.

Landon Wright's eyes lit up when he took a bite. "O.M.G., these are freaking awesome."

Ava pressed her lips together to hold back a laugh at his friends' slack-jawed expressions. Erin was rubbing off on the shaggy-haired Landon. The two were best friends.

"Tell me I didn't just hear 'O.M.G.' come out of your mouth?" one of the guys said.

"Seriously, Wright, you just lost your man card," the tallest of the three said.

His cheeks a telling pink, Landon ignored his friends. "If you promise to make these cookies every day, I'll marry you, Ava."

"I'll pass your proposal on to my Aunt Rosa, Landon. She's the one who—"

A large hand and muscular forearm appeared from behind her and the tray disappeared. For a big man, her ex-husband moved quietly and quickly. He glanced from her to the three firefighters. "Back off, boys. They're mine."

Liam sauntered over to stand beside them. His hair was

darker than Griffin's, his eyes just as blue. He was six foot two to his brother's six-four, leaner, too, but just as devastatingly handsome. All the Gallagher men were.

"You better do as he says, boys. My brother's pretty possessive of his *cookies*. And don't be embarrassed, Landon—you're not the first guy to propose marriage over a cookie. My brother did the same. Didn't you, Griff?" Ignoring his brother's killing glare, Liam grinned and took a cookie. "O. M. G, these are freaking awesome. If Ava's were this good, I totally get why you proposed to her, big brother."

Ava didn't know how Griffin reacted to his brother's teasing remark because she was too busy scowling at Liam...who winked at her.

"No way can you eat all of those," the tall firefighter challenged Griffin.

Griffin raised an eyebrow and slowly brought a cookie to his mouth. The way in which his strong, white teeth bit into the pastry seemed to give the younger men pause.

Landon nervously tugged on his friend's arm. "Let's go see if Erin can hook us up."

"You never did like to share," Liam said to his brother. "Can't say I blame you though." He helped himself to three more cookies. "Leave it to me to fall in love with the only DiRossi who can't cook. Speaking of my wife, I think I'll take my cookie break with her."

"Make sure it's only a cookie break you're taking, baby brother. I wanna get this wall done today," he called after Liam, who shot him a grin over his shoulder. Griffin shook his head and placed the tray on the scaffolding. Leaning against the steel bars, he crossed his arms. "Why haven't you told Kitty about your arm?"

Ava drew her gaze from the black armband tattoo that circled his left bicep. "Because it's nothing." She nodded at the dessert cart where the other men had gathered. "There's coffee. Would you like a cup?"

"You can't distract me that easily, Ava. I want to know why you haven't told anyone you're hurt. You shouldn't be working."

"Why are you making such a big deal of this? It's just—"

"You tell Sophie about it?"

"No, and would you please just give it a rest?"

"Tell Sophie and I will."

"Fine."

He half laughed, half huffed. "I wasn't born yesterday. I know what it means when a woman says *fine*. You tell Sophie or I do." He took another cookie, studying it instead of eating it. "So, Rosa's trying to butter me up in hopes I'll vote to keep Greystone in the family, is she?"

Ava wasn't surprised he'd clued in. He was a smart and observant man. She was just glad he seemed to believe the cookies had to do with the estate and not her. "Yes, and I'm sure she won't be the only one. You know, Griffin, Greystone isn't just important to the Gallaghers. The manor's important to everyone in town."

"The town will survive. If the condos go for what I heard they will, you'll have a lot of rich folks running around town with money to burn."

"What about Liam, Kitty, and Sophie?"

"What about them? They'll be rich too." His mouth quirked at the corner. "You cursing me out in your head?"

"Maybe. A little." She made a face. "I'm sorry about earlier. I really do appreciate the shoes. Thank you."

"Told you before, it wasn't a big deal." He averted his gaze from hers and pushed away from the scaffolding. "I should be getting back to work."

"Why are you helping out if you want to sell?" She wished he hadn't come, and not just because of the book. Spending time with him, being this close to him, reminded her of what she'd given up. It was like being lost in the desert, dying of thirst, and he was a mirage—a cool blue, shimmering lake that was just out of reach. It was simpler, easier, when he visited her in her dreams.

"My old man. He's the only reason I'm here. He's got enough on his plate without dealing with this too," he said, his tone clipped and harsh, just like it had been yesterday. He briefly closed his eyes and drew a hand down his face. "Sorry, I didn't get much sleep last night. I'm not trying to be an ass about this, Ava. I do understand what the manor means to all of you. It's just that feelings won't pay the bills. You're going to work your asses off and sink a pile into this place with no payback. The developer's just going to tear down the manor.

"You need all ten of us on board, and my uncle's girls hardly spent any time here. They have no loyalty to Harmony Harbor or Greystone. You're all too close to see just how much work the place needs, but they will, especially if you put them in Colleen's suite. I'm surprised I don't have frostbite. I could see my breath this morning."

"Why? I brought you firewood. Didn't you use it all?" she asked, and heard the anxious note in her voice. She hoped he didn't.

"I couldn't get the damn thing to light."

It took everything Ava had not to make a mad dash to his room. "I'll take care of that for you."

He crossed his arms and cocked his head. "*You* are going to take care of it for *me*, a Navy SEAL?"

Her lips tipped up at the offended look on his face. She gave his arm a playful pat. "It's okay. I won't tell anyone." At the feel of his warm skin and hard muscle, an electrical zing of desire shot through her, and she had to force the teasing smile to stay in place. She raised her eyes to meet his, but he was looking at her hand. Her hand that was still on his arm. She jerked it away. "I'll, um, go and—"

"Ava, just the person I was looking for," Dana said, giving them both a smile.

Ava's own fell from her face. If she wasn't mistaken, along with the smile, Dana had a matchmaking glint in her eyes.

And that's how Ava got stuck spending five hours watching her ex-husband hammer one hundred and one twelve-by-twelve tiles to the wall. Supposedly she was doing so for quality control. To be fair, four of the one hundred and one tiles had been slightly crooked. Although she may have missed one or two because she spent as much time watching the play of muscles across Griffin's back and the powerful flex of his bicep when he hammered the nails into the wood. And as though to prove to her that he was a SEAL, the man refused to take a break. Which, in one way, was a good thing because he hadn't gone to his room.

"Pizza's here," Liam called from the open doors.

"Thank God," Ava murmured. She was pretty sure she heard Griffin say the same. Her eyes went wide when he jumped from the scaffolding. "You were a SEAL, not Superman," she informed him tartly.

Beneath his heavy scruff, she caught the wink of his dimple. "Pretty much the same thing."

She rolled her eyes. "While you go feed your oversized ego, I'll put the fire on in your room."

He laughed, then grew serious. "You're going to eat before you do."

"Ava, can you help me out here?" Sophie called, holding up a pizza box.

Griffin grabbed her hand as she went to walk away. "I'm not joking, Ava. You have to eat."

"Why? Because you think I'm too skinny? I know I am. But there's nothing wrong with me if that's what you're implying." She didn't have an eating disorder. Food just didn't hold the same appeal for her anymore. It all tasted and smelled the same—bland. Half the time she was too busy or too tired to eat anyway.

"You never used to be," he murmured, gently rubbing his thumb over the finger that once wore his ring. He raised his gaze and met hers. "Ava—"

Jasper appeared from out of nowhere. "Master Griffin, there's a call for you in the study. It's your wife."

Chapter Five

♥

Colleen wanted to wrap her hands around Jasper's neck and squeeze. If they wouldn't pass right through him, that's exactly what she'd do. He'd just ruined Ava and Griffin's moment. Her great-grandson was so close to realizing he was still in love with Ava that Colleen had about done a jig. Though she highly doubted the straight-laced Jasper even knew how to dance, the smug smile he tried to hide made it clear he was doing some celebrating of his own. He'd accomplished exactly what he'd set out to—Griffin looked guilty and Ava stricken.

Colleen was torn between following after her great-grandson to listen in on his conversation with his ex-wife and following Ava when she begged off pizza duty to finish up the guest rooms. With Ava unable to hear her, it wouldn't be much use offering the girl comfort. At least with Griffin, if the conversation went in a direction Colleen didn't like, there was a possibility she could interrupt it. "Come on, Simon, I might need your help messing…" Her gaze narrowed on Ava, who tracked Griffin across the lobby, then hightailed it up the grand staircase when he disappeared from view.

The girl was up to something.

"Change of plans. You go with Griffin. Pull the phone jack out of the wall if it sounds like Lexi's trying to convince him to leave. It'll buy us some time at least." Simon blinked up at her, which she'd come to interpret as *Have you lost your bloody mind?* in cat-speak. "What? You got Kitty to the ballroom in time for her to intervene with Jasper earlier. Just bite through the phone cord if you have to. Off you go now," she said, and hurried up the grand staircase.

"What are you up to, Ava my girl?" Colleen wondered aloud as she caught up to her on the third floor. She hadn't stopped for a service cart, so it wasn't as if she planned to clean rooms. As Ava's footsteps rang out on the spiral staircase to the tower, Colleen realized what she was about and chuckled. "Well now, I have to say I'm impressed. I didn't think you had it in you. A well-planned seduction is just the ticket to get things back on track with Griffin."

Ava glanced over her shoulder as she slid her passkey into the door.

Worried that Jasper might have followed them, Colleen also looked over her shoulder. There was no sign of the man she now thought of as her nemesis.

She followed Ava into the room. "I used to be a dab hand at seducing my Patrick. It's too bad I can't remember where I put the candles," she said when Ava closed the door and pulled a lighter from her breast pocket.

Ava headed for the fireplace and the wrought-iron candelabra with the rows of candles.

"I suppose that'll work. Though you should close the draperies to set the mood. More romantic, you know." Colleen's eyes nearly bugged out of her head when, instead of lighting the candles, Ava moved them aside and stuck her head in the fireplace. "For the love of all that is holy, please tell me you're not trying to set my book on fire."

That's exactly what the girl intended to do. As Ava held the flickering flame to the small space between the two bricks, Colleen blew with all her might. She did it two more times before Ava stopped to hold the lighter upside down, shaking it. "Don't do it, child. You have no idea what you're about. There's information in the book that can't be lost. It'll cause more heartache than you know."

Colleen yelled, "Stop!" at the top of her lungs to little effect. She'd used up most of her energy blowing out the flame. Ava, of course, was oblivious and tried again. This wasn't going to be as easy as with Griffin. If possible, Ava was more stubborn than he was. Colleen prayed the girl ran out of lighter fluid before she ran out of air.

Thankfully, fifteen minutes later, that's exactly what happened. Ava released a defeated sigh and leaned against the fireplace, rubbing the tip of her scorched thumb. "Why did you do it, Colleen? Why did you record everyone's secrets?"

Colleen heard the censure in Ava's voice and sat beside her. "I didn't mean to hurt anyone. You have but one secret, and look what it's done to you. Try carrying around as many as I have. I needed to get them out of my head, and some things needed to be recorded. I'd planned to pass my book on to a member of the Widows Club. Someone I could trust to keep the secrets that needed to be kept and make right on the others. A man died because of me, and I'd vowed never again to meddle in anyone's affairs."

She glanced at Ava. Her expression hadn't changed. She was still angry with her. Colleen imagined she wasn't the only one. But that wasn't something she could concern herself with now. She had to ensure the book didn't fall into the wrong hands, at the same time protecting it from those who would destroy it.

Griffin returned to the ballroom and grabbed the last piece of pizza from the box.

"Everything okay with Lex?" Liam asked.

"Yeah…No, I don't think so," Griffin admitted because he was worried. "Something's up with her but she won't talk about it over the phone. She said it can wait until I get back to Virginia."

"Is that why she called? To find out when you're going home?"

"No, she said someone left her a message to call that number. She thought it was me."

"Weird. I wonder who called her."

"I have a fairly good idea who." He lifted his chin to where Jasper stood in the lobby, talking to the cat. "Jeeves. Anytime I'm around Ava, he goes into watchdog mode." Griffin didn't like it, but he understood why. In Jasper's mind, Ava had hurt one of his own.

"You're probably right. He's Sophie's number one fan now, but it wasn't always the case. He tried to warn me away from her too." Liam glanced over his shoulder and frowned. "Is he lecturing Simon?"

"Looks like. Simon bit through the phone jack trying to pull it out of the wall in the study."

"Huh. Simon's usually smart enough to stay off Jasper's radar. You must have done something to tick him off."

"I didn't do anything. And the cat's not as smart as you think. Last night he managed to get stuck in the fireplace and wouldn't shut—" Both Griffin and Liam startled when Jasper appeared between them. Liam widened his eyes while grinning at the older man. Griffin knew what his brother was getting at and held back a laugh. The way he seemed to appear out of nowhere, Jasper reminded them of the butler in *Mr. Deeds*.

"I couldn't help but overhear, Master Griffin. Did you say Simon got stuck in the fireplace in Madame's room?"

"Yeah, and he wouldn't shut up."

The old man's eyes narrowed on the cat before returning to Griffin. "I see. Well that explains why you complained about not getting any sleep last night."

The cat had nothing to do with his lack of sleep. He wasn't about to admit that to Jasper though. If Griffin believed in ghosts, he'd lay odds GG's room was haunted. He spent half the night being woken up by a voice whispering in his ear that Ava needed him. Since he didn't believe in ghosts, the only explanation he could come up with was that it was his subconscious. As much as he wished it weren't true, he could no longer deny that he was concerned about Ava…or that it was beginning to feel like something more.

He hadn't been able to stop thinking about her, of the

girl he remembered. And being around her wasn't helping. There had been small signs that, if he dug a little deeper, pushed a little harder, he'd find the woman he'd once loved beyond reason.

He mentally shook the thought from his head and responded to Jasper. "My lack of sleeping had nothing to do with Simon. Guess you missed the part where I told Liam and my dad that I froze my ass off last night, Jeeves. Come to think of it, that's probably why Simon was sitting in there meowing his head off. He was cold too. Every time I lit a match, the wind would blow it out. So you better add repairing the cracks in the chimney to your mile-long to-do list."

"I'll take care of that straightaway, Master Griffin," Jasper said, looking like a man on a mission as he left the ballroom.

"Come on, it's not a mile long," said his brother, who was firmly on the Save Greystone Team.

Griffin raised an eyebrow.

"Okay, admittedly, we still have some work to do. Speaking of which, we're getting the evil eye from the guys." Liam nodded at his buddies from the firehouse. "We better get back to it."

"You get right on that. I'm finishing my slice," Griffin said, taking a bite of the pizza. He wiped his mouth, looked around, and then followed Liam. "You seen Ava around?" he asked his brother casually. Jasper referring to Lexi as his wife had upset Ava, and Griffin wanted to know why.

"You seen Ava around?" Liam mimicked, chuckling as he climbed onto the scaffolding. "I know you too well, big brother. Cut the act. At least with me."

"What are you talking about? I just asked you a simple question," Griffin muttered before polishing off the rest of the slice. He should have kept his mouth closed.

"When are you going to admit you never got over her, not really?" Liam asked when Griffin joined him on the scaffolding.

He opened his mouth and then closed it. Liam knew him too well. And his baby bro might have a point. Because really, how do you get past something like that? One minute you're happily married and head over heels in love, and the next, you're being served divorce papers. Sure, there'd been small signs that something had been eating at Ava, but never in a million years did he expect her to end their marriage. She'd cut him out of her life completely, turned his upside down with no real explanation. The only way he'd been able to move on was to box up his memories and his feelings for her and nail it shut. They were still there though. For better or worse, they always would be.

So yeah, it wasn't a conversation he wanted to have with his brother. He picked up a wooden tile. "You're as bad as Lex. Hand me that hammer, will—"

"Where is she? Where is my daughter?"

Griffin turned at the raised, gravelly voice and was surprised to see Ava's father, Gino DiRossi, wheeling his chair into the ballroom. The old man wore a navy knit hat and padded plaid jacket. His pal Jimmy followed behind. The two men used to work on the boat together. The way Jimmy was twisting his hat in his hands, he'd obviously brought Gino and was second-guessing the decision. Griffin understood why when Ava's old man wheeled farther into the room. Gino was drunk and...

beside himself with fury. "Ava!" the old man bellowed at the top of his lungs.

"You might want to stay out of his way," Liam murmured before climbing off the scaffolding.

His baby bro was right again. Ava had been the light of her father's life. It'd been just the two of them for so long that Gino hadn't been overjoyed to discover there was another man in his daughter's life. Especially when that man turned out to be a Gallagher. He'd been even less happy when Ava got pregnant at eighteen and they got married. Griffin would have married her even if she hadn't been pregnant. Gino had softened a bit when they lost the baby six months later. Griffin believed it was because the old man finally realized how much Griffin loved his daughter.

Sophie rushed into the ballroom. Either she heard Gino or someone had alerted her to the situation. "Uncle Gino," she said as she reached his side. Gino squinted at her, and she added, "It's me, Sophie. Tina and Giovanni's daughter. Why don't we go to my office, and I'll—"

Stabbing a finger at her, Gino snarled, "I know who you are. You're just like the rest of the Gallaghers. Trying to steal my daughter away from me. I'll not have it, you hear. I'll not have it!"

Liam, who had quickly crossed the room to his wife's side, drew her away from Gino. "Calm down, Mr. DiRossi. No one's trying to take Ava from you. Sophie will go get her now." Liam turned to his wife. "Soph." She glanced at her uncle, nodded, and then hurried off.

Everyone in the ballroom pretended to be working, but no one was talking, no one was hammering. They were waiting to see what would happen next. Griffin's gut twisted at the thought of how Ava would feel if there was a scene. He didn't want to draw Gino's attention to him—he was pretty sure it would make matters worse—but he wanted his brother to take the old man somewhere private. "Liam," he called out, lifting his chin at the entrance.

His brother nodded. "Why don't we get a drink at the bar while we wait for Ava, Mr. DiRossi?"

Gino's lip curled, his bloodshot eyes narrowed at Griffin. "You didn't think I saw you? Didn't know that you were in town causing trouble for my girl again?" He started to wheel the chair toward him.

Jimmy grabbed the push handles, turning the chair toward the entrance. "You don't want to do this, Gino. Come on. Let's go have a—"

Gino shoved Jimmy's hands away and spun the chair around. The old man had obviously retained his upper-body strength. He'd been a strong man back in the day, short and barrel-chested with powerful hands the size of baseball mitts.

"I'm not here to cause trouble for anyone, Mr. DiRossi. I'm just helping out my family. I'll be gone in a couple days. Why don't you go with Jimmy and Liam—"

"I don't believe a word out of your mouth, Gallagher. You ruined Ava's life once. I won't let you ruin it again."

Griffin clenched his jaw to keep from laying into the old man. If anyone had ruined Ava's life, it was Gino. Every phone call home before his mother and sister died, his mother would find some way to mention Ava. His mother had almost been as heartbroken as Griffin when their marriage ended. She'd loved Ava like a daughter and was worried about her. She never admitted it to him, but her knowledge of Ava's life was too intimate to have come from town gossip. He'd always suspected they remained close after the divorce. His fingers tightened around the hammer he picked up, and he turned away before he said something he'd regret.

"I'm talking to you. Don't turn your back on me!" Gino shouted.

"Papa, what are you doing here? Is something wrong?" Ava rushed to her father's side, her face flushed with what Griffin imagined was embarrassment. He prayed Gino would let it go now that she was here.

A dark look came over the old man's face, and Griffin slowly lowered the hammer. There was something in Gino's eyes that Griffin recognized from a time when he'd drowned himself in the bottle—an uncontrollable rage.

"She told me, she told me what's going on, and I won't have it, do you hear? Do you hear me, Ava Marie DiRossi? I won't have it!" His meaty fingers closed around Ava's bruised forearm.

At her pained cry, Griffin moved, the anger pulsing through him and taking on a life of its own.

Gino shook her arm, oblivious to her anguish. "You're leaving with me—"

Whatever he meant to say was lost in a muffled groan when Griffin grabbed his upper arm with one hand, releasing Gino's grip on Ava with the other. Once he got her arm free, Griffin gently pushed up the sleeve of her sweater. "Look, look what you've done to her, old man."

People gasped, and Ava tried to pull her arm away, pleading, "No, Griffin, no. Please…please don't do this."

He released her arm, but he couldn't, wouldn't let it go. Everything made sense to him now. The reason why she wouldn't tell anyone about her arm, the reason for the dark circles under her eyes, and her too-slim, fragile frame.

Sophie and Liam drew Ava away. "Griff, come on—"

Griffin ignored his brother and held the old man's gaze, closing his hands over Gino's on the armrests. "You did that to her, old man. Her own father, a man who's supposed to protect her. It's not enough that you're working her to the bone; you're abusing her too." There were gasps, a cry from Ava, a flush working its way up Gino's thick neck to his face. Consumed with fury, Griffin barely registered any of it. "I don't care if you're in a chair, you lay one finger on her again, and I'll—"

"All right, that's enough." His brother pulled him away.

His anger still out of control, Griffin whirled on Liam. A firm, heavy hand landed on his shoulder. "Calm down, son. Think of Ava," his father said quietly.

He hadn't seen his father come in. Griffin drew in a deep breath and nodded. His father and brother let him go. Gino sat slumped in his chair, his face pale. Griffin couldn't work up any sympathy for the old man, not after what he'd seen. He didn't regret what he'd said or done, but as he calmed down, he realized he hadn't protected Ava from embarrassment; he'd made it worse. His grandmother, Sophie, and Dana were with her, talking in low, comforting voices.

An older woman in a winter white coat walked toward them, a stricken look on her face. "I'm so sorry, lovey," she said when she reached Ava. "It's my fault. I shouldn't have mentioned that Sophie wants you to manage the restaurant."

Jimmy held Griffin's gaze as he reached for the push handles. "I didn't know," he said, and then wheeled Gino away. Griffin's father followed them from the ballroom.

"Neither did I," his brother said, looking to where Ava stood a few yards away. "None of us did. We would have stepped in if we had." Liam glanced at him. "You went too far, Griff."

"Yeah? What would you have done if it was Sophie?"

Ava's arm ached, and her heart hurt for her father. Her eyes filled as she watched Jimmy wheel him away. She wished Dorothy hadn't told him about Sophie's offer. But she understood why she did. Just as she understood why Griffin had done and said what he did. Though she wished with all her heart that he hadn't. He'd humiliated her father...and her. Soon everyone in town would know.

"If you don't mind, Sophie, I need to leave early. I need to go home."

Her cousin gently rubbed Ava's shoulder. "Maybe it would be best if you stayed with me and Liam for a while. Just until—"

"I know what it looks like, but it was an accident. My father—" Out of the corner of her eye, Ava saw Griffin walking toward her. She didn't want to talk to him. Not here, not now. "I need to get my things. Dorothy, would you mind driving me home?"

"Of course not, lovey. I'll wait for you here."

She heard Dorothy reassuring Kitty, Sophie, and Dana that she would stay with Ava tonight. She cringed at what they must think of her, of her father. She wanted to turn and tell them to stop talking about them. Her father wasn't a monster, and she wasn't a victim. She didn't

want their sympathy, their pity. Instead she hurried from
the ballroom, pretending that she didn't hear Griffin calling her name. She quickly gathered up her belongings
from the staff break room.

The way her day had started, she should have known
it was bound to get worse. The thought reminded her of
her futile attempt to light Colleen's memoirs on fire. She
glanced toward the ballroom, heard what she thought was
Griffin's voice, and decided that she had to try again before she left. She couldn't bear the thought of him finding
the book, especially after today. His temper was one of
the reasons she hadn't told him about Damien. She was
afraid Griffin would kill his childhood best friend and
spend the rest of his life in prison. What she'd just wit-
nessed in the ballroom seemed to justify her long-ago
fears.

As the elevator rattled its way to the tower, Ava placed
her bag on the floor and leaned against the rail. She took
off her shoes and put on her boots, shrugging into her
coat. At least she'd be ready to leave as soon as she'd
taken care of the book. As close as it was to the supper hour, she hoped the ballroom would have cleared
out when she returned. She knew Griffin well enough to
know he wouldn't leave until he'd spoken to her. Somehow she'd figure out a way to get Dorothy's attention
without alerting him to her presence.

The elevator jerked to a stop on the fourth floor. She
peeked around the door as it slid open. No one was
around. She drew her passkey from her pocket, as well as
several of Julia's book club flyers from her bag, and then
opened the door. Setting her bag on the bed, she rolled the
flyers tight. At least this time she'd come prepared.

Ava rounded the bed and started toward the fireplace. She froze midstep. The candelabra had been moved, and there was a large footprint outlined in soot. Her pulse quickened, and her muscles unlocked. She ran to the fireplace, going down on her knees. Taking her lighter from her pocket, she put her head inside. There was no longer a gap between the two bricks. They sat perfectly flush inside the chimney.

The book was gone.

Chapter Six

♥

Looked like his reprieve had ended, Griffin thought as Liam crossed the empty ballroom with a grim expression on his face. Griffin hadn't been fit company for anyone and had stayed to finish up the walls instead of joining his family in the dining room. He figured Liam was ticked because Griffin had yet to apologize to Ava. He'd planned to, but somehow she'd managed to leave Greystone without him seeing her.

"Don't bother giving me grief. I'll call her in an hour. Gino should be passed out by—"

"Sophie just got off the phone with Rosa. They can't find Gino. Jimmy says he dropped him off at his place. He wasn't there when Ava got home."

"What's the big deal? He probably went to the Salty Dog. It's just around the corner." In Gino's place, it's something Griffin would have done. At least back when he'd used the bottle to deal with his own crap.

"You don't get it. Gino rarely leaves the house. They've already called the bars in town. I'm heading out to look for him. I thought you'd want to come along."

"Why? Because it's my fault he's missing? That's what you think, right?" Griffin came down off the scaffolding. There was no question he'd help look for the old man. Guilt didn't play into it though. Someone had to call out Gino, stand up for Ava. She was the reason he'd help look for her father.

"You accused him of abusing his daughter in front of everyone, Griff. A man like Gino…the man he used to be, that's not going to be something he can live down. Not in this town."

"So, what, I was supposed to keep my mouth shut? You saw her arm."

"She told Sophie it was an accident."

"Yeah, right," he said, heading for his room. "I'll meet you in the parking lot."

Ten minutes later, Griffin's face was pelted with snow and sleet as he walked to his brother's idling Jeep. The wind whistled through the trees, the iced branches clattering as the storm that had been threatening since late afternoon hit Harmony Harbor full force.

Sophie sat in the passenger side of the Jeep.

"Hey, Soph," Griffin said as he got in the back. He frowned at her muffled "Hi." It sounded like she'd been crying. "What's—"

His brother stroked Sophie's long, dark hair, meeting Griffin's gaze in the rearview mirror as he pulled out of the parking lot. "Jimmy and his buddies went looking for Gino. They found his wheelchair on the dock. Jimmy's boat is missing."

Griffin swore under his breath, fighting the urge to put his fist through the window. *Of all the stupid...* His inner rant at Gino broke off at the thought that, if something happened to the old man, Ava would never forgive Griffin. The muscles in his chest constricted, making it difficult to breathe. It hit him then that what he'd been feeling for Ava was a lot more than just concern. The realization made him as angry as her father taking out a boat in a winter storm. He beat back the raw emotion to focus on what needed to be done and dug his phone from his pocket, scrolling through his contacts until he found the name he was looking for—Joe Sullivan.

Griffin and his old friend had planned to grab a beer when he was in town. Sully was with the Coast Guard and coordinated search-and-rescue operations. "Hey, man. It's Griffin."

"Thought I might be hearing from you. Hang on." Griffin heard the buffeting of the wind in the background and Sully shouting orders before coming back on the line. "Hell of a night down here, buddy. I've got three men down with the flu, and a distress signal came in five minutes before we got word about Gino. We've got a boat taking on water north of the Cape. Cutter is heading out now with most of my senior crew."

"Any word on Gino?"

"Yeah, and it's not good. You heading to the South Shore docks?"

The sea-foam-green and sky-blue Colonials along Main Street whizzed by the window. "Yeah, we'll be there in under ten."

"Okay, if you weren't who you are, and I wasn't in a bind, I wouldn't ask. But I could use you out there tonight, Griff. I need a rescue swimmer. My guys have gone up with the chopper."

"You don't have to ask. I planned on going out with you anyway."

"Kinda thought you might. Listen, Jimmy told me what went down at the manor. Think you better talk to him so you know what you're up against. Jimmy," Sully called out, then added, "Cutter should be here in ten. See you when you get here."

The Coast Guard station was located west of Starlight Pointe.

"Griffin, it's Jimmy. Gino, he was in bad way after we left the manor. I shouldn't have left him on his own. He was off his head, talking stupid. He talked about it before, after the accident, you know? But I never thought…I gave it to him good after hearing what he did to Ava. Shouldn't have. Should have kept my mouth shut."

"Spit it out, Jimmy."

"He said he was gonna end it. That Ava was better off without him."

As Jimmy confirmed his worst fear, Griffin released a vicious curse. Liam glanced at him. "Griff?"

He held up a finger. "Where would he go, Jimmy?"

"I don't rightly know. Me and the boys have been racking our brains. Still can't believe he managed to take out the boat all on his own."

"Focus, Jimmy. There has to be a place that means something to him."

"Lots of places he liked to fish, but a night like this, doing what he planned to…Jumping Jesus, I know. I know where he'd go. Should have figured it out before now. Didn't think of it until you said—"

"Jimmy," Griffin said, frustration leaking into his voice.

"Okay, okay, there's a little spit of land near Twilight Bay. He spread his wife Maria's ashes there. Said it was their special place."

"Let Joe know." Griffin disconnected, his fingers tightening around the phone.

"What's going on, Griff? Why are you—"

He met his brother's eyes, lifted his chin at Sophie, and shook his head. She twisted in the seat to look at him. "I want to know what you know. For Ava's sake, I have to be prepared. Please, Griffin."

By the time Liam pulled alongside the road just down from the docks, Griffin had repeated his conversation with both Jimmy and Sully. "I'm going with you," Liam said.

Once again the muscles in Griffin's chest banded tight. Given that his brother fought fires for a living, the reaction was over the top, but Griffin couldn't help himself. Liam was his baby brother, after all. Nothing was going to happen to him on Griffin's watch.

He hadn't been able to protect his mother and sister; he'd damn well protect his baby brother. "No. It's going to be rough out there tonight, Liam. I can't be worrying—"

"Griffin's right. You're not…"

One look at Sophie's face and Griffin figured her argument would carry more weight than his. So he got out of the Jeep and left her to it. He weaved his way through the emergency vehicles, the flashing lights illuminating the crowd gathered along the rocky incline above the docks.

He spotted Ava. The wind whipped around her long, curly hair, snowflakes dotting the dark strands. His dad stood beside her. Her Aunt Rosa stood at her other side.

The older woman from earlier today was there, too, as well as a group of younger women who had shops on Main Street. Griffin knew from his family and from what he'd seen for himself that Ava didn't have much of a social life. A sharp contrast to the girl who used to be the most popular girl at Harmony High. Ava probably couldn't see it, but these women, these people, they were here for her.

Several of them turned as he approached, giving him half-smiles in greeting, a couple of *Hey, Griffin*'s rising above the wind and the chatter of the crowd.

He returned their greetings and approached his dad and Ava. She raised her gaze to meet his. The guilt he'd been denying sucker punched him in the stomach. "I'm sorry," he said.

She nodded, tears swimming in her bottle-green eyes, her chin trembling as though she tried to keep them in check. He cupped her cheek with his gloved hand and stroked it with his thumb. "If it's the last thing I do, I'll bring him back to you."

Her eyes widened, and she grabbed his hand, her fingers tightening around it. "You're going out with the Coast Guard?"

"Yeah." He glanced over his shoulder. Sully was waving him over to where he stood at the end of the dock. "I gotta get going."

She looked at him as though memorizing his face, a tear sliding down her cheek and onto their joined hands. "Be careful."

He smiled. "Always."

His dad pulled him in for a hug, whispering in his ear, "Don't be a hero. If he's…Look after yourself, son."

He knew what his dad was getting at but couldn't bring himself to say. Not with Ava standing right there. Griffin couldn't make that promise. Dead or alive, Gino was coming home to her. "I'm good at what I do. You don't need to worry about me, Dad."

"Wait until you have kids of..." His father winced as though realizing that was unlikely to happen. Ava had lost their baby seven months into her pregnancy. After two failed marriages, Griffin wasn't looking to get married again or start a family.

He gave his dad's shoulder a reassuring squeeze and began walking away.

"Wait." Ava's aunt caught up to him. With her curly, dark hair, Rosa DiRossi reminded him of Ava.

"I really gotta go, Mrs. DiRossi."

"*Sí*, I know." She took his hand and turned it to place a gold chain with a medal in his palm, closing his fingers over it. "St. Peter, he's the patron saint of fishermen. He will protect you." She glanced at Ava, then looked up at him. "You did a good thing. It needed to be said."

He appreciated Rosa's support. Guilt was riding him hard. He didn't realize until then how much he'd needed someone to tell him he'd done the right thing. He bent and kissed her cheek. "Thanks, Rosa." He wasn't sure she'd feel that way once word got out what Gino intended to do.

As though she'd read his mind, she said, "This was his choice. If you must make one, you come home safe."

"Gallagher." Sully waved him over as the lights from the forty-seven-foot MLB—motorized lifeboat—came into view.

Griffin put the chain in his pocket. "Take care of her, Rosa," he said, and then started to jog down the dock.

"Griffin!"

He stopped with a sigh, turning to his grandmother and brother, who hurried down the dock. When they reached him, he kissed his grandmother, hugged his brother, and promised to be careful. "Now, I really do have to go."

Liam held his gaze. "No heroics, big brother."

Losing their mom and sister to a drunk driver on a cold October night had left its mark on Griffin and his brothers. One minute their mom and sister were there, and in the next, they were gone.

"Any more family members to see you off?" Sully asked with a grin when Griffin reached him. He drew Griffin in for a one-arm hug. "Not under the best of circumstances, but it's good to see you, buddy. It's been a while."

"Too long." Griffin rarely came home. There were too many memories in Harmony Harbor. It was easier dealing with them in his nightmares than being blindsided by them when he came home.

As the cutter cruised up to the dock, Sully introduced Griffin to the five-man crew. They wore orange wet-weather gear, helmets, and black goggles. "Griffin's going to take the lead on the rescue." When the petty officer looked like he might voice an objection, Sully lifted his chin to where the searchlights lit up the heavy seas and breaking surf. "He's a decorated Navy SEAL, Johnson."

That seemed to be enough for the petty officer, who began giving orders to the rest of the crew. Griffin boarded and immediately headed belowdecks to get changed. He checked the gear, choosing to go with a dry suit instead of a full wet suit. Once he was ready, he made his way to the enclosed bridge. The lights of Harmony

Harbor winked behind them. Hampered by the winds and surf, Griffin estimated they were less than a mile from shore. "Any sign of him?" he asked Johnson, who operated the cutter.

Gino probably had a good hour on them, but given his drunken state and his physical limitations, Griffin figured he would have wasted at least forty of those extra minutes just to get the boat under way.

Johnson shook his head in response to Griffin's question. "If we find anything, it's most likely to be wreckage. Don't know the locals well. I just transferred to HHCG a couple weeks ago. But seriously, the guy must have had a death wish to go out tonight."

Gale-force winds and four-foot waves pummeled the cutter and hampered visibility. His gaze searching the dark and stormy seas, Griffin said, "I think he does."

Johnson swore under his breath and then asked, "You know the guy?"

Griffin understood the anger underlying the question. They were risking their lives for a man who didn't care about his. "My ex-father-in-law. He took out his best friend's boat, the *Lady Lou*. She's a green twenty-foot wooden Faroe, old but seaworthy. Just like DiRossi. He knows what he's doing. He grew up on these waters. He was a commercial fisherman for about thirty years."

"So if we find him, you're going to talk him out of it? That why the chief sent you?"

Griffin was the last person Gino would listen to. "Sully needed a swimmer, and I needed to at least try and save the old man." Now they had to find him. If he was close enough to Twilight Bay, the chances of them getting to him in time…"How far out are we?"

"About ten—" Johnson broke off to focus on steering through the breaking surf. As if they were a toy boat, the wave picked them up and slammed them down. From the chatter coming over the radio, the other rescue team was facing a lot worse. The waters off the Cape were notorious—the Bermuda Triangle of the North Shore.

"Man overboard!"

The shout wasn't coming from the radio. Johnson powered down as Griffin ran from the wheelhouse.

"There!" one of crew shouted, grabbing a life ring.

Within seconds, Griffin had sized up the situation. The young auxiliary member in the water was inexperienced and panicked. There was only one way he was going to make it out alive. Griffin dove into the churning, frigid water. He came up about fifteen feet from the kid. If he didn't act quickly, the sea would pull them farther apart.

"Hey!" Griffin shouted, raising an arm to get the kid's attention in hopes of calming him down. Yeah, that wasn't going to happen. He was beyond reason, screaming and choking on the water. Griffin swam toward him. He kept his body a good distance away so the kid didn't drag him under. Griffin grabbed the front of the jacket with his left hand, then, with his right, delivered a measured blow to knock him unconscious.

Griffin got him in a rescue hold, battling the wind and waves to get them safely to the boat. One of the crew members grabbed the kid while another helped Griffin over the side. Breathing hard, he lay flat out for a minute before hauling himself to his feet. The kid was already coming around.

"We've got it from here," one of the crew members assured him while another half dragged the kid toward the victim's shelter. As Johnson powered up the engines, Griffin leaned over the rail, looking for some sign of the *Lady Lou*. When he didn't see any, he made his way be-lowdecks to strip out of the dry suit and pull on another one. He grabbed a thermal blanket and headed back to the bridge. The petty officer glanced over his shoulder as the door slammed closed behind Griffin.

"Glad we had you with us, Gallagher. Nice work out there."

"That kid had no business being on board tonight. What the hell was Sully thinking?" He planned to ask his friend the same question when they got back to shore.

"Chief didn't have much say in the matter. The kid you just rescued is Admiral Donohue's great-grandson. Rec-ognize the name?"

Everyone in town knew the Donohue name, and the Admiral. The old man looked like Colonel Sanders of the chicken empire. The family had been in Harmony Harbor almost as long as Griffin's. The Admiral was a legendary figure in the Coast Guard. "Thought the old man died."

"Still kicking. Drops by the station every couple of days. He's determined that at least one member of his family will be with the Guard before he dies. If anything had happened to the kid, the chief would have gotten his ass handed to him."

"I might just hand old man Donohue his. He didn't put just his great-grandson's life at risk tonight."

"Let me know when you do. I'd like…" Johnson squinted. "You see that?"

Griffin leaned forward. "It's the *Lady Lou*. She's tak-ing on water."

"Looks like. She's wedged on a rock. Too dangerous

to bring the cutter in close enough to board. We'll use the life raft." Johnson relayed the plan to the other members of the crew through their headsets. One of them scrambled onto the outer bridge. Gripping the rail, the crew member announced the Coast Guard's arrival and rescue plan to Gino through the megaphone.

They were close enough that the searchlight clearly lit up the boat. Griffin made out Gino, watching their approach from where he lay outside the wheelhouse, propped against the side. The tension that had been stringing Griffin's muscles tight lessened at the sight. He wouldn't have to tell Ava that her father died tonight. He was minutes away from fulfilling his promise to her.

Griffin headed for the door. "I'll give them a hand with the life raft."

"What the hell is he doing?" Johnson said.

The crewman was yelling in the megaphone. "Stay down, sir! Remain on the floor!"

Griffin turned to see Gino dragging himself up the side of the boat.

Chapter Seven

♥

His eyes locked on Gino, Griffin willed the life raft over the next wave. They were still too far out. If he went over now…A wall of water crashed over them, and Griffin lost sight of Gino for a matter of seconds. It was all it took. When his vision cleared, Gino had managed to pull himself halfway over the side. One more good pull…

"Sit your ass down, old man!" Griffin yelled, trying to make himself heard over the howling winds and crash of the surf. Gino's head came up, turning their way. That's it; just a minute or two more was all Griffin needed. "Don't do it. Think about Ava!"

The *Lady Lou* dipped and rolled, and Gino went over the side. There was barely a splash as he slid into the water.

Griffin cursed, signaled he was going in, and rolled over the side of the life raft. A wave lifted Gino from the water, flinging him against the side of the boat. Mind blank of anything but saving the old man, Griffin powered through the water. A foot from where Gino disappeared, he dove deep. Even with the lights from the cutter and life raft, the water was dark and murky, offering no sign of Gino.

Griffin's lungs burned the deeper he dove. He stopped swimming, turning in a circle to search the dark depths. He was beginning to wonder how long he'd be able to hold out when he spotted something. Four powerful strokes brought him to the unconscious man. Wrapping his arms around Gino, Griffin kicked his way to the watery light on the surface. They broke through the churning water several feet from the lifeboat. Griffin pushed Gino's upper body into the boat, then lifted his legs. One of the crew was working on him when Griffin finally managed to pull himself into the raft. Gino's heart had stopped.

"We didn't go to all this trouble just to lose you, old man," Griffin said through clenched teeth as his body reacted to the cold and rush of adrenaline. He had basic medical training and took over chest compressions.

He felt a flutter of a pulse at the same time he heard a familiar *whoop whoop*. "Thank Christ," he muttered. The Coast Guard helicopter had a defibrillator on board; the cutter didn't. As they reached the cutter, the chopper hovered overhead. Within minutes, Gino was strapped into the lowered basket and on his way to North Shore General.

By the time Griffin and Sully finally arrived at the hospital, it was well past midnight. The late hour and snowstorm didn't seem to matter to the press who were gathered outside the doors leading into the trauma center.

"Play nice," Sully warned him.

"I'm too tired to be nice," Griffin grumbled. He didn't add that he didn't want to waste time answering questions he'd already answered down on the docks. He wanted to see Ava and check on Gino. They got word he'd coded a second time on the flight back. Last they heard, Gino was in critical but stable condition.

"Yeah, two cold water rescues in one night is enough to take it out of anyone. Old man like you must be bagged," Sully said with a grin.

Griffin flipped him off. Five minutes later, he was close to flipping off the reporters who wanted a minute-by-minute replay of both rescues. Knowing him as well as he did, Sully took him by the arm. "That'll be all for now, folks. Mr. Gallagher—"

"Is a true hero," said an older man with a gleaming head of white hair, batting the reporters aside with his cane to make his way to Griffin. It was the Admiral.

Out of the corner of his mouth, Sully said, "Let it go for now."

Griffin nodded. He'd learned his lesson. He didn't plan to embarrass the old man in front of the press. He'd talk to him about his great-grandson later. In private.

The Admiral gave Griffin a hardy slap on the back. "We breed our men tough here in Harmony Harbor. Gallagher is a prime example of the best of the best. A true Guardsman. We're proud to call him a member of our Coast Guard family."

Griffin raised an eyebrow at Sully, who was trying to keep a straight face. "Just go with it or you'll be stuck arguing with him for an hour. From firsthand experience, you won't win," his friend said loud enough for only Griffin to hear.

"Reminds me a little of myself. You've probably heard…"

Sully nudged Griffin, and the two of them escaped into the warmth of the hospital while the Admiral regaled the reporters with stories of his youthful exploits. "You realize he's going to be on my case to hire you, right? So what do you say you do a bro a major and accept my offer?"

Sully had offered him a job as soon as the cutter docked and again when they were driving to the hospital. Griffin had said thanks but no thanks both times. It wasn't that he found the idea of working for the Coast Guard unappealing. It was the idea of moving back to Harmony Harbor.

So he wasn't sure if Sully had purposefully set out to put him on the spot just now when he made the offer loud enough for Griffin's approaching brother, father, and grandmother to hear. He knew they had because the three of them were looking at him with hope shining from their faces, and damned if he didn't want to say yes for them. As hard as it was to be in Harmony Harbor, it was just as hard to be away from his family. He'd missed out on a lot—time with his great-grandmother that he couldn't get back, and his Grams and father weren't getting any younger.

Then his eyes went to the real reason he was second-guessing his decision not to accept the job—Ava. She stood with her back to him between the waiting room and admissions desk. Her Aunt Rosa, Dana, Sophie, and the older woman in the winter white coat were with her.

Once Gino was airlifted off the cutter and on his way to the hospital, Griffin had had time to think. Whether it was out on a storm-tossed ocean or on one of his many missions as a SEAL, there was always a chance he wouldn't make it back. Sometimes, like tonight, it made him reevaluate his life, where he was going and what he regretted most. One of his biggest regrets was letting Ava go. He sometimes thought he could have fought harder. But at the time, he'd been shell-shocked, and then angry, and then hurt. As tonight had proven, his feelings for her weren't all in the past. He found himself wondering if they had a shot at a second chance.

"Son?" his father said, looking concerned.

Griffin drew his eyes off Ava, at the same time speculating on how much of the conversation he had missed. "Sorry, I'm a little out of it. What did you say, Dad?"

"That as long as Sully was offering you a desk job, I think you should take it."

"He couldn't pay me enough to be a desk jockey. Don't start getting your hopes up. I haven't said yes."

Liam cocked his head. "But you haven't said no?"

"He has, twice. So I'm taking this as a good sign. Keep working on him, folks. I'm going to speak to Ava before heading out." Sully shook Griffin's hand. "All kidding aside, that was one hell of a performance out there tonight. We'd be honored to have you as a member of our team. Plus, I could use a good wingman at the bars."

As Sully walked away, Kitty wrapped her arms around Griffin's waist. "I'm so very proud of you and so very happy you came back to us unharmed." She lifted her head from his chest. "But do you think you might consider staying onshore? It's not easy being the grandmother of Harmony Harbor's heroes."

"You love it, and you know it. You'll have something to brag about at the next Widows Club meeting," his father said to Kitty, throwing an arm over Griffin's shoulders. "Proud of you, son."

"You know what? Maybe you shouldn't take the job with HHCG. Dad and I will have to share the spotlight with you." Liam grinned, giving Griffin a playful punch on the arm. "You couldn't be satisfied with saving just one life; you had to save two. You always were an overachiever."

Griffin smiled, reminded once again of how much he'd loved and missed his family. "Thanks, guys. Now would you mind telling me how Gino's doing?"

The three of them shared a look. "You should talk to Ava, dear," Kitty said, adding, "Colin, we better be leaving. Liam, you and Sophie stay as long as Ava needs you. Mia's in good hands."

Once his father and grandmother headed for the exit doors, Griffin turned to his brother. "Something I need to know?"

Liam rubbed his stubbled jaw. "Yeah. Jimmy got a little emotional when they brought Gino in. He told Ava what Gino had planned to do. So she's…Oh, shit," his brother said when Sully lifted his chin in their direction and Ava turned. "Okay, whatever she says, don't take it—"

Focused on the woman striding their way, Griffin tuned out his brother and walked toward her. "Ava, I—"

She shook her head. "I don't want to hear your apologies and excuses. Because of you, my father nearly died tonight. You took away his dignity, embarrassed him in front of his friends. If he d-dies, it's your fault!" Her eyes were bloodshot and swollen, her face pale, the finger she stabbed in his chest shaking.

He closed his hand over hers. "You've gotta believe I never meant—"

She jerked her hand away, raising it as though to slap him, and then she clasped it with her other hand. "Go. Just go. Get out of here," she demanded, her voice rising hysterically on each word.

Sophie hurried toward them with her grandmother following close behind. His sister-in-law reached for Ava. "Come on, honey. Let's go sit down." Sophie cast Griffin an apologetic glance as she tried to steer her cousin away.

"No, he needs to get out of here. He needs to leave!"

Rosa reached for Ava's hand, giving it a gentle shake. "*Cara*, that is enough. Griffin, he doesn't deserve this. You owe him your thanks. Your father is alive because of him. He risked his life to save Gino's."

"He's the reason my father is even here. He's the reason he's fighting for his life!"

"No, *cara*, there is only one person responsible, and that is Gino. The drink, it has made him *pazza*."

She put up her hand. "Don't. You always hated my father. You—"

Rosa cut Ava off. "Griffin only said what someone should have said years before. What I should have—"

Her intentions were good, but Rosa was making matters worse. Griffin gave the older woman's shoulder a gentle squeeze. "It's okay. I'm leaving."

"Good. Go. Go, now!" Ava practically shouted at him.

Rosa brought her hands to her cheeks, shaking her head as she watched Sophie lead Ava away. "What's the matter with her? She's acting crazy."

"She's afraid she's going to lose Gino, Rosa. She's angry at me."

"Angry? You went out in a storm and risked your life for him. You all did. He's a no-good, selfish somabitch."

Ava obviously heard her aunt and turned to shoot daggers at Rosa. Sophie forcibly dragged her cousin to a chair while holding her husband's gaze. She nudged her head at her grandmother.

Liam nodded and said to Rosa, "Why don't I take you home? It's getting late."

Rosa ignored his brother and pressed a firm hand to Griffin's cheek. "You're a good man. Don't let her push you away. She needs you."

"She doesn't want me. She hasn't for a long time," he said without thinking, grimacing when he caught the sympathetic expressions on his brother's and Rosa's faces. He reached in the pocket of his leather jacket for the gold chain and placed it in Rosa's hand, closing her fingers around it. "I appreciate everything you said. But Ava needs you. Don't drive a wedge between the two of you because of me. I'm good."

He might not be good right now, but he would be. He'd needed the reminder of just how deeply Ava could wound him. The twist in his gut, the ache in his chest, they were nothing compared to how much he'd suffered twelve years before. He still bore the scars. And the reason why he'd never set himself up for that kind of heartache again. He knew when to cut his losses, and this was one of those times. He hoped his family hadn't gotten their hopes up, because he wasn't taking the job with HHCG.

Ava held her father's hand. Her eyes felt like they were rubbing against sandpaper as she tracked the shallow rise and fall of his chest, listened to the steady beep of the monitor. It had been two days since that horrible, awful night. Other than to change into the clothes Sophie had brought her and use the washroom, Ava hadn't moved from Gino's hospital bedside. Every time she left his side, she was overcome with panic, terrified that he was going to die. Afraid that if she stopped willing him to live, willing him to fight, he'd let go and slip away.

"How is everyone doing this morning?" a cheery young nurse Ava hadn't met before asked.

Her chirpiness was annoying. Ava wanted to say, *How do you think we are?* She could read her father's charts. He had pneumonia. There'd been no improvement. He'd barely regained consciousness. But she'd done her clinical practicum in a hospital and knew how difficult the job could be. She forced herself to respond politely. "Fine, thank you. How's your morning going?"

The nurse gave her a wide smile. "Aw, that's sweet of you to ask. I'm having a great morning, thanks. The snow has finally let up, and the sun is shining. And my patients are all in a good mood. I guess in your case, my patient's family." She unhooked Ava's father's chart from the end of the bed. "Oh, wow, now I know who your father is. My best friend's brother was rescued by the same man who rescued your dad." Her face took on a dreamy expression. "He's been in all the papers. He's so brave. God, I'd love to meet him. Has he come to see your father?"

"No, he hasn't." *Because I screamed at him and kicked him out of the hospital.* She wondered what the young girl would say if she told her. Probably look at her like her aunt had, like she was an ungrateful lunatic. Her face burned at the memory. She'd acted like a crazy person. Only an hour before Griffin had arrived at the hospital,

Jimmy had told Ava that her father meant to take his own life. After the anguish of waiting on the docks for news, it had been too much to deal with.

She'd taken her fear and anger out on Griffin. And he'd just stood there and taken it. She'd hurt him. She knew she had. But she'd been so ashamed, so embarrassed and afraid for her father…She'd been angry at him too. Because Rosa was right. Griffin had put his life on the line for Gino and so had the other men.

"Maybe he'll come by today." The nurse smoothed her hair from her pretty face and then looked down at her powder-blue scrubs. "I should have worn my other uniform."

"I wouldn't worry about it. He won't be coming today either."

"I bet he'd come if you called him. I can find out his number for you. I'm sure—"

Ava was back to being annoyed. Her father may be taking his last breaths, and all this girl could think about was Griffin. "That isn't necessary. I have his number. He's my husband."

The nurse's eyes went wide. "Oh, um, I should probably check on my other patients." She hurried to the door, then pivoted. "I'm really sorry. I shouldn't have been going on about your husband like that. But you probably get that all the time, don't you?"

. *Husband? Had she not said* ex*? Why wouldn't she have said* ex*?* "Ex. He's my ex-husband."

"Really?" The girl broke into a wide smile. "That's awesome." Her smile faltered. "I mean, wow, that sucks for you. I'm sorry for your loss." Ava thought she must have made an aggravated noise in her throat because the girl looked startled and flapped her hand. "I'll just go now."

Ava forgot about being annoyed when her father's eyes fluttered open. For the first time, they held hers, and she saw awareness there. He made an anxious sound in his throat, lifting his hand to the tube in his mouth. "No, you have to leave it in, Papa. Calm down. Everything's going to be all right." She rubbed his hand while reaching to press the call button for the nurse.

He shoved her hand away and pulled at the tubes in his arms, his eyes wild. "No, Papa." She tried to take hold of his hands but he was beyond reason and fought her. "Help, I need help in here!" she called out.

He sat up and shoved her out of the way. She lost her balance, tripping over the chair. It overturned, and she fell on top of it.

And that was how the young nurse, her Auntie Rosa, Dorothy, and Dr. Bishop found her. The nurse and Dr. Bishop ran to the other side of the bed to subdue her father while Rosa and Dorothy helped Ava to her feet. Another nurse rushed into the room to administer the sedative Dr. Bishop had called for.

Her face flushed with anger, tears in her eyes, Rosa cried, "Now you see. Now you see what Griffin tried to protect you from."

Ava knew her father hadn't meant to hurt her, but it was like everything crashed in on her at once. Her father nearly dying, the hurtful words she'd shouted at Griffin. And underneath all of that there was something else, something she didn't want to admit even to herself. Her fear that her father was going to live, and she would never ~~~ able to leave him alone in case he tried to hurt himself again. She'd have to quit her job to care for him full-time. She'd grow old in the house on South Shore Road.

"No, lovey, don't cry. You know he didn't mean to hurt you. You know that," Dorothy crooned, taking her in her arms.

"Come, we'll go to the cafeteria. You have something to eat. You'll feel better," Rosa said.

Ava drew back from Dorothy and self-consciously wiped at her face. "I'm okay. I need—"

"Rosa's right. Let's get out of their way. If they need you, they know where to find you," Dorothy said.

Ava glanced at her father, who'd calmed down, and numbly allowed herself to be led to the cafeteria. She sat in a plastic chair, barely able to hold herself upright. She couldn't remember the last time she'd slept. Rosa returned with a cup of coffee and a chocolate donut.

Taking the seat beside her, her aunt's anxious gaze searched Ava's face. "Enough, *cara*. You can't go on like this. You must go home at night."

"I need to be here, Auntie Rosa. The nurses are busy. I can—"

"If you don't agree, I will talk to Dr. Bishop and have him ban you from your father's room."

"You can't do that."

"*Sí*, I can. Dr. Bishop, he likes me, and he likes my lasagna." She gave Ava a smug smile.

"You're going to bribe my father's doctor to keep me out of the hospital. Is that what you're telling me?"

Dorothy pressed her lips together as though trying not to laugh, and then her eyes went wide. "Rosa, Dr.—"

"No, I'm going to seduce him. That's what I'm telling you." Rosa ignored Dorothy frantically trying to get her attention and took Ava's hand. "You see the lengths I would go to protect you? I love you, *cara*. I'm tired of seeing you this way. It hurts my heart. So for me, please, please, do this. Or *sí*, I will seduce Dr. Bishop."

"As intriguing as I find the idea of you seducing me, Rosa, it won't be necessary," a deep voice said from behind them.

Rosa blushed, glaring at Dorothy as Dr. Bishop took the seat across from them.

Dorothy shrugged.

"Your aunt's right, Ava. I've allowed this to go on long enough. I should have stepped in years ago. You can visit your father during visiting hours, but you have to…"

Ava strained to hear the words coming out of Dr. Bishop's mouth. It was as though he were talking underwater and in slow motion. She swayed on the chair and everything went black.

Chapter Eight

♥

Griffin looked out the back window, debating whether or not to go for a run around the lake. It was a cold and rainy forty-five degrees. Crappy weather had never stopped him in the past. For some reason, today it did. He wasn't himself. Ever since he'd left Harmony Harbor, he'd felt...Hell, he didn't know what he was feeling. Something just felt off. He wasn't even sure it had anything to do with Ava ripping him a new one at the hospital.

His family had tried to convince him to go back that morning and talk to her. Instead, using Lexi as an excuse, he'd headed home to Virginia Beach. She was dropping by after work, so he had at least an hour to kill.

He looked around the open layout of the two-bedroom bungalow for something to do. The landlord had been going for a cottage look, he supposed. The walls were cloud white while the built-ins and kitchen cabinets had been painted a dusky blue. It was kind of girlie. He liked the potbellied stove sitting inside the river rock fireplace though. About the only thing the place needed was some furniture. He'd moved in after he and Lexi had split and hadn't brought much with him. What he did have didn't really suit the place—it was too dark and masculine.

Rent was reasonable though, the view of the lake was great, and it was an easy bike ride to Little Creek. But other than hanging out at the base with his crew, he had no real reason to be there. He was retired. Jesus, God, he was retired at freaking thirty-eight. What the hell had he been thinking?

That he'd put in his time. That his luck would hold out for only so long. On their last mission, he'd lost a member of his team. It made him reevaluate his life. And now he was a civilian with no idea what to do with his time. He flicked a piece of peeling ocean-blue paint from the window frame, reminding himself of Sully's offer. The guy hadn't let up. Maybe that's why Griffin couldn't get the reason he wouldn't take the job out of his head. At least since he'd gotten home he wasn't constantly being woken up by a voice telling him Ava needed him. Now it was just his own conscience bugging him—wondering how Gino was doing and if she was okay.

Griffin gave up fighting the need to know and walked to his favorite chair. He made himself comfortable, pulling up the wooden lever to raise the footrest. An image came to him, sitting there with a book in his hand and a bottle of beer in the other. Is that really what he wanted to look like ten years from now?

He pushed the thought away. Everyone deserved

some downtime. He'd only been nonactive for a month…
*It's January, dumbass. You've been sitting on yours since
November.* Scowling, he thumbed through his contacts on
his phone. Instead of texting his brother, he decided it
might be better to talk to someone rather than talking to
himself.

"Hey, I was just about to call you," his brother said as
soon as he picked up.

An uncomfortable feeling twisted in Griffin's gut at
the serious tone of his brother's voice. Maybe this wasn't
a good idea after all. "What's up?"

"Ava was just hospitalized."

Griffin slammed the lever down and shot to his feet.
"What the hell do you mean she was hospitalized?"

"Jesus, you just about blew out my eardrum. Chill. It's
nothing serious."

"Chill? You tell me something like that and you expect
me to *chill*? And since when did you start saying shit like
chill?"

Liam snorted a laugh. "Blame Mia. It's her favorite
new word."

"If you don't tell me why Ava was hospitalized, you'll
be hearing my favorite word."

"For a guy who says he doesn't care, you sound pretty
worked up about this."

"Liam," he gritted out.

"Okay, okay, she has a hairline fracture in her arm."

"Goddamn, the woman's stubborn. I told her it wasn't
just a bruise."

"Yeah, well, here's the thing. It was just a bruise, a bad
one. But, uh, Gino woke up, and he wasn't himself. He
was ripping—"

"Swear to God, I'm going to kill that old man. He hurt her again, didn't he?"

"Seriously, big brother, you've gotta calm down. It wasn't intentional. Gino was off his head and pulling out the lines. Ava tried to stop him, and he pushed her. She tripped."

Griffin sat on the arm of the chair and dragged a hand down his face. "They wouldn't hospitalize her for a hair-line fracture. What else is going on?"

"She fainted. She's been at the hospital since they brought Gino in and hasn't slept. Before you give us grief, we all tried to get her to go home. Like you said, she's stubborn."

"Are they sure that's all it is? I've gone without sleep for forty-eight hours. I'm sure you have too. I didn't faint. Did you?"

"Hello, I've never gone without sleep for that long. And you're a SEAL; nothing affects you. But it's not just the past two days. Dorothy, their next-door neighbor, says Ava hasn't had more than a couple of hours of sleep a night since she moved in beside them. Over the past month, Gino's been drinking more and staying up all night. Ava's afraid he'll hurt himself and doesn't go to bed until he does. Then she's up at the crack of dawn get-ting him and his meals ready for the day. Doc Bishop says she's burned out. He's beating himself up for not recog-nizing the signs and stepping in sooner. We're all feeling pretty bad. We've seen the changes, the weight loss, signs that she might be depressed, and none of us took her aside and talked to her about it."

"Take it from me, it wouldn't have done you any good. She would have told you she's fine."

"That what she did with you?"

"Yep." He watched the rain stream down the window-pane, remembering how hard he'd tried to get her to open up all those years ago. "In the end, this is probably the best thing that could have happened to her. She won't be able to pretend anymore. How long is Doc keeping her in the hospital?"

"A few days."

"Gino?"

"He's got pneumonia, and they're monitoring his heart. Looks like he's going to make it though. He's a tough guy. If he continues to progress, Doc figures he'll be released in a couple of weeks."

And unless someone got through to Ava, she'd end up back in the hospital. Only next time it might be worse. But there wasn't much Griffin could do about it. He was the last person she'd listen to. There was something he could take care of though. "I need Sophie to do something for me. Other than you, I don't want anyone else to know." When his brother agreed, Griffin continued. "Give Ava a month paid leave. I'll cover the cost."

"You're forgetting the DiRossi pride. She won't take it."

"Make something up. Tell her she hasn't used up her holidays, and if she—"

"She's never taken holidays, Griff. She takes the money instead."

"Are you telling me that Ava hasn't taken any time off in over ten years?"

"That's what I'm saying. You gotta know we've been thinking about what we can do to help her too. Grams said she's always refused time off. She thinks it's because coming to work is Ava's escape."

From her father. Griffin wanted to go to the hospital and shake her, ask her why she couldn't open up, let him in, and let him help. "So tell her if she doesn't accept, she's fired."

"That's a little harsh, don't you think?"

"What other choice do we have?"

"I'll talk to Sophie about it. Maybe we can figure out something else. By the way, I saw Sully this morning. He says you've been avoiding his calls."

"I've been busy. I'll get back to him."

"You got a job I don't know about?"

He chose to ignore his brother's wiseass remark because Liam probably had a few comebacks he'd been saving up about Griffin's interest in Ava. So Griffin took away his opportunity by saying, "I've gotta make dinner for Lexi. Call me when you've come up with a way to handle the Ava situation. I'll transfer the money to you."

"I'll probably get back to you tonight. Say hi to Lexi for me."

"Will do." He disconnected and stood up, glancing at the time on his phone. He thought about calling Sully and then decided to put it off, telling himself it was because his old friend would ride his ass for rejecting the job offer. But lying to yourself never really worked, at least for long. After hearing about Ava, there was a part of Griffin that was almost desperate to take the job.

With the aim of killing time and shutting off thoughts of his first ex, he walked into the kitchen to figure out what to make for his second one. Lexi was easy to please. As long as she didn't have to make it, she'd be happy with whatever he served for dinner. He opened the refrigerator, almost hoping he didn't have the ingredients for a meal and he'd have to head to the store. Shutting down thoughts of Ava wasn't working out as he'd planned. His conversation with his brother kept playing in his head. The changes in Ava had started months before her father was paralyzed in the accident. Nothing to the degree they were seeing now, but the signs had been there.

Griffin scrubbed his hands over his face. He couldn't go there again. Refocusing on the contents of the refrigerator, he decided to make a chicken stir fry…which would take him all of fifteen minutes to prepare. Right then, he solved the mystery of that feeling of unease that had been hovering over him. He was bored. He wasn't the kind of guy who would be happy sitting on his ass or working out twenty-four-seven. He was the kind of guy who needed a purpose, a focus, to make a difference.

A message pinged on his cell. He dug the phone from his front jeans pocket. Lexi was bringing takeout. So much for his killing-time plan. And that's the thing with too much time on your hands—you do something stupid like calling your ex's doctor.

"Hey, Doc, Griffin Gallagher here."

"I had a feeling I'd be hearing from you. Your brother told you about Ava?"

And that was the thing about growing up in a close-knit community—people knew you too damn well. Because of patient confidentiality, Doc Bishop couldn't tell Griffin much more than his brother had. But those same rules applied to what Griffin told him, so for the first time in twelve years, he opened up about the month leading to the end of his and Ava's marriage.

The doc had some interesting insights. Things Griffin

hadn't factored in, like their ages when they married, the loss of the baby, the amount of time they spent apart, and the stress they were both under—Ava with school and Griffin with the military. And being a man who'd been the Gallagher's family physician for what seemed like forever, the talk eventually turned to the loss of Griffin's mother and sister and how he'd dealt with it.

By the time the call ended, Griffin felt like he'd gone through an intensive therapy session. He wasn't sure he liked the feelings Doc Bishop had stirred up. But Griffin had accomplished the goal he'd had when he'd initiated the call. The doc was now aware that the changes had started in Ava long ago. More importantly, he was aware of Griffin's concerns for her safety. Though the older man didn't believe Gino had, or would, intentionally hurt Ava, he had some concerns of his own. So when Griffin suggested that Gino deal with his alcoholism and anger issues in a rehabilitation center instead of at home, Doc Bishop agreed the idea held merit and that he'd look into it.

With his mind somewhat at ease over Ava, Griffin's thoughts turned to Lexi. He'd called her yesterday, thinking she'd come over right away. He hadn't seen her in months, not since his great-grandmother's funeral, which wasn't unusual. They were both busy with their careers and lives. She was at least. But she'd put him off until today. It was late, and she was tired. At least that's what she'd said. She'd sounded more nervous than tired. Lexi wasn't the type of woman who got nervous. And that worried him. It didn't escape his notice that he was spending an inordinate amount of time lately worrying about his ex-wives.

At the sound of a car pulling into the driveway, Griffin walked to the window. Lexi sat behind the wheel of a blue sedan. A sun-kissed blonde with chin-length hair and brown eyes, she was pretty in a girl-next-door kind of way. She had a long, lean frame and kept herself in great shape. He'd been gun-shy after his split from Ava, but Lex had managed to break down his barriers. She was tough, no bullshit, and he liked that about her. They had a lot in common. It was one of the reasons he'd convinced himself to give marriage another shot. Ava and Lex were complete opposites, so he'd figured they stood a good chance of making their marriage work. At least they were still friends.

He frowned when Lexi didn't immediately get out of the car. He went to the door and opened it. She gave him what looked like a forced smile and got out of the car. "Hey, Griff," she said, walking toward him with a takeout bag in her hand.

"Hey, yourself," he said, pulling her in for a hug when she reached the porch. *What the…* He slowly drew back, looked down at what had felt like a football between them, and then lifted his eyes to hers.

She pulled a face. "Surprise."

"Seriously? You're pregnant?" he said as he drew her into the house. She nodded with that wry expression still on her face. Griffin laughed and pulled her in for another hug. "That's fantastic. I'm happy for you, babe."

There was nothing Lexi wanted more than a baby. She'd wanted one so bad that she'd made Griffin promise they'd make a baby together if neither of them was in a relationship by her thirty-ninth birthday. Lexi'd made it clear she wanted his sperm and nothing more. Griffin hadn't known how he felt about that, but he'd agreed. He loved Lexi and had felt guilty that they couldn't make their marriage work. It was his fault. He hadn't loved her the way she deserved to be loved. And Lexi wasn't the type to settle. She was an all-or-nothing kind of girl. He didn't blame her.

She'd turned thirty-nine last June. Since neither of them was in a relationship back then, she'd called in her marker. They'd tried for a few months. He was a guy, he loved sex, and he loved Lex, but it got weird fast. And it sure as hell wasn't fun. It was like he was a baby-making machine.

Lexi became obsessed. It was all about charts and timing and temperatures. So he was over the moon that she'd found someone to make her dream come true. Maybe even a little relieved that it wasn't him. Still…

He stepped back. "I thought you agreed to let me interview the baby-daddy candidates."

"Yeah, about that—"

He crossed his arms. "Do not tell me he's army." There was a friendly rivalry between the branches. Okay, sometimes not so friendly. Since Lexi was army, every so often it had leaked into their relationship.

She didn't answer him right away. Instead she placed the takeout bag on the console table and took off her black coat, hanging it on the hook by the door. "No, he's not army." She turned, her hand resting protectively over her baby bump. "He's navy, a SEAL."

"All right, that's more like it." Only he was afraid it wasn't. She wouldn't meet his eyes, and her face was flushed. "Lex, don't tell me it's one of my guys. You know I love them, but they're players. None of them are ready to settle down. Jace might be though. You two always got along. Is it Jace?"

She shook her head, pushing her sun-streaked bangs from her eyes. "No, it's, um"—she lifted a shoulder with that wry smile back on her face—"it's you."

What the...

Afraid his legs were going to give out, he reached behind him for the console table. He sat down and then, worried it wasn't going to hold his weight, stood up. At least he tried to but his legs were like wet noodles, so he parked his ass on the table again. He met brown eyes that appeared to be filled with amusement. Lex always did have a dry sense of humor.

He let out a relieved laugh that cracked a little with residual nerves. "You had me going there for a minute, babe."

She wrapped an arm around her expanding waist and brought her other hand to her mouth, chewing her thumbnail. "I'm not joking, Griff. You're the baby's daddy."

"You're serious?"

She nodded. "I get it if you're not happy—"

He didn't know what he was, but he sure as hell wasn't going to take away from Lexi's happiness by acting like an ass. "Of course I'm happy. I'm just surprised. This is...wow...this is so...cool." Jesus, he was completely blowing it.

He always told Lexi the truth, so he stood up and took her hand, leading her into the living room. He needed to sit down for this. "I really am happy for you. Whatever you and the baby need from me, you've got. I'm here for you, for both of you. I'm just kind of surprised. You never said anything. We were at GG's funeral in November—"

"I didn't know then. I wasn't keeping it from you, honest. I just thought I was going through the change of life early or something. I went to my doctor a few weeks ago, and…and that's when I found out." An emotion flickered in her eyes, and then it was gone. Because he knew her so well, he could have sworn it was sorrow.

He gently tugged her onto the couch, taking both her hands in his. He searched her face. She looked tired, a bluish tinge under her eyes. She looked like she'd lost a little weight too. "Are you okay, Lex? There isn't anything wrong with the baby, is there?"

"God, no. The baby's perfect." Her face lit up, and she gave him a watery smile. "I'm having a baby. Can you believe it?"

He smiled, truly happy for her. "You'll be an amazing mom."

"You're going to be an amazing dad. If you want to be, I mean. I know I said—"

"Do you want us to live together, get married again?" As he waited for her to answer, it felt like he stood on a cliff with a foot dangling over the edge. He knew why. If that's what Lexi wanted, he'd do it. He'd marry her. And Ava would be lost to him for good.

There it was—another answer. No matter how hard he'd tried to deny it, he still had feelings for Ava; he'd never gotten over her. He didn't know if he wanted closure or a second chance, but after talking to his brother and Doc Bishop, he knew he wanted to be there for her.

"That didn't really work out the first time," Lexi said, playfully nudging him in the ribs, and then she grew serious. "But I want you to be the baby's father in every sense of the word. I want the baby to have your name, and if…if anything ever happened to me, I want you to raise him or her."

"Don't talk stupid. Nothing's going to happen to you," he said, his voice sharper than he intended. Maybe because he knew better than anyone that bad things happened to good people. One minute they're laughing and smiling, giving you grief for not tagging along, waving goodbye, telling you not to eat all the cookies, that they'd be home in a few hours from their early Christmas shopping trip in Boston. Only they never came home. And Harmony Harbor never felt like home again.

As though she realized where the underlying anger was coming from, Lexi rubbed his arm. "None of us like to think about it, honey. But with a baby on the way, sometimes we have to talk about the hard stuff."

"I'd rather talk about the fun stuff. But you want to talk about the hard stuff, okay then. You know there's no way this kid is enlisting in the army, right?"

She laughed. "Okay, I think you're getting a little ahead of yourself."

"Just putting it out there."

"There's something I want to put out there too." She looked down, her hair falling forward to hide her face. "I want the baby to grow up with family close by."

Lexi didn't have any family. She'd been an only child of only children. A late-in-life baby whose parents had both died before she was nineteen. Griffin tucked her hair behind her ear. "You know my family loves you. We can visit anytime. Grams and Dad are going to be over the moon."

"No, I mean, I want us to move there." At what he imagined was a look of shock on his face, she hurried on.

"I love your family. I love Greystone. I seriously love everything about Harmony Harbor."

She was forgetting one thing, one person, because she definitely did not love his ex. But he sure as hell wasn't going to be the one to bring up Ava.

"What do you think?" Lexi asked, a hopeful expression on her face. Actually it was a little beyond hopeful, and he was kind of wondering if more was going on than she was telling him.

"So you do want us to live together?" he asked, his chest tightening once again.

"I was thinking maybe you could live in one of the cottages on the estate, and I can live in one a couple doors down. That way you won't get in my space, and I won't get in yours."

His family would love it. Though seeing Lexi was pregnant, they might not be too happy with him. They'd no doubt expect him to marry the mother of his child. "I guess. What about your job?"

A shadow crossed her face but was gone so quickly he thought he must have imagined it. "I thought I'd apply with HHPD. Just part-time though. It'd be a lot less stressful than my job now. And I'm eligible to retire anyway. I'd collect my pension and make some money on the side." She looked at him, an expectant expression on her face. "What do you think?"

There were some pros to moving to Harmony Harbor. He liked the idea of raising his child in his hometown and being close to his family. And being around if Ava needed...

Yeah, not something he'd share with Lex. "It's a good idea. I think we should do it."

"Really?"

"Yeah." He laughed when she threw herself into his arms. She wasn't a demonstrative woman. It had taken a while for her to get used to his family's easy display of affection.

Pulling back with a wide smile on her face, Lex looked happier than he'd seen her in a long time. "Okay, so don't get offended, but, Griff, you've gotta get a job. You're too young to retire. It's not healthy."

Leave it to Lexi to put her finger on his problem. At least one of them. "I've been offered a job in Harmony Harbor with the Coast Guard. All I have to do is accept."

"That would be perfect for you. But don't you have to train or something?"

If they were really going to do this, he had to tell her what happened. She'd find out about it anyway. As he told her about Gino and Ava, she stiffened. When he finished, she crossed her arms and stared across the room for a few minutes. Then she looked at him, pink blotches spreading on her cheeks. She was ticked. "I need you to promise me one thing."

"Okay." But he was thinking it might be far from okay.

"You need to stay away from that woman. You can't have anything to do with Ava DiRossi. She's your kryptonite, Griffin."

"I think you're exaggerating, babe. But you don't have to worry about Ava. The last thing she'd want is to see me again. She'll probably try to have me run out of town."

Looking every inch the cop that she was, Lexi said, "She'll have to go through me first."

He said his favorite word in his head.

Chapter Nine

♥

The clock on Ava's nightstand ticked down the minutes until her father came home. In a little more than an hour, the peaceful silence would be replaced with the creak of a wheelchair rolling across the parquet floors, the tinny voices on the television, a gravelly male voice demanding his meals, a blanket, his whiskey.

The sweet scent of pink roses on her dresser, of cinnamon buns in the oven, and crisp air wafting through her open bedroom window would soon be buried under layers of stale cigarette smoke. Hours upon hours of blissful freedom, of reading, of catnaps, of visits with friends would be replaced with the mundane routine of seeing to her father's needs and working at the manor.

Life in the bungalow on South Shore Road would return to normal. Ava's holiday was officially over.

"Stop," she murmured, feeling churlish and petty. She should be happy, grateful that her father was alive and coming home. It had been only three short weeks since she'd nearly lost him in the dark and stormy seas. She prayed that night had changed him. Over the past week, she'd seen signs that it had—glimpses of the father she remembered. Fleeting, but they'd been there. They'd given her hope that things would be different.

She was different. That night had changed her. Maybe not that night exactly, but the days that followed certainly had.

She'd been angry and embarrassed when she came to at the hospital. But anger had won out over embarrassment when Dr. Bishop informed her he was admitting her. Not that it had done her much good to argue. She hadn't had the strength to fight with Rosa and Dorothy, and her rubbery legs wouldn't have made it to the exit. Besides, Rosa and Dorothy would have chained her to the hospital bed if she'd tried to leave. They didn't have to. Ava was out as soon as her head hit the pillow. She'd slept for twenty-four hours straight. And every night since she'd been released, she slept a solid twelve hours with even a few catnaps in between.

Dr. Bishop had limited her visits with Gino to two hours in the morning and three hours in the evening so she'd had lots of time to rest. She'd had even more time to herself that first week. Gino had thrown a fit, cursing out Ava and pitching his breakfast tray at her before Dr. Bishop intervened. He'd informed Gino that he didn't care if he was on his deathbed; he wouldn't stand for him verbally abusing Ava.

As she was wont to do, Ava had been about to come to her father's defense. Before that moment, she'd never thought of his belittling name-calling as abuse—something that she was embarrassed to admit now because she wasn't a stupid woman. In her nursing program, she'd been trained to look for the very signs both she and her father exhibited. Signs she'd ignored.

That wasn't entirely true. She hadn't ignored them, not exactly. They had started small, a little dig here and there, and then over time slowly became more abusive. But it was like she'd become immune to his hurtful words and his fiery temper. Maybe because she'd been in a zombie-like state. Now she was awakening to what her life had truly been like. She took a nervous swallow. What if she slid back and it started all over again?

With that worrisome thought in her head, she moved the hanger that held the hoodie and sweatpants she'd intended to wear today to search deeper in her closest. Maybe if she made small changes to herself, they'd protect her from a backward slide. She found the jeans she was looking for and pulled them off the hanger. She'd bought them six years earlier after a meeting with the Widows Club.

Grieving the loss of Mary and Riley had brought Colleen and Ava closer, and Colleen had invited her to become a member of the Widows Club. The older women's stories of what they had accomplished despite their ages and losses had been inspiring, and they'd sparked something in Ava. It was after her third meeting that Ava made a decision to take her life back.

She'd heard Griffin was coming home to sing with his brothers at the Salty Dog in a fund-raiser for MADD. She went out and bought the jeans, a pair of sexy red heels, and a pretty T-shirt. She took extra time with her appearance, putting on some makeup and Griffin's favorite scent. She'd waited until her father was asleep and snuck out of the house.

She remembered laughing at herself—a woman of thirty having to sneak out to meet up with the man she loved. Only, when Ava arrived at the Salty Dog, the man she loved was singing their song to another woman. After he'd finished to whoops and cheers, Griffin pulled Lexi onto the stage and introduced her as his fiancée.

Colleen had found Ava crying in a guest room the next day. She'd poured out her heart and her secrets to the older woman. The same secrets that she was positive Colleen had recorded in her book. A book that someone now had in their possession.

Ava had stopped by the manor after she'd been released from the hospital, but Sophie and Kitty had insisted she go home. They'd forced her to take a paid vacation, threatening to fire her if she refused.

For the first week, she'd waited for the shoe to drop. But when there was no mention of Colleen's memoirs being found, Ava began to wonder if whoever had repaired the chimney had inadvertently sealed the book inside. Either that or whoever found it had secrets they didn't want revealed. As long as Byron hadn't found the book, she thought she was safe. She was almost positive he hadn't.

When he'd stopped by the hospital to interview her father, Byron had brought Ava flowers and books. In hopes, he'd said, that she'd convince Julia to let him join the book club. Ava didn't believe him. He may not have found *The Secret Keeper of Harmony Harbor*, but his subtle questions made her think he was trying to discover *her* secret.

"Lovey, Julia's dropped by with your coffee. The cinnamon rolls are out of the oven," Dorothy called.

Ava would miss her morning visits with Julia, Dorothy, and Rosa. Kitty, Dana, and Sophie usually stopped by too. But with the bridal fair only a week away, they were probably too busy.

"I'll be right there," she called, shimmying into the jeans. She kept shimmying, but nothing happened. She lay flat on her back on the bed and sucked in her stomach. A stomach that was no longer concave and hips that were more round.

Mio Dio! How much weight had she gained? She got off the bed, shuffling to the closet. She moved the hangers, finding a pair of jeans from her freshman year of college. She'd been voluptuous back then, all butt and boobs. She looked down at herself. Why hadn't she noticed the changes until now? It wasn't difficult to figure out. All she'd been wearing were pajamas, jogging pants, and hoodies. And thanks to Rosa and Dorothy, all Ava had been doing was sleeping and eating.

She took off the six-year-old jeans and shimmied into the fifteen-year-old pair. They went on easily. They were well-worn and faded, a little loose in the butt and at the waist, so she pulled a belt off the hanger. Pairing the jeans with a high-neck, plum-colored sweater, she went on her knees to dig a pair of high-heeled, black suede boots from the back of her closet. Small changes, she thought, once she was dressed. She looked at herself in the mirror on the dresser. Giving her hair a quick brush, she added a touch of mascara and lip gloss.

Julia and Dorothy looked up from where they sat at the kitchen table and did a double take when she walked into the kitchen.

Self-consciously, Ava lifted a shoulder. "They're old

and a little baggy, but I didn't have anything else to wear." She did, but she thought it might sound silly if she explained that she was using her wardrobe change to remind herself that she had changed on the inside too.

Dorothy smiled. "Lovey, you look beautiful."

"Dorothy's right, Ava. You look amazing," Julia said.

"Thank you," she murmured, trying to ignore the anxious knot pulling tight in her chest. After so many years of doing her best to fade into the background, she supposed it was only natural she'd be a little uncomfortable with the attention. If this was going to work, if her changes were going to stick, Ava had to get used to putting herself out there.

As she took a seat at the table, the mouthwatering scent of cinnamon and chocolate enticed her taste buds. "I think I've gained twenty pounds."

Dorothy laughed and put two cinnamon rolls on a small plate, passing it to her. "Rosa will be pleased to hear that. It looks good on you, lovey."

Julia handed her a pretty lilac ceramic thermos. "Chocolate cinnamon latte is from me. The thermos is from Byron. He says a pretty woman needs a pretty thermos. I think he has a crush on you."

Ava suspected he felt sorry for her. She didn't know which would be worse, if Julia was right or if Ava was. "He's hoping I can convince you to let him join the book club."

"I already did. He's going to run a monthly column in the paper about it." She lifted a shoulder. "I couldn't pass up the free advertising."

"So you're going ahead with it?" Ava asked.

"Yes. We have close to twenty members. Most of the Widows Club joined. First meeting is the week after the bridal fair. You're coming, right?"

"I don't know. I'll have to wait and see how my father is doing," she said, picking at a cinnamon bun. Her stomach pitched and rolled as she saw her world shrinking again.

"That won't be a problem now that…" Dorothy pressed her lips to together and shared a glance with Julia. "You know, we probably should get going."

Julia stood up. "I have to go too."

"But Auntie Rosa said she's meeting us here," Ava said.

Dorothy busied herself sweeping up crumbs with a napkin. "She's going to meet us at the hospital instead," she said without meeting Ava's gaze.

"Is there something you're not telling me?"

"Thanks for the cinnamon buns, Dorothy." Julia turned to look at Ava. "Call me later if you need to talk, okay?"

Ava nodded, narrowing her eyes at Dorothy when the door closed behind Julia. "Why was Julia looking at me like she was going to cry? Has something happened to my father?"

"Of course not, lovey." Dorothy's smile didn't quite reach her eyes. "I've got a peacoat that will look lovely with your outfit. I'll be right back."

Ava sat across from Dr. Bishop wearing Dorothy's lovely winter-white peacoat. Ava wondered if the older woman had given it to her to make up for stabbing Ava in the back. Dorothy, sitting to Rosa's left, twisted her hands in her lap.

"If you don't mind, I'd like a few moments alone with Ava," Dr. Bishop said, rising from his chair.

Rosa stood. "We're not doing this to hurt you, *cara*."

Ava turned away. She couldn't look at her aunt right now. If Ava didn't agree to their health-care plan for her father, they were going to Judge Monahan to ask that Rosa be appointed Gino's conservator.

A hand stroked her hair. "Your mother was my best friend, you know," Dorothy said. "We wrote to each other once a week, and you were all she ever talked about. She wouldn't want this life for you. If Maria were here, she would have done exactly what Rosa and I did."

Her mother never would have torn their family apart by sending her father to some horrible institution to be taken care of by strangers. "This is a mistake. You're wrong about my father. You and Rosa hate him because you think—"

Dorothy shook her head with a sad smile. "No, lovey. Rosa doesn't hate Gino, and neither do I. One day I'll tell you why I left Harmony Harbor, and you'll understand that I wouldn't do this if I didn't think it was truly best for your father. But for now, I hope you'll listen to Dr. Bishop. No matter how difficult it is, Ava, you have to do this for both you and Gino."

Dr. Bishop closed the office door behind Dorothy and took the seat beside Ava. "This wasn't an easy decision to make. But Dorothy's right. Gino needs help that you can't give him."

"But he's getting better. He hasn't had a drink in weeks, and he—"

"All right, let's say Gino goes home with you, and tomorrow he asks you to buy him a bottle of whiskey. Will you be able to say no, Ava?"

"I…Yes, of course," she said, though truthfully she wasn't sure how long she could hold out. Right now she was strong and rested. What would happen months from now when she was functioning on two hours' sleep?

"Ava, you've been enabling your father's drinking for many years now." At her gasp, he held up his hand. "I'm not judging you. I know of very few children who would be able to, or be willing to, provide the level of care you have for your father. But now your physical and mental well-being are being compromised. I'm as concerned for you as I am for Gino."

"You don't have to be. I'm going to take better care of myself."

"I'm sure you will, for a week or two, and then in-evitably you'll revert to the same pattern. Gino's overly dependent upon you, Ava, and you've allowed him to be. It's become unhealthy. There's no reason he can't be self-sufficient. You're his crutch, and he's yours." He reached for a pamphlet on his desk and handed it to her. "This is a private facility in Boston."

She flipped through the glossy brochure. The rooms and dining area looked like they belonged in a high-end hotel. There were several therapy rooms, a gym, and two pools, and the grounds were lush with trees and gardens. She looked at Dr. Bishop. "There's no way we can afford this."

"They've accepted Gino into the program. Between his monthly pension checks and insurance, the cost is cov-ered," he said, focusing on the pamphlet in her hands.

She crossed her arms, wincing at the ache radiating down her forearm. The brace she had to wear for another few weeks typically made her more careful.

He sighed and looked up. "All right, some strings were pulled. For your father's sake, don't look a gift horse in the mouth. This is a second chance for him, for you both."

She glanced at the brochure again and read the testimonials from former residents. She wanted her father to regain his independence and reclaim his life. But he'd hate being a charity case as much as she did. "Who pulled the strings? Dana didn't put up a GoFundMe page for us, did she?"

"No, but I'm sure she would have. Just as I'm sure people in town would have been happy to contribute. There's no shame in taking or asking for help, Ava. You would do the same for anyone else."

She would, but that wasn't the point. They didn't need help. They paid their own way. "I'm not saying this wouldn't be a good thing for my father. But it's only fair that he gets a say. I want to talk to him first." She stood up. "Before I do, I need to know who pulled the strings." If there was money involved, she'd work three jobs in order to pay them back.

Dr. Bishop stood and started for the door. "I know the director. He made an exception for me."

Since he had his back to her, Ava couldn't tell if he was lying. But as she walked to the door, concerns about money were replaced with thoughts of her father. "How long would he have to stay there? When would he leave?"

"The van is here to pick him up. The length of his stay will depend…"

Ava was out the door before Dr. Bishop finished. "You can't just take him away like that. He hasn't agreed," she yelled at him as she ran to the open elevator. Her finger shook as she stabbed the button to the fourth floor.

She wrapped her arms around herself, ignoring the pain in her arm, willing the elevator not to stop on another floor. When the doors opened on the fourth floor moments later, she raced to her father's room.

She was winded, her legs shaky when she pushed open the door. She almost collapsed against it when she saw her father sitting beside the bed in his wheelchair, his head bowed. Tears filled her eyes at the sight of the suitcase at his feet.

He lifted his head. He looked tired and sad.

She went to sit on the edge of the bed and took his hand. "I didn't know, Papa." The words were little more than a whisper as a tear slid down her cheek. "I'll go to Judge Monahan. They can't do this. It's not right."

He looked down at their joined hands and then met her gaze. "What's not right is that I didn't see what I've done to you. What I was doing to you."

"Don't talk foolish. You—"

"No, you listen to your papa now. I'm going to this place. And while I'm there, I don't want you to visit."

"Why? What have I done? Are you mad at me?" she choked out on a sob, unable to ask the question she wanted the answer to: *Don't you love me anymore?*

"Now who's talking foolish?" He reached up to wipe the tears from her face. "I'm going to work hard to get better. I want you to do the same, *luce dei miei occhi.*"

Her throat ached when he uttered the endearment she hadn't heard in years: *light of my eyes.*

"You take the chef job at the manor." He tugged on her hand. "Promise."

"*Sí*, Papa. I promise." She looked up at the knock on the door.

"You all set, Mr. DiRossi?" A large man filled the doorway, the name of the facility on the pocket of his quilted navy jacket.

Her father bent to pick up his suitcase. Ava got off the bed to help him.

The man at the door cleared his throat, giving a subtle shake of his head. Ava lowered her hands to her sides. Her father placed the suitcase on his lap, his eyes roaming her face. "*Ciao, bella.* Make your papa proud," he said, his voice gruff.

He didn't want her to see him off. She didn't know if she could. "*Ciao*, Papa. I love you."

She stood in the empty room, feeling lost and alone.

Dorothy and Rosa peeked their heads around the door and then came inside. "Are you all right?"

Ava shook her head, and Rosa took her in arms. "In time you will see it's for the best, *cara*."

Dorothy rubbed Ava's back. "They'll take excellent care of him, lovey. He's lucky they were able to take him. They have a two-year waiting list."

"It was not luck, Dot. The director is one of those fish people too. He's Griffin's friend. Griffin asks, and he says *sí*." Rosa frowned at Dorothy. "Why are you flapping your hand at me?" Then her aunt grimaced. "Oh, *accidenti*. I forgot. It was a secret."

Chapter Ten

♥

Ava searched the pockets of her jeans and Dorothy's coat. She hadn't been thinking clearly when she jumped in the cab idling alongside the curb at the hospital. If she had been, she would have called Sophie from her father's room to get Griffin's number. "Sorry, I forgot my wallet. I'll be right back with your money," Ava said to the cabbie, sliding across the backseat to reach for the door. She'd borrow twenty dollars from Sophie.

"No problem," the older man said, getting out of the cab. "I could use a smoke break anyway."

Ava's fingers tightened around the handle as she closed the door. She hadn't had a cigarette in ten days. One more of the small changes she'd recently made. She glanced at the cabbie leaning against the hood of the black car, a look of utter contentment coming over his craggy face as he took his first drag. Oh, what she wouldn't give to feel the way he looked. It wouldn't really count if she only had a puff or two. "Would you be able to spare—"

He looked at her and coughed, a deep, wet sound.

"It's okay. Don't worry about it. I'll just be a minute," she said over her shoulder as she hurried up the walkway. Before she opened the door, she pinched her cheeks and smoothed her hair. She wouldn't let them see how hurt she was that they'd all plotted behind her back to send her father away. She couldn't let them know how angry she was at Griffin for orchestrating the whole thing either. They wouldn't give her his number if they knew.

Drawing in a deep breath through her nose, she opened the door. Of course the first person she ran into was Jasper. He didn't notice her right away. He was talking to Simon, nudging the cat away with the edge of his black shoe. She opened her mouth to tell him he shouldn't be shooing Simon away like that, but closed it in hopes she could sneak by him. She'd make it up to Simon later. Ava turned to head for her cousin's office.

"Miss DiRossi."

She swallowed a groan, stopping to face him. "Yes?"

He blinked, an emotion she couldn't read crossing his face. "Sophie is showing Mr. St. John around. Is there something I can help you with?"

"Thank you, but I'll just wait in her office if that's all right."

"Quite." He hesitated and then approached. "Perhaps you would like to"—he removed a starched white handkerchief from the breast pocket of his black suit and handed it to her—"clean up a bit. Your mascara—"

"Is it all over my face?" she asked, self-consciously bringing the handkerchief to her cheek. The odd look the cabbie had given her when she'd jumped in his car now made sense.

"No, just…Here, allow me." He gently removed the handkerchief from her hand.

Ava didn't know why—maybe because Jasper had never said so much as a single kind word to her before now—but a tear rolled down her cheek. "They took my father away today," she said as a way of explaining the emotions she couldn't seem to get under control.

"Yes, I know. I'm sorry," he said, holding her chin to dab at her cheeks. It reminded her of something her father would have done when she was a child, and her bottom lip quivered as she tried to keep the tears at bay. "Come now, there's no need to cry. Your father will be home before you know it, miss."

She gave her head a tiny shake. "They don't think I can care for him. They think it's my fault he hasn't gotten better. It's my fault he tried to…he tried to kill himself." She told this man who'd never been a friend what she hadn't told anyone else. The thing that hurt most. Her father had tried to take his own life. She'd tried convincing herself it had been an accident, a mistake. He was drunk and not thinking clearly. But she'd been fooling herself. Dr. Bishop was right. She'd enabled her father, and now even Gino didn't want her. At the thought, a sob broke in her throat, and she started to cry.

Jasper drew her awkwardly into his arms and patted her back. "There, there now," he murmured.

Seconds later, Ava found herself wrapped in another pair of arms. There was nothing awkward about the way this man held her. She should have felt uncomfortable, anxious that a tall, powerfully built man, a man she didn't know, was holding her so close, so intimately. She didn't. She felt like she'd come home. And there was only one man who'd ever made her feel that way.

She lifted her head and met her ex-husband's indigo gaze. "What are you doing here? I thought you left weeks ago," she said, at the same time thinking she'd completely lost her mind.

Because instead of staring into that beautiful, familiar face, she should be pushing him away, yelling at him for the part he'd played in all of this. Yet she couldn't bring herself to move from his warm, comforting embrace.

"We can talk about that later. Right now, I want—"

Someone cleared their throat. "Master Griffin, perhaps Miss Ava would be more comfortable in the study."

Oh God, she'd broken down in the entrance to Greystone, right there for everyone to see. She did a face-plant into Griffin's chest, making an embarrassed sound in her throat.

Griffin stepped back and put an arm around her shoulders. "Do me a favor and bring a pot of coffee to the study, Jeeves."

"No, I should go. I have a taxi waiting for me." Ava couldn't borrow money from him. She was already in his debt for something she didn't even want—a debt she no doubt couldn't afford to pay.

"You mean the cabbie I just paid? He's long gone."

She took in his brown leather jacket and boots. The two large, black duffel bags off to the side. He must have come in when she was crying in Jasper's arms. Heat rose to her cheeks. "Why did you—"

"You were here to speak to Sophie, miss. I'll let her know you're awaiting her in the study," Jasper intervened, reminding Ava of why she'd come here in the first place. Only the man she'd planned to call was standing right here in the flesh, all six-foot-four gorgeous inches of him. She wished he wasn't looking at her with an expression that softened the strong, chiseled angles of his face. It made it difficult to remember why she was mad at him.

He'd always had that effect on her. They'd be fighting about something, and then she'd look at him, and he'd look at her and say, *"Why are we wasting time arguing about this shit? I love you. Nothing else matters."* That's what it always came back to—they loved each other.

They weren't *them* anymore, the boy and girl who thought their love could withstand anything. Back then, the world could have fallen down around them and they wouldn't have noticed. But Griffin no longer loved her. And right now, it felt like her world had imploded, and he was partially to blame. If he hadn't confronted her father in the ballroom that day and then made arrangements for Gino at the rehab center, her life would have gone back to normal.

Ava moved away from him and touched Jasper's arm. "Thank you." She hoped she managed to convey how much she appreciated his earlier kindness. She glanced at Griffin. "I need to speak with you."

"Thought you might," he said as he followed her down the hall. "Rosa called me."

Ava stopped outside the study door to stare at him. "Why does my aunt have your number?"

"Why do you think?" he asked, a wealth of meaning behind his words. He opened the door, ushering her inside.

"Because it wasn't enough you accused my father of

abusing me? You couldn't leave it alone." She took a seat.

He angled the other chair toward her and sat down. He didn't say anything, just looked at her.

Feeling uncomfortable under the weight of his steady gaze, she crossed her arms. After so many years apart, so many years of loving him from afar, it was difficult not to fall into old habits. She had to remind herself that he didn't share her feelings.

He leaned over and carefully uncrossed her arms. "You shouldn't do that."

"My arm's fine," she said, though she didn't recross them because he was right. The movement had caused a dull ache to travel from her elbow to her wrist.

"Really. So why are you still wearing a brace?"

She opened her mouth to tell him because the doctor said she had to. He stood up, and she frowned. "That's it? You're just going to look at me and leave without explaining why you had my father put away?"

He raised an eyebrow and walked to the door, opening it for Jasper. Obviously he'd heard what she hadn't. It wasn't a surprise given his training with the SEALs. Griffin was always on alert. He noticed things before anyone else did, the slightest movement and sound, the minute changes in a person's facial expressions and body language. He was a hard man to fool. Something she needed to remember.

Griffin accepted a silver tray that held a plate of cookies and a pot of coffee from Jasper. "Thanks, Jeeves."

Setting the tray on the desk, Griffin glanced at her. "To answer your first question, I gave Rosa my number when you and I split up."

She blinked, the news catching her off guard. When

Griffin was done, he was done. Or so she'd thought. For weeks, he'd tried everything possible to change her mind, and then he'd just stopped. He'd never contacted her again.

He poured her a coffee, adding sugar and cream, then handed her the mug. "Don't look so surprised."

"I don't understand why you would—"

"Don't even go there. You knew I was still in love with you back then, that I was worried about you." Taking a seat, he cradled his own mug in his big hands. "I shouldn't have called your father out in front of everyone. I'm sorry that I did. I can't take back what happened, Ava. I wish I could. But don't expect an apology from me for suggesting Doc Bishop look at the rehab center."

Most of what he said floated over her head. She was stuck on his *I was still in love with you*. She wasn't surprised he'd still loved her back then. It was his use of the past tense that grabbed her attention and wouldn't let go. Which was silly since he'd obviously moved on from her years before.

How many times had she reminded herself these past few weeks that he didn't love her? Too many times to count. But then he'd do something like buy her shoes, overreact to the bruise on her arm, look at her like he used to, hold her like he had only moments ago. They didn't feel like the actions of someone who didn't care. They made her wonder if he still had feelings for her.

And for some reason, the thought that he might made it easier to forgive him. No matter how misguided or hurtful the outcome had been, Griffin had been trying to protect her. He'd always been fiercely protective of those he loved. In his place, she probably would have done the same.

"Honey, are you okay?"

The endearment warmed her, soothing the lingering resentment at what his interference had cost. "I'm sorry I yelled at you at the hospital. You risked your life for my father that night. You didn't deserve my anger; you deserved my thanks. I am grateful, Griffin."

He cocked his head and his mouth lifted at the corner. "But…"

"No, no *but*…Okay, maybe a small one." He smiled, the dimple she loved deepening in his cheek. "It wasn't fair that you all went behind my back. I didn't deserve to be blindsided like that this morning. To have Dr. Bishop, Rosa, and Dorothy threaten to go before Judge Monahan and have my aunt named my father's conservator if I didn't agree to their health-care plan."

His smile faded. "Hold on. All I did was recommend the rehabilitation center and smooth the way for Gino with Adam. What exactly happened today?"

When she finished telling him, he gave his head an angry shake. "No way did I have anything to do with that. It's bullshit. They can't—"

"It's okay. My father wasn't upset. He wanted to go." She dropped her gaze, tears welling in her eyes as she recalled the conversation with her father.

She sensed Griffin rising to his feet and heard him placing his mug on the desk. And then he was there, crouched in front of her. He took her mug, setting it on the floor before he gently smoothed the rough pads of his fingers over her cheek. "You know it kills me to see you cry."

"Still?" she murmured without looking at him.

"Yeah, looks like," he said, sounding as though the admission cost him.

A tiny flicker of hope ignited inside her. She smothered it, unwilling to put herself in the position of being disappointed. She didn't think her heart could withstand another blow today.

"I know you did more than smooth the way for my father, Griffin. I don't believe Gino's monthly pension checks and insurance will come close to covering the cost. I need to know what I owe you. I doubt I can pay it all at once, though, so maybe we could come up with a monthly payment plan?"

At her suggestion, a muscle pulsed in his clenched jaw, and his eyes narrowed. She was familiar with that look. It didn't bode well for her repayment plan. And maybe because of that small hope that refused to be denied, she raised her hand to trace his stubbled jaw with her finger. "You know that look always annoyed me," she said, thinking back to how long it had been since she'd touched him this way.

"Yeah, and you always knew how to get rid of it. Never could hold out against you for long." His eyes darkened as though remembering their standoffs always ended in bed.

"What are we doing?" she whispered, the heat in his eyes weakening her resolve. She had to know if it was just her imagination. She'd deal with the consequences later.

"I—"

The study door swung open, and her cousin rushed in. "Ava, are—Oh, I…" Sophie's gaze moved from Griffin to Ava. "Am I interrupting?"

Griffin rose to his feet, and Ava didn't know if it was relief or regret she saw on his face.

He glanced at his watch. "I better get going. I have to meet up with Sully."

Ah, so it had been relief after all, she thought, fighting to keep the disappointment from showing on her face.

Sophie smiled, stepping in front of Griffin as he walked to the door. "Welcome home," she said, giving him a hug. "We're so glad you took the job."

"Job?" Ava asked, and there it was again, hope. Only this time it came out in her voice.

Griffin turned with his hand on the doorknob. "Sully offered me a job with the Coast Guard. Thought it was about time I came home." He held her gaze. "We'll talk later. If you need me, call."

Sophie stared at her, openmouthed. "He…You." Sophie found her voice and looked from the door to Ava. "What did I just interrupt?"

"I'm not sure," she murmured, glad she was sitting, otherwise her legs might have given out.

Sophie looked at her more closely and winced. "Nonna called. I'm so sorry, Ava. I should have told you. We've just been so worried about you that it seemed like the best possible solution for you and Uncle Gino."

"Maybe it will be. I don't know anymore. I'm confused about a lot of things."

Sophie rested her hip against the desk. "When Jasper said you wanted to speak to me, I thought you were going to yell at me or disown me. Nonna and Dorothy are afraid you'll never speak to them again."

"I know. I'll call them later," she said, her mind occupied with the promise she'd made to her father. She wasn't sure how she felt about it. Then again, she wasn't sure about much right now. She felt a little like a rudderless boat lost at sea. Maybe taking over the restaurant at the manor was a good idea. One more change. One more way to anchor herself and take her life back. The added income would be helpful too.

Whether Griffin wanted her to or not, she was paying him back. It wouldn't be hard to find out the true cost of the rehab center. She took a deep breath, straightened in the chair, and smiled at her cousin. "I have some news I think will make you happy. I'll take over the kitchen. I'm not promising anything, but if it goes well, I'll think about leasing the space. We'll give it a couple months to see how it works."

Ava frowned when her cousin simply stared at her. She'd expected Sophie to be at least a little excited. It had been her idea, after all. But she looked to be on the verge of tears…or was it laughter? "Why are you looking at me like that? You're getting your wish, aren't you? I can cater the bridal fair like you wanted me—"

A man wearing skintight black pants and a silky, purple-and-black paisley shirt swanned into the study. He posed with one hand on his hip and one turned out. "*Zee* castle is *magnifeco. Zee* kitchen, *comme ci, comme ca.*" He moved his hand back and forth. "*Zee* Helga woman must go. *Zee chat* too." As though just noticing Ava, he tossed his dark, heavy bang as if he were in a shampoo commercial. *"Qui etes-vous?"*

He may be wondering who Ava was, but she had an uneasy feeling she knew exactly who he was. She looked to Sophie for confirmation. Her cousin gave her a pleading look at the same time saying, "Gaston, this is my cousin Ava. She, ah, works at the manor. Ava, Gaston has—"

"Monsieur Gaston St. John at your service. I am *zee* manor's new head chef."

* * *

"Does he expect Ava to kiss his hand or shake it?" Colleen said to Simon from her perch on the windowsill in the study. "And what is with the *zee* nonsense? If that boy is French, I'll eat my Easter bonnet. What?" she said when Simon looked up at her. "Easter bonnets were quite the thing in my day. I'll show you my…I don't like how he's looking at you, Tomcat. Come on, let's find Jasper and see if we can get the goods on this Gaston fella."

Colleen hopped off the windowsill and walked toward the door. She stopped beside Ava. "Chin up, my girl. I'm on the job. I'll make sure everything works out for you. Griffin is home now. And after what I saw going on between you two in here, it's only a matter of time before you're back together."

She narrowed her eyes at the new chef. "There's something familiar about you, Monsieur Gaston St. John. My memory might not be what it used to be, but I'll figure it out. Of that you can be certain."

Jasper looked up from polishing the round entryway table and sighed. "Not again." He glanced around as though checking to be sure they were alone. "Madame, you can call off your familiar."

Colleen snorted. "Witches have familiars, and I'm not a…" She put her hands on her hips. "I don't find you amusing, my boy."

"If you're here to pester me about your memoirs, you can forget about it. I'm not giving them back. They're dangerous. And no, I didn't read them. That would be dishonorable, and I am an honorable man. I've locked them away for safekeeping."

"Well, you may have a point. But not where Ava is concerned. She and Griffin are getting closer. If they're going to make this work, he needs to know about Damien." Jasper got back to his polishing, ignoring her, which was easy because of course he couldn't see or hear her.

She blew on the table, smiling when a white mark appeared.

He polished over the mark.

"You're a hardhead," she groused. "But your heart is in the right place. I saw you with Ava. You felt sorry for the girl today, and rightly so. She needs our help, Jasper." He stood back from the table to admire his handiwork. Obviously, she wasn't going to get anywhere with him. She'd have to recover the book on her own. It had to be somewhere in his room. Colleen started to walk away. "Come on, Simon. We…" She turned at the chef's approach.

"*Garcon.*" Gaston St. John snapped his fingers at Jasper as he walked toward the entryway. "My *chapeau* and coat, *si'l vous plais.*"

Jasper's nostrils flared, and he turned on his heel. The new chef studied his reflection in a bronze plaque while he waited, leaning in to smooth his left eyebrow and then the right. Colleen leaned in to study him too. The shape of his smooth, clean-shaven face, the hazel eyes, reminded her of…

Jasper returned with a black fur coat and fedora, releasing a sigh when Gaston held out his arms. Once Jasper had helped him into his coat, Gaston placed the hat jauntily on his head. "*Au revoir* until tomorrow, *garcon.*"

Jasper practically slammed the door behind him. "What has Sophie gotten us into?"

Colleen wondered the same and made a run at the front

door. She didn't go through it as she'd hoped. It appeared she was still bound to the manor. She hurried back to the study, walking through Ava, who was leaving, pretending that she wasn't upset about Gaston St. John taking her job. Colleen couldn't worry about that now. Something was nagging at her, and she wanted another look at the lad.

She rushed to the window and watched the new chef walking across the parking lot. He glanced over his shoulder as though checking to be sure he wasn't followed. A silver Lincoln Navigator pulled up to the front gate. St. John rushed toward the waiting vehicle and jumped inside.

"Trouble, my boy," Colleen said, responding to Jasper's earlier question. "Trouble with a capital T." She recognized the vehicle and the woman behind the wheel.

Paige Townsend was up to her tricks again.

Chapter Eleven

♥

Griffin sat across from Sully at a table in the far corner of the dining room at Greystone, bracing himself for the approach of their waitress. It was Ava. Only not the Ava he'd hauled from the shower weeks before. No, the woman making her way toward their table looked more like the girl he'd married than she had in years. She wore black shoes with a small heel, a black skirt that hugged her hips and thighs to fall below her knees, and a white blouse that was sheer enough you could see her black arm brace under the sleeve.

He wasn't feeling much like smiling, but he did. "Hey, Ava, I didn't know you were working in the dining room."

If he had, he would have suggested they eat elsewhere. He'd been doing his best to avoid her. Which must have come across in his greeting because Sully kicked him under the table with a what-the-hell look on his face.

Her long, ebony curls piled on her head in some kind

of a bun thing, Ava handed Griffin a menu without looking at him. "I started yesterday." Sully got a small smile along with his menu. "Hi, Joe."

"Hey, Ava, if I knew you were working here, I would have stopped by sooner." Sullivan gave her the same smile he'd been flashing at girls since high school, the one that, according to Sully, had gotten him laid more than their entire crew combined.

Griffin said his favorite word in his head, and not because he was worried Ava would fall victim to Sully's supposed panty-dropping smile. It was because he was pretty sure she'd been expecting him to call her and finish the conversation they'd been having the other day in the study. The day he'd come close to kissing her. He'd planned to call after he'd met up with Sully. He'd wanted to, but…

Another kick to his shin interrupted his thoughts. "What the…," he began without thinking. He caught Ava looking at him, her brow furrowed. He gave her a sheepish smile. "Sorry, did you say something?"

"Are you all right?"

"Yeah, sure, just didn't get a whole lot of sleep last night." Because he'd been thinking about her. Just like he had the night before, and the one before that. He glanced at her brace. "Isn't it a little soon for you to be back to work?"

"The rehabilitation center my father has been placed in is expensive. I can't afford to be off," she said, giving him a pointed look. Then, as though remembering Sully was there too, a flush worked its way from her chest to her cheeks.

"Yeah, I hear it costs a crap—" Sully shrugged when

Griffin gave him a shut-it look. "She was married to you, so I'm sure Ava's heard worse than *crap*. Sorry if I offended you though," Sully apologized to Ava. "What I was going to say was that, whatever it costs, it's worth it. At least that's what I've heard."

"I hope so." She gave Joe another small smile. "Would either of you care for a drink before you order?"

"That'd be great. Bring us a couple of North Shore ales when you have a chance. We'll order in a bit," Sully said, giving her another one of his lady-killer grins.

Griffin watched Ava walk away with a subtle sway to her hips. Her walk had been the first thing that had drawn his interest in high school—even as a teenager she'd exuded sensuality and confidence. He'd been at football practice, and she'd been walking across the field with a bunch of girls. He'd casually pointed her out to a friend and asked who she was, shocked to discover it was Ava and not some new girl in town.

He was a couple years ahead of her in school, but he knew who she was. Until that moment, he just hadn't paid much attention to her. She'd grown into her nose and lost the baby fat. She'd lost the braces too. The one thing that hadn't changed was her laugh. She was always laughing and smiling. She'd been the happiest, most passionate girl he'd ever known.

Ava stopped to talk to the other waitress. Erin said something that made Ava laugh. God, he'd missed that husky, low laugh.

"Are you done salivating over your ex yet?"

Griffin caught himself raising his hand to check for drool and scowled at Sully. "No, I—"

"Yeah, you were." Sully glanced at Ava and then

looked at Griffin. "You're still in love with her, aren't you?"

"I don't think I ever fell out of love with her," he reluctantly admitted, in part because he could use a sounding board who wasn't a Gallagher. Aside from his brothers, Griffin had mainly hung out with four guys all the way through grade school and high school: Sully, Damien, Caleb, and Ryan. He'd been closest to Sully.

"So what are you going to do about it?" his friend asked.

Griffin looked around the dining room. It was fairly busy for a Thursday night, but the tables nearest them were empty. "Nothing I can do about it right now," he said, and told Sully about the bombshell Lexi had dropped on him three weeks earlier.

She'd asked Griffin to keep the news to himself for now. Because Ava had lost their baby late in her pregnancy, he understood where Lex was coming from. He didn't want his family to get their hopes up, only to be disappointed. They'd dealt with enough loss over the years. He trusted Sully though.

"I'm happy for you, man. That's great news. But I can see how it complicates things for you and Ava. Does she know?"

"No, she doesn't know any of it. Lexi's not exactly a fan of Ava's. She basically warned me to stay away from her." She'd called him the night he'd arrived at Greystone, checking to make sure he got in okay. Griffin had always been honest with Lex and thought it best to come clean about the time he'd spent with Ava hours earlier in the study.

Up to a point. He didn't tell her he'd begun thinking

about a second chance with Ava. But no matter how innocent he'd made it appear, nothing he said placated Lexi. Which was why he'd been avoiding Ava and would continue to do so. Until Lexi had the baby, he couldn't contemplate a relationship with her.

"Not that I'm an expert on women, but are you sure Lexi isn't hoping you two get back together?"

"I asked her straight out, and she said no. She's overprotective. She thinks Ava messed with my head."

"I wasn't exactly happy with Ava when it all went down either. But Lexi didn't know you guys when it was good. And it was really good, man."

"Yeah, it was," he said, and the memories of how good it had been swamped him. Movement out of the corner of his eye interrupted the trip down memory lane. His brother intercepted Ava as she walked toward the table with their beers. "This stays between us, okay? Family doesn't know."

"You know me better than that. I—Hey, Liam, they got you working as a server?" Sully asked, accepting a bottle of beer.

Liam pulled out a chair and sat down heavily. "No, I just finished setting up for the bridal fair." He lifted the bottle of beer to his mouth.

"Get your own," Griffin said, reaching for the bottle.

Liam moved it out of his reach. "Ava's bringing another one. I told her to order our meals too."

"Who said you could join us? And we haven't even looked at the menu," Griffin said.

"My wife. She wants me to keep an eye on Ava, and I ordered the specials. You got a problem with that?"

Sully grinned around his beer. "I'm good."

Griffin shifted in his seat to watch Ava enter the kitchen. "Why does Sophie have you keeping an eye on Ava? Is it because of her—" A high-pitched male voice followed Ava out of the kitchen. She rolled her eyes when the door closed on the sound of pots banging and more yelling. Then she delivered orders to a table of three businessmen.

"That's the reason." His brother pointed at the kitchen. "You'd know what's going on if you hadn't been making yourself scarce the past couple of days."

"I've been busy. So I'm not exactly getting what the problem is?"

Liam lifted his chin to where Ava stood a few tables away from the businessmen she'd just served, intently watching them eat. His brother leaned in. "Sophie's been after Ava to take over the restaurant for months. Ava always refused, using Gino as an excuse. Soph finally gave up on her a few weeks ago and started putting out feelers for a head chef. She hired him a few hours before Ava said she wanted the job."

Griffin's gut twisted as he looked at Ava. She and Erin were talking behind their hands as they now watched a table of four eat their meals. "When?"

Liam grimaced. "The same day Gino went into rehab."

The same day Griffin had promised to call her. "Fire him."

"He's got a contract. We can't afford to buy him out."

"I can," Griffin said, pushing back his chair with every intention of firing the man himself.

"That's the thing, you can't. Sophie explained the situation, and he wouldn't budge. Said something about Greystone inspiring his muse, whatever the hell that's supposed to mean. The other thing is the guy's actually qualified. He trained in Paris and worked with some world-renowned chef Dana got all shiny-eyed over."

"You saying that just because this guy's trained, he can cook better than Ava?"

After sharing a knowing grin with Sully, Liam said, "No, because I like my face the way it is and so does my wife."

Sully chuckled into his beer. Griffin scowled at the two of them. "This isn't something to joke about. I've never met anyone who can cook as well or who was as passionate about food as Ava. She needs this, Liam. It'd be the best thing for her. Sophie—"

"Feels bad enough as it, so don't say anything to her about this. And don't do or say anything to wreck this guy's 'muse.'" Liam made air quotes. "We need the bridal fair to be a success. Besides, Ava seems fine with it."

Griffin sat back in the chair and crossed his arms. "Is that right? Then why are she and Erin sniffing each of the meals they serve and watching everyone eat?"

"Looks like we're going to find out," Sully said, aiming his beer bottle at Ava, who approached with a loaded cart. "Um, are we expecting anyone else?"

"I didn't order all that, did I?" Liam asked, staring at what appeared to be at least five entrées.

Ava shrugged. "I wasn't sure which of the specials you would prefer, so I ordered all of them. You don't have to eat everything. Just maybe a sample of each. I can bring the rest back to the kitchen."

"Won't that hurt the chef's feelings?" Griffin said, fighting a grin. Her accent always became more pronounced when she was nervous or excited.

She snorted. "He has no feelings."

"Don't hold back, honey. Tell me how you really feel."

Ava's gaze shot to him, a hint of pink flushing her cheeks. Until that moment, he hadn't noticed that she'd lost the gray cast to her olive skin. He'd been focused on the tantalizing way she filled out her blouse and her skirt. The weight gain that had rounded her chest and hips had also filled out her face. She looked healthy and well rested, and at that moment, she also looked confused.

He wasn't; he knew exactly what he wanted. He wanted to turn back the clock to the day in the study and find out if her feelings for him were still there. If she wanted him as much as he wanted her. Then he reminded himself it didn't matter what he wanted, at least until the baby was born.

Ava didn't respond. Though his brother gave him a knowing grin. Only because Liam had no clue what was really going on. Sully, who did, gave Griffin a sympathetic smile. Ava's arm brushed his as she placed a dish in front of him. Griffin felt sorry for himself too. She was close enough that he could smell her perfume. Sweet and sexy, warm and alluring, it reminded him of the confident, flirty girl he'd married.

This wasn't doing him any good. He had to snap out of it. "What is this exactly?" he asked, poking his fork at the lump of golden pastry sitting in congealed gravy.

"Le fricandeau," she said, the words rolling off her tongue. She had an ear for languages and spoke several.

He didn't and raised an eyebrow.

"Braised veal. It's been slow cooked with pickled pork, white wine, and stock, and covered with bacon."

"Sounds"—he was going to say *great*, because in his book anything with bacon was great, but one look at Ava's face and he changed it to—"good."

"We'll see," she said, and placed a plate in front of Sully. *"Canard a la orange."*

"Some kind of orange bird, right?" Sully said, eyeing his plate with consternation.

"Duck," she informed him, and then picked up a platter with a white sauce and mushrooms covering what looked to be fish. She rounded the table to serve Liam. *"Sole Normande."*

"Okay, I got this. Norman sole, like the fish, right?"

"Yes, and mussels."

"Perfect. I love…" His brother looked up at Ava and, because he was a smart guy, said, "I kind of like mussels."

She pursed her lips. "Hmm." Then walked back to the cart, lifting the lids on two other dishes. *"Cote de porc Normande.* Pork chops in cider. And *boeuf bourguignon.* Beef cooked in Burgundy wine."

Both dishes looked more appealing than the one in front of Griffin. From the expressions on Liam's and Sully's faces, they thought so too. The three of them looked at Ava, who was standing with her arms crossed. *"Mangia. Mangia."*

Griffin had barely chewed the first bite when she asked, "How is it?"

He cut off a piece, offering it to her instead. "You tell me." He wasn't stupid either.

Well, that's what he thought until she leaned in and he smelled her perfume again, and she opened her mouth to accept the piece he offered her from his fork. She closed her eyes and delicately chewed, making a familiar humming sound in her throat. He couldn't take his eyes off her lips. They were plump, moist, and perfect.

Sully kicked him lightly in the shin. Griffin didn't get a chance to react because Ava opened her eyes.

She moved her head from left to right and then said, "It's okay. The pastry is good, but the veal is overcooked, and the gravy…" She shuddered.

"Maybe you should try another piece." Griffin held it up to her. He stepped on Sully's foot to avoid another kick in the shin. He already knew he was playing with fire, but if this was all he had to hang on to until the baby arrived, he'd take it.

She nodded and leaned in again, her teeth closing on the fork tines—perfect, white teeth. Her eyes and lips closing as she savored the taste, he savored every inch of her gorgeous, expressive face, waiting for her to make that sound again.

His brother, who'd been staring at him, laughed out loud. Ava's eyes shot open. "Choking," Liam said, covering his laugh with a cough.

Ava straightened and picked up a bottle of sparkling water from the cart, walking to Liam's side to fill the crystal goblet. "How is the sole?" she asked his brother as she went to fill Griffin's and Sully's glasses.

"It's"—he glanced from Ava to the half-empty bottle in her hand—"good." He looked relieved when she placed the sparkling water on the middle of the table.

She picked up a fork and knife from the neighboring table. "Do you mind?" she asked Liam.

"Nope, not at all."

She cut off a big chunk and, cupping her hand beneath it, leaned toward Griffin. "You loved my *tilapia scaloppini*. See if this compares." He leaned in and removed the piece from the fork with his teeth. While he chewed the sole and mussels, she moved her mouth like she was too. "So?" she asked when he swallowed.

"Not even close." It wasn't bad, but then again, he really did love her *tilapia scaloppini*. "Why don't you give it a try?"

She nodded and cut off a piece. He was a little disappointed at how quickly she ate and swallowed this time. She didn't make that sound in her throat either. He understood why when she scooped up Liam's plate.

His brother stared at her, knife and fork poised in the air. "Hey, where are you going with that?"

"The mussels are undercooked. Do you want to get sick?" she asked, muttering under her breath in Italian as she practically slammed the platter on the cart. Griffin found himself grinning at the familiar curse words rolling off her tongue.

"Here," she said, taking the lid off the pork chop dish. She stuck her finger in the sauce, licking it off as she walked toward Liam. "It's still warm."

Liam stared at her. "You just stuck your finger in my food."

She lifted a shoulder. "Fine. Here, you won't mind. You eat it." She removed Griffin's veal, replacing it with the pork chops.

If he could get her to take a bite, he didn't mind at all. Right now, though, her attention was on Sully, who was studiously avoiding her gaze. She cleared her throat, smiling when Sully looked up. "How's your duck, Joe?"

Sully sighed and nudged his plate. "Have at it."

He didn't need to tell her twice. Ava picked up the

knife and fork from the place setting in front of her and cut off a piece. They all watched as she closed her eyes. She made that small humming sound again, only longer this time. She swallowed and opened her eyes, then slowly licked off the sauce glistening on her lips with the tip of her tongue. Griffin inwardly groaned. At least he thought it'd been in his head until three pairs of eyes turned his way.

"Bone in my chop. I bit my tongue."

Liam covered the side of his face with one hand while Sully snorted a laugh, but Ava wasn't paying attention to any of them. She'd turned when Erin approached the table four over with their order. "Erin," she called out, hurrying to the other waitress's side. She removed the sole dish from Erin's hand, apologizing to the guests.

Sully pointed his fork at Griffin. "If she comes back and offers you a piece of my duck, say no. This shit is good."

Ava returned with the plate, setting it down beside Liam's on the cart. She checked their progress. "I'll bring you a platter of pastries for dessert."

"Bring lots," Griffin said with a smile. Ava used to love her pastries. Which meant, if he was lucky, more humming sounds.

"Ava, you know, it might be best if I take those dishes back to the kitchen," Liam said, wiping his mouth with a napkin as he pushed back his chair.

"Don't worry, Liam. I'm not going to hurt his feelings. I'll just educate him on how to properly prepare mussels so he doesn't kill our guests." She turned to push the cart determinedly toward the kitchen.

Liam swore and set off after her. "Ava, hang on."

Griffin laughed, settling back in the chair. "This should be good."

Sully looked at him. "When's the baby due?"

Griffin's laughter faded. "April." He never should have promised Lexi he'd stay away from Ava.

"Good luck with that," Sully said.

Chapter Twelve

♥

Ava had seriously miscalculated the benefits of mindless work. She would have been better off stopping by the corner store on the walk home and buying a pack of cigarettes, she thought, as she moved the steamer in a slow, rhythmic motion over the hardwood floor.

She'd volunteered for the job in hopes it would relax her. She'd needed to relax after her stressful first day as a server. Not only did she have to deal with a fake French chef, but she also had to wait on Griffin. She'd tried to hand off his table to Erin, but the younger woman had apparently thrown in with Greystone's matchmakers and refused.

Without anything else to keep it occupied, Ava's mind was playing a constant loop of her interactions with Griffin tonight. It was as though her brain was using the images and his words as evidence, trying to sway a jury.

The left side using them as proof he didn't love her, the right side as proof that he still did.

She wondered if the jury was as confused as she was.

Though the last image, the one where Griffin had decided he was too full for dessert and gave her an offhand "See you around," should have been enough to clear the confusion. It would have been if she hadn't made the mistake of looking into his eyes. Indigo eyes that had darkened with the same desire she'd seen earlier, only this time the want and need seemed to be accompanied by frustrated regret.

She used both hands to maneuver the steamer into a corner of the octagon dining room. Obviously she was frustrated, too, because she rammed the black head against the baseboard, sending a shooting pain up her arm. She did a quick scan of the now shiny hardwood floors, relieved to discover she was done and a little disconcerted to realize she'd gone over the floors twice.

More than ready to go home to put her feet up and ice her arm, Ava turned off the steamer. Her arm had begun to twinge toward the end of her shift. Thanks to the forceful contact between the steamer and baseboard, it had grown into a bone-deep ache. She made a mental note to bring Advil with her tomorrow. It was the first day of the bridal show and would no doubt be busier than today.

Carrying the steamer to a storage closet near the window, Ava glanced at the stars studding the black velvet sky, a half-moon shining down on Kismet Cove. At least her walk home would be a pleasant one. Over the past week, the temperatures had been slowly climbing, melting most of the snow.

She pressed on the door that was hidden in the wall and set the steamer inside. Turning to flip off the sconces that graced the stone walls and the three burnished gold chandeliers hanging from the exposed beams of the ceiling, she frowned. The light was still on in the kitchen. Erin and the other server had left an hour ago. And Gaston had left an hour before they did.

As Ava approached the kitchen, she heard someone softly crying. She pushed open the door. It was Helga. Wiping her eyes on the sleeve of her white chef coat, the older woman hadn't noticed her. Ava began to tiptoe backward and then sighed. Helga might hate her, but Ava's conscience wouldn't let her leave until she made sure the older woman was all right.

"Helga, are you okay?"

Short and heavy-set with dyed red hair that looked almost orange in the fluorescent light, the older woman covered her face and shook her head.

Ava approached, taking in the two trays of pastries sitting on cooling trays. She gingerly placed a hand on Helga's shoulder, fully expecting to be rebuffed. "Is there anything I can do?"

Helga lowered her hands, a hopeless expression on her heavily powdered face. "He's going to fire me." She lifted her quivering double chin at the pastries. "I've been making dozens of these things all day, and he says he wouldn't serve them to a dog. A dog, he says."

Since the day Sophie had taken over at Greystone, her cousin had been thinking of ways to get rid of Helga. Not only was the older woman cantankerous and contrary, but for the past several months, the guests had also been complaining about the food. But Helga had worked in the manor's kitchen for decades, so as much as she may want to, Sophie would never fire the older woman.

"Don't listen to him. He doesn't know what's he's talking about. He nearly poisoned three guests with undercooked mussels, and the veal was overcooked." Ava picked up a pastry. "Are these for the bridal fair?" They were to serve hor d'oeuvres to the attendees throughout the three-day event.

Helga nodded. "He says I have to have sixteen dozen of them made by tomorrow morning. If they don't meet his approval, he's says I'm done."

Ava took a bite and then wished she hadn't. The pastry was thick and doughy. The filling, what little there was, had no taste. She worked the pastry down her throat with several hard swallows, forcing a smile for Helga, who watched her closely. "They're not too bad. What exactly did Gaston say he wanted? Did he leave you instructions or a recipe?"

"Some puff things with brie and mushrooms and a palmier with ham, Gruyère, and mustard." Helga pulled two pieces of lined paper from under a stainless steel mixing bowl.

Ava didn't need to look at the recipes to know what the problem was. She took them anyway. "A palmier is made with puff pastry, Helga. Not regular pastry. I'm guessing Gaston forgot to mention that." Either he assumed that Helga knew what a palmier was or he was trying to sabotage the older woman. For now, Ava would give him the benefit of the doubt. He knew how important the bridal fair was to Greystone.

"I don't know how to make puffy pastry, just the regular stuff."

Ava smiled and slipped off her shoes. "You're in luck because I do. You make up new batches of the fillings, and I'll get started on the pastry."

Helga stared at her. "Why are you helping me?"

"Because what Gaston did to you wasn't right. Someone needs to teach that cocky little man a lesson. He thinks just because we don't have his fancy schooling that we can't cook? Ha. We'll show him. He can't just come in here and ride roughshod over all of us."

"I'm getting a taste of my own. I was no better to you and your cousin a few months back. Worse, truth be told." The older woman raised her red-rimmed, tired eyes. "I'm sorry. It's no excuse, but I thought Sophie was trying to get rid of me. Probably past time I did retire. But I love this old place, you know? It's home. I don't have any family. This"—she lifted a hand, her fingers swollen and bent with arthritis—"this is all I've got."

Knowing only too well how Helga felt, Ava spoke around the lump in her throat. "I don't blame you. In your shoes, I probably would have acted the same."

Now that she thought about it, wasn't that exactly what Ava was doing to Gaston? She'd been upset when she'd learned that Sophie had hired him, resenting him for stealing her opportunity to fulfill her promise to her father. But more than the promise to her father, it had been the loss of the opportunity to make more money. Money she needed to pay for Gino's care. Maybe Gaston really was the best person for the position.

In her opinion, his culinary skills could use some work, but at least he was actually passionate about his job. Which would serve Greystone well. In the end, that's all that really mattered.

An hour later, Ava discovered that, while Helga appreciated her help, she was still a cantankerous old lady. She slapped the back of Ava's hand with the spatula. "Get your fingers out of my filling."

Ava ignored her, pinching some of the ham and Gruyère between her fingers "You have to taste it. How do you know if it's good if you don't?

Helga elbowed her out of the way. "You just follow the dang recipe."

Trying not to make a face as she forced herself to swallow the filling, Ava asked, "So, how many teaspoons of honey mustard did the recipe call for?" She had a feeling she may have discovered the reason why Helga's meals had been drawing complaints over the past few months. And it wasn't only because the old lady needed to start tasting what she made.

Helga picked up the paper, squinting at the recipe. "Honey mustard? I thought it said mustard, mustard."

Testing her theory, Ava tapped her finger on the line. "It's more the amount than the type of mustard." Which wasn't entirely true. "How many teaspoons does it say?"

"You can't read?" Helga retorted.

"Yes, I can read. But I'm beginning to think you can't see." There, she'd said it.

"What are you talking about? Look, right there, it says eight tablespoons."

"Helga, it says three teaspoons."

The older woman brought the paper within an inch of her nose and then put it down. "Teaspoons, tablespoons, what does it—"

Ava scooped some of the filling onto a teaspoon and shoved it in the older woman's mouth.

Helga scowled at her as she chewed and then looked at the filling in the bowl. "I guess it does matter."

"It does. So until you get glasses, you need to taste what you make, and tell Gaston."

"No, there's something off about that man. I'm not telling him nothing."

Ava crossed her arms.

Helga pulled a face. "I know I said the same thing about your cousin, but this is different. He's up to something, mark my words."

"All right, if he gives you another recipe, bring it to me. I'll go over it with you and rewrite it so you can read the amounts and ingredients."

"What we should do is get rid of him, and then you and me will take over the restaurant."

She didn't like the glint in Helga's eyes. Ava had enough experience with crazy old ladies to know what kind of trouble they could get up to once they set their mind on something. "Once I've paid off my father's rehab bill, I'll go back to housekeeping," she said, taking off her brace in hopes of relieving the throbbing ache. She'd had it on too long anyway.

"Nothing wrong with an honest day's work, but you've been given a talent. Seems wrong to waste it cleaning toilets."

Two hours later, Ava found herself thinking about what Helga had said. She'd sent the older woman home not long after she'd made the comment. Not because Ava didn't want to continue the conversation, but because the older woman was exhausted. Ava wasn't, and she knew why.

For the first time in a long time, she was enjoying

herself. Tonight, cooking didn't feel so much like a chore as a pleasure. She'd turned on the radio when Helga left, pounding the butter with the French rolling pin to the beat of '90s rock music.

She'd found herself moving in time to Pearl Jam's "Black" while kneading the flaky, light-as-air pastry, taste testing a few other fillings she'd experimented with while singing—quietly so she didn't wake anyone. She loved the textures, the smells and flavors. Quitting smoking had apparently reawakened her taste buds. Something her expanding chest and butt could attest to.

The oven timer dinged, signaling the moment of truth. Did she still have it or not? If she were to listen to her cousins and aunt, she did. But to Ava's mind, the dishes she'd made back in late November and December were missing something. She couldn't put her finger on what it was, but the food had lacked that special indefinable ingredient. Her Auntie Rosa would say it was love. But Ava wasn't sure she'd added that intangible element to the five pastries—each with a different filling—that she'd popped into the oven twenty minutes earlier.

She was about to find out, Ava thought, as she bent to open the oven door. She pulled out the tray and smiled. They were perfect, beautiful and golden brown, and they smelled delicious too. Something else occurred to her as she straightened to place the baking sheet on the cooling tray; there wasn't a speck of tension in her body.

Yes, her arm ached, but other than that she was calm and relaxed. She hadn't spared a single thought for Griffin in hours.

"Ava?"

She closed her eyes on a groan. Would she have to spend every minute of every single day, cooking just to keep the blasted man out of her head? "Go away. I'm done thinking about you. You're making me crazy."

"Yeah, well, I'm done with you acting crazy. It's three-thirty in the morning, Ava."

She slowly turned. And there he was in the flesh, perfectly beautiful and golden. As he prowled toward her, she caught a whiff of a delicious lemony scent. It wasn't her pastries. Her gaze moved from his bare feet to his plaid sleep pants to the navy T-shirt that hugged his wide chest, stopping at his firm, sculpted lips. She wondered if he would taste delectable too.

She lifted her gaze to meet his before she gave in to the temptation to find out. "I'm not acting crazy. Helga needed help with her hors d'oeuvres for tomorrow. So I helped her."

He looked around the kitchen. "Where is she? You lock her in the cooler?"

The Gallagher grandchildren were well acquainted with Helga. "No, I put her in the oven," she quipped, hoping to distract him from remembering what she'd said when he first entered the kitchen.

His lips twitched. "Funny girl." He nodded at the tray. "So Helga browbeat you into doing her work for her and toddled off home. Never thought I'd have to say this to you, but you have to start standing up for yourself, babe. You can't let people take advantage of—"

No, what she had to do was stop letting his casual endearments reignite the he-loves-me-he-loves-me-not debate in her head. "Despite what you think, I'm perfectly capable of standing up for myself, *babe*." She mentally gave herself a pat on the back when his eyebrows shot up to the messy golden brown hair that flopped over his forehead. "Helga wasn't browbeating me. Gaston was browbeating her. He made her cry."

"You know what they say about karma. None of her assistants ever lasted more than a month." Griffin leaned in and sniffed. "I probably should be giving you hell for staying up half the night to help her out, but damn, those smell good. Can I have one?"

"If you promise not to tell anyone you saw me here tonight, yes, you can." She frowned as she slid a red silicone spatula beneath the golden-brown triangle. "What are you doing up? The music isn't that loud, is it?"

He raised his hand to rub the back of his neck, the movement causing the hem of his T-shirt to rise, giving her a mouthwatering glimpse of sculpted abs. Maybe she was more tired than she thought because she had an almost uncontrollable urge to brush her lips over the golden skin that was lightly dusted with dark hair…

She drew her gaze back to his face, only her eyes took a detour and got stuck on the flex of his impressive bicep.

"Every time I fell asleep, I was woken up by…my stomach telling me I was starved." A touch of color flushed his stubbled cheeks.

"I don't know why you're embarrassed. It's no wonder you're starved. You didn't eat enough tonight. You should have had dessert." She offered him the pastry. "Careful, it's…" He'd already popped it into his mouth. "Good?" she asked when he swallowed.

"Good? Are you kidding me? That was amazing. What was in it?"

"Ham, Gruyère, and honey mustard." She handed him a square pastry. "See what you think of this one. It's chicken, cream cheese, and a sweet chili relish."

He chewed slowly, a familiar expression coming over his face. She recognized the look. He'd worn it when they made love. Feeling a little flushed herself, she cleared her throat before asking, "Good?"

"You really need to increase your repertoire of adjectives, Ava. Because that…that was…I might have seen stars."

He seemed closer. She wasn't sure who was closing the distance between them—him or her. The one thing she knew for sure was the kitchen was growing warmer. She leaned back to turn off the oven. She already had. "Would you like another one?" she asked without looking at him.

"We'll share." He reached for the circular-shaped pastry and brought it to her lips.

"It's Gorgonzola and mushroom," she said, and took a bite. She closed her eyes, savoring the light-as-air pastry, the sharp tang of the full-bodied creamy cheese, and the chewy texture of mushroom. It was almost perfect. Something was missing though—that intangible ingredient. She opened her eyes to the missing ingredient in her own life.

Holding her gaze, he gently wiped the corner of her mouth with his fingers. "You missed a bit."

Out of habit, she licked the corner of her lips. His eyes darkened, and his nostrils flared as he tracked the movement. He cleared his throat. "This is wasted on me. I'm not a fan of blue cheese, even Italian blue cheese," he said, his voice gruff as he brought the half circle to her mouth. She had to tip back her head to look at him. They were only inches apart. She took it from his fingers, and they lingered on her lips.

Afraid he'd move away if he saw the depth of emotion in her eyes, she closed them. She wanted to wrap her arms around him. She wanted him to…

"What's this one?" He held the small bundle between his large, blunt fingers.

"Spicy sausage and potato." Her voice was husky, barely a whisper.

"I'm not sharing." He watched her as he put it in his mouth and slowly chewed. His Adam's apple moved in his throat when he swallowed.

She brought her fingers to the corner of his mouth. "You missed a little." She fed him the flakes, barely a crumb. He sucked the tip of her finger into his warm mouth, and she shivered. Without breaking eye contact, he took her hand, gently nipped her finger, and then brought it to his shoulder. "Why did you say you're done thinking about me?" he asked, placing her other hand on the opposite shoulder.

A groan escaped from between her lips, not only because he'd remembered what she'd said, but also because there wasn't a whisper of space between them now. Every inch of his hard, muscular body was pressed against her. "Because you're making me *pazza*."

His lips curved, the dimple showing up in his cheek. "How am I making you crazy?" His voice was both gentle and rough.

"I don't know what you want from me."

"No?"

She shook her head. "No."

"Would it make it easier if I show you?" he asked, moving his hands to frame her face.

She nodded, her eyes drifting closed.

"Open your eyes, Ava. I want you to see me when I kiss you. I want to look into your gorgeous eyes when I have my mouth on yours."

She did as he asked. Her knees softened, going weak at the heat in his indigo eyes. She clung to his shoulders, releasing a tiny sigh of complete and utter joy as he lowered his mouth to hers. His lips were…

"Master Griffin, I…Oh, my apologies for the interruption."

With a low, frustrated sound in his throat, Griffin stepped back from her and lowered his hands. "What is it, Jeeves?"

"Your father's waiting for you in the study. He received word from Doctors Without Borders that the hospital Master Finn is working at in Central Africa was attacked by armed rebels. There are casualties."

Colleen paced the study behind Colin and Kitty, who sat in the chairs across from the desk. Kitty was wringing her hands, her face pale. "Griffin will get through to his friend. He'll find out what's going on, what's happened to Finn," Colin reassured his mother, rubbing her shoulder.

Griffin sat behind the desk, holding a phone between his shoulder and ear at the same time he typed on the computer. Colleen's fears eased somewhat watching her great-grandson take control. He had a way about him, their Griffin did. As the oldest, he'd always looked out for his brothers and got them out of their scrapes. Just like he was doing now. His watchful eyes moved to his father and grandmother and then to his brother, who was standing by the window with Sophie.

The person he'd been holding for must have returned. Griffin responded to whatever was being said in a calm and even voice. No indication on his face that anything was wrong. It didn't mean that there wasn't because Griffin was good at hiding his emotions. Even as a lad he'd been hard to read. He was different than his brothers that way. He took after his mother in looks, his father in temperament. Griffin had been the serious, responsible one, and Ava had been the only one able to bring out his lighter side.

It was a shame their moment had been ruined. He could use Ava right now. Jasper had driven her home after delivering the news.

"Thanks, call as soon as you have anything else." Griffin hung up the phone. "It looks like most of the staff and patients managed to escape. But it'll take them at least a few days to get someplace safe. The rebels are still in the area, so they have to be careful. Good news is there's a Special Forces team about a hundred miles north of there. I'm working on a way to reach out to them. But if we don't have a definitive answer as to Finn's whereabouts in forty-eight hours, I'll be wheels up. I've got a couple friends who've offered to come with me."

The last thing Colleen wanted was for another of her great-grandsons to fly off to the war-torn country. Griffin wouldn't be deterred though. As they all knew, once his mind was made up, there was no dissuading the lad. If anyone could find Finn and ensure his safety, it was Griffin.

Once he'd finally persuaded everyone to head to their beds, Griffin got back to work on the computer and phone.

Colleen parked herself on the corner of the desk. "If I'd known how the night would turn out, I would have let you get some sleep, my boy." She'd kept him awake half the night yelling in his ear. Instead of telling Griffin that Ava needed him, this time she'd told him he was hungry, ravenous. Worked as well as any food commercial on TV.

Shame no one else could hear her. She was beginning to wonder if it had something to do with her suite of rooms in the tower. Griffin had heard her there, but nowhere else. She'd have to get Jasper in there to test her theory. Badger him into giving her memoirs back. Though it wouldn't do a whole heck of a lot of good until she learned to hold an object in her hands. She really needed to work on that.

An hour later, Griffin called the family to relay an update that alleviated some of their fears. A UN security force had met up with the convoy and were escorting them to safety. As Griffin made his way to his room for some much-needed sleep, Colleen started on her rounds of the manor. She'd just passed by the bar when the front door creaked open and someone crept inside.

"What are you up to, Gaston St. John?" Colleen murmured, following him through the great room to the dining room. He looked over his shoulder before entering the kitchen. Colleen walked through the door...and him. A satisfied smile curved her lips when he shuddered.

He walked to the long counter where a lone pastry sat on the baking sheet. Picking it up to examine it, he took a tentative bite. "Oh my God," he moaned, and took another bite. Licking every last crumb off his fingers as he made his way to the cooler, he opened the door, staring openmouthed at the trays of hundreds of perfect pastries under clear wrap.

"There's no way the old battle-ax made them herself. The pastry is perfection," he said without a trace of an accent. Fisting his hands in his hair, he turned in circles, looking around the kitchen. He stopped midturn. "I should have known." He raced to the counter. Flinging Ava's brace across the room, he pulled out his phone.

"Yes, I know what time it is. I'm at the manor. We have a problem. I came here to check on Brunhilda's hors d'oeuvres. Helga, I'm talking about Helga. You know, our fall guy. Anyway, Ava DiRossi must have decided to play Helga's fairy godmother and made the pastries for her. If the rest are as incredible as the one I just ate, they're going to get rave reviews from the bridal show's attendees."

He winced and held the phone from his ear, counting to ten under his breath before he said, "I tried. That Italian Nigella Lawson wrecked that plan too. Ava, Ava DiRossi. She swooped in and saved the guests from food poisoning and then had the nerve to try and give me a lesson on cooking mussels. I…What? Get rid of her? That's a little extreme, don't you…Give me a minute."

He opened the cooler and moments later started to nod. "All right, I have it. You're lucky you hired a genius, Paigey. Did I tell you…All right, all right, take a pill. Here's the new plan. Ava was upset I took her job, so when the attendees get sick on *her* hors d'oeuvres, I'll suggest to the Gallaghers that she did it to get me fired."

He nodded. "Thank you, I sometimes amaze myself. Okay, I've gotta get to work and get out of here before anyone comes in. I think I'll sleep in today. Whatever." He rolled his eyes, laughing when he disconnected. "Little do you know, Paigey. I'd do this job for free. The Gallaghers are going to pay for what Colleen stole from me."

Chapter Thirteen

♥

P sst, Ava."

At the frantic whisper, Ava put out her arm to stop the door from sliding shut and stuck her head outside the elevator.

"Hurry, I have to talk to you, and no one can see me." Erin waved her over, furtively looking around the second-floor hallway.

She wasn't surprised that Erin didn't want to be seen with her. Ava was persona non grata at the manor. Even Kitty, who walked around with a perpetual smile on her face, had given Ava the side-eye when she'd arrived for work. Given that the family was worried about Finn, Ava had tried not to let the slight hurt. The same as she did when she felt the staff's accusatory stares stabbing her in the back. She couldn't believe they were falling for Gaston's lies, taking his side over hers.

Sophie had woken Ava up with the news this morning

that every single one of the pastries she'd slaved over had been destroyed. According to Gaston, upon learning that he'd found her fillings bland and had doctored them up, she'd destroyed them in a fit of jealous rage. And now they were scrambling to replace the hors d'oeuvres in time for the bridal fair's opening this afternoon.

When Ava pointed out the holes in his accusation, Sophie assured Ava that she believed her. Ava wasn't so sure that she did because Sophie had refused her offer to help and had given in to Gaston's demand that she not be allowed within ten feet of the kitchen or dining room. Sophie had even suggested she take a few days off until everything calmed down. Ava refused. She thought it would make her look guilty, and she needed the money.

She dragged the service cart out of the elevator, parking it alongside the wall. Erin peeked her head around the corner. "Hurry, I left the new waitress they replaced you with alone."

So it looked like Ava could kiss her waitressing position and tips goodbye. Which would make it harder to pay back Griffin in a timely fashion. She should probably start looking for a second job. She worked to keep the hurt and frustration from showing on her face as she rounded the corner.

Erin grabbed her arm, half dragging her to the nearest guest room. Then Erin nearly strangled her by sliding the passkey Ava wore around her neck into the door.

"The room's not occupied, is it?" Erin asked as she turned the handle.

"A little late to be worrying about that now," Ava said, following the blonde into the room. "What's going on?"

Erin closed the door and then pulled a sheaf of folded

papers from her bra. "Sorry, I couldn't let anyone see me with them. Helga let me in on her secret. I offered to recopy them, but she wanted you to look at the recipes first. She doesn't trust Gaston." Erin looked at Ava. "We don't believe him, you know. Helga says he probably smashed the pastries. She says not to worry; she's going to fix him."

"You tell her to keep her head down and do her job. I'm fine," Ava said, a nervous catch in her voice. With Ava's luck, she'd be blamed for whatever retribution Helga cooked up for Gaston. Ava unfolded the papers and scanned the recipes, looking up to find Erin studying her.

Her head cocked, Erin said, "You do look fine. Better than fine, actually. Your eyes are shiny and your skin's all glowy. If I didn't know better, I'd say you look like a woman—"

She cut the younger woman off before she could say that Ava looked like a woman in love. Which of course she was, and had always been, and it hadn't done much for her looks the past decade. No, if she was glowy, it was because of her hope that maybe, just maybe, they were going to get a second chance. That hope had gone a long way in making the whole situation with Gaston bearable. A hope she wasn't ready to share with anyone just yet.

"Anger will do that, you know," she said to Erin while walking to the desk.

Ava pulled out the chair and sat down. "Once we rewrite the recipes in large print, Helga won't have a problem with them. I can't believe he's serving such mundane fare to the attendees though." She flicked the recipes with her fingers. "Mini cheese balls, egg rolls, and pigs in a blanket are not going to earn the reviews we're hoping for. Does Sophie know what he's sampling?"

"Between what happened with you and Liam's brother, she seems a little distracted."

Ava bowed her head and picked up a pen. "I don't know what you're talking about. Nothing happened between me and Griffin," she said, her heart beating a little faster. If Griffin told his family about them, that was huge. It meant their almost-kiss hadn't just been a blip. He really was…

"You and Griffin? No, I meant what happened with you and Gaston, and then what happened to Finn. Sophie says that he's safe, but they don't know if he's injured. They're hoping for more news soon."

Ava berated herself for getting her hopes up and thinking of herself and Griffin when his brother was in such a precarious position. "Yes, that was good to hear at least." Griffin had started his job with the Coast Guard this morning, so Ava hadn't talked to him yet. Sophie had shared the news when she'd called.

Ava held out the recipe for pigs in a blanket to Erin. "The ingredients all check out. It'll go faster if you copy one."

Erin joined her at the desk. Feeling the young woman's gaze upon her, Ava looked up from scanning the mini-egg-roll ingredients. "Why are you looking at me like that?"

"Don't take this the wrong way, but are you sure you didn't grab someone else's uniform?"

Ava self-consciously tugged at the front of her maid's uniform. The black buttons that lined the front of the dress were straining at her chest and hips. "No, it's mine, but I need a new one. I've gained weight. My neighbor and my aunt drop off pastries every morning. I can't seem to stop eating them." It was getting out of hand—her weight gain and her aunt and Dorothy.

She knew they were trying to make up for the part they'd played in sending her father away. Even though she'd told them she'd forgiven them, they obviously didn't believe her because they'd both shown up on her doorstep again this morning while Ava was having a cigarette after receiving Sophie's call. It was either that or eat a tray of cinnamon buns. She'd had two when she was explaining the situation with Gaston to her aunt and Dorothy. Given their reaction, Ava should have kept her mouth closed. She prayed they didn't show up at the manor today.

"Tell them to drop them off at my place. I can't gain weight no matter how hard I try."

"Enjoy it while it lasts," Ava said as she stood up. She handed the recipes to Erin. "You shouldn't be worrying about your weight. You look great though."

"Thanks, but I'd rather be curvy like you." Erin smiled and held up the pages. "And thanks for these. Helga really appreciated your help, you know. She tried to get a petition started among the staff to…" Erin grimaced. "I'm sure it'll blow over as soon as the bridal fair is over. Everyone knows how important it is to the manor. Are you going to stop in after work?"

Until today, she'd been looking forward to the fair. "As long as Gaston won't be there, I might."

"You should be okay. The waitstaff is taking turns doing the tastings." She glanced at the alarm clock on the nightstand. "Yikes, I better run."

As Erin hurried off, Ava took one last look around the room. The manor was almost at full occupancy for the weekend. Satisfied everything was in its place, she closed the door and headed for her service cart. The elevator doors opened, and one of the other maids stepped out.

Trudy had been the only staff member who hadn't snubbed her this morning. Ava frowned when the other woman turned to pull her cart from the elevator. "The rooms have all been done on this floor, Trudy."

The other woman wouldn't look at her. "Jasper asked me to check to make sure…" Her apple cheeks flushed, Trudy lifted a shoulder and mumbled, "Sorry."

"It doesn't matter." Only it did, a lot. Ava worked hard and took pride in her job. Today was no exception. It hurt that Jasper had asked someone to check up on her. He never had in the past. The other staff would hear about it.

Forcing a small smile for Trudy, Ava let her pass before pushing her cart onto the elevator. The box of red-foiled chocolate hearts on her cart called to her. They were putting them on the guests' pillows in honor of the bridal show and Valentine's Day, which had been three days earlier.

Ava looked down at her uniform's straining buttons and pushed the tower floor button.

She'd reversed the order of the rooms and had done Griffin's first thing this morning, hoping to catch him before he left for work. He'd already gone. She'd spent more time than normal cleaning his room, lingering over his pillow, breathing in his scent, comforted just by being there.

The elevator jerked to a stop, and she got out. Doing her best to ignore the chocolates' siren song, she left the cart outside Colleen's suite and entered. Griffin wasn't there. She sat on the edge of the bed, feeling jumpy and out of sorts, hoping the room and thoughts of Griffin worked their magic again. They didn't, and five minutes later she couldn't take it anymore. She got up and walked to the French doors that opened onto the balcony. Maybe the brisk sea air would clear her head.

She stepped outside and closed the door. Wrapping her gray sweater around her, she leaned against the sun-warmed granite wall, watching the seagulls' pinwheel in the crystal-blue sky. Their familiar high-pitched *ha ha ha* and the swooshing sound of the white-foamed waves rolling onto shore washed over her, calming her. She looked past Kismet Cove and the red-roofed lighthouse to where a fishing boat headed into the harbor, reminding her of her father. She closed her eyes.

It was easier not to think about him. But now he was there, too, in her head, mixed up with everything else that had gone wrong today. Her eyes misted, and she blinked the moisture away. She managed to stop the tears, but she couldn't resist the temptation any longer and withdrew the pack of cigarettes and a lighter from her sweater.

There was an iron planter in the corner, and she went to stand beside it. She lit the cigarette and rested her elbows on the stone balcony's ledge. Looking out to sea, she inhaled deeply, waiting for the calm to settle over her. It didn't happen right away. Not like it usually did. She shouldn't be surprised. Nothing in her life was usual anymore.

She tipped her head back and closed her eyes, letting the sun's fading rays warm her face as she inhaled deeply of the cigarette. The French door opened, and she gave a guilty start. She turned to see Griffin filling the space.

He wore an admiral-blue long-sleeve shirt with U.S.

COAST GUARD stitched in white on the right side of his chest, a T-shirt the same color underneath, as were his pants that were tucked into black lace-up boots.

"You look handsome," she said, the words slipping easily off her tongue. At the serious expression on his face, she realized it wasn't something she'd said to him in a long time. Maybe he didn't want her to say it to him now. Maybe their almost-kiss had been a blip. She caught the direction of his gaze and grimaced. "I'm sorry, I shouldn't be smoking on your balcony." She leaned over to butt out the cigarette.

"You have a bad day, sweet face?" he asked as he stepped outside, pulling the door shut behind him.

Afraid she might cry—and she didn't want to cry in front of him again—she pressed her lips together and nodded. She hadn't thought she'd ever hear him call her *sweet face* again.

"You gonna tell me what's wrong?"

Straightening, she shook her head and wrapped her arms around her waist. If she opened her mouth, the only thing that would come out was a sob. She could feel it warbling at the back of her throat. And if she didn't get herself under control, words he might not be ready to hear would follow. Words like *I love you. I never stopped loving you. I need you. I want you. Don't let me go again. Don't let me walk away from you.*

He placed his hands on her shoulders and turned her to face him. She kept her head down, focusing on his boots.

"I hate your sweater. It's ugly."

Her head jerked up. "Why would you say something like that?"

He smiled. "To get you to look at me."

"So you don't really think my sweater is ugly?"

"Yeah, I do. And once the weather gets warmer, you and me, we're going down to the beach, and I'll build a big-ass bonfire, and we'll burn it." He leaned back and opened the door. "Now, you just keep scowling at me and come inside and tell me what happened."

"You're not making any sense. Why would you want me to scowl at you?" she asked, following him inside.

"You know how I feel about you crying. If you're scowling, you can't."

She stared at him, wondering how he could read her so easily after all this time. Still, she tried to deny what he obviously knew. "I wasn't going to cry."

He raised an eyebrow and went to sit on the end of the bed, patting the spot beside him. She sat down, and he put his arm around her. "All right, tell me what's going on. Why aren't you working in the dining room? Be warned, if you tell me it's because you're working two jobs to make extra money to pay for your dad's stay at rehab, I'll be—"

"No, it's because I'm not allowed within ten feet of the kitchen and dining room." She told him what happened with Gaston.

He laughed. "You're shitting me, right? This is some kind of joke?"

"No, and other than Helga and Erin, everyone believes his lies. Even your grandmother, and I think Sophie might too. I guess it's no surprise that Jasper does. He even has the other maids checking on my rooms to make sure I've done my job." She twisted her hands in her lap, turning her head to sniff as quietly as she could, willing away the pinch in the backs of her eyes.

He swore under his breath and stood up.

"I'm not crying. I just sniffed."

He frowned. "What are you talking…" His expression softened, and he crouched in front of her. "My reaction had nothing to do with you, other than that I'm pissed off on your behalf." He touched her cheek. "Stay here. I'm going to talk to Sophie and Grams and clear a few things up. They didn't taste your pastries; I did. No way in hell St. John was doctoring them up. He was jealous and didn't want you to steal his thunder today."

"I appreciate what you're trying to do. I really do. But I already told Sophie my side of the story. She did what she thought was best, and I think your grandmother agreed. So it's not like anything you say can make a difference. I don't want to be the cause of hard feelings between you and—"

"Sophie might be the manager, but, babe, I own this place. So I damn well do have a say in what's going on and how the manor's being run."

Maybe something good would come out of this after all. "Technically, you own one-tenth, and until you become a member of Team Greystone, I don't think your opinion will carry much weight. Now if you did sign on, they'd have to listen to you because you have a vested interest in seeing the manor succeed. Right now, you're in the enemy camp." She smiled, hoping he'd take the bait.

He laughed. "Points for giving it a shot, but it's not happening. It'll take more than increasing occupancy rates and a bridal fair to give the old place the influx of cash that's needed. I, for one, don't intend to throw my savings into a pit of quicksand."

"No, you'd just sell out your family's legacy to make

a quick buck." She lifted her chin. "You act like you care about me losing my position in the dining room, yet, if you get your way, I won't even have a job. None of us will."

He sat beside her and took her hand in his, giving it a gentle tug to make her look at him.

"If you don't think I care about you, you haven't been paying attention."

"I'm sorry, you're right. I appreciate everything you've done for me and my father. I just—"

"I wasn't talking about that. Though we probably should before you go out and get another job to replace your tip money."

"How did you—"

"I know you. And you know me well enough to know that I'm not taking your money. You didn't take anything when we split up, and you could have."

She watched as his thumb rubbed her ringless finger. She'd left her wedding ring on his dresser the morning she'd moved out of his place in Virginia Beach. But she'd taken things, small things, mementos of their time together. She didn't take much because she carried the most important thing in her heart—her love for him. "We didn't really have anything."

"We had everything, everything that mattered."

He was right, and she'd thrown it all away because she couldn't look at him without remembering that night.

Griffin tugged on her hand. "I didn't mean to upset you. It was a long time ago. We were young. We both moved on."

He'd moved on, but she hadn't. She'd stayed stuck in the past. She nodded because she knew that's what he expected and she couldn't speak. Her throat was so tight she could barely breathe.

"But I can't just erase how I felt about you, Ava. You matter to me. You've gotta know I feel partially responsible for what happened with your dad that night. So let me do this. It's as much for me as you. The rehab center doesn't cost as much as you think. Adam gave me a deal."

Each word was like a pin stabbing the shiny pink, hope-filled balloon in her chest, the emotion leaking out, leaving her deflated. She'd read too much into their almost-kiss. "You're not to blame. You did nothing wrong, Griffin. You never have. It was always me."

"Hey, where's this coming from?"

"I'm just tired. I should probably go," she said, and went to stand up.

"Hang on a sec." He pulled her back beside him and reached in his pocket for his phone. "I know it's been bothering you not to talk to your dad, so I gave Adam a call." He punched in his password and swiped his finger over the screen and then handed it to her. "Even though Gino's your dad, Adam probably broke some privacy laws sending these. So this stays between us."

There were pictures of her father working out with a medicine ball, pulling himself up between two parallel bars, and one of him sitting in the dining room with another man. They were laughing. The photos blurred. She turned to surreptitiously wipe at her eyes and then cleared her throat. "He looks…happy."

Griffin leaned into her. "In that one he does." He swiped his finger over the screen.

"Looks like he's plotting how to kill the therapist in this one. Kidding aside, Adam says your dad's working hard. Says he's a pain in the ass and stubborn, too, but he thinks you'll be impressed by his progress when you come visit."

"He doesn't want me to visit him. He doesn't even want to talk to me."

"Wait a sec. You think your dad doesn't want to see or talk to you?"

She nodded. "That's what he told me."

"Because he didn't have a choice, honey. It's one of the stipulations in the application. It has nothing to do with you. Adam finds that clients settle into a routine better if they don't have contact with family members for the first couple of weeks."

"Oh, I thought…" She smiled. "Thank you for this, and for getting my dad in your friend's center. I don't know how I can ever repay you."

"Smile at me like that once a day, and we're good."

"I can do better than that. I'll make you some more of the chicken pastries you liked. I can make you lasagna too. You always loved my—"

He rubbed his hand along his jaw. "That's something else we should probably talk about."

She jumped to her feet. She didn't want him to spoil this moment. She was relieved, happy to see her father doing so well and to know he hadn't intentionally shut her out of his life. She didn't want Griffin to ruin it by telling her he'd made a mistake when he'd almost kissed her. "It's fine. It wasn't important. I really need to go," she said, heading for the door.

"Ava, you've got my phone."

She turned and walked back to him, holding it out. His fingers closed around her wrist, and he slowly drew her closer. "So you're telling me that you didn't feel anything when I held you in my arms, when we almost kissed?"

"Yes, but…Did you?"

"Yeah, of course I did." He shook his head with a laugh. Probably because she was smiling like a crazy person.

Then his laughter faded, and he rubbed his jaw again. "Here's the thing though. There's stuff going on that I can't share with you. So for now, it's probably best if we don't spend a lot of time together. Just for a couple months until I get things sorted out."

"Months?"

He grimaced. "Yeah, I know. It's not ideal. I wish—"

"Is everything okay with Finn?" she asked, assuming this was about his brother. Finn had never forgiven her for hurting Griffin. When he was in town and saw her on the street, he'd cross to the other side. But the thought couldn't take away from the happiness bursting inside her. It was all she could do to keep it from showing on her face. It was inappropriate to be this happy when he was worried about his brother.

Griffin glanced at his phone. "They arrived at the hospital a few hours ago. Finn was hurt, but his injuries aren't life-threatening. I'm expecting a call in the next twenty minutes with an update as to when we can fly him out of there. But he's not…" He looked like he'd changed his mind about whatever he'd been about to say and instead lifted his hand to tuck her hair behind her ear. "I want a second chance, Ava. And I don't want anything to screw it up. I want to do it right this time."

She stared at him. "This feels surreal. Like I'm dreaming. If it is a dream, please don't wake me up."

"You're not dreaming, sweet face. I'm right here, and so are you. Do you want this, Ava? Do you want to give it another shot?"

Covering his hand with hers, she pressed it to her cheek. "Yes, more than you'll ever know."

"Honey, could you maybe not look at me that way?"

She smiled.

"Yeah, don't do that either." He bowed his head and swore under his breath. "This is going to be tougher than I thought."

"So if I can't look at you or smile at you, what can I do?"

"I know it's a lot to ask, but wait for me."

That was easy. She'd been waiting for him for more than a decade. "I can do that."

"I'll make it up to you. I'll take you to that restaurant you love in Boston for our first date."

"We're going to date?"

"That and a whole lot more. So pencil me in for April twenty-first…What's wrong? You got plans?"

"It's not that. It just seems so far away."

He looked like he was counting the weeks in his head. "We'll shoot for the first week in April. If I can work this out sooner, I will, Ava. I wish I could take care of it tomorrow."

"Is there anything I can do to—"

"Uh, no, believe me, you do not want to get between me and…" He took her by the shoulders and steered her toward the door. "You should go now. I'll call you tonight."

"We can talk on the phone?"

He grinned. "We used to do a whole lot more than talk, sweet face."

Ava pushed the cart into the elevator, remembering their steamy conversations from the past. She fanned herself and then pinched herself, still finding it hard to believe this was real. Maybe it was because their relationship would be in limbo for months. Ava had spent almost half her adult life in limbo so she didn't relish the idea of being stuck there again.

"Psst, Ava!"

The frantic whisper greeted her as she pushed the cart from the elevator onto the main floor. Expecting Erin, she was surprised to see Dana poking her head from behind a potted palm, waving her over.

Ava left the cart and hurried to the redhead's side. Dana wasn't always a redhead though. She had wigs of all colors and lengths in her room. She also had a wide assortment of sleeping and pain pills, which Ava knew from cleaning her room. But Ava hadn't seen the telltale glazed look in her friend's eyes for months. Today they were light green and framed with thick lashes.

Ava crouched behind the potted plant. "What's going on?"

"Look," Dana said, poking a finger through the leaves at the waitress leaving the ballroom with what appeared to be a barely touched platter of egg rolls. "Everyone's turning their noses up at the hors d'oeuvres from the manor, and Mackenzie says they're going to run out of their sample cakes."

Mackenzie's desserts were as truly scrumptious as the bakery's name indicated. "Can't she have her staff make more?"

"They are, but we have to get through all day tomorrow and six hours on Sunday." Dana reached for the iPad by her feet. "After what happened with Gaston, I hate to even ask you this, but I really need your help. Some of the Widows Club went to the bridal fair in Bridgeport to snoop around. Look what they're serving."

Ava angled her head. "Um, I think these might be your personal pics because that looks like a man's naked butt cheeks."

Dana turned the screen and blinked, then leaned in. "Definitely a man's butt cheeks. But I've never seen them before. Mrs. Fitzgerald must have sent it by mistake." Dana scrolled through more pictures. "Okay, so maybe it wasn't a mistake." She turned the screen to Ava. A bare-chested waiter was passing around hors d'oeuvres to some very excited women.

Ava squinted. "I think I see Auntie Rosa and Dorothy in the crowd." She supposed she should be thankful they were there and not here stirring up trouble. Though…"This isn't good. We need to do something."

"It's even worse than I thought. Please say you'll help me, Ava. I understand Sophie and Kitty are upset about Liam's brother, and I don't blame them, but I can't get them to commit to anything or to help come up with a solution." Dana chewed on a manicured nail. "This is my first big event as Greystone's event planner, and it's going to be a bust."

"No, it's not. We've got this. I can have enough simple but elegant hors d'oeuvres ready within an hour. You just have to drop me off at the deli. Hopefully Marco will be there, and he can help too. They'll get you through tonight. I'll call in reinforcements to help make enough to cover the next two days. But, Dana, you have to clear this with Sophie."

"No, I don't. I'm making an executive decision and contracting out to DiRossi catering. And you're billing us, Ava."

She opened her mouth to refuse and then closed it. She'd have extra money to go shopping for her date with Griffin. It would give her something to look forward to. She thought of something else to look forward to and smiled. "I think I've solved our eye candy problem. We'll get Griffin, Liam, and some of the firefighters to act as waiters." But she didn't want the women ogling her half-naked soon-to-be boyfriend, and she knew the men would never agree anyway. Then she came up with a way to keep everyone happy. "They can wear their uniforms."

Chapter Fourteen

♥

I bet you have a very big hose," an older woman said to Griffin with a lascivious wink.

"I'm with the Coast Guard, ma'am. My brother here is the firefighter. His hose isn't that big though."

Liam shot him a dirty look, and Griffin grinned.

"Size isn't all that—" the older woman began, sighing when a younger version of herself hurried over.

"Mother, leave the men alone. Sorry," the woman apologized, dragging her mother away.

Griffin watched as the two women were swallowed up by the hordes of attendees swarming the tables lining either side of the ballroom, thinking their cover was probably blown. After five hours of mingling with the mostly female crowd, he and his brother had found a quiet corner at the back of the ballroom beside the raised platform, staying in the shadows of the red velvet curtains that were serving as a makeshift backstage. *Quiet* being a relative term when you put more than a hundred women in a room, even one as big as this.

Liam forced a smile for the group of women now finger-waving at them from the table for A Spoonful of Sugar, the town's local candy shop. "Thanks for the shot about my *hose*. You can knock it off now. I apologized to Ava," his brother said out of the side of his mouth.

Griffin returned the women's finger-waves with a resigned smile. "It was too good to pass up. Besides, you owe Ava more than an apology. She saved your asses, baby brother. She spent half the night making the samples for today."

Which meant the late-night phone conversation he'd been fantasizing about hadn't transpired. It had lasted all of five minutes and was disappointingly PG-rated. Maybe that was a good thing. Sexy talk time would have been fun, but it undoubtedly would have left him frustrated and desperate for the real deal. It'd been okay when they were married and separated by hundreds of miles. It wouldn't be the same now.

But he wouldn't risk Lexi and his baby's well-being by upsetting the mother of his child. Once Lexi got to know Ava, she'd recognize her for the kind, loving, bighearted woman she was and not the coldhearted bitch that Lex thought her to be. Ava didn't have a mean bone in her gorgeous, curvy body, and Lexi was a good judge of character. All she needed was to spend some time around Ava.

"Yeah, and thanks to her, we're spending our Saturday being pinched and patted down by a bunch of..."

Griffin crossed his arms, and Liam rolled his eyes. "All right, I'll concede that it was a good idea, and while Ava didn't literally save our asses, because I guarantee mine is bruised, she figuratively did. We owe her big-time, and we've all been trying to make it up to her. Well, most of us are anyway. The thing is, big brother, you're making a bigger deal of it than Ava."

"It was a big deal. You didn't see her yesterday, Liam. She was hurt. And you didn't see her working till three-thirty in the morning to help out Helga and the manor, only to have all of you turn around and accuse her of—"

His brother raised his hand. "We didn't. Gaston did. And he didn't leave Sophie much choice. It was just hours before they opened the doors, and he threatened to hold the hors d'oeuvres he'd made hostage. So Sophie did what she had to do to appease him."

"And to hell with Ava. Nice."

His normally easygoing brother stiffened, and his expression hardened. "Watch it. Soph's been dealing with more than what's going on at the manor. She doesn't need you giving her grief over this too."

"What's going on with Sophie?" He may be unhappy with how she handled the situation with Ava, but he liked his sister-in-law. She was good for his brother and made him happy.

"I'll tell you about it later," Liam said as Sophie made her way through the crowd toward them wearing a red dress. "But if it makes you feel better, Soph is meeting with George Monday morning to see if there's a way to break the contract without Gaston suing us."

"I can be pretty persuasive. Why don't you let me take a shot? Save on George's legal fees."

His brother snorted. "Yeah, right. Your idea of persuasion would get us sued for sure." He smiled at his wife. "Hey, beautiful, everything okay?"

"Everything's fine." She kissed Liam's cheek, then glanced around. "Where's Mia?"

Liam frowned. "I thought she was with you at Grams and Rosa's workshop."

"She was until their How to Live Happily Ever After lecture became How to Keep Yourself Happy Without a Man. When I overheard Nonna asking Mrs. Fitzgerald where the box of toys was for the demonstration, I told Mia to come find you and help you serve the samples." She looked from her husband's half-full platter to Griffin's empty one. "It looks like you could use some help. Maybe you should take some pointers from your brother."

"Hey, it's not my fault. The women love me. They just aren't crazy about pickled beet deviled eggs."

While his brother and Sophie were talking, Griffin was scanning the crowd for his niece. "There she is." He pointed to where Mia stood on her tiptoes at the candy table, reaching past several giggling women. She wore a red ruffled dress with her long, chestnut-brown hair pulled up in two ponytails. The kid was adorable and reminded Griffin of his sister Riley.

"Oh no," Sophie said, and rushed off in their daughter's direction.

"Come on, Soph," Liam called after his wife. "A little sugar once in a while won't hurt…" His brother's jaw dropped when Mia turned around and waved a cellophane-wrapped pink sucker at her mother. "Tell me that's not what I think it is."

"I'm not sure what you think it is. But it looks like a pink penis to me," Griffin laughed.

Sully, wearing his dress blues, walked toward them, his face a picture of consternation. "Uh, seeing a little girl with a penis sucker is bad enough, but the way that older woman is looking at us while she's licking hers is giving me the creeps."

"What the hell is Zoe thinking?" his brother asked, referring to the owner of A Spoonful of Sugar. Though he looked relieved when Sophie finally managed to get their daughter to exchange her penis sucker for a heart sucker.

"That she's in the business of making money and, from the looks of it, those suckers are gonna sell," Griffin said.

"Maybe you should give them away with your eggs," Sully suggested to Liam, and fist-bumped Griffin. "The Guard's beating out the firefighters. Liam and two of his buddies still have samples to get rid of."

"It's not a competition, you know," his brother said.

"Yeah, it is. Guard's handing out Ava's hors d'oeuvres, and you guys are passing around Gaston's. She's winning," Griffin said.

"No, the manor's winning because…Oh, Jesus, here he comes. Take some of my deviled eggs or I'll never hear the end of it," Liam said when Gaston entered the ballroom wearing red pants and shoes with his white chef coat and hat.

"They're purple," Griffin said, eyeing the egg. He took a tentative bite.

"Ladies and gentlemen, *zee* crab cakes with *zee* remoulade have arrived," Gaston announced, posing with the tray in the air.

"Ava better hurry up with those samples or Gaston will win by default," Sully said.

Griffin hadn't seen her all day. She'd been working out of Rosa's kitchen, sending the food back with her aunt and Dorothy. "She lost her runners. Rosa and Dorothy are at the workshop."

"I saw her fifteen minutes ago," Sully said. "Arianna was trying to convince her to wear one of Tie the Knot's dresses…" His eyes went wide. "Ah, wow, looks like Arianna succeeded."

Popping the rest of the egg in his mouth, Griffin turned…and choked. Ava stood at the entrance wearing a scarlet dress with a deep V neckline that gave a tantalizing glimpse of creamy skin and cleavage and showed off her narrow waist and rounded hips, her long, shapely legs enhanced by a pair of sky-high black heels.

Griffin was having a hard time catching his breath and he didn't think it had anything to do with the egg caught in his throat. He swallowed hard. "Jesus, God," was all he managed to groan.

His brother grinned.

Sully gave him a commiserating pat on the back and said, "Looks like the battle of the chefs is on."

As Ava and Gaston worked opposite sides of the room, they'd glance over their shoulders every few seconds as though gauging the reactions of the women tasting their competitor's samples.

"I have a feeling they're both going to lose," Liam said, lifting his chin to where his brother-in-law Marco strolled into the ballroom wearing his turnout gear, his jacket opened to reveal he was shirtless and, if Griffin wasn't mistaken, well oiled.

Marco grinned at the room at large and held up two trays. "Ladies, the Italian Stallion has arrived. Come get me and my pizza."

Ava laughed, shaking her head at her cousin. Then, as

though she sensed Griffin watching her, she looked his way. She nudged her head in Marco's direction and rolled her eyes, sharing a joke like they used to all those years ago. He didn't feel like laughing. Ava and Gaston weren't the only ones who had lost the battle. Griffin had lost his too. There was no way he could stay away from her until April.

Gaston had disappeared behind the red velvet curtain at the back of the ballroom as though someone had hooked a shepherd's crook around his neck and yanked him off-stage like they used to do in the good old days of vaude-ville.

Colleen glanced at Ava and Griffin as she made her way to the curtains. She didn't know what nonsense Griffin had gotten in his head to put off Ava for months. He'd never been a foolish boy, but for the life of her, she couldn't come up with another reason to explain his behavior. It was obvious he still loved Ava. From the heated glances flying across the ballroom between them, she didn't expect him to hold out much longer. A good thing since they had an enemy in their midst. Two, she corrected when she walked through the curtain.

"What are you doing? I'm paying you to ruin Greystone's reputation, not enhance it! Everyone's raving about the food," Paige Townsend said in a furious whisper, her face red against her blond hair.

"Really?" He preened. "What exactly are they saying? Did you happen to hear what Basil Brisiel thought? He's the tall, elegant man wearing the double-breasted navy blazer and jeans."

Paige looked like she wanted to throttle him. "I have

no idea who this Basil Brisiel person is or why you're even talking about him." She held up her phone. "The Gallaghers wouldn't let me through the front gate. I have spies sending me updates, you idiot. Now explain yourself or you're fired."

He gave her a cocky smile. "You can't fire me. You have no one else who can do this job. And let's not forget that I know a little something about you."

"You don't know anything—"

He tapped his cheek and batted his eyes. "Let me see, it had something to do with a fire…" He dropped the act and gave Paige a don't-mess-with-me look. "A fire that just happened to burn down the carriage house on the estate and nearly claimed the lives of Sophie, Mia, and Dana."

Colleen gasped. It didn't give her pleasure to know that her suspicions had been correct. Truth be told, it worried her. Paige didn't care who she hurt to get her way, and Colleen was beginning to think that Gaston St. John was just as dangerous.

"It was an accident. I didn't think it would catch fire that quickly, and I had no idea Dana had moved out of the manor or that Sophie and Mia were there at the time. They usually stayed at the house on Breakwater Way. Anyway, the case is closed. They ruled that faulty wiring was the cause. Who knows, I may have saved them from something really terrible happening."

"A little evidence shows up and they might reopen—"

"You're threatening me? You'd have nothing without me. I'm the one who stood by you all those years ago and bailed you out last month. So stop with the threats or I will stop paying, and you, Gaston St. John, need the money." She sneered in a way that told Colleen that was not the man's name and, given her earlier comment, the two had a past. They were connected somehow. But for the life of her, Colleen couldn't place him.

Paige continued. "You better tell me that this is all part of your plan or I'll start looking for—"

"All right, all right." He screwed up his face. "I had a plan, and Ava DiRossi ruined it. As much as it pains me to admit, the Italian she-devil can cook. She was making me look bad in front of Basil, and I just couldn't have it. I had to up my game, and every time I upped mine, she upped hers."

"Who. Is. Basil?" Paige said from between clenched teeth.

He clasped his hands to his chest. "A living food god. He's the Midas of the restaurant industry. Every, and I mean every, restaurant he's been involved with has three Michelin stars. Three." He shook three fingers in Paige's face. "Do you know what a feat that is? And he's here, Paigey. Right here with his Food Network producer fiancée."

"They're actually thinking of booking their wedding at the manor?"

"Oh my God, you're right. I could be catering the King and Queen of the Food Network's wedding. It'll make my career. I'll be a star," he said, looking like he might faint.

Paige grabbed him by the shoulders and shook him. "They can't have their wedding here, you idiot. That'll make Greystone a star as much as it would you." She let him go, her fingers flying over the keys on her phone at the speed of light. "Please, please, tell me they're looking at…" There was a ping from her phone. "Oh thank God," she said, sagging in relief. "They were at the bridal fair in Bridgeport too. From what my source says, your friend Basil wants to book their wedding with them, but his fiancée likes the old-world charm of Greystone. The idiot. We need to come up with a way to make them choose the Bridgeport Marquis while publicly destroying Greystone's reputation at the same time."

As she rubbed her temples, another message pinged on her phone. She glanced at the screen and her mouth compressed, a flush working its way up her neck to her face. "The *Harmony Harbor Gazette* has just proclaimed Greystone the winner of the bridal fair wars."

"Isn't a little early to announce a winner? It's not over until tomorrow. And I thought Byron Harte was in your pocket."

"So did I. But ever since…" She lifted a shoulder. "It doesn't matter. The bridal fair in Bridgeport opened Thursday and ends today." She closed her eyes, tapping her finger on her lips. "There has to be…" Her eyes popped open. "I've got it. Instead of a bridal fair war, we'll have a food war between the manor and the Marquis. Basil will be the judge, and the winning hotel, which will be the Bridgeport Marquis of course, will host their wedding and comp them for all the publicity they've received. We should be able to get some coverage from the local stations in New England, morning shows and the like." She laughed. "Greystone will be ruined."

Colleen wanted to wrap her hands around Paige's overlong neck.

Gaston was staring at the real estate agent, looking like he wanted to do the same. "Are you mad? I'll be ruined."

"Not if you blame someone else, you won't," Paige said with a smirk.

Swaying from side to side, Gaston moved his hand in a downward motion. "Ava DiRossi, you're going down."

Guilt ridden, Colleen watched Paige slip out a side door. Gaston straightened his chef's hat and then pushed aside the red-velvet curtain to walk back through the ballroom. Because of something Colleen had done in the past, Gaston, or whoever he was, would do whatever was necessary to bring Greystone down—Greystone and Ava.

Colleen had already caused Ava enough pain. First by keeping her secret from Griffin, and then by smashing the pastries in the cooler after Gaston had meddled with them. Her actions may have saved the bridal fair's attendees from food poisoning, but Ava had paid the price. Colleen wouldn't allow someone else to suffer because of her interference—not again.

The good Lord should have taken her back in November. She was making a hash of things here, she thought dejectedly. She sat slumped on the slate floor, unable to even bury her face in her hands and have a good cry like she wanted to.

Meow.

She lifted her head to see Simon looking at her. He might only be a cat, but there was something regal about his bearing as he sat in front of her. His piercing blue gaze held hers, and he lifted his chin. He did it again with a slow stretch of his neck.

Colleen half sobbed, half snorted. "If I didn't know better, I'd say you were telling me to keep my chin up."

His ears twitched, and if a cat could smile, that's what Simon appeared to do.

"I appreciate you trying to cheer me up, Tomcat, but

they'd be better off without me." Apparently Simon took offense to the remark and sauntered off, leaving her alone. Colleen was feeling very alone these days.

She supposed if there was a bright spot in all of this, it was that Griffin would be there to watch out for Ava, and there was very little her great-grandson missed. And Ava, along with Sophie, Liam, Kitty, Jasper, and Dana, would do their best to protect the manor.

Maybe if she just closed her eyes, she'd...

"Hi, GG."

Colleen opened her eyes to see Mia. The little girl sat down beside her, straightening her pretty red dress before crossing her legs at the ankles. She smiled at Colleen. "I can still see you, you know. Not as good as before, but I can't let Mommy and Daddy know."

Simon hopped onto Mia's lap, looking very much like the cat who'd swallowed the canary. "You're a smart one, I'll give you that," Colleen said to him, and smiled at Mia, who was nattering on about the bridal fair now. Colleen was content just to sit and listen to her sweet voice.

She paid closer attention to what Mia was saying when a familiar name came up. "Mommy shouldn't have hired that new chef. He's mean to Auntie Ava and Helga. You should make him leave, GG. Scare him. I'm not scared of you because you're my GG, and I love you. But a lot of people are afraid of ghosts. Will you do that? Will you scare him away?"

It was a good idea. The lad looked the type to scare easily. Colleen nodded and smiled. "I'll scare the living bejaysus out of him, poppet." She supposed it was a good thing Mia could only see her and not hear her.

The curtain opened. "Mia honey, who are you talking

to?" Liam asked, a concerned expression on his face as he looked around.

Mia cupped the side of her face with her hand and winked at Colleen. "Just Simon, Daddy," she said, then patted the purring cat.

Oddly enough, the purr sounded like a chuckle.

"You'll have to continue your chat with Simon later. Mommy's looking for you. Arianna wants you to try on your dress for tomorrow's fashion show."

Mia lifted Simon off her lap. "Yay! Can I see Auntie Ava's wedding dress? Mommy says it's beautiful."

"That's a secret, remember? Auntie Ava doesn't know she's in the fashion show."

"Does Uncle Griffin?"

Liam laughed. "Nope, he's in for a big surprise. And your Uncle Griffin isn't a fan of surprises. It's going to be fun times."

"Do you like surprises, Daddy?" Mia asked.

"Sometimes, but I guess I'm a little like your uncle." Liam looked down at his giggling daughter. "Sweetheart, is there something I should know?"

She made a zip-it motion with her finger across her lips and skipped off.

Liam chased after her, calling for his wife.

"It sounds like we won't want to miss the fashion show tomorrow, Simon," Colleen said, feeling a renewed sense of purpose. "But for now, we have a chef to scare."

Chapter Fifteen

♥

"Why does Mia keep looking at me and giggling?" Ava asked her cousin as she lifted Sophie's hair to zip up the dress she was wearing in the fashion show. Arianna was showcasing Tie the Knot's new spring line. All the dresses were gorgeous with layers of sheer fabric in various pastel hues. Sophie's was petal pink, and Mia's was robin's-egg blue.

"She's just excited about the fashion show and to hear her daddy sing," Sophie said.

"Her daddy didn't seem as excited as she is. Neither did Griffin or Colin." Ava wouldn't admit it to her cousin, but she was excited to hear Griffin sing. Just to sit for a few uninterrupted minutes and watch and listen to him would be a joy. She'd been too busy preparing food for the bridal fair to spend any time with him. And then there was the whole keeping-their-distance thing. Their brief nightly conversations had been unsatisfying too. She supposed she should be grateful though. After all, this was more than she'd dreamed possible.

Sophie laughed. "Don't let him fool you; he loves to perform. He just didn't want to wear a tux. Now Colin and Griffin, they weren't as crazy about being in the spotlight. Not to sound boastful, but don't you think it was a brilliant idea? What better way to make *Harmony* Harbor stand out in the bride-to-be's minds than to have three beautiful men singing a capella?"

"It was inspired. But you do realize that every bride who books their wedding at the manor will expect them to sing at theirs, don't you?"

"Yes, and because Liam has a very healthy ego, he's positive all the women will want them to, and just as sure I'll say okay to seal the deal. Which means his Saturdays will be tied up for the foreseeable future."

"And we all know you'd do anything to seal the deal." Ava patted her shoulder. "You're all zipped up."

Sophie turned and hugged her. "Thank you for working so hard to make the bridal fair a success. I hope you know how much we all appreciate it."

"I do, because every time I run into you, Colin, Kitty, or Liam, you all keep telling me. So you can stop now. You know the manor's success is just as important to me."

"We do. That's why I feel so bad I caved to Gaston." Sophie glanced around the sitting room where the women had all gathered to get ready for the fashion show. Her cousin lowered her voice. "I've been dealing with some things I didn't want to talk about, and between that and Finn and the bridal fair, I didn't handle the situation as well as I should have. I'm going to take care of that tomorrow. I'm meeting with Mr. Wilcox, and we'll figure out a way to break Gaston's contract without him suing us." She took Ava's hand in hers. "Please tell me you'll take over for him."

What a difference a few months make, Ava thought when the prospect of taking over as chef caused her heart to give an excited thump instead of an anxious twist. "I'd love to. Thank you."

"Oh God, don't thank me. I'm just glad you're willing to consider it after everything."

Ava thought back to her cousin's earlier comment. "You mentioned that you were dealing with some things. Are you okay?"

"This is totally under the dome, because, well, I'm not, but I thought I was pregnant. I've been really tired and nauseous and realized I'd missed a period. I let myself get excited. Thankfully Liam and I didn't tell anyone because I got my period last week. And the next day, after months of radio silence, my mother calls. Her boyfriend dumped her for another yoga instructor, and now she's thinking about moving back to Harmony Harbor."

"I wouldn't tell your brother or Rosa about Tina before you know for sure. Maybe she'll change her mind." Ava looked around, leaning into her cousin. "Did you take a pregnancy test?"

"No, I'd been planning to, and then…" She lifted a shoulder.

"You can have intermittent bleeding during pregnancy, Sophie. Especially in the early stages. It's much lighter than your period though. So if that's what you're experiencing, you might want to take the test." Ava didn't know this only because of her training; she knew from personal experience.

Before Sophie had a chance to respond, Arianna turned from where she'd been helping her sister Serena into the bridal gown. "We need a new bride."

Serena pulled the front of the bodice from her chest. "Preferably one with boobs." She glanced over her shoulder. "And a butt."

Everyone turned to look at Ava. She narrowed her eyes at the women and held up her hands, almost positive she was being set up. "No."

Twenty minutes later, Ava was standing in front of a mirror wearing one of the most exquisite bridal gowns she had ever seen. The full bell skirt and tight bodice was made up of layers of vanilla-white, tissue-thin material, and small pastel flowers were appliqued on the outer layer with intricate embroidery creating the leaves and stems. Each flower had a tiny crystal bead at its center that matched the beading on the delicate pink high heels and the line of crystals that were attached to the fabric at the nape of her neck down to the base of the backless gown.

Dorothy and Rosa stood on either side of her, their hands pressed prayer-like together, the tips of their fingers touching their lips. They didn't speak, just stared at her through shining eyes.

Ava forced a laugh and said for them as much as for herself, "It's a fashion show, not a wedding."

"Father O'Malley's here. He's right up at the front. So we can have a real wedding," Mia said, giving Rosa a thumbs-up in the mirror.

Ava groaned. "Auntie Rosa, you didn't!"

"Didn't what? Father O'Malley can't come to a fashion show now?" Rosa shrugged and lifted her two hands, palms up. "And if someone decides to get married, he's here. It's all good."

No, it was very bad. The last thing Ava wanted was Griffin to think she had an ulterior motive for playing the part of the bride in the fashion show. "I can't do this."

"Nonna and Dorothy, why don't you go check and make sure everything's organized in the ballroom? You too, baby," Sophie said, ushering them out of the sitting room.

Arianna walked over with a pale pink flower that had strands of crystals hanging from it. "Please do it for me, Ava. No one can make that dress look half as stunning as you do. You're the perfect advertisement for Tie the Knot."

"Guilting me is how you got me into the dress in the first place."

"I know. It worked so well, I thought I'd try again. But it's not a lie. I guarantee when you walk out there, I'm going to be besieged by women wanting that gown."

Ava sighed. "All right."

"Thank you. And I have a feeling you'll be thanking me by the end of the day, once a certain someone sees you." Arianna moved Ava's hair to the side so that it cascaded down the front left of the bodice, and then she clipped the flower in Ava's hair to hold it there.

Maggie, an attractive fiftysomething redhead, who was appearing in the fashion show in a pale yellow dress, picked up Ava's bouquet off the table and handed the pastel-colored roses tied together with matching ribbons to her. "You have to let me paint you in this dress, Ava. If that's okay with you, Arianna."

"Pass up the opportunity to have one of my gowns

featured in a Maggie Stewart original painting? Are you kidding me? Schedule us in, right, Ava?"

Maggie was not only a talented artist, but she was also a lovely woman whom Ava was fond of. They'd gotten to know each other at the Widows Club's meetings, and lately Maggie had seemed to be going through a difficult time. Ava thought it might be because she was no longer dating Griffin's father. Though they'd never come out and said they were actually dating.

At Maggie's and Arianna's expectant looks, Ava didn't feel she had a choice but to agree. "That would be nice. Thank you, Maggie." Then Ava thought of something. "I get to keep the gown on, don't I?" Maggie was famous, or infamous as the case may be, for her nudes.

Maggie laughed. "Whatever you want."

Dana hurried in wearing a mint-green dress. "Showtime, ladies." She hooked her arm through Ava's. "You have nothing to be nervous about. You look absolutely stunning. If you need a distraction, just look at Griffin. Because I guarantee that man won't be able to take his eyes off you."

Dana was right, Ava thought a few moments later when she entered the ballroom. And so was Arianna. Using a white runner decorated with pink and yellow rose petals, Dana had created an aisle between the rows of chairs. Everyone on both sides of the aisle came to their feet, whistling and clapping. But Ava only had eyes for the man standing beside his brother—his father behind them—on the platform.

The three men wore black tuxes from Tie the Knot. Griffin had forgone the black bow tie both his brother and father wore, leaving the top two buttons of his white shirt open to expose his corded neck. Griffin and Liam began playing their guitars, and the crowd quieted and took their seats. Colin rested a hand on each of his sons' shoulders, and the three men began to sing "I Swear" by John Michael Montgomery.

Everything faded, the whispers, the *oohs* and *aahs* over the dresses, the people, the room, until all she saw and heard was Griffin, singing the words of "I Swear" directly to her as she slowly made her way up the aisle toward him. As he sang the lyrics, she wanted to ask him *Do we have to wait?* More than ever she didn't want to. They'd wasted too many years already.

And she knew as he promised to never break her heart, that he never would have. She'd done that, and she wanted nothing more than to make it up to him. He didn't need to know the secret she'd kept from him, the secret that had torn her and them apart. It wouldn't make a difference now. That part of her was long gone, dead and buried. All that was important now was the future, their future together. From the soft expression on his face to the shimmer in his beautiful eyes, she knew he wanted one with her too.

Sophie and Mia walked to the left of the stage, Maggie and Dana to the right. The four of them smiled at her as Ava continued to make her way up the aisle. She smiled back and then returned her gaze to Griffin. Love shone from his indigo eyes as he sang the chorus to her one last time, and she tripped on the edge of the runner.

Father O'Malley came to her aid, but Griffin reached her first, steadying her with his hands on her arms. "Ava," he breathed, looking into her eyes.

"Stop, stop!" a woman yelled from the back of the

ballroom. "I object, and more importantly, your baby objects, Griffin Gallagher. You can't do this. You can't let her ruin your life again!"

Looking determined and furious, Lexi stormed up the aisle toward him. He knew he should be worried about her and what effect her over-the-top anger was having on both her and the baby. But it was the woman standing before him who worried him more. Only seconds ago, her beautiful face had been alight with happiness and love. Now she looked devastated. Her legs buckled, and he tightened his grip on her upper arms. "Honey, it's not what you think. Just give me a chance to ex—"

Ava raised her gaze, the stricken look in her eyes punching a hole in his chest. "She's having your baby?"

"Yes, but—"

She made a small, desperate sound in her throat and tugged her arms free. Lifting her gown, she ran down the aisle. "*Mi dispiace*. I'm sorry. I didn't know. I'm sorry," he heard her say to Lexi as she brushed past his ex-wife, breaking his heart as she did.

People turned to watch her leave, several of them pressing their fingers to their lips. Rosa shot him a furious glare before hurrying after Ava with Dorothy following close behind. He needed to go after her too, but first he had to calm Lexi down.

Her lip curled as she glanced over her shoulder. Then she looked up at him. "I cannot even begin to understand what you see in a woman like that. She's a mouse and a coward, sniveling and apologizing instead of standing—"

"Don't," he gritted out, holding on to his temper by a thread. "What you saw is a decent woman who thinks that you and I are together and having a baby. She'd never come between—"

"We are, and she did. Got anything else before you explain to me what you're doing marrying that…that *woman* when you promised you'd have nothing to do with her?"

"Calm the hell down, Lex." Griffin kept his voice low. People were giving them space, but they were listening to their every word. "We weren't getting married. Look around, it's a fashion show."

She frowned. Then a touch of pink flushed her cheeks. "Oh, I…" She shrugged. "What was I supposed to think?"

That was Lex. She'd never apologize or admit when she was wrong. It used to drive him nuts, but it was doing more than that now. "Really? Because I routinely lie to you and don't keep my word so of course I'd just up and get married without talking to you about it first."

"God, don't get all sanctimonious on me, Gallagher. Not when it was obvious to everyone what was going on here." She rose up on her toes and stabbed him in the chest with her finger. "You promised to stay away from her."

From behind him, he heard Mia say to Sophie, "Mommy, we have to find Auntie Ava. She has nobody to look after her. No daddy, no mommy, no kids, no nothing. We're her family. She needs us."

"It's okay. Don't cry, baby. I'm sure Nonna and Dorothy are with her. We'll go check on Auntie Ava as soon as we pass out the gift bags and draw the winning raffle tickets. Come on, you can help me. Excuse us," Sophie said quietly, keeping her head down as she brushed past them.

Mia didn't. She stuck out her tongue at Lexi.

Lex rolled her eyes. Always the hard-ass. She didn't care what people thought of her, and she sure as hell wouldn't care that Ava was hurting.

"Could always count on you to make an entrance, Lex," Liam teased, and walked over to give her a hug. Leave it to his baby brother to defuse the situation. He obviously knew Griffin was riding the knife edge of his temper. Liam drew back. "So, looks like you two have been holding out on us."

"Do you mind if we do this somewhere private? I think we've provided enough entertainment for one day," Griffin said, his voice tight with anger and laced with the sarcasm he didn't bother trying to hide.

"You know what, I do mind. You're trying to make me feel bad because your girlfriend is upset and you feel guilty because you went back on your promise."

"No, I didn't. Did I want to? Yep. Was I considering doing just that when you walked in here? You bet. But here's the thing, Lex. I was going to call you first and talk about it. And that was a courtesy because we haven't been a couple in years. You're my best friend, and I care about you, and your opinion matters to me. But when it comes to Ava, you have your head so far up your ass you can't—"

A heavy hand came down on his shoulder. "That's enough, Griffin," his father said, then went to Lexi and pulled her in for a hug, saying something to her in a low, soothing voice.

Whatever his dad said seemed to cheer her up, a small smile touching her lips as she nodded. And that made Griffin nervous. But it was nothing compared to how he felt when his grandmother did the same. Whatever Kitty said to Lexi caused his ex to meet his gaze with a familiar look in her brown eyes. The same look she got whenever she won an argument or a challenge—self-satisfied and triumphant.

Jasper walked toward them. "I've delivered Miss Lexi's bags to your room, Master Griffin," the old man said, shooting Griffin a hard stare that softened when he looked at Lexi. "After your long drive, I thought you might be hungry, miss. There's a tray of refreshments awaiting you."

"Thanks, Jasper. That was very thoughtful."

Griffin thought his head might explode if he stayed there much longer. "If you guys don't mind, Lex and I have to talk."

Surprisingly, she didn't argue with him. Probably because she figured his family would now be on his case, which his dad more or less proved when he said, "Griffin, we'll be in the study waiting for you."

"You'll be waiting awhile. I have something to take care of first." Ava. If he'd thought Lex'd show up like this, he would have told Ava about the baby. But he knew, no matter how he broke the news to her, it was going to hurt. He'd wanted to put that off for as long as possible. And because he had…

"It wasn't a suggestion. It was an order," his father clipped out.

Griffin opened his mouth to set his old man straight, then closed it when he saw the uncompromising expression on his father's face. Beside him, Lexi snorted a laugh.

"Glad you find it amusing, Lex," Griffin said as they

walked out of the ballroom. The bridal fair attendees were gathered in the lobby.

A touch of regret shadowed her eyes, and then she lifted her chin. "It's not my fault your family's ticked at you because you're making an ass out of yourself over a woman who dumped you more than a decade ago."

"You're the one making this about Ava. It has nothing to do with her, and you know it. This is about you and me and the baby. Maybe, if you hadn't made such a big deal about keeping your pregnancy a secret, we could have avoided this. It might have been nice if you let me know you were planning to visit, Lex." He pushed the button on the elevator.

"I'm not visiting. I got an offer on the house that I couldn't refuse. So I packed up my stuff, and here I am."

"And you didn't think you should tell me? What about your job?"

"I don't know why you're making such a big deal out of this. You were all for the idea before you moved back." There was something desperate about the way she added, "You can't change your mind now. This is happening. We're doing this. It's important for the baby to have family nearby. He'll—"

"He'll? We're having a boy?" Griffin hadn't let himself think about the baby. He didn't want to get his hopes up again. But hearing he was having a son suddenly made it all seem real, and he felt a small measure of excitement stirring inside him.

Lexi stepped inside the elevator and nodded. He frowned at what sounded like a sniff. He followed her inside the elevator, took her by the shoulders, and turned her around. "Lex, honey, is something wrong with the baby?" He ducked to look her in the eyes.

She swiped at her damp cheeks. "No, he's doing great. The doctor says he's going to be a big, healthy boy."

"Why are you crying then?" Probably a stupid question after what just went down in the ballroom, but Lexi rarely cried.

She scowled at him. "I'm not crying. I'm mad at you. You spoiled my surprise and made me feel like you didn't want me here. Didn't want us here." She touched her rounded belly.

"I'm sorry." He took her in his arms and kissed the top of her head. "We'll work it out. Everything will be fine."

She'd been right earlier. None of this was her fault. He should have told Ava and explained the situation. Eased Lexi into the idea that Ava would be a part of his life. Waited until the baby had arrived and they'd settled into a routine. Who was he trying to kid? He couldn't have stayed away from Ava if he wanted to.

Lexi drew back. "Just don't expect me to have anything to do with that woman."

"That's going to be a little tough, babe. Ava works here."

"So she can get a job somewhere else. I don't want to run into her every time I turn around. It shouldn't be that difficult for her to get one. She's just a maid."

Chapter Sixteen

♥

Griffin walked up to the side door of the white bungalow on South Shore Road. It looked different than he remembered. The house might be small and modest, but Gino's pride of ownership had always shone through. So had Ava's love for the gardens that her mother had started decades before. Now the house just looked unloved and uncared for with its peeling paint, crumbling sidewalk, and a roof in obvious need of repair. There was no sign of the gardens under the small patches of snow. Ava must have given up on them too.

The last memory Griffin had of being in the house was a late August morning before Ava went back to school and he deployed. It'd been about six months before she'd asked for a divorce. A warm breeze had been blowing off the harbor, ruffling the white lacy curtains and filling the house with the scent of lavender and basil from the herb garden in the flower boxes outside the kitchen window. Gino had already left for work, and Ava had been making Griffin breakfast, experimenting with some kind of omelet. It didn't matter what she made, it was always amazing.

She'd been laughing herself sick over something as she stood by the stove with sunlight dancing in her long, curly hair, her eyes lit up and her skin tanned and glowing. He couldn't remember what it was that made her laugh, probably because he'd been looking at her and thinking how crazy beautiful she was and how much he loved her and how he couldn't wait for the day when they were living together full-time.

Ava had only been eighteen when they married, and he hadn't felt right asking her to move away from her family and friends with a baby on the way and him set to deploy. And then she'd lost the baby, and he felt she needed their support even more. So when she decided to go to school for her nursing degree and received a scholarship from the university in Boston, they'd both agreed she should accept. She'd spent long weekends and holidays with him in Virginia or at one of the cottages at the manor when he was on leave. It wasn't perfect, but they'd made the best of it. That August morning they'd been planning their future, counting down the days until she'd finish her degree. Only none of those plans came to fruition. He never did get to eat the omelet either.

He shook off the memories as the door started to open and Rosa appeared. Afraid she'd slam the door in his face when she saw who it was, he raised his hand. "I have to see her and explain."

She stepped back. Dorothy was at the table and gave

him a wan smile. "I hope you can get through to her, Griffin. She's—"

"I've only seen her like this twice before, the day her mother died and the day she lost the baby. Her heart, it's broken." Rosa sat down, placing an elbow on the table to rest her face in her palm. Until that moment, he'd never thought of her as old.

If he'd been worried about Ava before, he was doubly so now. "Is she in her room?"

Reaching across the table to pat Rosa's hand, Dorothy nodded. "Don't give her a chance to turn you away. Just go in."

He strode through the house, barely registering the changes as he made his way to Ava's bedroom. Her room looked the same as he remembered. Ava lay on top of the double wedding ring quilt her mother had made for her daughter before she died. She'd used fabric from Ava's summer dresses and her own to make the colorful rings. Ava used to bring it with her when she came to visit him. She was curled on her side away from him, still wearing the wedding gown. He started across the room, and then his eyes caught the framed photos on her nightstand, and he couldn't move.

He stared at their wedding photo, at a picture of him surfing, one of Ava pregnant with him standing behind her, his arms around her. He half turned to her dresser, almost afraid to look. It was the same as her nightstand, covered with framed photos of them, her mother and father, Griffin's mother and sister. Something told him that the photos weren't recent additions, and his legs went weak at the thought. He reached for the edge of the bed, slowly lowering himself onto it.

The movement must have alerted Ava to his presence because she turned. She looked like she'd cried herself to sleep. "What are you doing here? You shouldn't be here," she said, her voice husky and tinged with panic.

The way her eyes darted from him to the nightstand, he didn't think the panic had anything to do with Lexi. Ava didn't want him to see the photos. His head was spinning with what that seemed to imply. Something inside him said to let it go. That he didn't really want to know.

But he couldn't let it go and leaned over to pick up their wedding photo, the one of her pregnant. "Why, baby? I don't understand. If you didn't love me anymore, why would you have all these pictures of us, of me?"

Some of the pain, the frustration from the past, leaked into his voice. He'd deleted their photos from his computer and his phone. Boxed up the others, along with his memories of the moments, and put them away.

"It doesn't matter anymore. You have a wife and a baby on the way." She rolled onto her back, swiping away the tear that slid off her cheek and into her hair. "You should have told me," she said, her gaze on the photos in his hands. "It was wrong. What we did and said, it was wrong."

He was close to losing it, walking a tightrope between hope and fear, frustration and relief. "Lexi and I aren't married. We've been divorced for more than three years."

He felt the need to reiterate that even though she knew exactly how long it'd been. Then he explained the promise he'd made to Lex the night they'd met up to sign the divorce papers, sharing some laughs and a bottle of wine. He shared a bit about how the baby came to be. Not enough to make either of them uncomfortable, but enough that she'd understand that he hadn't done anything wrong. He ended with the reasoning behind their decision to move back to Harmony Harbor and raise their son. "I should have told you, but Lexi wanted to keep it quiet until she was further along. If I'd known she was coming today, I wouldn't have waited."

"You're going to get the baby boy you always wanted," she said, a soft, wistful smile on her face. She lifted her gaze from the photo in his hand. "I'm happy for you. You'll be a wonderful papa."

And there it was, the reason he'd put off telling her. "I wish—"

She reached over, giving his hand a gentle squeeze. "Don't. It wasn't meant to be. You've got a second chance. Enjoy every precious moment of it."

The doctors hadn't been able to find a reason as to why their baby boy was stillborn. But they did discover that the doctor who'd delivered the baby via C-section hadn't been qualified to do the surgery. Ava not only lost the baby that night, but she'd also lost the ability to conceive another one.

He looked down at the photo in his hand, of Ava heavy with their child, her beautiful, radiant smile. "I will, but it doesn't mean I can or want to forget what we almost had. He's a part of me too."

She nodded, her small smile forced as she fought back tears. So brave, so good, so kind. He placed the photos on the nightstand and stood to remove the black jacket from Tie the Knot. He hadn't taken the time to change after the meeting with his family. As he was reminded of the conversation with his dad and grandmother, the anger that had been riding him since Lexi arrived spiked.

His grandmother had all but chased down Father O'Malley, and his father hadn't been far behind. The only thing that had kept Griffin from losing it on them was his baby brother, who'd acted as the voice of reason. At least in Colin's and Kitty's presence. Liam had kinda blown it when he'd walked Griffin to his truck. His brother had appointed himself Lexi's protector. Liam didn't know Griffin's ex as well as he did. There was only one woman who needed protection, and she was lying in the bed looking up at him.

"What are you doing?" she asked as he toed off the black dress shoes.

He carefully moved the reams of flowered fabric. "I'm hoping to do what I've wanted to since I moved back to town," he said, and lay down beside her. "I forgot how small your bed was."

She shifted onto her hip. He took it as a good sign when she rested her cheek on his chest and didn't object to his arm going around her. "You used to say it was cozy."

He laughed. "I lied. Now"—he gently tipped her face up with two fingers—"let's get the hard stuff out of the way so we can get to the good stuff."

"Can we reverse the order?" she asked, placing her hand on his stomach.

Holding her gaze, he moved his fingers along her jaw until they tangled in the mass of her long, dark curls. He touched his mouth to her soft lips, smiling against them at her sweet, breathy sigh. He drew back just enough to look in her eyes. "You aren't trying to distract me, are you?"

Slowly smoothing her hand up his stomach to his chest, she gave a tiny negative shake of her head and stroked her fingers in the opening at his neck. "I didn't put the photos away because I wanted you, us, to be the first thing I saw when I opened my eyes in the morning and the last thing I saw when I closed them at night. I never stopped loving you. I never will." She lowered her head to replace her fingers with her warm lips.

He lay there, unable to speak, unable to move. He'd been trained to act quickly, efficiently, eliminate the threat without thought or emotion. That last month with Ava all those years before he'd been in a battle—for her and for her heart. He hadn't known who or what he was fighting. He'd done everything, tried everything, and still he'd failed, both her and himself.

She lifted her hand to stroke his face, pressing her mouth to the underside of his jaw. Her lips trembled against his skin, a hot tear splashing on his neck, and then she trailed small kisses all the way to his ear and whispered, "It wasn't your fault. You did nothing wrong. There was nothing more you could have done to help me. I had to help myself."

Her admission cut the thread that had been holding his anger in check, unlocking his muscles, his voice. "No, all you had to do was let me in. We said the vows, made the promise to be there for each other in sickness and in health, in the good times and in the bad. That's the promise I made to you, Ava." He cleared the emotion from his throat, his eyes burning. "You didn't let me keep it. I shouldn't have let you go. Should have fought harder."

"I tried to fight. I did fight, but I wasn't strong enough. I never meant to break my vows. I never meant to break my promise to you." Her fingers clutched his shirt, her eyes desperate and pleading. "I loved you. I love you. You are the only man I've ever loved. You have to believe me. You have to—"

She was beside herself, almost beyond reason. Why couldn't he have just left it alone? He pulled her into his arms and rocked her. "Shh, it's okay, baby. It's over. It was a long time ago. We'll put it behind us, okay? We'll start over." His gut twisted as he remembered what a mess he'd been when he'd lost her. He couldn't go through that again. Smoothing his hand down her hair, he rubbed her back, waiting until he felt the tension release. "Ava, baby, look at me a minute."

Her groan vibrated against his chest, and then she raised her head. "You said we were putting it behind us."

He smiled. Her reaction was more typical of the woman he remembered. He took her face in his hands and kissed her long and deep, feeling a little panicked as his need for her almost overrode the need to protect his heart. He slowly drew back, searching her face, relieved to see the color in her cheeks and the dazed and heated look in her heavily lidded eyes.

"We are putting the past behind us. I won't bring it up again. But before we do, I need one promise from you."

She gave him a wary look. "What?"

He kissed her again, a little longer, a little deeper, and then like she had done to him, trailed his lips along her delicate jaw to her ear. He gently nipped the lobe, then soothed it with a kiss before whispering, "All I ask is that, if you ever feel yourself slipping, you have to talk to me. You can't try and deal with it on your own. If it happens again, we'll deal with it together and see a professional. I talked to Doc Bishop about it, and he thinks it wasn't just one thing that led to your depression."

She pushed herself onto her knees. "You talked to Dr. Bishop about me?"

"Yeah, when you ended up in the hospital for exhaustion," he said defensively. "And don't tell me it wasn't my place because—"

Her face softened. "It's okay. I understand why you did and why you're worried. But you don't have to be. It won't happen again. But I promise, if I have any concerns at all, I'll talk to you about it. And I'll talk to Dr. Bishop."

"You won't try to diagnose yourself again? Because, babe, you have a tendency to think you know better than the doctors."

She arched an eyebrow, took his arm, and unbuttoned the cuff, pushing it up to reveal the thick scar on his forearm. "The quack stitched this," she said, referring to the medic on the base. Leaning in, she traced the barely visible scar that bisected his eyebrow. "I stitched this."

He laughed, pulling her on top of him. "Okay, so you're good at taking care of other people, just not yourself." Wasn't that the truth, he thought, thinking about her father. But right now he wanted to stop thinking about anyone else but them. "Time for the good stuff now?" He waggled his eyebrows, trying to make light of a moment he'd been dreaming about for years.

"Ava, Griffin, the lasagna is ready," Rosa called through the door.

"We'll be right there, Auntie Rosa." Ava smiled when he groaned his frustration. "The good stuff will have to wait. She needs to know I'm okay. I worried her." She got off the bed. "Would you mind undoing me?"

"Is that a trick question?" he asked, coming to stand behind her. He moved her hair over her shoulder, pressing his lips to her nape. "You never looked more beautiful than you did today, Ava. That song was for you. I meant every word."

She shivered as he trailed his fingers up and down her bare back, then turned her face to look up at him. "Will you stay with me tonight?"

"There's nowhere else I'd rather be."

Ava had a feeling Griffin would rather be anywhere else than at her kitchen table being grilled by her Auntie Rosa.

"So, you're in love with our Ava again. Is that what you're telling me?"

He wasn't the only one who'd rather be anywhere but here.

Griffin looked across the table at Ava, his dimple deepening in his cheek. "No, not again. I never stopped loving her."

In a way, she was surprised Rosa even had to ask with the meaningful glances Griffin had been sending Ava's way since they sat down. Despite looking like a hot mess with her bloodshot eyes and disheveled hair, Griffin hadn't taken his eyes off her.

Rosa patted his arm. "Okay, now I understand."

Looking pleased that he'd finally gotten through to her aunt, Griffin started eating again.

Rosa leaned down and came up with her cell phone in her hand. As she typed impressively fast with two thumbs, she said, "You were married on the beach last time, so this time, maybe in the church, *sí*?" She waved her hand at what must have been Ava and Griffin's slack-jawed expressions. "It's okay, Kitty and I will look after the detail—"

Griffin choked on his lasagna while reaching for her aunt's phone. "Don't send—" He groaned at the sound of a message being sent.

"What's the matter with you?" Rosa crossed her arms. "You don't want to marry our Ava?"

"Rosa, they've just gotten back together and, well, Griffin is expecting a baby with his other wife. It might be best if they waited...All right, don't mind me," Dorothy said when Rosa shot her a dirty look.

Ava understood Griffin's reaction to the thought of marriage not more than thirty minutes after they declared their love for one another, but she had to admit to being a little hurt by it. She also didn't appreciate being reminded of his *other wife*. Which might have been why she said, "Griffin and I have no plans to marry. Not now, not ever."

He put down his fork and cocked his head. "Is that right? Maybe I'm missing something because I don't remember having that conversation."

"We didn't need to. Your reaction said it all."

"Ava, honey, you don't understand what Rosa telling Grams—"

"Now look what you've done. You hurt her feelings, and she breaks off the engagement."

"We're not engaged," Ava and Griffin said at almost the same time, although Ava's denial was more vehement than his.

"Would anyone like a cup of...I guess not," Dorothy said when they all shot her a look.

Rosa's phone pinged with a message, and then Griffin's phone rang. He looked at the screen and rejected the call.

"Who does she think she is telling me not to interfere?" Rosa gasped, staring at Griffin. "She says you're marrying the mother of your child."

"I'm not marrying anyone. Oh, for Chrissakes," he said when his phone rang again. Griffin looked at the screen. "Sorry, I have to take this." He pushed back from the table and got up, walking into the living room. "Hey, is everything…Calm down, Lex. I'm not getting…All right, that's enough. Yeah, I am, and…"

Ava couldn't make out any more of the conversation. Griffin had walked down the hall. She got the gist of it though, and it left her with a queasy feeling in her stomach.

"We should go. Griffin and Ava need some time alone, Rosa."

Her aunt waved Dorothy off without lifting her head, her thumbs flying over the keys. Ava had lost count of the zings and pings going back and forth between Rosa and Kitty.

Ava got up and began clearing the table. She needed something to keep her mind off Griffin's conversation with Lexi and her aunt's war of words with Kitty. To think, only a month ago, she'd been upset about Kitty matchmaking, and now she was upset that she wasn't. Well, she was, just not for her and Griffin. Ava didn't want to think what life would be like at the manor now that Griffin's ex was here to stay.

"Lovey, we're leaving now," Dorothy said, half lifting Rosa from the chair. She took the phone from Rosa's hand. "Stop that. You're going to make matters worse for Ava."

Ava didn't think they could get much worse. She didn't say that to Rosa or Dorothy though. Despite the doubts roiling around inside her, she put on a brave face and said goodbye, assuring them she was fine. Obviously Rosa saw through her and pulled her in for a fierce hug. "You are a DiRossi. You don't let them push you around, *capisci*?"

"Auntie Rosa, don't renew your feud with Kitty over this. Just let it go." Before Sophie had moved back home, the two older women had been in a bitter feud for years. They'd put their differences aside to save Greystone and bring Liam and Sophie together. Until now, they seemed to have renewed their childhood friendship. They'd once been best friends.

"No, you don't mess with one of mine and get away with it. I'll show her. I've called a secret meeting of the Widows Club to discuss revoking her membership."

She tried to talk Rosa out of it, but it was no use. Ava needed to warn Sophie that the feud was back on. Closing the door, she pressed her forehead against it.

"Run away with me," Griffin said from behind her, wrapping his arms around her.

She wished they could go away, even for a few days. She wanted time alone with him, just the two of them. No fighting families and no…"We can't. You have responsibilities, a baby on the way." She ignored the dull ache in her chest. She'd hadn't been lying earlier; she truly was happy for him. But it hurt, just a little, that Lexi was the one giving him his heart's desire and not her.

She felt his chest rise against her back, his warm breath ruffling her hair. Then he pulled out a chair from the table, sat down, and drew her onto his lap. He gathered her in his arms and rested his chin on the top of her head. "I'd be lying to you if I said this was going to be easy, babe."

"Lexi decided she wants you to marry her, hasn't she?" Ava was surprised she got the words past the lump in her throat. What if she got him back only to lose him again? She hadn't been surprised when Griffin told her he'd offered to marry Lexi. She would have been more surprised if he hadn't. He was an honorable man. Lexi refusing? That had been a shock. Ava didn't understand how any woman who'd been loved by Griffin Gallagher wouldn't have immediately jumped at the chance to get him back.

"No, once Lexi makes a decision, she doesn't change her mind. About anything. And therein lies our problem. Because, honey, she doesn't like you very much."

It didn't escape Ava's notice that he didn't say, even if Lexi had changed her mind, the offer of marriage was off the table. She refused to let the thought get a toehold in her mind. They had enough to deal with. "But she doesn't know me."

"I'm not saying this to hurt your feelings, but you need to know what we're up against. My brothers and father weren't exactly your biggest fans after we split up. Aidan, and especially Finn, blamed you, unfairly, for a lot of the crap I went through. They shared that with Lex."

He might not have meant to hurt her feelings, but he did. "Your mom didn't blame me. She still loved me," she said defensively.

His arms tightened around her. "I know she did, honey. She used to bring you up every time I talked to her. She was worried about you."

"I think she'd be happy we're back together."

He lifted her hand to his mouth, kissing her palm. "I know she would be. That's something we'll hold on to when everyone else is giving us grief. We're in for a rough week or two, and it's going to be toughest on you because you work at the manor."

"Maybe if I talk to Lexi and try—"

"Sweet face, she'd eat you alive."

Ava crossed her arms. "I'm not a wimp, you know. I can stand up for myself." She supposed she could see why he might think she couldn't though. She hadn't done a very good job of standing up for herself the past few years.

He laughed. "You forgetting I was married to you? I know you're strong when you need to be. But Lex, she's a military cop and as tough as they come. The woman will never admit she's wrong or back down from a fight. She's a protector; you're a caregiver. There's a difference."

"I can be tough when I want to be. I—"

He gently pressed a finger against her lips "What you are is the kindest, most caring woman I know. You have a way with people. You have a way with me. I've missed you, sweet face. I don't want to waste any more time talking. I want you naked and in my arms." He stood up, taking her with him. "Interested?"

She waited for her pulse to become erratic, for sweat to slick her hands and body, for the paralyzing fission of nerves to hit her limbs at the thought of Griffin touching her, making love to her. But there was nothing except a warm sensation low in her stomach, heavy and needy. She looped her arms around his neck and tipped her face up. "I might need a little persuading."

If she didn't know him as well as she did, she would have missed the small telltale sign that he was worried, the way he mentally took her pulse, searching her face without seeming to. She wasn't the only one who remembered how their last weeks together had been. She needed him to know she was all right, for both their sakes.

She reached up, sealing her lips over his. She didn't take it slow or give it to him sweet. The kiss was hot and wet and long and deep. With every nip, lick, and slide, she gave him a taste of the love she'd been stockpiling since the day she'd left him.

She slowly broke the connection. "Okay, I'm interested."

They'd gotten no farther than the living room, and he leaned against the wall, his breathing labored. "I think…I think I forgot to mention you were also the most passionate woman I know, and one hell of a good time in bed."

"We probably should see if I still am," she said, laughing when he practically ran to her bedroom and tossed her on the mattress.

It was her old laugh. Big and joyful, and totally absent of worry and fear.

Chapter Seventeen

♥

Everything was going to hell in a handbasket. Colleen didn't know if she should be throwing her support behind Ava or Lexi. She'd always been a sucker for the underdog, and if anyone was an underdog in the game that was in play, it was Ava. But Lexi was carrying a Gallagher. In Colleen's eyes, that meant she and Griffin should be tied together in holy matrimony. Granted, things had changed since her time. Kids nowadays seemed to put the cart before the horse. They had their babies and then got married. Or didn't.

It had taken no arm twisting at all on Griffin's part to get Ava to marry him when they'd discovered they had a baby on the way. And what a heartbreak that had turned out to be.

"Ava, my girl, you've withstood more heartache than most," Colleen murmured, recalling the shattered expression on Ava's face when Lexi, bold as brass, arrived at the manor. That decided it for Colleen. She was captain of Team Ava. She'd not allow the girl to be hurt any more than she already had been. With one quandary settled, she moved on to the next. And it was a doozy.

Twenty minutes earlier, Gaston St. John had summoned the family to the dining room and made his big announcement. He was now firmly established as King of the Kitchen with the news. Sophie's appointment with the lawyer was off, and the food war between the manor and the Bridgeport Marquis was on.

Basil Brisiel had agreed to judge, along with two up-and-coming chefs from celebrated New England restaurants. Basil and his producer fiancée planned to air video clips of each competition—of which there were three—on their popular social media pages. Chronicling Greystone's spectacular failure for all the world to see.

In Colleen's mind, there was only one way to save the manor from a PR nightmare they'd unlikely recover from anytime soon. Unless she figured out a way to replace Gaston with Ava, all the business they'd drummed up at the bridal show would disappear.

As Colleen had discovered, the lad didn't scare off easily. Though it probably had more to do with her inability to move things around and make her presence known. She had to get better at this ghost gig, and she had to do it fast. The first round of the competition was in two days' time.

Jasper fussed with an elaborate floral arrangement on the round table in the entryway, eyeing it from several angles to make sure it was just so. No doubt about it, the lad loved his flowers.

Colleen grinned. "Jasper's been messing with me; it

seems only fair I mess with him. What do you think, Simon?"

Meow.

"All right, here it goes." Focusing, visualizing the result she wanted, Colleen pinched a lily between her fingers. They didn't go through the flower. "Half the battle's won, Simon," she crowed, and got a testy meow in response. "Quiet now. You have to celebrate the small victories." Small might be the answer. Instead of the entire flower, she moved her fingers to the petal and tugged. The white petal fell from the stem to the table. "I did it!" she cried.

Jasper frowned, bending down to study the lily, then narrowed his eyes at where she was standing. "If that was your handiwork, Madame, I suggest you find something else to occupy your time."

"Ha." She focused her energy and latched onto a rose. "Give me back my book, and I'll think about it." A red petal fluttered to the table. She chuckled with delight and kept plucking.

"Stop that this instant, Madame." Jasper picked up the vase and clutched it to his chest. The front door began to open, and he set the vase back down, casting a warning look in her direction. His mouth compressed in a thin line of disapproval when Griffin and Ava walked into the manor together. They had eyes for only each other, their pinkie fingers latched together. Griffin hadn't looked this relaxed and happy in Colleen didn't know how long. Wait, she did. It was when he was married to Ava. If Colleen hadn't already made her decision to support Ava, the look on her great-grandson's face would have decided it for her. On Ava's too—the girl was beaming.

Of course Jasper would go and ruin it. "Master Griffin, the rest of your things arrived this morning. I've taken the liberty of opening the second bedroom in Madame's suite for the nursery, and I'm having another bureau moved into the master bedroom for your use. I'm afraid I had to move your clothes to accommodate your wife's. I hope that meets with your—"

Colleen pushed the vase in a fit of pique, shocked when it wobbled and water sloshed over the side. Jasper's eyes went wide. He lifted his hand to hold it in place.

Griffin laced his fingers through Ava's. "Don't worry about unpacking for me, Jeeves. I'm moving out after work."

"I see. Do you have a preference to which floor—"

"I'm moving out of the manor and into the lighthouse."

Jasper lifted his chin. "Have you spoken to Miss Kitty and Sophie about your plans? They may have other parties interested in—"

"Good try. I've already cleared it with George. And, Jeeves, you might want to remember who you're dealing with." He turned to Ava, briefly touching his mouth to hers, and said, "I better get going or I'll be late for work. Meet me at the lighthouse after your shift. We'll—"

Jasper tapped his watch. "Miss DiRossi is already late. Sophie is waiting on you in the study."

"I'll see you later," Ava said to Griffin, going up on her tiptoes as though to kiss his cheek. Jasper cleared his throat. Ava patted Griffin's chest instead and then made her way toward the study.

Colleen gave the vase another frustrated push, blinking when once again water sloshed over the edges and onto the table. "Would you look at that, Simon? I think I've got it," she said, somewhat shocked she'd managed it twice in a row.

"You're walking a fine line, old man," Griffin said to Jasper before calling after Ava, "If any of them give you trouble, sweet face, you know who to call."

Jasper steadied the vase, muttering under his breath, "I know who I'd call. The ghostbusters."

"Jeeves," Griffin called over his shoulder as he walked away. "You might want to put a shim under the table."

"You better be careful, Jasper, my boy. The better I get at this, the more trouble I'll cause for you. Especially if you try stirring it up between Ava and Griffin. Though, from the looks of those two, it would take a better man than you to…" Then Colleen remembered. It wasn't a man she had to worry about; it was a woman. She hurried down the hall toward the study, wondering if Sophie had broken the news to Ava.

Ava sat across from Sophie. "I understand the competition is a coup for Greystone and why you felt you had to keep Gaston on. What I don't understand is why Lexi is providing security for him. What does that even mean?"

Colleen grimaced and took the seat beside Ava. Simon padded into the room to sit at her feet. "This isn't going to go well, Tomcat."

"Lexi gets bored easily, I guess. So she asked us to give her a job. She loves the manor." Sophie smiled over her coffee cup at her cousin, then took a drink, looking like she'd rather be anywhere than here.

Ava snorted.

"No, she really does. She promised to do whatever it takes to get Griffin…" Sophie sighed and put the mug down. "I get why you don't like her, but she's actually very nice. If you gave her a chance you…Um, okay, maybe not. Anyway, she's going to do her best to convince Griffin to vote to keep Greystone in the family. That's what we all want, right? So it doesn't really matter who convinces him—"

"I don't understand what any of this has to do with her providing personal security for Gaston?"

"Well…um, Gaston is a good chef, but you, you're amazing. Your hors d'oeuvres, they were to die for. Everyone said so."

"Ava's no fool, Sophie, my girl. You're going about this all wrong. Look at her face. You can't butter her up."

"So I'm the better chef. What does that have to do with Lexi…" Ava's eyes went wide. "Me, it's me she's protecting him from, isn't it? And whose idea was that?"

"Here we go. You might want to cover your ears, Simon. I know they're sensitive."

Sophie shuffled the papers on her desk and mumbled, "Lexi may have suggested it."

Ava made an aggravated sound in her throat, and Sophie hurriedly added, "But only after Gaston told her about you ruining his hors d'oeuvres and writing out the wrong recipes for Helga to follow." Sophie put up her hands. "Don't yell at me. I had your back. I told Lexi flat out there was no evidence to prove you had anything to do with it. But then Jasper and Kitty questioned your innocence…

"Crap, I didn't mean to tell you that. Double crap! I didn't mean to say that either. Oh God, I hate this." Sophie did a face-plant on the stack of papers on her desk.

"It's too bad I dropped dead before I had a chance to

work with you, Sophie. You're making a hash of this, you truly are. Keep it up, and Lexi and Ava will be at each other's throats in no time at all."

Sophie lifted her gaze. "Aren't you going to say anything?"

Ava pressed her lips together and shook her head.

This was worse than Colleen expected, but she supposed she shouldn't be surprised Ava was more hurt than angry. They were all turning against her in support of Lexi. "I'm here for you, my girl. I just wish I could give you a sign." She might not be able to comfort Ava, but she knew someone who could. "Simon, do your chin-up trick."

Simon padded to Ava and nudged her leg. When she looked down at him, he lifted his chin. Ava leaned over and picked him up. Cuddling him to her chest, she scratched behind his ears. Simon closed his eyes on a contented purr with what looked to be a lusty smile on his face. Colleen had created a monster.

Oddly enough, the thought made her think of Lexi. Oddly, because the girl was far from a monster. There was something going on with her though. The way she was acting about Ava was out of character. Colleen didn't know why Griffin didn't see it. It would be a different story if Lexi was *in* love with Griffin. She loved him, but more like a brother or best friend, someone she needed to protect. Thanks to Finn and Aidan, Lexi no doubt felt Griffin needed her protection from Ava. But the old Lexi wouldn't have been so quick to judgment. If she'd only give Ava a chance to show her what she was made of and how much she loved Griffin...

An idea came to Colleen. "Ava, my girl, I think I've

found a way to help you. I'm going to have a little chat with Lexi every night like I did Griffin. I won't let up until I've convinced her you're the one for him." She reached over to pat Ava's thigh, only to realize the girl was standing. "What did I miss, Simon?"

"Please reconsider, Ava. We can't afford to lose this competition. We need you in the kitchen too."

"Wait? She said no? How could she say no? We need her. Greystone needs her."

"I'm sorry, Sophie. I promised Griffin I wouldn't go anywhere near Lexi. Even if I hadn't made the promise, I couldn't work in the kitchen with her watching my every move."

For two days, Ava had managed to avoid Lexi. It wasn't easy. She could have sworn the woman was stalking her, trying to force a confrontation. Good thing Ava knew the manor better than she did. Which came in handy right now. Ava was hidden in the closet in the dining room, talking to Erin through a crack in the door.

"Helga cooked the green beans like you said, but Gaston told her to add more honey and maple syrup. She wants to know what you think." Pretending to tie her apron, Erin passed a green bean through the crack.

Ava took a bite, closing her eyes to savor the flavor. "The man needs to have his taste buds checked. It's perfect. Tell Helga to tell Gaston she did as he asked and to keep him away from the pan."

"Okay." There was a commotion toward the front of the restaurant and Erin stretched on her toes, leaning to her right. "They're here. One of the judges is pretty cute. I wish I was serving. Yikes. Lexi glanced this way, and she looks suspicious. I better…Oh, I almost forgot, how much balsamic vinegar was supposed to be in the reduction?"

Ava inched the door open. Lexi's long, side-swept bang fell over one of her eyes, but the other one was looking their way. She wore stylish cognac boots over her jeans and a black sweater with a pretty fringed black-and-blue scarf. "She doesn't look suspicious, she looks constipated," Ava said tartly, then remembered what Erin had asked. "Half a cup if he's cooking four steaks." Basil's wife had been added as a judge. One of her assistants was doing the filming.

"Oh. My. God. Ava, I'm pretty sure Helga said Gaston told her to use a cup."

"Why is he having Helga do the sides and reduction? He should be preparing the entire entrée. It's a competition, not a regular night in the dining room."

"He was making red velvet cupcakes and then changed to black-bottom cupcakes. He's kind of obsessed with desserts."

"Who's cooking the steaks?" Ava asked, a nervous hitch in her voice.

"The new sous chef. He looks like he knows what he's doing except…"

Because of the number of bookings from the bridal show, Sophie had hired the sous chef. Gaston had tried to fire him yesterday, but Sophie had overridden him. "Except what?"

"Gaston told him to blacken the bottom of the steaks. Kind of like a theme thing with his dessert. This isn't good, is it, Ava?"

She shook her head. "The only way Greystone stands

a chance of winning is if the Marquis's chef is worse than ours."

Two hours later, they found out the Marquis's chef was much better than theirs. Ava, Helga, and Erin were sitting in the break room watching the videos that had been uploaded to Basil's Facebook page. Helga slumped in the chair. "Look at Gaston pointing at me and the kid. The weasel threw us under the bus. He's trying to get us fired before the next round."

The three of them had been standing in front of the judges' table while they sampled the meal. And sample is all they did. All four judges had pushed their plates away after a single bite of the smothered steak topped with sautéed onions, the rosemary potatoes, and sweetened green beans. They ate the entire cupcake, though, pronouncing it divine.

Erin looked at Ava. "You think it's more than that, don't you?"

"I do, and I think it's about time we did some digging into Gaston St. John. We have a little more than a week before the next round."

"Forget digging into him; I'm gonna dig him a grave. On second thought, that's a lot of work. You two can dig the grave, and I'll choke him to death," Helga said.

As a way to ease their frustration and disappointment at the loss, they started coming up with more creative ways to get rid of Gaston.

"Wait, wait, I've got a better one," Erin said once they'd stopped laughing at Helga's suggestion to put a raw turkey over his head and sew it shut.

Erin's better idea took her five minutes to explain. It was kinky and involved ropes. "I don't even want to know how you came up with that. But simple is best. We snip some wolfsbane leaves into his salad. He'll die of asphyxiation just like that." Ava snapped her fingers. Helga looked at her, making an odd noise. "Yes, that's close to what he'd sound like, I think. The postmortem will blame an arrhythmia." Erin's foot tapped hers. "Yes, something like that, just faster...more like this." She tapped her foot on Erin's. "And that, ladies, is how you get away with"—Erin kicked her—"murder," Ava said, looking over her shoulder. *Crapola.* "Oh, hello, Lexi."

"It's not funny, Griffin. She tried to get me fired because of a joke!" Ava said into her cell phone as she paced the ramp in front of her house, barely noticing the cold night air that frosted the railing and the grass.

"Babe, I think it had more to do with you orchestrating the cook-off fail from the closet than with your plot to poison Gaston," Griffin responded in a slow drawl that was laced with amusement.

"You know why I was in the closet, and they do too. Helga and Erin told them everything. But who do Kitty and Jasper believe? Gaston and your ex-wife the cop." Ava snorted. "She couldn't solve a case if you spoon-fed her the evidence. If she had half a brain, she'd know who was really behind this." Ava took a long, satisfying drag on her cigarette. She'd given in to its siren call after she'd eaten the two cupcakes she'd snuck from the kitchen at the manor. Sadly, they were divine, and probably a thousand calories each.

"You didn't happen to say all that to Lex, did you?" Even over the phone, she picked up on his concern. Of course he wouldn't want her to upset his pregnant ex.

Ava scowled at the night sky and took another drag of her cigarette. "No, I sat there like a meek little mouse while they grilled me and fired their accusations at me." She blew smoke rings, stabbing the cigarette through each one. "And your *pazza culo* ex looked at me like I wasn't fit to shine her shoes. I hate that woman so much."

"Yeah, kinda getting that, babe. Is that why you're outside smoking?"

She grimaced at the cigarette. "No, I'm—"

A white Coast Guard SUV pulled alongside the road across from the house. Sully grinned at her from the driver's seat and gave her a two-finger salute. "You might want to reconsider what you were going to say," Griffin suggested with a touch of amusement in his voice as he rounded the front of the vehicle. He tucked his cell phone in his jacket pocket and strode across the road.

"I wasn't expecting to see you tonight," she said, her pulse quickening and butterflies taking flight in her stomach at the sight of him in his uniform. Her body reacted the same way every time she saw him. Sometimes she was afraid it was a dream and she'd eventually wake up. She slid her phone in her pocket and dropped her cigarette in the plastic cup of water by the door before running down the ramp. Throwing herself in his arms, she hugged him tight and lifted up on her toes to kiss him.

He leaned back, looking down at her, his blue eyes dancing, his dimple winking at her. "Sorry, babe, you've just had a cigarette in that mouth. I'm not kissing it."

She dropped down with a frown. "You're serious?"

"Yep, I figure that'll be incentive enough for you to quit." He touched his lips to the corner of hers and pulled back with a laugh. "You really are a sweet face," he said, tracing her lips with his thumb. He brought it to his mouth and licked it. "Chocolate."

She made a face. "Your ex is driving me to eat. I had two cupcakes as soon as I got home. I won't be able to fit in my jeans if I keep this up."

He moved his hands to her butt and gave a gentle squeeze. "Works for me." Sully beeped the horn. "I better take off. Just wanted to check and make sure you're okay."

"I'm glad you did. I'm going to miss you tonight." It was their first night apart because Griffin had to work late.

His expression grew serious as he stroked her hair. "I'll miss you too. We've got a lot of lost time to make up for." He looked over when Dorothy's front door opened. "Have fun at book club. Call me when you get home." He gave her a hard, quick kiss on the mouth. "No more smoking. I'll take care of your oral fixation tomorrow. I'm off."

"You look happy, lovey," Dorothy said when she reached her side, waving goodbye to Sully and Griffin.

"I am." She smiled, and then she remembered what had gone on at the manor today. She told Dorothy about it as they walked along Main Street. Rosa met up with them two blocks from Books and Beans.

At the same time Dorothy said, "I hate to say it, lovey, but I was afraid this would happen. You've got yourself in a difficult situation. You can't come between a man and the woman carrying his child."

Rosa slashed her hand in the air. "Foolish old woman. Don't listen to her, *cara*. She's letting her own decisions cloud her eyes."

"Rosa, this isn't the time—" Dorothy began, shooting a sidelong glance at Ava.

"It was your choice not to come back to Harmony Harbor when you found out Maria and Gino were expecting Ava. Your mama did nothing wrong, *cara*. Dot and Gino had decided to take a break when she went away to nursing school."

Ava looked from her aunt to Dorothy. "You dated my father? That's what you were talking about the day I accused you of hating him?"

"Yes, lovey. Gino and I—"

"Dating? They were engaged," Rosa interjected.

"Do you mind? It's my story to tell, Rosa."

"You're too slow. It doesn't matter anyway. This isn't the same. You and Maria were best friends." Rosa hooked her arm through Ava's. "This Lexi, she's hard as nails. So you, you have to be tough too. Mark my words, she has one goal in mind, and that's to break up you and Griffin. You stand up to her. Show her you mean business too."

Ava was still trying to deal with the fact that Dorothy had once been engaged to her father so it took a minute for Rosa's words to sink in. "I promised Griffin I'd stay away from her."

"I think that's a good idea, lovey."

"Eh, you're both *pazze*. You'll see I'm right. And once you do, you better rise to the challenge, *cara*, or that woman will walk all over you. Tonight, I'll show you how it's done. Kitty agreed that we would get you and Griffin together, and now she thinks she can go back on her word? Ha! She has another think coming."

Dorothy leaned into Ava. "Let's hope the only murder we're discussing tonight is the one in the book."

Chapter Eighteen

♥

Ava wasn't thinking about murder when she entered Books and Beans; she was thinking about her mother and Dorothy. "I don't understand how you were able to stay friends with my mother after she stole my father from you. I feel like I should apologize to you somehow," Ava said as they walked through the coffee shop to the bookstore.

"Your aunt has horrible timing. We'll talk about it another day. But you needn't worry your head over it, lovey. If things hadn't turned out the way they did, I never would have met my Rocky. As much as Maria was Gino's soul mate, Rocky was mine. I was just blessed to have him longer than your father had your mother." She lifted her chin to the children's section where the circle of empty chairs waited. "Let's put Rosa between us. That way we can each grab an arm if she goes after Kitty."

"Sophie's coming too. She'll help keep her in line."

Maybe. As Ava had discovered, her cousin wasn't herself these days. She hadn't been all that helpful putting a stop to Lexi and Gaston this afternoon. Then again, Sophie had probably been too busy formulating a strategy to deal with the unhappy couples who'd booked their spring and summer weddings at the manor. The manor's poor performance in the first round of the food wars had gone viral. As a result, two weddings and an engagement party had been canceled.

Ava was distracted from her thoughts by Julia, who walked over to give her a hug. "I'm glad you decided to come. I've missed you the past few mornings. I was worried about you after…well, you know."

No doubt news about the bridal fair's wedding crasher had hit the Harmony Harbor grapevine minutes after it had happened, but it seemed news of her reconciliation with Griffin hadn't. "I'm good. Really good. Griffin and I are back together." She smiled, feeling almost giddy.

It'd been more than a decade since she'd actually had news worthy of sharing with her friends. She'd listened to all of them talk about their love lives for years, and now, finally, she could too. Maybe it was a little high school, but she was glad she'd come. They'd want to hear all about it, all the romantic details, and she was more than happy to share at least some of them. It would be fun. After today, she could use some girl time and fun.

Julia reacted exactly as Ava had hoped. She gave an excited squeal and hugged her again. "I'm so, so happy for you. This is the best news." She frowned. "But how come I'm only hearing about it now?"

"It's just been a couple of days, and we've mostly been at my place or the lighthouse. So it's not like anyone has seen us together." And the ones who did know they were together, like Griffin's family, weren't spreading the news for obvious reasons. Neither had her family.

"Mac, Arianna, Lily, and Zoe are going to go crazy when they hear you two are back together. In their eyes, you guys were the perfect couple. They're going to want the scoop. And speaking of scoop…" Julia pulled Ava toward the chairs and lowered her voice. "I need to ask you a favor."

"Sure. What do you need?"

Julia glanced over her shoulder as though making sure no one was around, then asked, "Did you like the book?"

"I loved it. I was on the edge of my seat the entire time. I didn't want to put it down." It was probably a good thing she'd read the book while she was visiting her father at the hospital. With Griffin home, she wouldn't get much reading done for a while.

"Okay, here's the thing, I need you to pretend you hated it."

"Why? Byron picked the book for this month's read, and his brother's the author. I'm not going to say—"

"He picked it because he thought we'd hate it. And everyone I've talked to has loved it. I can't keep it on the shelf. I don't really know the whole story, but they have this intense rivalry and Byron always ends up on the losing end. Anyway, Poppy says he's going through a difficult time…" Ava cleared her throat as the Hartes approached, nudging her head in their direction.

Julia turned with a smile. "Hi, Byron and Poppy. Why don't you guys all take a seat? Looks like everyone's arriving now, so we'll be starting anytime."

At the steady chime of the front door, Ava glanced toward the coffee shop, waving to her friends who'd just arrived. Ava made out Dana and Sophie in the group of women, but she didn't know who the blonde...Lexi. Griffin's ex was here.

Byron took her arm. "Why don't we get a seat?" He didn't wait for a response, steering Ava toward her aunt and Dorothy. "I take it you weren't counting on your ex's ex being here?"

Ava's body practically vibrated with anger. She couldn't understand why Dana and Sophie would bring Lexi with them. They had to know how uncomfortable it would be for her. "No, no, I didn't," she said as she took the seat beside her aunt.

Rosa looked at her. "What's the matter...What's she doing here?"

Ava was gratified to know that she wasn't the only one who thought it wasn't right Lexi was crashing book club too, but it didn't mean she wanted her aunt to start something. Rosa was already gearing up for a fight, and her aunt's nemesis had just taken the seat beside Lexi. Ava elbowed Rosa and told her in Italian to behave.

Byron took the seat beside Ava and murmured, "Looks like this is going to turn into an interesting evening after all." He grimaced when she glanced at him. "Sorry."

Sophie, who sat on the other side of Lexi, looked across at Ava and made a what-was-I-supposed-to-do? gesture with her hands. Ava pursed her lips, then forced a smile when Mackenzie and Arianna spotted her and came over. They each gave her a quick hug. "We'll chat after, but you're good, right?" Arianna asked.

Ava didn't feel quite so excited about sharing her news now and just smiled and nodded.

"I brought cupcakes," Mackenzie said. "We'll talk after the meeting."

She'd tell them about her and Griffin then. "Sounds good," Ava said, returning Lily and Zoe's waves.

Several members of the Widows Club came in, glancing from Rosa to Kitty. Half sat on Kitty's side, half on Rosa's.

"So, it looks like you two not only have the same taste in men, but you also have the same taste in clothes..." Byron trailed off at what must have been the confused look on Ava's face.

She looked down at the purple and black scarf looped around her neck, the black sweater that hugged her curves, and her jeans that were tucked into her leather boots. Ava was mortified to realize she'd copied Lexi's outfit from this afternoon, the one she still wore.

"Okay, time for a subject change," Byron said when Ava glared at him for noticing and pointing it out. And if he'd noticed, so would...From under her lashes, Ava saw Lexi cross her arms while giving her an up-and-down look.

"You remember Lexi, don't you, Ida? Griffin's wife," Kitty said to Mrs. Fitzgerald, who'd taken the seat beside her.

Ava reached over and squeezed her aunt's hand when Rosa opened her mouth to no doubt correct Kitty's *wife* comment. Ava wanted to correct her too, but not here and now. And she definitely didn't want her aunt to. "No."

Dorothy said and did the same thing to Rosa.

"Of course I do. And when is the blessed event?" Ida asked, nodding at Lexi's baby bump.

Ida had opened the floodgates. Lexi barely had a

chance to respond to one question when another one was asked. No matter how hard Ava tried, she couldn't drown them out.

"Griffin must be over the moon. I hope he's taking good care of his baby mama," someone said.

Ava couldn't take it anymore. She had to leave. And not because she was jealous of Lexi or upset about the baby. Ava knew Griffin loved her, and she wasn't a jealous person to begin with. She was just hurt that these women didn't give her feelings a passing thought.

Rosa pinched Ava's thigh. "Do not let them know your feelings are hurt. Laugh. Now."

"I'm not...ouch. Stop that," she said when Rosa pinched her again. And then her aunt started laughing loudly and rocking in her chair like a crazy person.

Beside Ava, Byron's shoulders shook.

The conversation among the other women trailed off as everyone looked at Rosa, who was still laughing and holding her stomach, bent over at the waist. Ava felt an almost hysterical giggle bubbling in her throat, and then she was laughing too. The tears-streaming-down-your-face kind of laughter.

"If you can't beat 'em, join 'em. Ha, ha, ha, ha." Byron's laugh was so obviously forced and fake that Ava laughed harder.

The women in the chairs on the other side of the circle crossed their arms. "Perhaps you'd like to let us in on the joke," Kitty said.

"You...you are the—"

Dorothy was faster than Ava and covered Rosa's mouth with her hand.

Julia shot up from her chair. "All right, it looks like

everyone's here. Welcome to the first meeting of Harmony Harbor's book club. Truly Scrumptious has provided the snack for this evening. Thank you, Mackenzie." Julia clapped, and everyone joined in. "There'll also be coffee and tea for whoever wants some after the meeting. Now, all of you know Byron." He gave a jaunty wave. "He'll be writing a column every month about our meetings." She cast a nervous glance at Rosa. "So just be aware that some of your comments may end up in the *Gazette*."

Her aunt bent at the waist to catch Byron's eye. "I have some comments for you."

Byron grinned and held up his iPad. "I'm all ears."

"About the book, comments about the book," Julia said. "Okay, would anyone like to start?"

Several hands shot up, and it quickly became apparent that Julia had been right; everyone loved the book. It was as though each word of praise shot an arrow through Byron's heart, and he deflated right before Ava's eyes. She leaned into Rosa and whispered, "You hated the book."

"No, I loved—"

"No, listen to me. You thought it was *crapola*. Tell Dorothy she did too."

Ava straightened in her chair, opening her mouth to share her opinion with the group, but Mrs. Fitzgerald was speaking. "You must have been able to identify with the protagonist, Lexi, seeing as you're an officer of the law."

"What's a protagonist?" Rosa whispered to Ava.

"The main character. Charlotte Bean, the homicide detective."

"Oh, Charlie. I liked…I didn't like her?"

"No, you didn't." And Ava really didn't like her now that everyone was asking Lexi about her experiences as a cop. The whole night had become about Griffin's ex, and for once in her life, Ava had been hoping it would be about her. All she wanted was a few minutes, five minutes at most, to share her big news. And Lexi had stolen that from her.

"Sure Griffin worried about me, but he knew I was good at my job and could take care of myself," Lexi responded to a member of the Widows 'Club, and then laughed. "Well, there was this one time—"

Ava raised her voice to be heard. "I hated the book."

Everyone stopped talking and looked at her.

"It was overwritten. Pretentious and repetitious. There was no plot to speak of, and Sergeant Bean, pfft, so unbelievable it took me right out of the story." She held Lexi's gaze. "She couldn't solve a case if you spoon-fed her the evidence. If she had half a brain, she would have known Darryl Foote was behind the murder in chapter ten. It just dragged on, and on, and on. And the inner dialogue…all she wanted to do was talk about herself. The woman was so full of her—"

"Thank you, Ava," Julia cut her off. "Does anyone else feel like—"

"*Sí*, I do. I didn't mind Charlie, but her grandmother…*Oh, Marone a mi*, such a spoiled, vindictive, backstabbing—"

Byron was taking notes with a small smile playing on his lips.

"Um, thank you, Rosa," Julia intervened, then asked nervously, "Does anyone else…Yes, Dorothy?"

"I feel the same as Ava and—"

Kitty glared at Rosa. "I know exactly what you're doing, Rosa DiRossi. You can't pull the wool over my eyes."

Rosa opened her mouth, and Julia clapped. "Why don't we take a little break? We'll have some cupcakes and coffee and reconvene in fifteen…" She glanced from Rosa to Kitty. "Thirty minutes."

Byron shifted in his seat. "Okay, Ava and Mrs. DiRossi, Julia cut you off, so why don't you tell me how you really felt about—"

"Byron, I could use your help with the coffee and tea."

"Love, I'm working here. Now, if you said coffee, tea, or *me*…" He waggled his eyebrows at Julia.

She smiled prettily at him. "Well, we are behind the counter together."

"I'm so easy," he said, putting his iPad on the chair and following Julia to the coffee bar.

Sophie and Dana walked over. "Nonna, you stay right where you are. I'll bring you a coffee," Sophie said to Rosa, then looked at Ava. "I'm sorry. I didn't know what else to do. I felt bad for her. We were going out, and she just seemed so lonely and sad."

Ava pursed her lips and then nodded toward Lexi, who was laughing with Mackenzie and Arianna. "*Sí*, I can see how sad and lonely she is."

Sophie sighed. "I…Nonna, where do you…Nonna." Sophie and Dorothy hurried after Rosa.

Dana sat in Byron's chair and took Ava's hand, giving it a light squeeze. "I'm sorry. I'm sure after today the last thing you need or want is for Lexi to show up here, but Sophie's right. She really did seem sad earlier. And it's not like you can avoid her. You and Griffin are together now, and she'll be living in Harmony Harbor."

"I don't have a problem with her. Well, I didn't, but I kind of do now. I was more than willing to try to be friends, Dana. She's the one who hates me. I'm not over-stating things," she said when Dana cast her a doubtful glance. "You haven't seen her with me. If you were there today, you would have been impressed with my restraint."

Dana looked to where Lexi stood at the coffee bar. "Maybe she's worried about having a baby at her age. Being a first-time mother at forty must be a little worrisome, don't you think? Both her parents died when she was a teenager, and she doesn't have any friends here. All she really has is Griffin, and he loves you. Anyone can see that."

Ava groaned and leaned back in the chair. "Now I feel horrible, and none of this is even my fault."

"That's because you're a kind and caring woman. Come on, we'll just casually join in their conversation. This is a perfect opportunity to mend fences. Lexi's re-laxed, you're away from the manor, and—"

"Why do I feel like I've just been played?"

In response, Dana fluttered her lashes, and Ava had to stop herself from saying, *And why are your eyes violet to-day?* If she didn't know what it was like having a secret you couldn't share, Ava might have asked. Because there were times when Dana looked sad too. Ava stood up. "Okay, fine. But if this goes—"

Looking deep in thought, Byron approached carrying a cup of coffee. His expression cleared once he reached them. "Dana, is it? Do you mind if I talk to Ava alone for a minute?"

Avoiding Byron's gaze, Dana murmured, "Not at all. I'll go get a cup of tea."

"Sit," Byron said, handing Ava what smelled like a cin-namon chocolate latte.

He took the seat beside her. "First, I need you to tell me the truth. Did you really hate the book or did you just use it to get in a couple shots at your ex's other ex-wife, who I've just heard from Julia is no longer your ex, ex. I can't believe I just said that. But obviously you know what I mean."

"Umm…" She nodded and took a sip of the latte.

He cocked his head.

She grimaced. "I loved the book. But Julia was worried about you and asked me to say I hated it. That's good, right? She obviously cares about you, and you care—"

He aimed his finger at Julia and then at his chest. "You think I'm interested in…" He shook his head. "No, Julia's not my type. I'm fond of her—"

"Oh, I thought…Are you gay?" Because Ava didn't understand how any straight man wouldn't be interested in Julia.

"No, I'm not gay. Why would you think I am?"

"For one, Julia's an incredible catch. She's not only beautiful and smart, but she's also one of the sweetest women I know. So I don't know how you wouldn't be interested in her unless, you know…Then there's that whole thing you've got going on…" She circled her face with her finger. "You always look so perfect and put together." She leaned in to peer at his face. "Do you wear makeup?"

"I'm not sure whether I should be offended or flattered. No, I don't wear makeup, and Julia's everything you say she is and more, and that's the problem. She's too sweet. I like edgy women with attitude you don't have to worry about hurting. Like your archnemesis there. Which is what I wanted to—"

"I don't believe this. You want me to set you up with Lexi?" Ava lifted a shoulder. "No accounting for taste, but I can't help you with that. She—"

"I'm actually quite capable of getting a date on my own, thanks," he said sarcastically.

"Like Paige? What's our favorite Realtor up to these days? We haven't seen her around the manor lately." Ava frowned. Now that she thought about it, that seemed odd. Not that Paige wasn't snooping around the manor—she was persona non grata and banned from Greystone. But there was too much money at stake for her to simply give up and walk away. She had to be…"Are you still working with her?"

"Just because we went out a couple of times doesn't mean I was working with her. Why do you ask?"

Ava didn't miss that he'd neither confirmed nor denied his involvement in Paige's schemes. She had a feeling he could be as cagey as Colleen. But the next round of the competition was only a week away, and she didn't have anything on Gaston. She had to take a chance. So she told Byron what had been going on at the manor. "It fits Paige's MO, don't you think?"

He nodded. "It would definitely help make her case to the heirs who haven't signed on. If you get me something on the chef, like his driver's license, even where he went to school, I can do some digging around for you."

"You don't mind?"

"Are you kidding? The most exciting thing I've covered in weeks was the bridal show at Greystone."

"You didn't write about what happened with Lexi, did you?"

He gave her a look. "Obviously you're like half

the residents in Harmony Harbor and don't read the *Gazette*."

"Sorry, I've been distracted lately."

"Which brings me back to what I wanted to talk to you about in the first place. Does your ex's ex...I'll try this again before I confuse myself. Does she"—he pointed at Lexi—"know that you and Griffin are back together?"

"Of course. That's why she's being such a pain in the *culo*."

"Well, that pain in *your culo* just got bigger. She's auditioning women for Griffin."

Ava glanced to where Lexi stood talking to Dana and frowned. "What do you mean, auditioning women for him?"

"Girlfriend material? Marriage material? I'm not sure which, but I overheard her talking to Mackenzie and Julia. She asks the same questions. I saw her checking off some kind of list inside her copy of the book."

"What kinds of questions?" Ava asked from between clenched teeth.

"First, she opens with a little flirtatious talk about Griffin. Gauging if they're interested in him or not, I guess. That's where the laughter comes in. She's playing them, warming them up. And then she goes in for the kill, like what are their hobbies, education, health, net worth, that sort of thing. Oh, and most important, do they like kids. She's got good interrogation skills. But I guess she would, being a cop." He looked over at Lexi. "She really is hot, even if she is pregnant."

Ava elbowed him in the ribs.

"Hey, what did you do that for?"

"The woman is trying to get rid of me and all you can say is, she's hot?"

"You're being a tad dramatic, don't you think? I doubt she'd try and murder you. Then again, pregnant women can get a little crazy." He grinned at Ava and put his arm around her. "Thanks to you, I might just get the story of my journalistic career."

Chapter Nineteen

♥

Colleen followed Lexi as she paced from the canopied bed to the French doors, tapping a pencil on a pad of paper. The girl had on a pair of powder-blue pajamas and some kind of knitted sock slippers.

"Stop moving so I can get a look at the list you've made," Colleen grumbled.

Lexi had been agitated since she'd come back from Books and Beans. It annoyed Colleen to no end that she was tethered to the manor. She had a feeling she'd missed out on some good stuff tonight. She wouldn't call anything about Kitty and Rosa renewing their feud good though.

Back in December, Colleen thought she'd wiped that sin from her eternal soul. Now it was back like a bad penny. Stupid phrase, she didn't know what it meant or where it had come from. Obviously she was as overwrought as Lexi. Colleen hadn't made any progress with

Jasper, no breakthroughs on who Gaston was, and even though they'd lost the first round of the competition, no one was doing a single thing to get rid of the man.

Lexi sat on the end of the bed and glanced at Simon, who was grooming himself. "You're a smart cat. Who do you think would be Griffin's perfect match? I've narrowed it down to three: Julia, Mackenzie, and Dana."

Colleen buried her face in her hands, a little too forcefully since it went right through them. What did she expect? How was she to concentrate with Lexi making a statement like that? She supposed it was indicative of Lexi's mental state that she was deducing Simon's brain power from the way he was licking his…"Mind, there's ladies present. Stop that right now, will you? Sit up and look like you're paying attention. We need to know what she's about. How far she'll take her matchmaking."

Meow. Simon lifted his chin. When Lexi didn't respond the way he wanted, he did it again.

Colleen snorted. "Save it. She'll not pick you up and give you a cuddle like Ava. Lexi's a cool customer. She's not much for snuggles."

Lexi looked at the pad of paper. "All three of them get high marks for physical attractiveness. Shallow, but necessary, because the only reason I can figure that Griff would be gaga over the mouse is she's got that Eva Mendes thing going on." She made tick marks beside each of their names. "Mackenzie has the other two beat when it comes to working out and being a sports fan, which is important to Griffin. Extra points for that. Her cupcakes were great, so I imagine she can cook as well as bake. Another point to her, because Griff loves to eat and eventually the baby will too.

"Julia was hands down the winner in the stepmommy category. She'd be perfect. Except I get the feeling she's a pushover. Her imagination is a little off the charts too. Like seriously, what's up with dressing up for story hour with the kids? She has her masters in English and American literature, so that kind of cancels out the weirdness factor, I suppose." She glanced at the page. "I like that Julia and Mackenzie have their own businesses. Shows some drive and ambition. Dana beat them out in the class department though. She practically oozes it from her pores. I guarantee she has money, too, pots of it if I'm not mistaken."

"You're not mistaken, but that money came with a price and its own share of pain. Olivia Davenport, or Dana as you know her, isn't for Griffin. If you'd stop letting hate blind you, you'd see what's right in front of you. The qualities you admire in each of those women, put them all together and you have Ava. Except money and working out, unless you count walking to and from work. She's not much of a sports fan either. Never missed Griffin's games though. Distracted the boy to no end with her cheering."

Lexi lay down on the bed and tapped the pencil against the pad of paper. Colleen stretched out beside her.

"The biggest strike against all three of them is that they're friends with the mouse. In my book, that speaks to a lack of judgment." Lexi gave a short laugh. "Surprisingly, she did show some spine tonight." She made a face and ripped the page from the pad. Crumpling the paper, she tossed it on the nightstand and then rubbed her rounded belly. "Don't worry, we have a couple months, baby. I'll find someone who's perfect for you and your daddy." Looking up at the canopy, she blinked her eyes. "I just wish I knew what kind of hold she has on him."

"Love, Lexi, my girl. A love that's rare and true. My wish for you is that one day you'll find the same. Never doubt that Griffin loved you though. He still does. He'll be there for both you and the wee one." Colleen turned her head at Lexi's sniff. "Oh now, you're not one to cry."

The last time Colleen had tried to reach Lexi, she hadn't been able to. No doubt she'd used up her energy messing with Jasper. But she had to try again. The girl was working herself into a state over this, and it wasn't good for either her or the baby.

Colleen centered her energy, then brought her mouth near Lexi's ear. "Ava's his match," she yelled.

Lexi's hand froze by her cheek. She slowly sat up, her eyes darting around the room. "Relax," she told herself and lay back down, "it's just your imagination."

Colleen smiled and did it again. This time Lexi jumped off the bed. She put her hands on her hips, her eyes narrowed as she scanned the room. "You can't mess with me, DiRossi. I know you're behind this, and when I find out how you pulled it off, I'll bring you down."

Bejaysus, Colleen had gone and made everything worse. Again.

Griffin had fond memories of the whitewashed wooden footbridge that arched over the tide pools. It was where he'd first kissed Ava. He'd brought her to see his favorite place on the estate—Starlight Pointe. The windswept spit of land that jutted out to sea was home to the white brick lighthouse with its red roof. It had become Ava's favorite place too. Whenever they wanted to escape the prying eyes of family and friends, especially his brothers, they'd come here.

It was their secret place. A place where they'd shared their hopes and dreams. She'd told him she was pregnant here. He'd asked her to marry him here. It's where he'd said goodbye to her when he'd left for his military training. But he hadn't been back since their divorce.

Starlight Pointe was part of the estate, an easy ten-minute walk from the manor, but the family hadn't maintained the lighthouse. Money had been tight for a while now, and they'd put whatever they had into the manor and the cottages. It was going to take a crapload of work to refurbish the lighthouse and make it livable.

After his first night out here, Griffin had decided he was up for the challenge. He already felt more at home here than any place he'd ever lived. He just had to get the family attorney on board. George was giving him some legal mumbo jumbo about being unable to sever it from the estate.

Griffin figured he'd eventually wear him down. If he didn't, he planned on getting in touch with his cousins. They could sell out everything else, but no way was he letting this place go. Starlight Pointe had played a big role in his past with Ava, and he was hoping it would play a bigger role in their future.

The winds off the Atlantic rustled through the tall grasses on either side of the path. To his left, the waves crashed against the rocks, dampening his face with sea spray. His gaze traveled the crooked white steps down to the small sandy beach at the base of the bluff. He had a feeling Lexi wouldn't be all that comfortable with his choice of homes and added baby proofing to his long to-do list.

The door to the house opened, and Liam stuck his head out. "I've been searching all over for you. I was beginning to think the house ate you. Weren't you supposed to stay here last night?"

"Change of plans, wiseass." Given the state of the floors in the house, it wasn't beyond the realm of possibility that he could have fallen through the rotted boards. "I got a text from Ava after their book club meeting. She wasn't in a great place, so I stayed with her last night."

Understatement. He'd arrived after midnight to find her sitting at the kitchen table eating cupcakes. As soon as he'd walked in the door, she'd informed him that she was drawing a line in the sand. If Lexi crossed it, Ava's promise to him was off. She wasn't walking away or turning the other cheek anymore.

Griffin understood where she was coming from after she'd explained that Lexi was apparently on the hunt for his future bride-to-be. Something Griffin had a hard time believing. But Ava did, so he'd promised to talk to Lex about it today. Not exactly a conversation he was looking forward to.

Liam pulled out a chair at the table. "Grams and Soph weren't in a great place after the book club meeting either. I don't want Soph upset right now, Griff. It's getting out of hand."

"Something going on with her?" Griffin asked as he hung his leather jacket on the hook by the door.

"She's got a lot on her plate right now. Negative publicity from the first round of the competition means she's been fielding calls from nervous brides."

His baby brother had one of those faces that gave

everything away. It'd been Liam's downfall when they played poker. "And?"

"Okay, all right, but this is under the dome."

Griffin cocked his head. "Under the dome?"

"Wait till your kid's seven. You'll be saying shit like that too."

"Doubtful." He eyed his brother, thinking about the last time he'd seen Sophie. "So, when's the baby due?"

Liam grinned. "Always could count on you to figure it out. Now, I won't be lying when I say I never told anyone. But don't say anything. It's early days."

Griffin shook his brother's hand, bending to give him a one-arm hug. "Congrats, baby bro. I don't have to ask if you're happy about it." He straightened and walked to the kitchen with its crooked floors and crooked cabinets. Ava was right; it had to be gutted. "You have time for a coffee?"

"Sure. Thanks. Soph and I are over the moon about the baby. Which kinda got me thinking about you and Lex. Don't tear my head off, okay? I'm not taking sides. But this thing between Ava and Lex can't be good for either her or the baby. Any chance you and Ava could cool it for a bit?"

Griffin filled the coffeepot with water, working to keep his temper in check. The idea of staying away from Ava...He couldn't do it. More to the point, he wouldn't do it. And he didn't think it was fair that his brother even brought it up as an option.

"What you all seem to be forgetting is that Lex and I aren't together anymore, and neither of us want to be. If you think that's just me, you might want to ask Lex why she was trying to set me up with half the single women in Harmony Harbor last night. In case you're wondering, Ava wasn't one of them."

Liam groaned. "It's going to get worse, isn't it?"

"I'd say the probability of that is high," Griffin admitted as he scooped coffee into the filter. And that worried him, because Liam had a point. The stress wasn't good for Lex and the baby. Which Griffin had known all along and the reason he'd tried to keep his distance from Ava in the beginning. Since that was off the table, it was up to him to figure this out. He'd spent twenty years as a SEAL, how hard…He smiled. He knew exactly what to do. He dug his phone from his pocket and texted Ava and then Lex.

"I don't know what you're smiling about. This has shit show written all over it."

"Leave it to me. I've got it under control."

"Care to enlighten me?"

"I'm going to deal with them the same way I would members of my team who didn't get along. They need a common goal to work toward."

"You seriously think you can get Ava and Lexi to work together?" Liam looked around and lifted a shoulder. "Guess I shouldn't be surprised. You actually think you can make this place habitable."

"Yeah, I—" Griffin began as he walked to the counter to get the sugar…and fell through the floor. "Shut up."

Lexi stared at him from across the table in the manor's dining room, looking a lot like his brother had earlier today, only without the thigh-slapping laughter. Griffin had picked a public location for the meeting of his two exes in hopes it would keep the drama—i.e., yelling—to a minimum.

"Ten minutes is all I'm asking for, Lex. I promise, once I tell you and Ava what I have in mind, you'll be glad that you stayed to hear me out." He'd decided to put talking to Lex about her matchmaking scheme on the back burner. If this played out the way he hoped, it wouldn't be necessary. The last thing he needed was for her to get defensive, and she was already in a mood.

"You're lucky I've been craving a burger all day. Just don't expect me to talk to her." She picked up her burger just as Ava walked into the dining room, still wearing her uniform.

Ava spotted him and gave him a wide smile, which faded as soon as she saw his dinner companion. From the way her eyes narrowed as she strode toward the table, he had an uneasy feeling she was going to be worse than Lexi.

"Are you crazy?" She pried the burger from Lexi's hands.

"Jesus, God," he groaned. "Babe, give Lex her burg—"

Lexi stared from her empty hands poised at her mouth to Ava.

Ava put the burger on the plate, picked up a napkin, and held it to Lexi's mouth. "Spit."

Lexi looked at him. "I told you she's nuts."

At least that's what he thought she said but couldn't be sure because she'd yet to swallow the burger in her mouth.

"You want to get sick, fine. But you're not making Griffin's baby sick, so you spit that burger out of your mouth right now. Or I'll stick my finger in there and get it myself."

Lexi spat out the burger. "What are you talking about? It's a hamburger."

Ava folded the napkin and picked up the plate. "An undercooked burger. You want a burger? I'll make you one that won't possibly be contaminated with *Listeria* or *E. coli*." Ava lifted the bun and shook her head. "You can't have blue cheese. Did your doctor not talk to you about what you can and can't eat?" Apparently Lexi wasn't the only one on her shit list. Ava pointed at him. "You know better. You should have told her."

"I didn't know she couldn't eat it. You—"

She waved her hand and walked off, muttering in Italian.

"How does she know what I should and shouldn't eat, and why are you supposed to know better?"

He winced at the shouting coming from behind the closed kitchen door. Two seconds later, St. John stormed out with his chef's hat in his hand. No doubt off to tell on Ava.

Griffin drew his gaze back to Lex. "She did her clinical practicum in women's health." He didn't really want to get into why he should know better and hoped that would suffice. Lexi was already worried about carrying the baby to term. She didn't need to have her fears validated by their loss.

"You're telling me she's a nurse?" Lexi couldn't look more stunned if he told her Ava was Mother Theresa.

"She dropped out two months before she graduated." She'd planned to go on and get her MSN. He couldn't let himself think about all the dreams that had died in those few short months. He'd been doing his best to keep his promise to Ava and stay focused on their future.

"So why am I supposed to listen to her if she wasn't good enough to get her degree?"

"It had nothing to do with her abilities. She was on the dean's list. Several of her profs suggested she go on and get her medical degree."

Lexi looked confused. "I don't get it then. Why did she drop out?"

And that was the million-dollar question. "I don't know."

Lexi put her elbow on the table, cupping her face with her hand, a look in her eyes he was familiar with. Nothing the woman liked more than solving a puzzle. "When did she ask you for a divorce?"

"A month before."

"And the plot thickens," she murmured.

"Do me a favor and leave it alone, Lex. It upsets her to talk about it."

"But don't you want to know…" She straightened when Ava approached the table with two platters.

She placed one in front of Lexi, the other in front of him. "*Mangia*," she said, pulling out a chair to take a seat.

Lexi looked from her platter to his. "Why do I get a salad and he gets fries?"

"Because you're carrying his son, he isn't." She plucked three fries off his plate and put them on Lexi's. "Happy now?"

Lexi pursed her lips, then lifted the burger to her mouth, taking a bite. She slowly chewed, her eyes went to half-mast, and she moaned. Obviously unintended because she glanced at Ava after she swallowed and said, "It's pretty good."

"Uh-huh, I moan when my food is *pretty good* too." Ava picked up a fry and took a bite. Griffin grinned around his burger. Ava had never lacked confidence, and when it came to her cooking, she was downright cocky.

She had reason to be; the burger was amazing. "Best burger I've eaten in a long time, babe."

"Let me taste." She leaned in and took a bite, closing her eyes to savor the taste. She swallowed and nodded with a smile that lit up her gorgeous eyes. "I've got it back. I found my missing ingredient."

He didn't understand what she meant, but the way she was looking at him made it seem like it had something to do with him. She looked so happy he wanted to kiss her but he wouldn't rub their relationship in Lexi's face.

Lexi looked completely horrified. She never did like to share her food. "That's gross."

Ava shrugged, picking up another fry from his plate. "You wanted to talk about something?" she asked him.

He nodded, feeling more confident about his idea than he had earlier. Probably because Lexi and Ava had managed to sit within a foot of each other without drawing blood. "I've come to a decision I thought you'd both want to know about. The two of you have been after me to sign on to keep the estate in the family, and I'm willing to do that if…"

"If what?" They asked at almost the same time, glancing at each other when they did.

"If the manor wins the food war competition." He raised his hand when Ava sputtered a protest and Lexi opened her mouth to no doubt do the same. "It's non-negotiable, ladies. If the manor doesn't win, it's going to take at least a year to recover from the negative publicity. There's already been two wedding cancellations for this summer. I'm not willing to back a lost cause. If the manor wins, it stands a chance of eventually operating in the black."

He took a bite of his burger, feeling pretty pleased with himself. His chances of getting George to back him in buying Starlight Pointe were higher if he was on Team Greystone. And knowing his two ex-wives as well as he did, they would do everything in their power to win the food wars.

Lexi looked at her burger and sighed. "All right, we have to convince Gaston to let you help with the next competition."

"When are you going to start listening to me? Gaston won't let me in the kitchen because he doesn't want the manor to win," Ava said.

Griffin happily ate his burger and fries while the two of them hashed it out, confident they'd get on the same page eventually. Ten minutes later, as he popped the last fry in his mouth, it sounded like they had.

"I still say you're wrong about him. But if you can prove he isn't who he says he is, I'll keep an eye on him until we have enough to make a case to get rid of him. We need actual proof though," Lexi said.

Griffin's cell phone rang, and he glanced at the screen. "I've gotta take this. It's about Finn." Griffin picked up, and his contact turned him over to the doctor looking after Finn. Problem was, the guy spoke French and Griffin didn't. "*Une minute*. Babe, can you talk to Finn's doctor for me? I can only make out one or two words every few sentences."

"No, but I know who can." Ava's smile said she was up to something. She pushed back her chair and went to stand up. "Perfect timing." She waved over the chef, who was heading for the kitchen, looking about as unhappy as when he left. "Gaston, Griffin needs you for a minute."

The man approached the table warily. "*Oui, vous* wish to have speaks with me, monsieur?"

Griffin handed him the phone. "My brother's doctor speaks French. I need someone to translate."

"*Tres bien.*" Lexi gave Ava an I-told-you-so look when he put the phone to his ear. "*Bonjour. Non. Oui. Une minute. Zee* dialect is one I'm unfamiliar with. Apologies," the chef said.

Ava raised her eyebrows at Lexi with a smug smile curving her kissable lips and then took the phone from Griffin, looking at St. John while she conversed with the doctor in perfect French.

Lexi's eyes followed Gaston as he hurried off; then she looked at Griffin. "I know what you're doing, and if you think we're going to become friends because you've got us working for a common cause, you'll be disappointed."

Ava, who'd pulled a pen from her pocket and was writing on a napkin, glanced at Lexi. "Eat your salad."

Lexi scowled at Ava and picked up her burger. "You're going to be a pain in my ass, aren't you?"

Chapter Twenty

♥

Lexi was a pain in Ava's *culo*.

"Just stand guard at the door and be quiet," Ava said from where she crouched behind her cousin's desk in the study. She took the small screwdriver from her uniform pocket and fit it in the tiny hole beneath the filing cabinet drawer.

"You don't have to get pissy. All I said was you could give lessons to petty criminals. It was a compliment," Lexi said, her eye pressed to the crack in the door.

Ava snorted as she reached for a book on Sophie's desk. "Yes, after you asked me how long I'd served for breaking and entering." Ava smacked the end of the screwdriver with the book. It popped open on the second try.

"Can you blame me? You broke into Gaston's locker as fast as you just broke into the filing cabinet. And let's not forget that you wired my room and kept telling me you're Griffin's match in that creepy-ass voice."

"For the third time, I didn't wire your room. I wouldn't know how even if I wanted to. You're eating too much crap, and it's giving you crazy dreams."

"I was awake."

Ava flipped through the employee files. "I've had dreams where I thought I was awake." She used to have them often after the rape. She hadn't had one in years though.

"I was writing out…Anyway, I was definitely awake."

"Have you had them since I gave you the food guide to follow?" She'd made a what-to and what-not-to-eat list for Lexi two nights ago when they got home from the manor. Griffin hadn't been all that supportive. He said he didn't want her to rock the Lexi boat after the productive first step in his plan to smooth the waters between them. While Ava admired his optimism and his willingness to join Team Greystone in order to bring her and Lexi closer together, she didn't tell him his plan was doomed to fail. At least where she and Lexi were concerned. They were complete opposites. There was no way they'd ever be friends.

"No, I haven't heard you whispering in my ear since that night. But your list sucks."

"You want a healthy baby boy, you make sacrifices."

"Easy for you to say. Try having cravings for a smoked meat sandwich in the middle of the night."

"I had cravings. Mostly for—"

"What do you mean you had cravings?"

Ava straightened with Gaston's file in her hand. "When I was pregnant, I craved lots of things." She frowned at the look of surprise on Lexi's face. "Griffin didn't tell you we lost a baby?"

"No, I had no idea. Shit, I'm really sorry, mouse…" She winced and cleared her throat. "…Ava. When did it happen?"

Ava wasn't hurt that Griffin hadn't mentioned the baby to Lexi. They'd shared a lot about their years apart these past few weeks, so she knew he'd locked away his memories of their life together. She told Lexi about the pregnancy.

"You lost your baby boy at eight months?" Lexi asked, her hand moving anxiously to her stomach. "Were there any signs? Anything you could have done—"

"They never confirmed the actual cause. But in two-thirds of cases, a stillbirth is linked to placental insufficiency. At our last ultrasound, the baby was measuring a little small for his gestational age, so that kind of points to problems with the placenta. It's uncommon, Lexi. Griffin says your baby is a big, healthy boy." She gave the other woman a reassuring smile. "Everything will be fine."

"He kicks all the time. He's really active."

"See, there you go. You have to keep up your prenatal care though. Have you made an appointment with Dr. Bishop?"

"I'll do that. I'll do that today."

Ava opened Gaston's file, avoiding eye contact with Lexi. She didn't want to make matters worse, but she had to say this for Griffin's sake. "I know you're mad at Griffin for being with me, but I hope you'll include him in your appointments, Lexi. It's a special time for both of you. I don't want him to miss out because of me."

"Yeah, yeah, of course, I'll let him come. And stop being so sweet." She pressed her eye back to the door and muttered, "I knew you were going to be a pain in the ass." And then jerked back. "Hurry up, Sophie's coming."

Crapola. Ava didn't have time to write the information down and pulled her phone from the breast pocket of her uniform. Zooming in on Gaston's social security number, phone number, address, and references, she took several pictures before quickly replacing the file in the drawer. Grabbing the screwdriver off the floor, she put it in her pocket and returned the book to the desk.

She hurried to the chair beside the one Lexi occupied. "You're a little too good at this stuff, mouse."

"Thank you, hard-ass."

They were both chuckling—probably from relief that they hadn't gotten caught—when Sophie entered the study. Sophie had refused their request to see Gaston's file. Her cousin was a stickler for the rules and protecting Greystone's employees' privacy. Even after they'd explained that Gaston was fake French.

Sophie gave them a narrowed-eyed stare, then glanced around her desk. "Why are you two laughing? What are you up to?"

"Just joking around. Passing time while we waited for you," Lexi said.

Ava sighed when her cousin turned to open the filing cabinet. "You're not very good at this," she said out of the side of her mouth to Lexi. "Sophie, I have to get back to work. Did Gaston agree to me working in the kitchen or not?"

As Ava had noticed, her cousin was easily distracted these days. In this instance, it worked to their advantage. Sophie took a seat behind the desk instead of opening the filing cabinet. "Yes, as long as Lexi continues to provide security and you do exactly as he tells you."

Ava stood up at the same time as Lexi. "Okay, we better get going then. I'm sure he wants to get a practice run in before tomorrow."

"All right, but just promise...Oh, God." Sophie groaned and jumped to her feet. She didn't make it very far, leaning over to throw up in the wastebasket.

Fifteen minutes later, with her cousin taken care of, Ava and Lexi walked toward the entrance of the manor. "I can't believe it doesn't bother you to clean up puke. You've got this cool, competent thing going on. Why did you quit nursing school?"

"It's not important," she said, waving a dismissive hand. "We have to get this information to Byron. Give me your number, and I'll send you the photos of Gaston's employee file and his license. The *Gazette*'s on Main Street, just down from Books and Beans."

"Why don't you just send it to him?"

"He'll get on it right away if you're there. And you're a cop, so you'll probably pick up on things he doesn't."

Lexi cocked her head. "You're up to something, mouse. Just not sure what it is."

Ava smiled. "Tell Byron he's welcome and that he owes me."

"Hey, what was that for?" Griffin said. They were in the dining room at Greystone waiting for the second round of the competition to begin. Griffin had just gotten there, and the judges were expected to arrive any minute. Lex had greeted him with an elbow in the ribs.

"For not telling me you and Ava lost a baby. Why would you keep something like that from me?"

"Honestly, it wasn't intentional. At least back then. I buried those memories deep, Lex. I couldn't let myself think about them. I considered telling you the other night, but you're stressed as it is. You know you don't have to worry about it, right?"

"Yeah, the mouse did her best to put my mind at ease. It's too bad she quit school. You should have seen her with Sophie yesterday…What's with the smug smile?"

"You like her. No, don't try and deny it. I can see through you. But could you do me a favor and stop calling her mouse? At least to her face."

"She likes it. She calls me hard-ass, and it doesn't bother me."

"Yeah, 'cause there's nothing you like better than to be thought of as tough." He put his arm around her and kissed the top of her head. "I know this hasn't been easy for you. I appreciate you trying to get along with Ava."

She shrugged. "It's not a big…Here comes Gaston." She pushed open the kitchen door.

Over Lexi's head, Griffin saw Ava barefoot in her chef's uniform wiggling her hips and shoulders in time to the music as she stuck her finger in something on the platter. Helga was watching her with her arms crossed and a scowl on her face. "You already tasted it."

"Quiet, old lady. I just have to—"

"Stop tasting and get a move on. Gaston is coming," Lexi said.

Ava turned with her finger in her mouth. Griffin grinned at the adorable picture she made. Well, he was grinning until she gave him a smile that sucked the air right out of him.

"For God's sake, mouse. Get with the program and move it." Lexi stepped back and, because he was unable to take his eyes off Ava, she bumped into him. Lexi scowled at him and then Ava. "You two are ridiculous. Now move it, both of you." The door closed just as Gaston reached them.

Lexi leaned against the door frame, blocking the chef's way. "Everything okay, Gas? Nothing urgent, I hope."

"*Non*, it was another prank call." He waved her away from the door.

Lexi lifted her chin. "The judges are here. Maybe you should go over and say hello to Basil. Butter him up."

"I suppose it couldn't hurt." He pivoted on his red shoes, effusively greeting the judges.

"You gonna tell me what's going on?" Griffin asked as Dana, Sophie, and his grandmother joined Gaston to organize the judges and the cameraman.

"Ava's in charge of the risotto. Every time we got rid of Gas, she made the entrée too. She's switching up his with hers right now. No way we're going to lose this one."

Fifteen minutes later, the judges' reactions seemed to prove Lexi right. All four of them proclaimed the chicken scaloppini with morels and spring vegetables in a sherry cream sauce perfection. Ava's risotto got high marks too. As did Helga's cheesecake mousse with blood orange gelée.

"How does she stand there smiling away while the little dick takes all the credit and praise?" Lexi asked.

"Ava's a team player. She doesn't need the credit or praise." As if to prove him right, she glanced over her shoulder and gave them a thumbs-up. Griffin noticed the cameraman hadn't taken the lens off her for nearly the entire time. In his shoes, Griffin would have done the same. He winked at Ava. She rewarded him with a blinding smile in return.

"I see it now. I get why you love her," Lexi said.

"Yeah? So no more interviewing potential brides for me?" he teased.

"No, she's your one." Her smile was quiet and, if he wasn't mistaken, a little sad.

And that made him a little sad too. "Lex, honey, what I feel for Ava doesn't take away from what you and I had. I loved you, don't ever doubt that. I still do."

Colleen sat on the counter in the kitchen watching Gaston throw a hissy fit. If Sophie, Kitty, and Jasper were here, they'd see Ava's and Lexi's suspicions were right. But it was late and no one was around. He'd told them all he was working on a menu for the third and final competition that would guarantee a win.

Ava, Lexi, and Helga would have to up their game. Gaston knew he'd been had. Helga forgot to dump his entrée in the trash. He'd discovered it five minutes ago, hence the hissy fit.

His cell rang. "What?" He sighed. "Yes, Paigey, I know we lost. I did sabotage my entrée, but the Italian she-devil pulled a switcheroo. How is it my fault? I had no choice but to let her in the kitchen. I had to throw off their suspicions. She guessed I'm not French. Of course I wanted to lose. What do you mean you don't believe me? You listen to me, Paigey, I have as much reason as you to want to see Greystone fail. Why? Because of Colleen Gallagher, Great-grandfather disinherited me, and I lost the only man I ever loved. Ricky's parents sent him to live with his grandparents when they heard about us kissing."

Bejaysus, it was Paige's cousin, little Theo Townsend. Colleen should have recognized him. And there it was, another sin she had to wipe from her eternal soul. She hadn't thought she'd get the opportunity to make amends to the lad. She hadn't meant to hurt him though.

It was different in her day, and she'd been as fool-minded as the rest of them. She'd seen Theo and Ricky the week before the church social having a snog down at Kismet Cove. She wouldn't have said anything, mind you, but her dander had been well and truly up the day the old codger, Theo's great-grandfather, had made a derogatory remark at the church social about one of her great-grandsons. Colleen had quipped, *"At least he's not a pansy like your Theo."*

"So what if we were only sixteen? True love can happen at any age. What do you mean it's off? Byron Harte was asking about me? Why didn't you tell me that in the first place? Tell the manager at the Marquis I can start right away. I can beat the Italian she-devil. I know I can. What do you mean you can't get me the job? You promised me...I've ruined my reputation because of you! You have to give me a chance to...Paige. Paige!"

Colleen looked over as the door of her suite creaked open. Ava glanced at the still-sleeping Lexi and tiptoed inside carrying a cream-colored box that had yellowed with age, a blue ribbon tied around it.

Colleen sat up in bed with a smile. She'd stayed the night with Lexi, whispering in her ear that Theo Townsend deserved a second chance. She had no doubt Lexi and Ava were close to discovering he was Paige's cousin and all that implied. This was Colleen's chance to make amends to the boy.

"Griffin chose your nickname well, Ava, my girl. It's a sweet thing you're doing. Any other woman might have been bitter and jealous, but not you," Colleen said as Ava placed the box on the end of the bed and then crept out of the room.

Her great-grandson had chosen well both times. He was a smart boy, their Griffin was, coming up with his plan to bring the two women he loved together. It did her body good seeing the beginnings of a friendship blossoming between Ava and Lexi. Colleen was close to wiping another sin from her eternal soul, two if her plans for Theo worked as she hoped.

Lexi sat up and rubbed her eyes with a scowl on her face. She looked around the room as though searching for a speaker. "I don't know what you're up to, mouse, but I'm going to find out. And the first thing I want to know is who the hell Theo Townsend is and why he deserves a second chance."

Colleen chuckled. Ava must have a good laugh every time Lexi calls her mouse. Rosa's pet name for her children was *topolino*, mouse.

"Don't you worry, Lexi, my girl. You'll find out soon enough who Theo is. I'm not sure he'll explain why he did what he did, but I hope my message stays with you and you take it to heart."

Simon tugged on the blue ribbon, drawing Lexi's attention to the box. Frowning, she drew it toward her. She pulled out the small card tucked under the ribbon, opening it to read.

"Damn you, Ava DiRossi," she said on a choked sob, swiping at the tear that rolled down her cheek. She untied the ribbon and opened the box, slowly removing each item. There was Griffin's christening gown, the beautiful blanket Mary had knit for her first grandchild-to-be, the Irish wool shamrock blanket Kitty had made, and lastly, the tiny U.S. Navy outfit Griffin had bought upon hearing the news he and Ava were having a boy.

With tears rolling down her cheeks, Lexi hugged the outfit to her chest and rocked in place. "It's not fair. He's all I've ever wanted and dreamed of, and I won't see him in this. You'll see him, but I won't. He won't remember me. All he'll know is you."

Beside herself with worry over Lexi's reaction, Colleen said, "Simon, hurry. Go to the door and make such a racket she lets you out. Get Ava, bring her here."

Simon leaped off the bed, his caterwauling bringing Lexi around. She rubbed the backs of her hands across her cheeks and got up, her shoulders hunched, her movements painfully slow. Simon took off as soon as the door cracked open.

Once Lexi let him out, she closed the door and crawled back into bed, curling into a ball. Her shoulders shook as sobs wracked her body.

"Come now, it can't be that bad," Colleen said, staring at the hand that went through Lexi's back as she tried to offer her comfort. "Hush now, it'll be all right." She kept repeating the words even though she knew Lexi couldn't hear her unless she yelled them in her ear, and she'd already used her energy up earlier. She was just about to go looking for Ava herself when she heard Simon outside the door.

"You can stop yowling at me. I'm coming," she heard Ava say, and then there was a knock on the door. "Lexi?"

"Go away. Just go away and leave me alone!"

The old Ava wouldn't listen; she'd charge right in at the sound of someone in distress. But the new Ava had buried her so deep that Colleen couldn't be sure that Lexi yelling at her wouldn't scare her away. "Don't let her leave, Simon. Nip at—" Colleen smiled when the door opened. "Welcome back, Ava, my girl. Welcome back."

Ava rushed to the bed, placing a knee on the edge to lean across and touch Lexi's shoulder. "What's wrong?"

Lexi brushed Ava off and sat up. She grabbed the blankets, christening gown, and the baby outfit and shoved them back in the box. Pushing it away from her, she said, "You shouldn't have given me these. Keep them for when you and Griffin have another baby."

Ava sat on the edge of the bed, reaching out to stroke the ivory lace gown. "I'm sorry I upset you, Lexi. I didn't mean to. This was Griffin's christening gown, and his mother and grandmother made the blankets. I thought you'd like to have them for your baby."

"I appreciate the thought." The words sounded like they were scraped from Lexi's throat. "But like I said, keep them for—"

"There won't be any more babies for me and Griffin. I can't get pregnant, Lexi. The doctor who did my C-section made a mistake. He damaged—"

"Oh God, I'm so sorry. I didn't mean—" Lexi covered her face, the rest of her words lost in a torrent of tears.

Ava climbed onto the bed and pulled Lexi into her arms. "Tell me. Tell me what's wrong. Why are you crying?"

"I have cancer. I'm dying."

Chapter Twenty-One

♥

After two days of trying to convince Lexi to tell Griffin she had cancer, Ava had changed tactics. The pressure was only stressing Lexi out, and that's the last thing Ava wanted. And really, who was she to judge? She'd back off for a couple of weeks. Hopefully by then, Lexi would be more willing to open up to Griffin.

But for now, Ava's goal was to get Lexi ready, both mentally and physically, to face her upcoming battle. And it would be a battle, but Lexi hadn't been handed a death sentence. Ava didn't blame her for being scared and going to the worst-case scenario. Cancer was scary, but knowledge was power. Lexi needed to feel she had some control. More importantly, she needed hope.

To put her plan into action without alerting anyone's suspicions, Ava had enrolled her cousin in the program she'd devised for Lexi. A program that included daily yoga and meditation classes, given by none other than

Sophie's mother. Who, thanks to Kitty, had arrived last night. Because despite Ava and Lexi's improved relationship, the feud between Kitty and Rosa was still going strong.

Tina had called to talk to Sophie and got Kitty instead. In Kitty's eyes, there was no better way to stick it to Rosa than invite her much hated daughter-in-law to stay at the manor. So far, they'd managed to keep Tina's arrival from Rosa.

That wasn't going to last for long, Ava thought as she walked into the atrium where the class was being conducted. Kitty and several members of the Widows Club were doing the downward dog. It looked like Surfside active wear must have had a sale on fluorescent spandex. From their laughing, flushed faces, the older women seemed to be enjoying the class. The baby mamas...not so much.

Lexi and Sophie glared at Ava from between their legs. Tina didn't look any happier about the interruption and came agilely to her feet. Ava didn't know if it was due to Botox or yoga, but Tina didn't look a day over thirty-five. Her glowing, unlined face was framed by fuchsia-streaked dark hair, and her black spandex yoga pants and fuchsia bra top showed off a lean, ripped body with surgically enhanced boobs. "Someone didn't see the *do not disturb our Zen* sign, did they? Wink, wink."

Ava held back an eyeroll and forced a smile. Tina might be in her fifties and look like she was in her thirties, but the woman acted like she was in her twenties. No wonder Sophie was stressed. "Sorry to interrupt, Tina. But it's time for Lexi's and Sophie's smoothies."

"Staying in this position is more appealing than what's on your tray," Lexi muttered.

Sophie went to move, then groaned. "I think I'm stuck."

"You must have gotten your inflexibility from the DiRossi side, baby. Because your mama still has the moves." And to prove that she did, Tina did the splits. Encouraged by the clapping Widows Club, she did a floor show, complete with a back flip.

Ava set the tray on a table and hurried to Sophie's side. Once she'd gotten Sophie to her feet, her cousin watched her mother's Olympic-worthy performance with an I-don't-believe-her expression on her face.

"Who is *that*?" a man's voice asked from behind Ava.

She turned to see Byron watching Tina. It was like Sophie's mother had hot-man radar and froze with a knee raised and arms in the air. Lowering her hands and leg, she gave him a sultry smile. "Now who do we have here? A new member to our club, I hope."

"You ladies are way out of my league, I'm afraid," Byron said, then cocked his head. "Well, most of you are. Lexi, love, you're looking a little flushed."

"Shut up, Harte, and help me up."

Sophie raised her eyebrows at Ava and nudged her head in the couple's direction. Yes, Ava had caught the *love* too and couldn't help notice Lexi's flush deepen when Byron helped her to her feet. Or that he was extremely attentive and gentle as he did so. Ava smiled. A new love interest might be exactly what Lexi needed to kick her endorphins into high gear.

As though the other woman read her thoughts, Lexi scowled at Ava and said, "Don't even think about it."

Ava grinned and waggled her eyebrows, then handed Lexi and Sophie their green smoothies. "Drink up, ladies."

Lexi handed hers to Byron, who took a sniff, then a drink. "It's not as bad as it looks."

Ava took the glass from him before he guzzled the nutrient-laden drink down, handing it to Lexi. "Unless you want salad instead of fries for lunch, drink it."

Sophie's eyes went wide. "Mrs. Fitzgerald, I don't think you're ready to do a headstand just yet. You either, Kitty," she called to the older women who were attempting to imitate Tina. Sophie handed Ava her glass. "I need to review our liability insurance."

"I have something else you should probably see first, Sophie." Byron drew his iPhone from the pocket of his jacket. Typing in his password, he swiped the screen. "Your chef isn't who he says he is. Meet Paige's first cousin, Theo Townsend, better known at the manor as Gaston St. John."

Lexi choked on her drink. "Did you say Theo Townsend?"

"Yes, do you know him?" Byron asked while patting her back.

"Stop that, I'm fine. And, no, I don't know him. If I did, don't you think I would have said something?"

Lexi's prickly attitude didn't bother Byron. If anything, he looked like he found it amusing. "One would think," he said. "But your reaction—"

Sophie cut him off, looking from Lexi to Ava. "So you two went behind my back and investigated Gaston…I mean, Theo—"

Ava and Lexi pointed at Byron, saying almost at the same time, "He did."

Lexi added, "But what does it matter who was investigating him? He obviously had something to hide."

"You're right, sorry." Sophie looked across the room. "Kitty, can you come here for a sec? We might as well get this over with before lunch service begins. I hope you're ready to take over the kitchen, Ava."

"Of course…" She noticed an odd look come over Byron's face and asked, "Is there something else?"

He rubbed his chin. "Yeah, there is. It seems Paige somehow got wind that I was asking questions about her cousin and stopped by the *Gazette* the other day when I was out. She asked my sister what I was working on."

"So? It doesn't matter now that we know…" Ava caught the glance he shared with Lexi, and the regret that crossed the other woman's face. Ava's pulse kicked up. "You were investigating me, too, weren't you? You both were."

"No, it's not what you think," Lexi said. "He was investigating you, and I mentioned that I found it odd that you quit nursing school around the same time you asked Griff for a divorce."

Sophie ushered them out of the atrium to stand near the elevators. She crossed her arms, her eyes narrowed at Byron. "Why were you investigating my cousin?"

"Would you just relax? I wasn't investigating her… Well, not really. You knew I was curious about Colleen's memoirs, Ava. I'd made a list of people in town who I thought had secrets, and you were one of many. I must have asked my sister if she knew anything about your story, and that's why she mentioned you to Paige." He sighed when Sophie continued to glare at him. Ava was trying to do the same in hopes they thought she was angry instead of terrified. "Look, I'm sorry. But it's not like there's anything for Paige to find, right?"

"Of course there isn't. It just would have been nice if you asked me instead of going behind my back." Ava was impressed that her voice came out calm and even. She pursed her lips at Lexi. "Both of you."

"I did, but you gave me the brush-off," Lexi said defensively.

Ava hadn't realized Kitty had joined them until Griffin's grandmother said, "I took you to be a serious-minded journalist, Mr. Harte. I'm surprised you've been taken in by those silly rumors that my mother-in-law actually wrote her memoirs. She was a hundred and four and could barely recall what day it was, let alone what someone told her decades ago. And I certainly won't have you coming here and upsetting Ava with such nonsense." Kitty touched her arm. "Are you all right, my dear?"

Over the past week, Ava's relationship with Kitty had been more or less back to normal. "I'm perfectly fine." She gave Griffin's grandmother a wide smile, which may have been slightly over-the-top given that Lexi watched her while tapping a finger on her lips. She needed a distraction. "Byron actually did all of us a big favor, Kitty. He looked into Gaston, who isn't Gaston. He's Paige's cousin Theo Townsend!" She groaned inwardly when they all looked at her. She had to get her nerves under control and stop worrying about this or she'd give herself away.

Paige had started college Ava's final year. She didn't know any of the people Ava hung around with at the time…Other than Harmony Harbor football star Damien Gray. But it's not like he'd say anything. Then she remembered someone else. The younger sister of Ava's roommate had started college with Paige. Even in the unlikely event Paige made the connection, it wouldn't do her any good. Ava hadn't told anyone, including her roommate. So the past would stay in the past where it belonged. The thought helped to slow her racing heart.

Ida Fitzgerald sauntered over. "Theo Townsend, did you say?"

"Yes, he's been masquerading as Gaston St. John." Kitty pressed a hand to her mouth, a stricken expression on her face. "Oh, Ava, he really was behind all the nonsense. I hope you can forgive us, my dear."

It had been hurtful when they took Lexi's side over hers, but that was water under the bridge. Thinking of what Lexi was dealing with made everything else seem trivial in comparison. "There's nothing to forgive. You and Sophie might want to confront Gas—Theo—though before he can do any more damage to the manor's reputation."

"Too bad we never did find Colleen's memoirs. You might have had some idea why the lad would come looking for revenge. His great-grandfather disinherited Theo when Colleen outed him at the church social."

Kitty cast a sidelong glance at Byron, who now had confirmation the book did indeed exist and tried to cover up. "It's difficult to find something that doesn't exist, Ida."

Ida looked at Kitty as though she'd lost her marbles. "What's gotten into you? Of course—"

Kitty took her friend by the arm. "Walk with Sophie and me to the dining room and tell us all you know about Theo so we have a better idea what we're dealing with, Ida."

Lexi looked like she was debating whether or not to go with them. She said something that sounded like *second chances* under her breath, then sighed. "I think I'll come along if you don't mind."

"Not at all, my dear. Ava, you should come too."

"Why don't I get an invite? I'm the one who uncovered—" At the sound of a woman yelling, Byron broke off to look in the direction of the entryway.

"Where is she? Don't you lie to me, you...you bag of bones. I know she's here somewhere."

Sophie bowed her head on a groan at the same time Kitty smiled gleefully.

"Go. I'll deal with Auntie Rosa," Ava said, shooing them away. As Sophie half dragged Kitty to the dining room, Ava noticed that Byron had used the distraction to follow after them.

Twenty minutes later, Ava headed for the restaurant. After fifteen minutes of ranting and raving at Tina in both English and Italian, Rosa had given up. It was difficult to have a satisfactory fight when the other person refused to take the bait. Ava had been impressed that Tina could meditate while someone yelled in her face. It wasn't until her aunt left that Ava realized Tina had buds in her ears.

One DiRossi down and one more to go, Ava thought. Rosa was no doubt on her way to let Marco know his mother was in town.

Erin hurried over to Ava as she walked into the dining room. "Did you hear the news?"

Ava nodded, glancing at the diners. "How loud did it get?"

"Other than Helga chortling madly and yelling for

Theo to be thrown out on his ear, not bad. There's been a lot of groveling on Theo's part though. He wants a chance to redeem himself. Something about the Gallaghers owing him. Lexi seems to be throwing her support behind him, suggesting they give him a second chance. They're waiting for you. Sounds like you're the deciding vote."

Erin was right. Everyone stood in the kitchen waiting for Ava's verdict. Lexi leaned into her. "Would you hurry up and make your decision? I've gotta pee."

Ava held back a laugh. This was serious business. The manor's reputation was at stake. Ava was positive Paige had been behind the scheme, but to hear Theo tell it, she hadn't been. Then again, she was his cousin. So maybe he was protecting her. Oddly enough, that played in his favor in Ava's book. Family stuck up for family always.

She also believed that he would do anything to prove himself to his idol—Basil Brisiel. And that played in Greystone's favor. "All right, we'll give you a second chance. But until you prove yourself, you are not to be in the kitchen alone. If I'm not here, you answer to Helga. None of your meals leave the kitchen without being taste-tested first." She put two fingers to her eyes and then pointed them at him. "I'll be watching you, Theo."

Lexi nudged her. "Keep this up, and I'll have to find another nickname for you."

Griffin had gotten off work two hours ago and had been waiting for Ava to meet him at the lighthouse. When she didn't show, he headed to the manor.

At the sound of hammering, he crossed the lobby to the ballroom. His brother was up on a ladder nailing the end of a rainbow to the wall. "Where's the pot of gold?" Griffin asked.

"Har har. You're a member of Team Greystone. Pick up a hammer and help a brother out."

A few days after Theo had been put on probation, they got word the final competition would be delayed. Basil had a restaurant opening or something. Two days ago, the management at the Marquis had pushed the date back again. They'd finally agreed to St. Patrick's Day and a green food theme. Everyone at the manor was thrilled because, of course, St. Paddy's Day was a big deal at Greystone. With Ava as head chef, no one doubted they'd win. They'd have a lot to celebrate that night since his brother Finn was scheduled to arrive that morning and Aidan was flying in to welcome him home.

"Sorry, no can do. I have big plans for the night. You seen Ava around?" She'd gone with Dorothy to see her dad today. Griffin would have taken time off work to go with her, but given what had happened the last time he'd seen Gino, he thought it best to hold off. Ava seemed to agree.

Liam came down off the ladder with a wiseass grin on his face. "Hate to be the bearer of bad news, but I think Ava threw you over for your ex. The two of them headed upstairs an hour ago."

"Ava seem all right to you?" he asked, worried the visit with her dad hadn't gone well.

"Yeah, they were loaded down with junk food and laughing their asses off. Guess she gave Lex the night off for good-eating behavior. I think Ava missed her calling. She should have been a drill sergeant. Or run a boot camp for pregnant women."

"She's doing something right. Both Soph and Lex look great."

"Don't get me wrong, I'm not complaining. Soph hasn't had a single bout of morning sickness since Ava took her in hand. She's way less stressed too. Even with her mother here." Liam grinned. "Gotta give you credit, big brother. You sure know your women. I never thought your plan to get those two on the same team had a shot in hell. And now look at them—they're inseparable."

"Shut up."

Liam laughed. "Worked a little better than you expected, I guess."

"Yeah, I feel like I'm competing with Lex for Ava's attention," he admitted, and it was starting to get to him. Especially tonight.

"I'm sure it's nothing to worry about, but have you noticed that Ava hugs Lexi quite a bit? A lot, really."

"Hugging her, like a lot? You don't think…Nah," Griffin said, messing with his brother's head.

Liam looked at him bug-eyed. "I was just busting your balls. You don't really think they're…you know?"

"I was just teasing. Ava calls it hug therapy. She's got me hugging Lex too. Something about increasing serotonin levels and strengthening the immune system. It drives Lex nuts."

He appreciated Ava's determination to keep Lex healthy. In the beginning, though, he'd been kind of confused by it. Then he figured out what was behind it. Because of what happened with her pregnancy, Ava wanted to do everything in her power to ensure Lexi didn't go through the same. Even though there was nothing Ava could have done to prevent their loss.

"If it's bothering you, talk to Ava about it. Tell her how you feel."

"I plan to." He lifted his chin at the six-by-six gray lump on the platform. "Is that supposed to be the Blarney Stone?"

Liam sighed. "Grams strikes again. She's driving Dana crazy. She and Soph are at the cottage right now trying to figure out how to keep Grams from turning St. Paddy's Day into a three-ring circus. We're scheduled to sing, by the way. The Gallagher brothers back together again."

"I'm looking forward to all of us being home. The performing, not so much. I'll give you a hand here tomorrow," Griffin said, and headed out the door.

"Good luck breaking up movie night."

Standing outside Colleen's suite, Griffin thought he might need it. He could hear Lex and Ava laughing their heads off. After knocking on the door for the fourth time, he pounded on it. "It's me. Open up!"

Ava answered the door wearing black dress pants and a long, pale purple top that tied at the waist with a bow, accentuating her curvy figure and sparkling eyes. "Griffin, is something wrong?"

No, other than that she'd have been naked and in his arms by now, if she'd come to the lighthouse two hours ago like she'd promised…"I've been out here for five minutes."

She laughed and pulled him inside. "Sorry, we're binge-watching *Modern Family*. Come join us."

"Hey, Lex," he said, returning her finger-wave. She was lying in bed wearing gray sweats and a T-shirt, with a bowl of popcorn resting on her stomach and a bottle of pop in her hand. He lowered his voice and said to Ava, "Babe, we had plans, remember?"

"Oh, I'm sorry. I forgot. We can do it another night, can't we?" She smiled up at him, taking him by the hand, completely oblivious to the fact he was ticked…and frustrated. The woman he loved was messing with his plans for the night. And they were important plans.

Thankfully, Lex had a better read on his mood. She threw a fistful of popcorn at Ava. "Get your ass out of here, mouse. It's past my bedtime."

"It's only eight…"

Lexi lifted her chin at Griffin, and Ava winced. She gave his hand a light squeeze before walking to the bed. Leaning over, she pulled out a bag of chips and chocolates from underneath the mountain of pillows behind Lexi's back.

Lex made a grab for the snacks. "Hey, give those back."

"You've had your allotted junk food for the week. Think how excited you'll be for the St. Paddy's Day party." Ava grinned as she picked up her coat and headed for the door. "Night, hard-ass."

They could hear Lexi grumbling from out in the hall. Ava turned to him and stretched up on the toes of her black, high-heeled boots. She kissed the underside of his jaw. "I'm sorry. I stopped to check on her when I came back from visiting with my dad, and she seemed a little down."

His frustration vanished at the soft press of her lips and the smell of her warm, sultry scent. He took her hand and brought it to his lips. "You can make it up to me," he murmured into her palm. Taking the bag of chips and chocolate from her while she shrugged into her black leather jacket, he curved his free hand at her nape, lifting the long, silky curls from under the coat's collar. "How did your visit go with your dad?" he asked, drawing her toward the elevator instead of the stairs.

She didn't look at him as they stepped inside. "Really good."

"What's wrong?"

"Adam moved him into a bungalow on the grounds last week. My dad does everything by himself, Griffin. He cooks, showers, and gets himself dressed. The bungalow was spotless, and they don't provide maid service. He does it all." She lifted a shoulder, a shimmer of tears in her gorgeous eyes.

Griffin put down the bags of chips and chocolates, then straightened to take her in his arms. "Don't beat yourself up over this. Sometimes things happen for a reason. Your dad got the wake-up call he needed."

"But if I wouldn't have babied him, done everything for him...He would have been better off without me. He would have taken his life back years before now."

"Same could be said about you, honey." He tipped her face up and kissed her, drawing back when the elevator doors slid open. "And not that the situation's the same, but in a way, you've replaced caring for your father with caring for Lex," he said, picking up Lex's junk food to set it on the table outside the elevator doors.

"Lexi needs..." She searched his face. "You're mad at me, aren't you?"

"More like frustrated and a little jealous." He put an arm around her and kissed the top of her head. "I appreciate everything you've done to take care of Lex and the baby. But between our jobs and this stuff with Lex, I'm not getting as much time with you as I want."

She wrapped her arms around his waist and hugged him. "I'm glad you told me how you're feeling instead of letting it build up until you were really mad at me."

He laughed, knowing what she was alluding to. "We were young when we were married, babe. I like to think I've matured since then."

"You've aged beautifully, Griffin Gallagher. And tonight when we cross Starlight Bridge, we're leaving everything and everyone behind but you and me."

"You read my mind, sweet face." He took a flashlight out of his pocket as they left the manor, careful not to disturb the small box beside it. "Let's make a promise to each other that the moment we cross the bridge, we leave the day's troubles and stresses behind. It's our special place, just like it used to be."

She stopped to look up at him. "Is there something you're not telling me? Did Mr. Wilcox agree to sever Starlight Pointe from the estate?"

"He did. It's one of the things I wanted to celebrate tonight." He lightly pressed his finger to her mouth. "No, I'm not saying anything else until we reach the bridge. So let's just enjoy our walk together."

"You've become romantic in your old age," she said, her eyes sparkling with amusement.

"And you've become even more impossibly beautiful, Ava," he said, scooping her into his arms.

"What are you doing?" She laughed, wrapping her arms around his neck.

"Getting to the good stuff faster. I've become an impatient man in my old age."

She opened her mouth, then caught sight of the tree arching over the bridge. He'd hung lanterns in the lower branches and placed LED lights up and down the handrails. "Oh, Griffin, it's beautiful. You went to all this work, and I ruined it. You should have—"

"There's only one way it'll be ruined." He set her on the bridge, drew the small box from his pocket, and then went down on one knee. "I wanna write a new ending to our story. One that has you growing old by my side. Will you marry me, Ava?"

She was smiling and crying at the same time, nodding her head. Her voice husky when she finally said the words he'd hoped to hear. "Yes, yes, a thousand times over." She'd gone down on her knees in front of him before he'd made it to his feet. "Hold me, kiss me. I need to know this isn't a dream."

The next morning, lying in Griffin's arms, Ava still needed reassurance that she hadn't imagined the night before. She lifted her hand. The ring was still there, sparkling in the sunlight seeping in through the bedroom window.

"Seriously? You're naked and in my arms and you need to look at the ring on your finger to know this is for real?" he asked, his sleep-laden voice husky with laughter.

"Oh, I can feel how real you are," she said, bringing her hand to his chest to teasingly trail her fingers over the hard slabs of muscle. "It's just the ring I was wondering about."

He brought her hand to his mouth, nipping at her fingers. "Keep that up, and we'll both be late for work."

He gave her a slow and thorough kiss before getting out of bed. "Don't move. I'll get your coffee and make breakfast."

"You don't have to pamper me."

"I want to, so get used to it. It's about time someone took care of you for a change."

She smiled as he reached for his boxers. "You took very good care of me last night."

"Forget breakfast. We'll grab some at the manor."

"No," she laughed, "I was just teasing. We don't have time. I have to have a shower."

"Me too. I'll join you." He winked at her as he walked out of what had once been the porch on the main floor off the kitchen. Griffin had converted it to a bedroom until the second story was renovated.

She heard the water come on in the kitchen while she admired her ring. "Are you sure your dad and Liam didn't mind you giving me your mom's engagement ring?" she called out, nervous about showing up at work with Mary's ring on her finger if they hadn't agreed.

Ava had been surprised to learn Griffin hadn't thrown away or sold her wedding and engagement rings. He still had them, but given how their first marriage ended...

Griffin appeared at the door with a coffeepot in his hand. "I'm the oldest. My mom would have wanted me to have her rings. And like my dad said, there's no one she'd rather have wear her ring than you. She loved you, sweet face. Dad knew that too. She wasn't fooling him when she'd visit you. Riley outed her when she got old enough to talk. She loved you too. And, yes, my dad's happy we're together again. They all will be, babe. So stop worrying about it."

"Finn and Aidan won't be. You should probably warn them before they come—"

"If it makes you feel better, I'll tell them. But seriously, all they'll care about is that I'm happy. It won't be hard for them to see that I am."

"I'm happy too, *amore mio*."

"It's been a long time since you've called me your love. Didn't know till now how much I missed it." His smile was soft, his eyes tender. He looked at the coffeepot in his hands. "We should have taken today off."

Ava glanced at the clock on the nightstand, shocked to see it was already eight o'clock. "You should have told me how late it was," she said, throwing back the covers.

"If I would have known you were going to jump out of bed like that, I would have." He winked and walked to the kitchen.

Ava had just turned on the water in the shower when Griffin called from the kitchen, "Babe, is your phone off or something? Soph's been trying to reach you."

"I must have left it in the lantern room. Why? Is something wrong?"

"No, good news actually. Damien Gray is a host on some morning show in Boston, and the Marquis's marketing team got him to agree to televise the final cook-off. I'll have to let Sully know. Maybe get the old gang back together for a drink."

Chapter Twenty-Two

♥

Ava sat across from the desk in the study with her arms wrapped around her waist, the sleeves of her sweater clenched in her fists, trying to keep the stomach-turning emotions from showing on her face at the mention of Damien's name. The same as she had six days ago.

"Ava, is everything okay? I asked if you were—"

"*Sí*, everything is fine. We're serving spicy BLT bloody Marys, green velvet soup, chicken ravioli with a lemon basil pesto, and a green apple sorbet with home-made chocolate squares to finish."

Sophie glanced at Dana and Lexi before saying, "Ava, you told us the menu a few minutes ago. I asked if you were going to be okay with the crew filming and Damien asking you a few questions while you guys were cooking?"

She'd been working out the scenarios in her head all week—how she'd avoid Damien, how she'd keep him from being alone with Griffin. Until now, she'd thought that would be the most difficult. "I don't know how Helga and Theo will feel. It's already stressful enough as it is."

"Is that what's wrong, Ava? You're stressed?" Dana asked. Like her cousin, she was watching Ava with concern. Lexi wasn't. Her arms were crossed, her jaw tight, blotches of pink on her cheeks.

Ava had to get out of there before she confronted her about what's going on. As the day of Damien's arrival drew closer, she'd done her best to avoid Lexi. "No, I've just had a lot on my plate with settling my father in at home and preparing for the competition," Ava said, telling another lie. Her newly self-sufficient father had come home two days ago. He didn't need or want her help anymore. She went to stand up. "I should get back to the kitchen. We have to—"

"Sit your ass in the chair now. Dana and Sophie, can you give us a minute alone, please?" Lexi said. She didn't give them a chance to argue. Going to the door, she held it open.

"I don't have time for this, Lexi. We have prep work to do before the competition," Ava said. She wasn't up for this, not now.

Dana and Sophie had barely made it out the door when Lexi slammed it shut behind them. "If I have to, I'll tie you to the goddamn chair. So if you really have stuff to do, you better come clean now."

She looked down at her hands in her lap. "I'm sorry I haven't had much time for you. I've been busy."

"You think this is about me? This is about Griffin. The man who you agreed to marry a week ago. The man who

is worrying himself sick about you. He says you're acting the same as you did right before you asked him for a
divorce, and just like then, he can't get you to open up."
Lexi sat down heavily in the chair beside Ava, looking at
her as though she wanted to wring her neck. "How can
you put him through this again? He's gutted, Ava."

She closed her eyes, a tear sliding down her cheek.
She'd been avoiding Griffin too, using her father as an ex-
cuse. Brushing the tear away, she said, "I'll talk to him.
I'm just overwhelmed right now. I'm sorry."

"You can't keep doing this to him. He deserves better."

"I know he does." As the minutes ticked by, she glanced
at Lexi, following the other woman's gaze to Ava's hands.
Unconsciously she'd been plucking at a loose button. She
tucked her hands in the sleeves of her gray sweater. "I
should really—"

"Looks like hell. Nails bitten to the quick. Hasn't eaten
or slept in a week from the looks of it. Dressing like shit,"
Lexi murmured as if talking to herself, then straightened
in the chair. "Let me see your arms."

"No. I'm not doing drugs if that's what you're thinking."

Concern had replaced the anger on Lexi's face. "Is
your father hurting you again?"

"No, no, he never hurt me intentionally." She pushed
up her sleeves. "See? No bruises, no nothing."

"Then I don't understand. You're not the woman I've
come to care about. That woman would never, ever,
knowingly hurt anyone, especially the man she loves.
And I know you love him, Ava. I see it every time you
look at him. Please, please tell me what's going on. Tell
me so I can help you like you've helped me." She looked
away and sniffed, wiping an arm across her eyes before

turning back to her. "I need you to be that woman, Ava. Because that woman is the only one I trust to be the mother of my child when I'm gone."

The emotions from the past—the fear, guilt, and shame that had caused Ava to withdraw into herself the last few days—were replaced with anger. "Don't talk foolish. You're not dying. You'll get the treatment, and you'll be fine."

"You don't—"

"I know. I was almost a nurse. I would have been a good one, a great one if I..." Her shoulders sagged under the weight of the memories. "It's Damien. It's because of Damien I haven't been myself."

"Damien Gray, Griff's best friend?"

Ava nodded, looking down at her hands twisting the loose button as though they were someone else's. "I'd been stressing over term papers, over Griffin being deployed. I went to a party and cut loose and had too much to drink. Damien was there and offered to take me home. When we got to my room, he backed me against the door and started kissing me. I pushed him away and told him to leave. I thought he had, but when I came out of the bathroom and crawled into bed, he was still there. He held me down and ripped off my pajama bottoms, and then...and then he raped me."

"Oh, Ava, no. All this time...That's why you left school and divorced Griffin, isn't it?"

"I couldn't tell him, Lexi. Damien threatened to tell him I'd come on to him. That I'd been fooling around on Griffin the entire time I was at school. His friends...He said his friends would back him up." She lifted a shoulder. "I liked to wear pretty clothes. I was friendly. Some people might say I was flirty. I was young, I liked to have fun. But I never looked at or wanted another man. Griffin was my first. He was my everything. I couldn't stand the thought of him wondering if I was telling the truth about that night. Couldn't stand the thought of him even picturing it in his head. I was disgusted with myself, ashamed, and guilt-ridden that I hadn't been able to stop Damien."

Lexi had moved out of the chair to crouch in front of Ava, taking her hands in hers. "It wasn't your fault. Griffin adored you. He never would have doubted your side of the story. He would have stood by you."

"I know that now. And maybe if my father hadn't been in an accident six months later, I would have gotten to that place sooner. But that's not what happened. I was depressed. I think I knew that even then. Sometimes knowing isn't enough though. I didn't think I'd be able to get past the fear and disgust when Griffin touched me. It got to the point where I felt like I was hurting him more by staying with him. And apart from worrying that his feelings for me would change if he ever found out, I was terrified he'd either seriously hurt Damien or kill him. Which would have jeopardized everything Griffin had worked so hard for."

Lexi squeezed her hands. "You have to tell Griffin. I know it'll be hard. But—"

She shook her head. "No good will come of dredging up the past. It happened more than a decade ago. There's nothing we can do about it. I've dealt with it. All I have to do is get through tomorrow."

"It's your decision, and I'll support you a hundred percent. Just like you've supported me. But, Ava, I think

Griffin has spent years trying to figure out what he did wrong. I'm not trying to make you feel guilty. I hope you know, really know, deep down in your soul, that none of this was your fault."

"I do. There was only one person at fault for the rape and that's Damien. But I allowed what he did to ruin my marriage and hurt the man I love. I was the one who left school because I couldn't face running into him on campus anymore."

"Again, not your fault. You went into a depression because of what *he* did to you. He shouldn't get off scot-free, not after all you've lost because of him."

"I've got Griffin back. That's all that really matters." She smiled. "And I've got you too."

"Yeah, you do. So what do you need me to do tomorrow to make this easier for you?"

"Don't let him be alone with Griffin."

"Done, and you've got yourself another sous chef. I'm not letting Damien anywhere near you without me by your side. So we better go to the kitchen and you can teach me to chop things." She pulled Ava from the chair, and then, the woman who'd never initiated a hug before, hugged her.

The next day Ava didn't know why she'd bothered to show Lexi how to chop vegetables. The only thing her friend had wielded the knife at was Damien when he came within three feet of Ava.

He hadn't changed. He was as handsome and charming as he'd always been. She supposed she shouldn't be surprised. Before that long-ago night, she'd never seen that other side of him.

Ava hadn't been left alone with him for a second. She'd barely responded to his questions, lapsing into Italian the one time that she did. At first Helga and Theo had seemed confused, and then, as though they'd picked up that something was wrong, they jumped in to fill the breach every time Damien asked another question.

When she forgot to add the dried split peas to the soup, Theo had covered for her, adding them himself. Same as when she forgot to add the lemon to the pesto. That time Helga had come to her rescue. As they mopped her sweaty brow, they complained about the heat. It was actually freezing. When the bell rang, signaling that their time was up, Ava's legs went weak with relief.

She didn't know how she managed to remain upright in front of the judges. She barely registered the crowd that had gathered in the dining room. All she knew was that Griffin, his father, and Liam weren't there. They'd gone to the airport to pick up Finn and Aidan, who were arriving at nearly the same time.

"We won! We won!" Theo bounced up and down and then hugged her. "Thank you, thank you, I'm your slave for life."

Because the Marquis had taken the slot earlier in the afternoon, the winner of the competition was announced at Greystone. "You more than proved yourself, Theo. Thank you, for today especially. We wouldn't have won without you. Or you, Helga." She pulled the older woman in for a group hug. The three of them went to the table to shake the judges' hands. When Basil mentioned to Theo that he might have an opening at one of his restaurants, she was surprised to hear him say, "I appreciate the offer, sir, but I think this is where I'm meant to be."

Sophie and Dana joined them, setting up a time to discuss Basil and his bride-to-be's wedding plans. Looking at everyone's happy, smiling faces, Ava was glad she hadn't bailed upon learning Damien would be here. Admittedly, the thought had crossed her mind. And in that moment, she was proud of herself. Proud that she hadn't allowed him to steal this from her too.

Sophie and Dana led the judges to the ballroom where the St. Patrick's Day celebration was getting under way. Damien glanced from Ava to Helga and Theo, then he hailed down Basil's fiancée for an interview.

"Go and enjoy yourselves. I'll clean up the kitchen," Ava said to Helga, Theo, and Erin, who'd just joined them. After the strain of the last hour, Ava could use a little time to herself.

"Oh. My. God, did you see how hot that Damien Gray is? I'm going to ask him—" Erin began before Ava cut her off.

"No," she said forcefully at almost the same time as Theo and Helga. The three of them looked at one another.

"Trust me," Theo said to Erin. "I've met his type before. That guy is bad news."

"He was a lecher when he was young, and I don't see any sign he's changed. He was practically undressing Ava with his eyes." Helga tapped her Coke-bottle lenses. "I don't miss much with my new specs."

Lexi pulled her in for a hug when the room cleared out. "It's almost over. Will you be okay if I go to the ballroom to keep an eye on things? Griffin should be back anytime now."

"Yes, please. I'd feel better if you were there."

"You have to come to the party. At least for a few

minutes for Griffin's sake. I'll pretend I'm not feeling well, and we can get out of there whenever you want to."

"Okay. I just need some time to decompress." After Lexi left, Ava thought about what she'd just said. She shouldn't need to decompress. She should be celebrating the win with everyone, celebrating her and Griffin's engagement. And beneath the worry and fear of earlier, something else bubbled up inside her, anger and resentment.

She slapped her hand on the kitchen door, pushing it open. Walking to the radio, she turned it up and kicked off her shoes in hopes the music would relax and calm her like it usually did. But when the song she'd downloaded for Lexi's afternoon walks came on—"Fight Song" by Rachel Platten—it had the opposite effect.

In his own way, Damien had won again. He'd stolen her joy, and she'd let him. It was time. Time for her to take her life back. And as she thought of everything she'd say to him, she scrubbed the counters in time to the music.

"There's the Ava I remember."

Her hand froze, and she slowly turned her head. It was Damien, leaning against the closed door with a glass of wine in his hand.

Simon yowled, and Colleen whipped her arms around, the movement sending the newspaper and half-full teacup off the nesting tables in Jasper's room.

"Stop that. Stop that right now. I'll get the memoirs," Jasper finally relented, muttering under his breath as he crossed the room. He removed an oil painting from the far wall to reveal a safe.

Colleen gave her head a frustrated shake when he carefully lowered the painting to the floor. He didn't understand the urgency of the matter. "Hurry up. Ava's in danger and no one knows. He's here. Damien Gray is here."

Lexi had been hovering around Ava, but despite the two being thick as thieves, Colleen didn't think Ava would share her secret. And it was killing the child. She was slipping back to her old ways. Colleen had seen her walking around with a hollow look on her face in that old, ratty sweater. Ava didn't deserve this. She'd finally gotten her second chance with Griffin. Colleen would be damned if Damien Gray was going to get in their way.

"You have no idea what you're up against, Damien Gray, but you're about to find out," Colleen said as Jasper removed the book from his safe. He sat on the edge of the bed, and she joined him. As soon as he opened the book, she blew on the pages toward the back of her memoirs. They didn't have time to waste.

"No, no, not back that far," she said, growing both impatient and nervous. She brought her finger to the page and focused on moving it. After all the energy she'd expended earlier, it wasn't easy. Once she managed to flip the first few, it became easier. Finally, she turned the page to six years earlier where she'd recorded Ava's story.

Jasper scanned the lines of the page, his angular face tightening as he read what Damien Gray had done to Ava. He briefly closed his eyes as he reached the bottom of the page and bowed his head. "You should have told Master Griffin, Madame. He deserved to know," Jasper said, and rose to his feet.

"You're not telling me anything I don't already know. But Ava needs us now."

He returned the book to the safe, removing an old Smith & Wesson revolver before shutting the door. "Don't worry, Madame. Damien Gray will pay for what he's done. I'll see to that myself."

Colleen gaped at him. Maybe this wasn't such a good idea after all. All it took was one look at Griffin to know he was a dangerous man. But what no one had realized, other than her, is how dangerous Jasper could be. She leaped from the bed and tugged on his arm. "You put that back."

Either the slight movement of his sleeve didn't register or he was ignoring her because he replaced the painting, stuck the revolver in the waistband of his trousers, and headed for the door. She'd seen the same coldly furious look on his face once before. Somehow she had to make him see reason. For the life of her, she didn't know how.

But as she hurried after him, something caught her eye. It was a copy of the *Harmony Harbor Gazette* lying on the floor. They'd done a feature on today's St. Paddy's Day celebration at the manor. It was on the front page and accompanied by a photograph of Kitty. Colleen tried to pick the paper up but couldn't make her fingers work. "Simon, come here. You need to bring this to Jasper, and you need to do it fast."

Jasper would get the message. He'd understand the point Colleen was trying to make. He was in love with her daughter-in-law and had been for a very long time. If he did something stupid and ended up behind bars, he would no longer be there for Kitty. And that's all the man lived for—Kitty and Greystone.

Simon picked up the paper and managed to slip through the door just before it closed. Jasper wasn't wasting any time and was almost at the second-floor landing when Simon caught up to him. Simon dropped the paper at his feet. Jasper stared at it for a moment and then nodded. "I know, Madame. I won't make that mistake again. But one way or another, Damien Gray will pay for what he did to Ava."

There wasn't much more Colleen could do. She hoped it had been enough to make him see reason. She walked beside him to the ballroom. If not for Damien, she could enjoy the spectacle of the celebration. She loved St. Paddy's Day, and the girls had done a right-fine job. The room was filled to capacity with friends and townsfolk enjoying the food and music. Like Jasper, she moved throughout the packed room looking for Ava and Griffin.

She found her family at a table at the far end. Griffin took a swig of beer, obviously angry at something his brother Finn said. Colin and Liam shared a worried glance. No doubt seeing what Colleen herself did. Griffin was hurting.

"I'm just saying what you're all thinking," Finn said. "What? Am I the only one who recognizes that look in his eyes? For Chrissakes, Griffin, cut her loose before it's too—"

Lexi, who'd been scanning the ballroom, got up from the chair beside Griffin. "You have no idea what you're talking about, so shut the hell up. You say one more word about Ava, and you'll be wearing your beer."

"Whoa, since when did you become her—"

Griffin slammed his beer bottle on the table. "Not

another word out of you, Finn." He twisted in his chair. "Lexi, babe, calm down."

She pushed her hand through her hair, frantically searching the ballroom. "Where's Gray? He was at Basil's table a few minutes ago."

"I think he headed out—" Liam began.

"Ava," Lexi said on a panicked whisper, pushing past the chairs.

"What about…Dammit, Lex." Griffin shot out of his chair to go after her. Colin and Liam did the same.

"What the hell's going on?" Aidan said as he approached the table.

"I don't know, but I think we better find out. Push this damn thing, will you?" Finn said, gesturing to the handles of his wheelchair.

Cluing in to why Lexi had said Ava's name, Colleen stopped searching the ballroom and rushed after them. Jasper must have figured it out before her and was running toward the kitchen. By the time Colleen caught up to them, they were all standing, stunned, in the dining room. At the sound of Ava's raised voice, Colleen understood why.

"I said no! I told you to leave when you shoved me up against the door and kissed me. Wanted you? Wanted you! The only man I have ever wanted is Griffin, and you knew it. You stole that from me, you violated me, you raped me!"

There was a low growl, and then Griffin said in a cold, menacing voice, "I'm going to kill him."

Lexi moved to stand in front of him and wrapped her arms around his waist, tears streaming down her face. Kitty was there now, too, crying. So were Sophie and Dana. "No, let her do this. She needs to do this. Please," Lexi begged him.

Jasper, who'd taken a step toward the door, stopped and bowed his head, drawing in slow, measured breaths.

Colin and Liam moved to Griffin. Colin placed a hand on his son's shoulder. "Lexi's right, Ava's been carrying this around for far too long. Let her get it out."

Griffin looked away, overcome with emotion, his shoulders shaking.

Colleen couldn't take it anymore and strode through the kitchen door. Her family's hands might be tied, but hers weren't. It wasn't as if the police could charge a ghost.

"You won't tell Griffin. He won't believe you even if you do. He knows what you were like back then, the good-time party girl in her short skirts and low-cut tops." Damien's lip curled, his eyes moving over Ava.

"And you were a good-time party boy in your skintight jeans who thought the world revolved around him. So tell me, Gray, if you had too much to drink and Becky Waters tore your clothes off you, climbed on top of you, and—"

"Shut up, it wasn't like that. It—"

"Was exactly like that. You knew I would never cheat on Griffin. You knew I had no interest in you. But no one ever said no to star quarterback Damien Gray, did they? You just took what you wanted. Well, no more. You're not going to get away—"

He snarled and grabbed Ava by the upper arms. "You say one word about this to anyone, and I'll make you—"

Overcome with fury, Colleen grabbed the frying pan off the stove.

Ava lifted her hands and placed her palms on his chest. "Don't ever threaten or touch me again," she said, and shoved him.

He stumbled backward, and his head hit the frying pan that was hanging midair. He went down with a loud thud. Ava stared at the frying pan, her eyes wide. Colleen dropped it just as the kitchen door burst open. Griffin stood there. "Ava…"

Ava's gaze flew past him to the people crowded in the doorway behind him. Her hand went to her mouth, muffling a sob. "No, no," she whispered, shaking her head. She frantically pushed past everyone, running from the dining room.

"Griffin, go after her," Lexi said.

Colleen watched as her great-grandson battled for control—his big hands balled into fists, the muscles in his chest and arms flexing. "Lexi's right, my boy. He's not worth it. Ava needs you now more than ever."

"I'll take care of him, Master Griffin," Jasper said.

There was a groan from the floor, and Damien slowly pushed himself to his hands and knees. "Bitch, I'm going to sue—"

Jasper lifted Damien to his feet and held him against the wall. He glanced over his shoulder. "Anyone mind if I take the first shot?"

"I do," Lexi said, and walked over to Damien, kneeing him hard in the groin.

"Don't put one foot on that bridge, Ava," Griffin called out to her, his voice ragged from holding back his emotions, his fury. It'd taken everything he had not to kill Damien with his bare hands.

"I'm sorry," he heard her say on a broken whisper as she turned from the bridge and walked past him with her head bowed, the edges of her sweater fisted in her hands.

He reached for her. "Sweet face, where are you going? I'm right here."

"You told me not to go over the bridge. I thought you didn't want me anymore."

"Jesus, God, no." He pulled her into his arms. "I'll always want you, baby. I never stopped wanting you, loving you. Even when I wanted to stop, I couldn't." He drew back and framed her face with his hands. "We made a promise the other night, remember? Nothing crosses that bridge but us. He doesn't get to come between us, and he sure as hell doesn't get to taint our special place."

She covered his hands with hers. "I'm sorry. I should have told you, but I was so afraid, so ashamed."

"I'm not going to lie to you. Even if it's difficult for you to hear, I'll always tell you the truth. So you listen to me now. The hardest thing I've ever done is stand outside that door and hear what happened to you. What he did to you. What he took from you, from us. I wish you had come to me too. But you had nothing to be ashamed of back then or now. You did nothing wrong. This is all on him." He kissed the tears from her face. "We'll get past this. I've waited too long to get you back to have anything come between us. You need to talk about this, we'll talk. You want us to see someone to work through this together, I'm there. But we don't walk back across Starlight Bridge until both of us have made our peace with this. Got it?"

"Got it." She reached up on her toes and kissed him. "I love you."

"I've never loved you more or been more proud of you." He held her tight and then drew back to take her hand.

"Griffin, I can't go back to the manor. They all heard. They all know..."

"It was long past time they did. And, honey, I know it'll be tough, but tomorrow, you and I are going to see your dad. He needs to hear it from you."

She nodded and looked up at him. "I'll have to tell my Auntie Rosa, Marco, and Dorothy too."

"Yeah, but not right now. We have something else we need to do."

"I don't know if I can go to the police, Griffin. I never told anyone, and…"

"If it was up to me, you'd be pressing charges. But I'll support whatever you decide to do. Right now, though, you and I have a date with a bonfire to burn your ugly-ass sweater. And I hope when we do, we burn up some of those memories too."

An hour later, Griffin sat with Ava in his arms on the beach at Kismet Cove, the flames flickering and dancing in the black velvet night sky, waves rolling onto shore, wood smoke scenting the air. "You cold? You ready to go up?" He wrapped his jacket around her.

"No, I could stay here all night and look at the stars."

"Do you remember how to find Polaris?"

She pointed to the sky. "There's the Big Dipper." She moved her finger down. "Dubhe and Merak." Then she drew a line straight across. "And there's Polaris." Turning in his arms, she smiled and trailed her finger down his jaw and neck to place her hand over his heart. "This is my North Star."

He lowered his head to kiss her. "And you're my—"

"Griffin, Ava, it's Lexi. She's in labor and losing it," Liam called out. "She thinks she's dying."

Chapter Twenty-Three

♥

Lexi had been in labor for more than twelve hours. The tension in the hospital room was so dense you'd need a flashlight to see through it. Griffin had retreated into a stony silence after learning what Lexi and Ava had been keeping from him. Ava sympathized with him. In less than twenty-four hours, he'd been dealt two devastating blows. But sitting beside the bed and refusing to speak wasn't helping. Neither, in her opinion, was Finn.

As handsome as his brother was with his wavy, dark brown hair, laser blue eyes, and square jaw, Finn had been barking orders at the nurses since they'd arrived. Initially, Ava had cut him some slack. Lexi's news and hers had hit him hard too. It was more than that though. His experience in Central Africa had changed him. The loss of Mary and Riley had changed him, too, as she imagined it had all the Gallagher boys.

Finn had been the brother who was always up for a

good time. If that included a little danger, pushing the limits of endurance and speed, he was on it. No doubt his injury was contributing to his surly behavior. Being confined to a wheelchair because of the cast that went from his foot to his thigh would wear on anyone, but Finn wasn't just anyone. It was like taking a wild horse and locking it in a four-by-four stall.

Ava slid her arm behind Lexi's back. "Up you go. Take Finn for a walk."

"Are you crazy? I'm having a baby. I'm not getting out of this bed. Go torture the perky redhead down the hall," Lexi said in a whiny, sullen voice.

"The perky redhead delivered her baby ten minutes ago. The walk will do you good. It'll help move things along." Ava managed to get Lexi into a sitting position. Then she looked to Griffin for help.

He was watching them with a muscle pulsating in his clenched jaw, his arms crossed over his powerful chest. Which was better than listening to him crack his knuckles like he had been for the past hour, but obviously she wasn't getting any help from him.

"Maybe the baby's not ready. He's three weeks early, you know."

As she planned to do with Griffin, Ava said something guaranteed to unleash Lexi's temper. "The doctor told you that, given his measurements, your dates were probably wrong. So maybe he's as lazy as his mama."

"You didn't just call my baby lazy."

"Yes, and you too. Now move your hard ass off this bed," Ava said, doing her best to hide her triumphant smile when Lexi got up and waddled to the wheelchair. "There, doesn't that feel better now?"

Lexi flipped her off. Ava closed the door behind them and turned to Griffin. "I'm not some fragile piece of glass. I won't break because you yell at me."

"What are you talking about?"

"I know you're mad at me for not telling you about Lexi's cancer. Get it off your chest, yell at me, do something because this silent act of yours isn't helping."

His eyes narrowed, and his muscles flexed, and then he looked away. "I'm not fighting with you."

She walked over, cupped his cheek in her hand, and drew his gaze back to her. "It was Lexi's choice. I had to respect that. And so do you."

"She chose the baby's life over her own."

"Yes, she chose to hold off treatment because she wanted this baby, your child, her child, to have a fighting chance. She's forty, Griffin. Between her age and treatment for the cancer, this might be her only chance to have a baby. You out of anyone know how important that is for her."

He scrubbed his face with his hands, looking at her over his fingertips. "I don't want to lose her. I love her. She's my best friend."

Ava sat on his lap, and his arms went around her. "She's mine too. We're not going to lose her. She's strong. She's a fighter."

"But what if it's a fight she can't win?"

"Then we deal with it. Together." She lifted her hand and tapped her engagement ring. "None of us know how long we have. So let's make the most of every day, store up the memories and the moments. Don't let your fear over losing Lexi take away from today. In less than a couple of hours, you'll be holding a tiny miracle in your hands. Yours and Lexi's little boy."

His hand curved around her neck. "I love you, sweet face. You know that, right?"

She nodded, smiling as his mouth came down on hers.

"I should have known why you wanted to get rid of me, mouse," Lexi grumbled, shoving Finn's wheelchair into the room.

"Jesus, Lex, watch where you're going. You knocked my leg on the door."

"Oh, stop your complaining. It was a little tap. Come talk to me when you've been in labor for a freaking day," Lexi said, waddling back to the bed.

Ava smiled at her. "Griffin and I were just talking about names. What do you think of Alphonso?"

And just as Ava had hoped, the name game broke the tension in the room. Kitty, Colin, Sophie, Liam, and Aidan arrived a few minutes later, and it continued with much laughter and some good-natured ribbing. Three hours later, baby Gabriel Gallagher made his debut, weighing in at a healthy nine pounds, six ounces.

The past three days had been great. It was like Lexi's room had become a cocoon, keeping the world out. Their tiny, confined space had only room for warmth and laughter and precious moments with his son and family. But reality had set in today, the words *breast cancer* and *treatment* ripping off the blanket. Griffin didn't know how Lex, Ava, and Finn did it. Discussing the pros and cons of surgery, chemo, and radiation in matter-of-fact voices. As though Lex's life weren't on the line.

"Please tell me you were able to pull some strings," Ava said to Finn.

They'd found a doctor, a renowned oncologist, who

both Finn and Ava believed was the best specialist to treat Lexi. Because he was the best, they'd been informed by his office that he wasn't taking on any new cases at this time. Ava and Finn had tried everything short of bribery to even get Lex on a waiting list.

"No one has an in with him that they can think of. We need someone with major clout." Finn had spent the morning on the phone with everyone he knew in the medical field, locally and abroad.

"I think I might know someone," Ava said, and walked over to the window with her phone pressed to her ear.

Griffin had to get out of there. He leaned over the bassinet and scooped his son into his arms, tucking the blue blanket around him and then fixing the knitted hat on his head. "I'm going to take Gabe for a walk. He's a bit fussy, and it's a beautiful day." Gabe was sound asleep.

Ava turned and gave him a soft smile. Whenever he held the baby, Griffin would look up to see her watching him with that same smile on her face. It'd been bittersweet the first time Ava had held Gabe in her arms. She got a faraway look on her face, as though remembering the day the nurse had laid their son in her arms. But that was the only time he'd seen any sign of her sorrow. Now every time she held the baby, she was either singing to him, rocking him, or trying to make him smile. It annoyed Lexi to no end that Ava was the only one who could get him to stop crying. Ava took great pleasure in reminding Lex of the fact every chance she got.

Griffin walked through the exit doors of the hospital, smiling down at his son, whose blue eyes had popped open. "Don't you worry, little buddy. Your Auntie Ava and Uncle Finn are doing everything they can for your mommy." Griffin might not have the same connections they did, but he could do his part. He walked to the bench near a weeping willow and sat down. And then he did something he hadn't done since his mother and sister died—he prayed.

Finn found him there two hours later. His brother maneuvered his wheelchair beside the bench. "Guess who just left Lexi's room and is taking her case?"

"Dr. Samuels?" She'd been Ava and Finn's second choice.

"Nope, we got *numero uno*, big brother. Or I should say Ava's contact did. The guy arrived within an hour of Ava making the call. To hear him, you'd think the sun rises and sets by this woman. Probably some high-society broad with a wing named after her," Finn said with a scornful twist of his lips. Griffin wasn't surprised by his brother's reaction. He'd been complaining about people with big bucks getting preferential treatment and serving on hospital boards since medical school.

"How does Ava know her?" Griffin asked.

"No clue. She's being tight-lipped about it. I've never heard of her. Name Olivia Davenport ring a bell with you?"

"No, but it sounds like we owe her. Did the doc seem optimistic about Lexi's prognosis?" He steeled himself for his brother's answer.

"Somewhat optimistic. Which in doc speak means it's looking good, big brother." He smiled, then his brow furrowed. "Uh, just one thing. Since Ava kept interrupting him to ask questions, he wanted to know what her relationship to Lexi was. She told him they were sister wives."

* * *

Almost two months to the day since the doctor had taken on Lexi's case, she sat on the bed in Colleen's suite grumbling as Ava tried another wig on her bald head. Ava stood back. "Ladies, what about this one?"

Arianna turned from zipping up Sophie's mint-green bridesmaid dress. "No, I liked the blond one better."

"I think she'd look good as a redhead. It'll go perfect with her maid-of-honor dress," Erin piped up as she helped Helga into her dress. Both women were standing up for Ava too.

When she'd told Griffin how many women were in her bridal party, he'd stared at her openmouthed, then shook his head with a laugh and kissed her. He was being a good sport about it since he'd been hoping for a small, intimate wedding.

"Dana, do you have another wig like the one you have on?" Ava asked. It was because of Dana that Lexi was being treated by the world-renowned oncologist. Less than an hour after Ava had made the call to Dana asking if she might know someone who could help, Dr. Wilson walked through the doors of Lexi's hospital room. So Ava's suspicions that Dana had money, and lots of it, seemed to be right. She couldn't help but wonder what she was running from. But as someone who'd kept her own secret for more than a decade, Ava didn't question Dana. She wanted to, especially lately. For the past week, she'd noticed that glazed, vacant look in Dana's eyes again.

Dana cast a nervous glance at the women gathered in the room. Then, as though she'd made an important decision, she reached up and took the auburn wig off. One question answered, but another one raised, Ava thought, when Dana revealed her own thick, gorgeous, long, blond hair. Ava had assumed Dana wore wigs because she'd lost her hair. Now more than ever she wondered who or what Dana was hiding from.

Which of course Lexi asked. "Why would you wear wigs when you have hair like that? Is there something you want to tell us?"

"No, I just wear them for fun," Dana said, handing over the wig. She took the other one from Ava. "I'll be right back."

"Is it me or does Dana not seem herself these days?" Lexi asked.

Ava was interested in Lexi's take on it. "How so?"

"Well, she's always warm and sweet, but she acts cool and aloof when Gabe's around. She doesn't ask to hold him or act like a complete loon like you do." Lexi mimicked the faces Ava made at Gabe when she was trying to make him smile.

"You're just jealous because he smiled at me first."

"It was gas."

"Stop your bickering. Anyone listening to the two of you would think you're sisters," Dorothy said, approaching with Ava's pale yellow wedding gown over her arm.

Lexi and Ava shared a glance and laughed. They'd had fun watching people's reactions when they told them they were sister wives. Griffin had put a stop to it when he started getting strange looks on Main Street.

"We're sisters from another mother." Lexi frowned at the dress Dorothy shook out. "Hey, how come you're not wearing the gown from the bridal show?"

"Griffin already saw her in it. It's bad luck," Arianna said.

Rosa, who'd been leaning toward a mirror putting on her makeup, pursed her lips. "He's not the only one who saw her in it. The whole town's talking about Maggie's painting. Really, *cara*, it should be hanging in your bedroom, not in the gallery for everyone to see."

Allowing Maggie to paint the portrait with the wedding dress more off than on had been another step in Ava taking her life back and becoming the girl she used to be. She was proud of that painting and what it stood for. So was Griffin. And so were her friends who'd wholeheartedly supported her.

She'd taken an even bigger step when she'd agreed to be interviewed for Byron's exposé on Damien. Through Byron, Ava had learned she wasn't Damien's first or last victim. No one had seen him since he'd left the manor that night. But with the to-serve-and-protect Gallaghers hunting him down, she had no doubt that one day he'd pay for what he did to her and the other women.

"When my baby bump gets bigger, I'm having one done, Nonna. I only hope it's half as beautiful as Ava's," Sophie said.

"I have my appointment booked with Maggie too," Dorothy said.

Rosa stared at her friend in the mirror. "What would you do that for? You're old."

Dorothy cast Ava a sidelong glance. "It's a birthday present for Gino."

Sophie hurried over and covered Rosa's mouth.

"I'm sure he'll love it," Ava said, happy that Dorothy and her father had decided to start dating.

Mia ran into the room. "Uncle Griffin said to hurry up or you'll miss the sunset."

Colleen stood on a table in the dining room, trying to get a glimpse of the wedding party. "I tell you, Simon, this being tethered to Greystone can be annoying. It looks like I've missed it," she said, noting the guests making their way back to the manor from Starlight Bridge.

She heard Theo calling orders in the kitchen, and then several waiters filed out carrying trays of hors d'oeuvres. The wedding reception was being held on the patio off the dining room. Dana had done a beautiful job. White lights were strung over the patio and decorated the trees, and the white tablecloths draped over the round tables were dotted with tiny stars that glowed.

The French doors leading to the patio opened. It was Jasper. He looked to where Simon meowed at her and walked over. "I have something you might like to see, Madame." He held up his phone.

She pressed her hands to her chest at the sound of her great-grandsons singing "I Swear" as the women in their mint-green dresses walked up the path, then stopped to line either side. Ava walked up the path in her beautiful buttercup-yellow gown with her father in his wheelchair at her side. She bent to kiss Gino when they reached the bridge, walking over it alone to where Griffin awaited her. Something in Griffin's smile said this moment was special to them in more ways than one.

"You're a good lad, Jasper, a very good lad indeed for thinking of me."

"Get down off the table, Madame. I'll leave the French

doors open so you can be part of the celebration. I moved the bridal party's tables close to the door."

Touched, Colleen did as he suggested, hurrying to the door as the guests began taking their seats. Mia sat between Sophie and Liam at a table close by. The little girl looked straight at her. Colleen smiled and waved, but Mia kept searching the entrance. She couldn't see her anymore.

"Ah, well, it was bound to happen sooner or later," Colleen said, feeling the loss more than she thought she would.

Meow. Simon raised his chin.

"You're right. I'm glad of your company, Tomcat. I truly am."

Jasper glanced from Mia to where Colleen stood and then walked onto the patio. He said something to Kitty, who nodded, and he wheeled the baby's pram inside.

"You figured I needed some cheering up, didn't you, my boy?" She leaned over the pram. Gabriel was wide awake, looking at her with his big blue eyes. "Oh, and aren't you a perfect wee mannie. Yes, you are. You are indeed. Can you smile for your GG?" She blinked. "Jasper, did you see that? He's looking right at me and smiling."

Jasper chuckled. "Well, Madame, it appears another of your great-great-grandchildren can see you. You'll be pleased to know I've suggested Miss Lexi and the baby remain at the manor instead of moving to one of the cottages, and she's accepted. At least for now."

"Did you hear that, little one? You and I are going to have lots of time to get to know each other." Colleen smiled at the baby, then straightened at the applause. Everyone stood up. "Sit down," she groused, unable to see over them. They did when the DJ started playing "A Thousand Years" by Christina Perri. Hand in hand, Griffin and Ava walked toward the dance floor, staring into each other's eyes.

Never had Colleen seen a more beautiful or happy couple. They were, and had always been, the perfect match.

Have you visited Christmas, Colorado?

Please turn the page for an excerpt from

Wedding Bells in Christmas

by Debbie Mason.

Chapter One

♥

Dear Heartbroken in Hoboken: Two years? Seriously, it's time for you to move on. Stop with the what ifs. Stop trying to figure out what went wrong. This guy has taken up space in your head and heart for way longer than he deserves. You have a job you love, family and friends who love you. Focus on that, embrace that, and start enjoying your life again.

Vivian Westfield stood in the long security line at LaGuardia airport rereading her responses to next week's letters from the lovelorn. Satisfied that they met her new criteria—the one where she no longer kicked butt but gently smacked it—she sent her Dear Vivi column off to her editor. At least Heartbroken had a job that she loved, Vivi thought as she shoved her iPad in her carry-on.

Vivi remembered the feeling. Oh, how she remembered it. Ten months ago, she'd landed her dream job as an investigative reporter for the *Daily Spectator*. All the long hours and hard work she'd put in at online newspapers had finally paid off. But she'd had only four lousy months to revel in the sweetness of her success.

While working on her biggest story to date—the story guaranteed to earn her editor's respect and, more importantly, protect her best friend Skylar O'Connor—Vivi's career imploded as spectacularly as a sinkhole opening up on Fifth Avenue in the middle of rush-hour traffic.

Looking back, and she'd done so every day since that bitterly cold November night, she realized where she'd gone wrong. She'd let Superman into her life. She should have known that someone who named himself after a comic book hero would turn into an overprotective wack job. In her defense, until that story, he'd fed her information she never would have gotten on her own. And over the months they'd spent texting each other on a daily basis, she'd found herself thinking about him all the time.

As embarrassing as it was to admit, she'd been crushing on Superman, fantasizing about becoming his Lois Lane. Which was ridiculous. She had no idea what he looked like. She hadn't even spoken to the man. The only thing she knew for certain was that in his misguided attempt to protect her, her sources had dried up overnight. And that's when her story went sideways. But Vivi was no quitter, and she'd tracked down the woman at the safe house to get the goods.

Lesson learned: bad guys don't quit, either.

The NYPD hadn't been happy… Okay, so that was an understatement. She was lucky they hadn't thrown her in jail and sued the newspaper for her interference in an ongoing criminal investigation. Actually, luck didn't have much to do with it. The credit went to the *Spectator*'s legal team. Too bad they hadn't been as successful when it came to her job. She was put on a six-month probation the same day ninety-year-old Hilda Branch, aka Dear Hilda, died in her sleep. Vivi'd sat across from the *Spectator*'s editor in chief, staring at him in stomach-dropping horror as he gave her her new assignment.

Everyone, other than the editor in chief obviously, knew that Vivi was the least qualified person for the job. And it wasn't because she'd never been dumped before. Of course she had, she was thirty for god's sake. What thirty-year-old hadn't been dumped, had a couple of those he's-just-not-into-you revelations that broke her heart? No, the reason Vivi wasn't suited for the job was because she was the most unsympathetic person north of Wall Street. And that was why, once she'd recovered, she didn't yell and she didn't argue. She smiled and graciously accepted the position. With her in-your-face attitude, she figured her stint as Dear Vivi would last... about a day.

But people obviously enjoyed having their butts kicked, because her column had been an overnight sensation. Which was why Dear Vivi's responses of late had gone from a butt kick to a light tap on the behind. She had no intention of being an advice columnist for forty years like Hilda Branch. One way or another, when Vivi's probation was up a few weeks from now, she was getting her old job back.

As the line in front of her moved forward as slowly as at Bagel Bagel on a Saturday morning, Skye's assigned ringtone jingled from Vivi's carry-on. She'd been expecting her call. Their mutual best friend Maddie McBride had already checked in with Vivi on the cab ride to the airport. The three of them had been friends since their first day of college. As they were only children— technically that wasn't true in Vivi's case, but it's how she thought of herself—they'd become the sisters they never had.

In the past eighteen months, Vivi's "sisters" had abandoned her. They'd moved from New York City to Christmas, Colorado. Maddie and Skye said they fell in love with the small mountain town. Vivi knew better; they fell in love with the town's most eligible bachelors. Vivi no longer believed in a one-and-only, but even she had to admit, if there was such a thing, Skye and Maddie had found theirs.

She missed them. New York wasn't the same without them. But that didn't mean she'd cave to their pleading and cajoling and move to Christmas. Vivi didn't do the great outdoors. Give her concrete, skyscrapers, Bagel Bagel, and Roasters Coffee down the street any day.

"Where are you?" Skye asked the moment Vivi put the phone to her ear.

She sighed. Her best friends expected her to bail at the last minute. And Vivi knew why—Chance McBride. She did her best to avoid the small town of Christmas when there was a possibility he'd be around. Since his father was getting married next week, the probability that Chance would be there was high. Then again, he'd been home only once in the last five years. Vivi knew why he avoided his hometown, and that knowledge was probably the reason her voice came out more raspy than usual. "Security line at the airport."

"Vivi! Your flight leaves in twenty minutes."

Checking the time on her phone, Vivi glanced at the ticket in her hand and grimaced. She was cutting it kind of close. "Relax, I'll make it."

"Don't tell me, you were working on your column and time got away from you. You're a workaholic, Vivi," Skye said in an exasperated tone of voice. "The week away will do you good. You can relax for a change."

Sometimes it was annoying how well Skye knew her. Only Vivi hadn't been working on her column before she left her apartment; she could dial those in. She'd been checking out a couple leads for a story. One that would knock her editor's socks off and get Vivi back her job.

She returned her attention to Skye. "Relaxing? I thought you guys said you needed me there to help with the wedding. 'Vivi, Maddie, and I will have nervous breakdowns if you don't come. We can't do this on our own. We're new mothers,'" she said, imitating Skye's angst-filled voice from three weeks ago.

"Hey, I did not sound whiny and hysterical."

"Yeah, you kinda did. But don't worry, I'm riding to the rescue in my big, white bird." Ten members of a seniors bowling team shuffled forward. "I have to take off my boots. See you soon."

"Okay, but don't, you know, tick off security. We really do need you here. Nell's driving us insane," Skye said, referring to Nell McBride, who looked like a sweet little old lady if you ignored the flaming red streak in her white hair. And no one should ignore that devil-red streak. The older woman was the biggest shit-disturber Vivi had ever met.

Vivi knew this because eighteen months earlier, she and Maddie got caught up in one of Nell's schemes. In the end, everything worked out well for Maddie. For Vivi, not so much. She was still in recovery mode. Which was the reason why she'd agreed to go to Christmas in the first place. Like Heartbroken, Vivi had a man who'd taken up too much space in her heart and head: Chance McBride.

She opened her mouth to respond when Skye said in a voice tinged with nerves, "Um, speaking of Nell. This was all her idea, okay? So don't get mad at me and Maddie. We had nothing to do with it. N-O-T-H-I-N-G."

Vivi froze, balancing on one foot as she took off her rubber boot. "What was Nell's idea?"

"Gotta go. Evie's crying," Skye said, obviously using her five-month-old daughter as an excuse, because there was no noise in the background.

"Skye! Skye, don't you dare hang—" Vivi broke off at the sound of a beep. "Call Ended" flashed on her phone's screen. "Dammit, dammit, dammit," she muttered at the same time the bald, mustached man in uniform waved her over.

And since Vivi was now in a ticked-off, panicked mood, she managed to tick off the security agents. By the time they got through with her, she was late for her flight. Her carry-on banging against her hip as she raced to her gate, she accidently bumped into several people, ensuring she'd now ticked off half the airport.

Breathless by the time she reached the woman standing behind the desk in front of her gate, Vivi waved her boarding pass, panting, "That's my flight." It was while she watched the woman scan the nonrefundable one-way ticket Skye had sent her that Vivi realized what Nell was up to. The older woman had decided to help Maddie and Skye in their bid to keep her in Christmas. She almost laughed in relief. She'd been worried Nell's current scheme had something to do with...

"It's your lucky day," the woman said, handing Vivi back the boarding pass with a smile. "There was a problem closing the cargo bay door. The plane was delayed."

To a white-knuckled flier, a malfunctioning door didn't sound lucky at all. "Are they changing planes?" Vivi asked, because while she had no problem writing about aircraft falling from the sky and people getting sucked out of them, she had no intention of being one of them.

"No, everything's fine. Get going. They won't hold the plane much longer." The woman gestured to the narrow corridor.

"Okay. Thanks," Vivi said, even as near-miss, landing, and takeoff accident statistics popped into her head.

Replacing those thoughts with the more pleasant one of seeing her best friends, she ran down the blue-carpeted corridor. A few feet from the plane's open door, a blast of hot, muggy air slammed into her. The earlier thunderstorm hadn't cleared out the mid-May heat wave that had blanketed New York for the last three days. One more reason to head to Colorado: she'd be able to breathe.

But when the flight attendant showed Vivi to her first-class aisle seat, she stopped breathing altogether. A long-legged, broad-shouldered man slouched in the window seat with a champagne-colored Stetson covering his face. Every time she saw a tall, exceptionally built man wearing a Stetson, she'd had the same reaction.

This was worse.

This was painful.

Because this man's scuffed, brown cowboy boots looked the same as the ones that had spent a week under her bed. So did the well-worn jeans that encased thighs that appeared to be as hard as the ones she'd run her bare foot along. She recognized the black T-shirt with the Rocky Mountain logo that hugged his wide chest. An extraordinary chest she'd kissed her way up and kissed her way down. Broad shoulders that she'd clung to. Muscular, tanned arms that had wrapped around her, and large hands that could easily crush a man but had caressed her gently, and at one time, she'd misguidedly thought, lovingly.

At the flight attendant's impatient sigh, Vivi dragged her gaze away. "Ah, is there another seat available? I'd rather not sit in first class. Too close to the front of the plane." The woman's black-penciled eyebrows snapped together when Vivi continued, her voice barely a whisper, "In the event of a crash, it's forty percent safer to be at the back." Safer for her. She needed time to prepare herself for the sight of his to-die-for face. She remembered that face, remembered kissing that face, falling head over heels in love with that face. And those amazing grass-green eyes of his wouldn't miss her reaction to seeing him for the first time in eighteen months. They'd never missed anything.

He'd know.

He'd know he'd broken her heart.

At least that was one positive thing that had come out of writing an advice column. Vivi had learned what she had to do to move on with her own life. She needed to prove to Chance as much as to herself that she was over him. That he hadn't ruined her for any other man. When Superman entered her life, she'd hoped that was the case. He'd been proof that all those soft, romantic feelings hadn't shriveled up and died. It didn't matter that he was no longer in her life. Everyone needed a rebound guy, and Superman had been hers.

Hopefully moving on from Chance would be as easy as moving on from Superman. Since the day Chance dumped her, she'd rehearsed her first face-to-face with him a million times. She knew exactly what she'd say and how she'd act. She'd even planned out what to wear. Which was so not Vivi. She was a jeans and T-shirt kind of girl. But she'd packed an outfit that oozed cool sophistication. It sure as hell wasn't the yellow rubber boots, black leggings, and seen-better-days, off-the-shoulder green T-shirt she currently had on. And a brief encounter with Chance on Main Street was not the same as being trapped beside him on the four-hour flight to Denver. Vivi's lungs constricted, and her face tingled. Good God, she was having a panic attack. And the flight attendant's tight smile and negative head shake was so not what she needed to see right now.

Maybe the woman at the gate was right and it was Vivi's lucky day. Maybe this guy who leaked testosterone from his pores wasn't Chance McBride after all. Her gaze went to the man's overlong, copper-streaked, dark-blond hair. No, it was not her lucky day. This was the second-worst day of her life. The worst day had been when she'd woken up to a note on her pillow. And the words "Take care, Slick" in Chance's bold, masculine handwriting.

Chance McBride kept his body relaxed even though everything inside of him tightened in response to that raspy bedroom voice. He didn't need to see her to know who it was. That voice was imprinted on his brain. It had made him want things he couldn't have. Made him forget things he had no business forgetting. It's why he'd left her without saying good-bye. He'd known he was in trouble the first time he'd laid eyes on Vivi Westfield.

A hollow ache filled his chest at the memory of the days and nights they'd spent together. Of her gorgeous, toned legs wrapped around him, his mouth at her pink-tipped breast while his hands kneaded her amazing ass. Her long, dark hair spread across the pillow as soft, sexy sounds escaped from her parted lips. Full, sensuous lips he could spend a lifetime fantasizing about. But it was her eyes, incredible violet eyes, that did him in. And those eyes were the reason he'd left her. The emotion that had turned them from violet to black.

She'd fallen in love with him. A man who had no love left to give. The death of his wife, Kate, and their baby girl had seen to that. If he'd met Vivi before Kate, it would have taken an army to drag him away from her. But he wasn't that man, and he'd walked away from her without a backward glance. Didn't mean he didn't think about her, keep tabs on her. He might not be able to give her the love she wanted and deserved, but she'd damned well needed his protection.

Vivi Westfield was a hothead. She had no fear. She was driven, ambitious, going after a story with no regard for her personal safety. She'd nearly gotten herself killed six months back. He'd done what he could, but she'd shut him down as quickly as he'd cut off her sources. She'd given the slip to the tail he'd put on her that night in November. If he hadn't been on another job halfway across the country, he would have protected her himself. Done everything he could to keep her out of harm's way.

At least he hadn't had to worry about her the last few months.

Thinking of her as Dear Vivi, his mouth twitched. He doubted she found the demotion amusing. And if she ever discovered who he was, she'd go ballistic. Her girls, Madison and Skye, they knew. Obviously they hadn't shared that he was Superman or Vivi would be straddling him right now, her hands at his throat. He shifted in the seat. He needed to get that particular visual out of his head.

Fucking Nell. He should have known his great-aunt was up to no good when she sent him the nonrefundable, one-way first-class ticket. She always had an agenda. Like the one that had put Vivi on his radar in the first place. He worked for an international security company and had been on assignment in New York when Nell tagged him to investigate Madison. A job that took him all of ten minutes. The rest of the time he'd spent with Vivi.

He'd assumed the plane ticket was Nell's way of ensuring he was there for his dad's wedding. If Chance didn't know it would break his father's heart if he was a no-show, Nell's nonrefundable ticket wouldn't have been enough to sway him. He'd been home only once since Kate and the baby's funeral. It had been tough being there. Tougher than he'd admit to anyone. Now with Vivi in town and his great-aunt apparently in matchmaking mode, it would be worse.

He took a moment to prepare himself, then pushed up the brim of his Stetson with a finger and forced a lazy, amused tone to his voice. "Hey, Slick. Long time no see."

About the Author

DEBBIE MASON is the bestselling author of the Christmas, Colorado series. Her books have been praised for their "likable characters, clever dialogue, and juicy plots" (*RT Book Reviews*). When she isn't writing or reading, Debbie enjoys spending time with her very own real-life hero, their three wonderful children and son-in-law, two adorable grandbabies, and a yappy Yorkie named Bella.

You can learn more at:
    AuthorDebbieMason.com
    Twitter @AuthorDebMason
    Facebook.com/DebbieMasonBooks

Fall in Love with Forever Romance

STARLIGHT BRIDGE
By Debbie Mason

Hidden in Graystone Manor is a book containing *all* the dark little secrets of Harmony Harbor...including Ava DiRossi's. No one—especially her ex-husband, Griffin Gallagher—can ever discover the truth about what tore their life apart years ago. Only now Griffin is back in town. Still handsome. Still hating her for leaving him. And still not aware that Ava never stopped loving him...

Fall in Love with Forever Romance

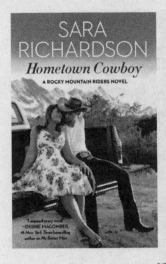

HOMETOWN COWBOY
By Sara Richardson

In the *New York Times* bestselling tradition of Jennifer Ryan and Maisey Yates comes the first book in Sara Richardson's Rocky Mountain Riders series featuring three bull-riding brothers. What would a big-time rodeo star like Lance Cortez see in Jessa Mae Love, a small-town veterinarian who wears glasses? Turns out, *plenty*.

THE BASTARD BILLIONAIRE
By Jessica Lemmon

Since returning from the war, Eli Crane has shut everybody out. That is, until Isabella Sawyer starts as his personal assistant with her sassy attitude and her curves for days. But will the secret she hides shatter the fragile trust they've built? Fans of Jill Shalvis and Jennifer Probst will love Jessica Lemmon's Billionaire Bad Boys series.

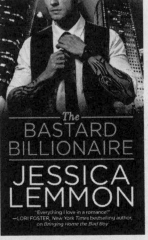

Fall in Love with Forever Romance

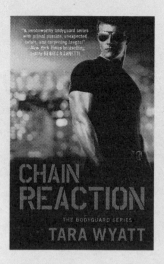

CHAIN REACTION
By Tara Wyatt

Alexa Fairfax is practically Hollywood royalty, but after she discovers a plot more deadly than any movie script, Alexa desperately needs a bodyguard. So she accepts the help of Zack De Luca, a true friend with a protective nature—and chiseled muscles to back it up. Zack is training to be an MMA fighter, but his biggest battle will be to resist his feelings for the woman who is way out of his league ...

IF THE DUKE DEMANDS
By Anna Harrington

In the *New York Times* bestselling tradition of Elizabeth Hoyt, Grace Burrowes, and Madeline Hunter comes the first in a sexy new series from Anna Harrington. Sebastian Carlisle, the new Duke of Trent, needs a respectable wife befitting his station. But when he begins to fall for the reckless, flighty Miranda Hodgkins, he must decide between his title and his heart.

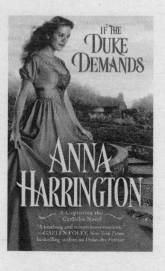